SEP -- 2014

Fic CULLUM
Cullum, Janice A.,
Vyrkarion :the talisman of Anor /

T3-ALT-474

WITHDRAWN

SEP - 2014

WITHDRAWN

Praise for J. A. Cullum

"Home to nine races of humans and near-humans, the world of Tamar lies on the brink of total war unless the living crystals known as the Karionin find young wizards capable of attuning themselves to the magic of the stones. First novelist Cullum begins her epic fantasy series with the tale of three young people destined to become bearers of the crystals. A unique approach to magic along with memorable characters makes this series opener a good choice for most fantasy collections."

— Library Journal review

"...a fantasy world rich in detail, with a large population of interesting creatures interacting with lifelike complexity."

— Poul Anderson

"Cullum takes a hard look at the results and the high price of ignorance, bigotry, and ethnocentrism in a thoughtful novel with an unusual piece of magic at the center of its story-a curse... placed on the protagonist to 'help' him see reason. Great fantasy with a conscience."

— Paula Luedtke, Booklist review

"Looking back, were I to read the book twenty times, there would be enough richness to sustain my interest and always something more for me to explore. This is a wonderful work of fantasy that readers of the Dune series might enjoy as the action jumps from place to place and characters dance on and off the stage for solos and different pairings.... At the last sentence of the book, when I saw there were no more words on the page, I felt bereft"

— Asta Sinusas at SFRevu.com

"Lyskarion is a fantasy, a family saga in a world where humans, shape-changers of different types, wizards and gods meeting on a playing field rather more level than the one we enjoy. It's a saga, and those who like the slow bringing together it intertwining lives (and plot lines) together with intelligent writing about an alternate world should like this one."

— D Jason Cooper

"I just loved your book Lyskarion. I do hope that it is the first in a series. I must know whether Elise and Errin reach their full potential and how Jerevan gets on. The world you created was a place I'd like to visit and the people took on lives of their own as I read... I read a lot of science fiction and fantasy and your voice is a truly enjoyable reading experience. Thanks so much for sharing your story."

— Rhané Vennes

"J. A. Cullum is a byline to watch carefully."

— Jacqueline Lichtenberg

OTHER BOOKS IN THE SERIES

PART THREE OF
THE CHRONICLES OF THE KARIONIN

VYRKARION

THE TALISMAN OF ANOR

BY

J A CULLUM

Alameda Free Library

1550 Oak Street

EDGE SCIENCE FICTION AND FANTASY PUBLISHING
AN IMPRINT OF HADES PUBLICATIONS, INC.
CALGARY

Vyrkarion - The Talisman of Anor

copyright © 2013 by J. A. Cullum
Release: Canada: Fall 2013 / USA: Fall 2013

This is a work of fiction. Names, characters, places, and
incidents are the products of the author's imagination or
are used fictitiously and are not to be construed as real.
Any resemblance to actual events, locales, organizations, or
persons, living or dead, is entirely coincidental.

Edge Science Fiction and Fantasy Publishing
An Imprint of Hades Publications Inc.
P.O. Box 1714, Calgary, Alberta, T2P 2L7, Canada

Editing by Shoshana Glick
Interior by Janice Blaine
Cover Illustration and Design by David Willicome

All rights reserved. No part of this book may be reproduced,
scanned, or distributed in any printed or electronic form
without written permission. Please do not participate in or
encourage piracy of copyrighted materials in violation of the
author's rights. Purchase only authorized editions.
ISBN: 978-1-77053-028-7

EDGE Science Fiction and Fantasy Publishing and Hades Publications, Inc. ac-
knowledges the ongoing support of the Alberta Foundation for the Arts and the
Canada Council for the Arts for our publishing programme.

Library and Archives Canada Cataloguing in Publication

Cullum, Janice A., 1944-
     Vyrkarion : the talisman of Anor / J.A. Cullum.
(The chronicles of the Karionin ; bk. 3)

ISBN ISBN: 978-1-77053-028-7
(e-book ISBN:978-1-77053-029-4)

     I. Title. II. Series: Cullum, Janice A., 1944- Chronicles
of the Karionin ; bk. 3.
PS3553.U34V97 2013   813'.6   C2012-906621-4

FIRST EDITION
(K-20130820)
Printed in Canada
www.edgewebsite.com

DEDICATION

For my daughters, who put up with me.

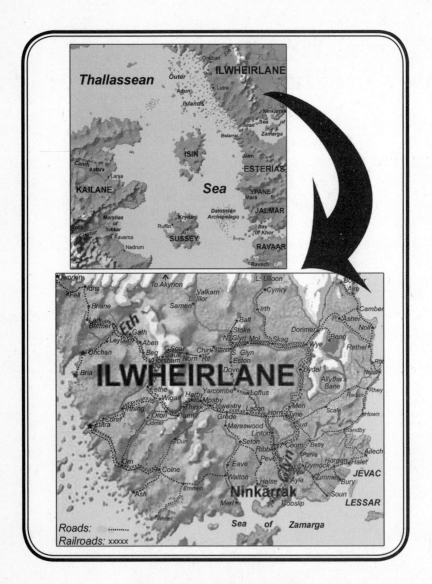

ILWHEIRLANE DETAIL

At the end of the Second Age of Tamar the Five Gods, the Lorincen, played with the dice of history. Tarat, self-styled ruler of the Gods, and Kyra, once the Chronicler, now the Destroyer, urged their worshipers, the larin, to war upon mankind.

Miune, the father of mankind, could do little to ward off the malice of his stronger kin, but he knew his children's hidden strength. He taught his worshipers to hate.

Maera of the Mists and Jehan, known as Player, sought a different path...

— FROM THE RED BOOK OF CHRONICLER RADAM IN THE 1111TH YEAR OF THE AGE OF EMPIRE

Book I

THE YEAR OF THE OX

Ilbekasar liac cain al at.

"The Ox pulls the wheel of fate."

— FROM THE BOOK OF YEARS

PROLOGUE

4730, 473RD CYCLE OF THE YEAR OF THE OX
MONTH OF INGVASH
> *Ilsha bor end itor;*
> *Len lorin cel ful cer.*

> "A great tree takes time to grow;
> Even gods begin with a seed."

— ESLARIN PROVERB

Inanda sat on Lutra's harbor wall, squinting in the glare from the ripe orange sun that, snared in the rigging of the ships, sank toward the sea. Her silver hair, thick and coarse, was pulled back in a braid that hung down her back to her knees. Her face was creased with wrinkles, like mud dried and cracked in the sun, her skin the color of teak, but her eyes were bright blue, her body still pliant as a girl's.

It was spring, the month of Ingvash when the ice breaks in the rivers of the north and the fishes called inglings die in their thousands and hundreds of thousands on the beaches. More, it was the first sunny day after a season of storms. The warmth, the blue sky and the lure of the sea had brought her to the harbor. Inanda loved watching the ships: galleons and frigates, schooners and caravels from all over Tamar, for Lutra was the second largest port in Ilwheirlane.

Over a hundred ships lay at anchor in the harbor or tied in the slips between the piers. Near Inanda's perch on the seawall stevedores unloaded a four-masted bark from Kailane full of bales of cotton for the cloth mills of Corin or Irthing. In the next slip a sleek schooner from the Isle of Sussey disgorged a cargo of oranges, lomcans, limes and barrels of wine. The sharp, citrus scent of the fruit mingled headily with the brackish smell of the sea. Inanda eyed the stocky crewmen. She wondered how it felt to change one's form whenever one wished, as many of the people of Sussey could do, and become a dolphin at ease in the sea.

Inanda's idle thoughts changed when she felt the stirring in her mind, the first sign of a vision to come. Her white robe marked her as one of the Kindred of Maera, but she was more, a sibyl chosen by the deity. Thus, when she felt the sense that was not quite pain but the warning of pain to come, she climbed down off the wall. She hoped to reach the Sanctuary of Maera before the sight came fully on her.

Although it was late afternoon, the area was still crowded. Merchants packed away receipts and bills of lading, and stevedores loaded or unloaded wagons. Inanda crossed the road through a gap in the line of vehicles and found herself in a square fronting the harbor.

The pressure in her head was building rapidly. Inanda paused as a group of young men pushed past, full of high spirits, come to mix with seamen in the dockside taverns. She could not make it to the Sanctuary; she had to rest. She wove her way through the crowd to a bench near the center of the square.

The pain grew. The color of health faded from her face, leaving her wrinkled skin the shade of ashes. A woman paused to ask if she were all right. Inanda gestured the stranger away. Speech was beyond her now.

The pressure built until it broke through her mind's instinctive defense. Then she saw, as Maera willed her to see, without the barriers of time and space, the unraveling threads of fate.

Her scream drew the crowd's attention and someone recognized her, for this was not the first time Inanda had been the vessel of Maera's will. People gathered around her, not touching, but watching, waiting; stilled by apprehension.

After the scream Inanda was silent for a time, her mind, a dry sponge in water, filling with visions. When she spoke her voice was soft, but her thin, clear tones reached everyone in the square. Two men, clerks by profession, wrote down her words.

"Iltheocan a Gand ba sanne danod…"

Not all her audience understood, for she spoke in Eskh, the high tongue, the language of gods and of eslarin, but not of men. It was the trade tongue all over Tamar and the language of scholars, so enough understood for it to be quickly translated for the rest.

"The Year of the Dragon is upon us. The time of peace is dead. The Banner of the Winged Snake has risen in the west. The Estahar shall die. A new emperor shall come from the north, a god-king who will never die save by the hand of that which he himself creates. Woe, people of Tamar! The heavens will cry with tears of fire. The Talisman must be brought from the south. The child must be saved. So many paths, so many, many skeins unrolling like colored threads. The new age will be birthed in blood. If the child dies, it shall be an age of chaos worse than any known before."

When she finished speaking, Inanda collapsed on the bench. A plump matron brought out smelling salts to revive her, and wine was brought for her to drink. A carriage was found, and she was escorted with honor to the Sanctuary of Maera. She remembered nothing but the pain of the pressure building in her head and then waking on the bench to find it gone.

I

4730, 473RD CYCLE OF THE YEAR OF THE OX
MONTH OF REDRI

> *So imo a ilde tortwe a cer andetwe wa lorin;*
> *Amid lu a ilde ba majaoda,*
> *Kor ilde tora...*

> "Beware the plant grown from seed sown by the gods;
> The first fruit of that plant is discord,
> But such a plant will grow..."

— FROM THE WRITINGS
OF THE WIZARD CORMOR

"Jerevan, I need to talk to you."

Jerevan Rayne, the Wizard of Leyburn, descending the steps of Ninkarrak after a less than amicable interview with Idrim, looked around and saw the Wizard Derwen crossing the courtyard toward him. His jaw clenched, but he forced himself to nod equably and say, "At your service."

"Not here," Derwen said, looking around at the guards. "Let's take a walk in the park."

Jerevan's eyebrows rose, but he said, "Very well, the park it shall be." Derwen was the man who had forced him to become a wizard by placing a curse on him. While he'd broken Derwen's curse over fifty years before, Jerevan could never like the man he had once dreamt of destroying.

Jerevan had punished Derwen in his own way. Derwen had forced Jerevan to become grotesque. Jerevan had simply changed Derwen's form to one pleasing to himself. Many did not think it a punishment at all, seeing Derwen's current tidy, slender form instead of the pudgy, untidy one they had once known. But it wasn't Derwen's natural form. Nor was it in his nature to be tidy. Yet now he was compelled to maintain the form Jerevan had given him, to constantly act in a way unnatural to him. Jerevan enjoyed the older wizard's frustration and humiliation. And Derwen was useful, being much better than him at dealing with Idrim and Idrim's court. When they were some distance into the grounds and out of sight of the guards posted around the Royal Park, Derwen said, "Sorry for the secrecy, but I have disturbing news. You know I've been observing Charden..."

Derwen broke off as two men and a woman stepped out from behind a large stand of rhododendrons slightly to the left of the path. "You!"

The woman smiled and said, "You weren't expecting us?"

There were spheres of bright light forming above her palm and those of both the men with her. All three had dark hair and swarthy complexions. Jerevan probed them. Isklarin! He raised his mental shields and grasped his crystal.

The woman had her right hand behind her back. Now she brought it forth and the sphere above it was already blazing. An arc of light reached out toward Derwen.

Jerevan blocked it with a hastily generated shaft of his own. "You take the man on the right," he told Derwen. "I'll handle the others." He didn't check to see if Derwen agreed. He was already too busy matching the force of the woman's will. She was strong and had been fully prepared for the confrontation. He was still shocked by the suddenness of the attack.

He forced himself to calm and drew up his own power. Derwen was weak; he wouldn't be able to hold even one of the opposing wizards for long. Jerevan would have to kill at least one of them quickly, or he'd soon be facing all three.

The man on the woman's left linked his lance of energy with the woman's, and Jerevan flinched at the increase in pressure. He wouldn't be able to fight another of equal strength.

Derwen managed to intercept the lance from the man on the right, but Jerevan could sense he was weakening rapidly.

"Link with me," Derwen said.

Even as Jerevan's intellect analyzed the fact that such a link might be their only hope of survival, his instincts slammed his mind shut against Derwen. He could not link with the man who had cursed him, not even to save both their lives.

In desperation he deflected the lance he'd been dueling with and sent his lance of will against the man attacking Derwen. He felt a sudden snap as the man's shield broke and knew then that he was called Akul. Then his will reached Akul's heart and crushed it.

The effort had drained him, however, and the lance he had deflected momentarily was back before he could fully shield himself. He felt a searing pain to the left side of his face. He slammed up his shield and matched the other lance with his own again, pushing it back. Derwen was staring at the dead wizard in shock.

"Get help," he gasped.

Derwen started, looked at him and nodded, but as he started to turn the isklar woman sent another lance after him.

Jerevan tried to deflect the attack on Derwen, but his will was already matched against the other lance now controlled by the surviving isklar male. He saw Derwen cry out and fall and tried to take advantage of the division of his opponents' strength. He felt that he hurt the woman, but all her will then snapped back into the linkage.

He sought desperately for someone to help him, but in Derwen's quest for privacy they had deliberately taken themselves out of sight of the guards. The Royal Park was huge and banks of shrubbery insured many private areas. There was no one nearby and wizard battles were, by their nature, silent. He could cry out, but he didn't think anyone would hear him, and even a shout would require energy he could no longer spare.

He fought on. He had no strength now for anything but simple resistance to the enemy lance. He would not succumb.

He lost track of time and place. There was only the force pressing against him and his will opposing it. He pulled up the very last of his strength and struck out. He thought he felt something give, but the world was growing dark around him. Then there was nothing left and he felt himself fall into the darkness.

II

4730, 473RD CYCLE OF THE YEAR OF THE OX
MONTH OF ILFARNAR

> Maera fair and Tarat dark
> They birthed a race that bore their mark,
> The women pale, with skin so light,
> The men with skin as dark as night.
> The eslarin, the first to wake,
> The first the gods saw fit to make.
> The first to yawn and look about,
> They were favored. There's no doubt.

> — EXCERPT FROM "THE ESLARIN" FROM *A CHILD'S GUIDE TO THE LARIN AND OTHER BEASTLY TAILS* BY ENOGEN VARASH OF ELEVTHERAI, 4557

Alanna Cairn, the Tamrai of Fell, set out for Ninkarrak in the first week of the month of Ilfarnar, as soon as this year's sylvith crop was safely harvested and stored. Agnes Maslow, her maid, accompanied her.

"I wish this trip weren't necessary," Alanna said as the carriage pulled away from her home and started down the long drive toward the highway.

"The Council chose you, my dear, to represent them with the Estahar. They trusted you to find a way to ensure that there will be future sylvith crops in the years ahead." Agnes said. She was a tall, angular woman in her middle fifties.

Alanna snorted. "Only because none of the merchants were willing to lose business to make the trip and all of the other nobles here in the mountains are known Jehanites, and therefore unpopular with Idrim. I'm an unknown quantity, and they all thought that my being young, and passably good-looking might help."

"Such things do help in dealing with men, my dear."

"But why is any of this necessary? Why have the eslarin closed their borders, and warned us that they won't fertilize the sylvith crop in future years when they've been doing it for millennia?"

"The Estahar will send wizards to fertilize the crops, don't you worry, dear. We shouldn't ever have depended on them from Arvonin. It's never wise to trust such folk," Agnes added, her mouth pursed tightly, as the coach turned onto the highway and headed southeast toward the lowlands and Ninkarrak.

"The eslarin wouldn't close their borders without reason," Alanna said, her eyes on the orchard of sylvith trees beside the road. Their beauty mocked her. They grew as tall and straight as elms, their boles and branches covered with smooth, silver-gray bark. In the summer their leaves were copper-colored, almost the same shade as Alanna's hair, but now, with the cold of autumn, the leaves had turned a deep maroon. The branches looked bare without the heavy burden of the pale chartreuse pods harvested in the previous weeks.

"Everyone in Arvonin will go hungry," she said. "The eagle folk depend on the sylvith harvest as much or more than we do and so do the eslarin themselves."

"I can't see where that should concern you, my lady. You've enough to worry about with our own people," Agnes said.

Alanna bit her lip. "The mountain folk, human and larin, depend on the sylvith harvest. How can I worry about just my own people when all suffer? But the worst of it is that the eslarin won't tell us why. They only make cryptic remarks about someone who shouldn't have been born."

"There's no knowing how larin folk think, my lady."

Alanna wanted to protest but thought better of it. No argument of hers would affect Agnes' entrenched bigotry. And yet, of all the races of Tamar, the eslarin had always been the least deserving of that hostility. She thought of the ones she had known, the gene-dancers who came each year for the fruiting. Male or female, dark-skinned or light, they looked like tall, slender humans until one got close enough to see the vertical slits, like a cat's, in the pale blue eyes. But the one thing that always struck her about them was their innate gentleness, their genuine love of living things. How could they have made a decision that endangered so many lives?

She sighed and turned to the view from the coach window. The sylvith orchards around Fell gave way to natural forest. It was fall in the Mallarnes and the mountain slopes wore their autumn motley of russet and citrine, cinnabar, maroon and gold.

The Wizard Myrriden buried his hands in Loyce's mane next to her warm neck and tried to flex fingers stiff with cold. The red and flame colors of the forested hills mocked him. Such hot colors, yet the air was so cold it burned his throat and made his bones ache. He had no energy left to heal himself. I'm too old, he thought, I've lived too long in the south.

His mind conjured a vision of Belkova, the White City, its walls and towers of white marble baking in the southern sun, its marketplace clamorous with the cries of hawkers, the air fragrant with the scents of spices: nutmeg, argerium, pepper, cuna, and ginger, and over all the musky scent of sweat and the sharp ammoniac odor of camel dung. He had lived there for more than eight hundred years. The hot sun had thinned his blood; the scents and sounds had become a part of him. Myrriden shook his head and the vision was gone, replaced by the icy, rutted mountain road bordered with dense forest and the thin, sharp feel of the frigid air burning his lungs. He would not live to see the south again, but Maera's prophecy had said to bring Vyrkarion north and he never defied the gods. His hand reached out to caress the bag that sat behind him on Loyce's back. Even through the thick leather he felt the warmth of the living crystal. It was all that sustained him in the cold of the high passes when he had crossed the Mallarnes into Ilwheirlane.

"*It will be warmer soon, rai, when we reach the foothills. The worst of the mountains are behind us,*" Loyce thought. She was one of the kariothin, the horned horses created by the eslarin. She wore no bridle. Her kind were sentient and served of their own free will or not at all.

"Are they still following? I'm too weak to find them now." Myrriden's voice was a harsh croak. The mind speech required more effort than he was willing to expend.

"*No, rai. They ride horses. There was no place for them to get fresh ones in Lachan. They're far behind us now, but there are enemies ahead.*"

"How can Aavik have sent wizards ahead of us?" Myrriden felt fear course through him, to have come so far only to fail and die in this cold, sunless land.

"*Not men of power, rai, merely servants. There are two of them around the next bend. They wait for us, but they do not understand what it is that they await.*"

Myrriden could hear the anger in the thought of the karioth. He drew on the remnants of his power and looked ahead. Two men waited, small and swarthy, dressed in the ragged homespun of peasants and mounted on shaggy hill ponies, but they were armed with muskets and swords and positioned to block the road.

"We can go around them through the forest," Myrriden urged, sitting back in the saddle.

"*Then they'll be behind us. You'll need to rest soon and they could catch up to us. It's better if we kill them now,*" Loyce thought fiercely, her stride lengthening.

Myrriden had no chance to protest further. Loyce swept around the bend and he just had time to deflect the musket balls fired at them before she charged between the two ponies, swerving at the last moment to knock the right hand pony off its feet before its rider could raise his sword.

"We're through them, now. You can outrun them," Myrriden cried.

"*They'd follow, rai, and here in Ilwheirlane they'll be able to buy fresh horses. It's better that they die.*" Loyce wheeled and charged again.

"I am not strong enough," Myrriden thought, clutching at Loyce's mane to keep his balance, but Loyce was too angry to heed. It offended her that such puny beings would dare to attack her master. She bore down on the second pony as it tried to wheel and face her. The rider had thrown down his musket, apparently realizing its futility, but before he could raise his sword, Loyce's sharp, pointed horn drove through his side. His scream died in a choking sound as blood gushed from his mouth. The pony fell from the impact of the karioth's shoulder, the body of its rider stuck to Loyce's head like a butterfly on a pin.

The rider of the first pony had fallen but retained his sword. As his companion died, he leapt to his feet and attacked Myrriden. Desperation lent force and quickness to his blade and he smote Myrriden from behind while Loyce was still blinded by his companion's body. Myrriden twisted in the saddle as the sword struck and the blow that would have killed him instantly drove into his shoulder instead. He lashed back at the man through the sword with all of the energy remaining to him and then fell into darkness.

East of Fell for hundreds of kilometers to the north and south of the road, the multi-hued hills stretched uninterrupted by signs of civilization, other than the occasional hunter's or ranger's cabin and a few small villages and sylvith groves tucked into high mountain valleys. Fell lay on the western frontier of Ilwheirlane only one day's ride from Dworkin, the last town before the border into Lachan. Although they had been traveling for several hours toward Idris, the nearest town, the mountains still absorbed Alanna's thoughts when the coach came to an abrupt halt.

She opened the window with one hand, her other going to the musket in its rack beside the door. Outlaws and highwaymen were rare but not unknown. "What's wrong?" she called to the driver. She had heard no shot or other unusual sound and could see nothing through the window that might have caused them to stop, but her angle of view was limited.

"I d-don't know, m-my lady," the coachman stammered, "but… but there's one of them h-horned horses b-blocking the road."

Alanna's hand dropped from the musket and she opened the door of the coach.

"Oh, my lady, you can't go out there. It might hurt you," Agnes protested.

"Nonsense! I've never seen one, but I understand they're intelligent and only dangerous if you mean them, or their riders, harm. I've always wanted to see one," Alanna added, jumping to the ground.

The horned horse was a mare. She had a dappled gray coat with black, cloven hooves and a spiral horn set in the middle of her forehead. Taller than a horse at the withers, but more slender, her limpid eyes studied Alanna as intently as Alanna studied her. Her head wore no bridle, but she bore a saddle with a large leather bag strapped to it.

"Well, you're a beautiful creature, aren't you?" Alanna murmured, approaching cautiously.

"Here now, my lady, you mustn't get too near. It could hurt you," protested the coachman. The groom was too bemused to do anything but gape.

Alanna hesitated, remembering all she knew about the kariothin. They and the karothin, the horned stallions, had come to Tamar with the eslarin millennia ago, long before mankind had arrived. It was said that the eslarin created the kariothin from a cross between horses and some other species but gave them intelligence and the ability to speak mind to mind. They could not be captured or ridden without their consent, but magic and power drew them and they could be summoned or would volunteer to serve certain people. What could this one be doing blocking the road so near the frontier of Ilwheirlane, and where was her rider? She bore a saddle; someone must have ridden her.

Alanna held out her hand, flat with the palm up, so the mare could examine her scent. The karioth lowered her head and sniffed. Her muzzle felt like velvet and Alanna had to check herself to keep from reaching out to stroke the plush neck. Kariothin could be fearsome in battle and, though this one seemed calm, there was no point in taking unnecessary chances.

The karioth raised her head as though sensing Alanna's hesitation. Then she nodded and, walking to the edge of the road, pointed down into the ditch with her horn. If she had been endowed with the power of speech, she couldn't have said more clearly, "Come and look here."

Alanna followed and looked down. The ditch was deep and three bodies lay at the bottom.

"There are men down here, Edmer. I must find out how badly they're hurt. Leave Jem with the horses. I'll need your help to get them up the bank." Alanna was a healer, trained by the Kindred of Maera. It was her duty to tend to the wounded wherever she found them. She fetched her medical kit from the carriage and started to climb down the side of the ditch, testing each foothold on the frozen, treacherous slope.

"Here now, my lady, you can't get down there. Jem, Jem, stop gaping like a loony and hold the horses." The coachman shook the groom until he roused enough to take the reins.

"Begging your pardon, my lady, but if one of them's that beast's rider, it may attack if you meddle with him. They're touchy about their riders," Edmer added, edging around the coach to begin his descent as far from the karioth as he could manage.

"She'd hardly have led me to them if she didn't want me to touch them. She must have stopped us because she sensed I was a healer," Alanna said as she reached the bodies.

Two of the men wore the rough homespun garments of peasants, but the third was dressed as a gentleman in buff riding breeches, a heavy frieze cloak, and leather riding boots. The two peasants were dead. One of them had a hole through his chest which could well have been made by the karioth's horn, Alanna thought, eyeing the mare more warily. The other was clutching a sword, but the hand he held it with was charred black and the rest of his body looked shriveled.

The third man lay face down in the ditch. She probed for his life force and was relieved to find that he still lived. He was a small man and, as soon as she assured herself that he had no broken bones, she turned him over gently. His skin was as dark and wrinkled as the skin of a walnut and he had soft, white hair that grew in tufts like cotton. His clothes were worn and cut in an archaic style, but of good quality.

His breathing was shallow and his heartbeat erratic. His life force was faint and had a brittle intensity unlike any she had met before. He'd lost a great deal of blood from a sword cut in his shoulder and blood and life force oozed from the wound.

She reached out with her mind. She could block the loss of life force, but it was beyond her skill to staunch the flow of blood in the same way. Only a first class healer or a wizard could see the reality of the flesh well enough to do that, and there had been no wizards available to teach her when she had taken her training.

Alanna shrugged off the old regret. Bemoaning the limitations of her talents served no purpose. She strove instead to concentrate on what she could accomplish. She took a pair of scissors from her kit and, after easing the wounded man out of his cloak, cut through the fabric of his jacket and shirt, exposing the wound. Then she bound up the injury with gauze and had Edmer carry him up the bank.

Although Edmer and Alanna both kept one eye on her during this proceeding, the karioth merely watched, sometimes nodding her head with seeming approval.

Alanna had Edmer place the man on the seat opposite hers and she wrapped him in a travel rug to keep him as warm as possible. As the coach lurched into motion once more, Alanna saw the karioth take up a position just outside her window. The mare's beauty raised her spirits, yet she was anxious. Her carriage was well sprung, but it still rocked uncomfortably on the irregular surface of the road. Frail as the old man's life force was, Alanna feared he wouldn't survive the journey to the Sanctuary of Maera at Idris, but there was no place closer she could take him.

His wound was no longer bleeding but he had lost a lot of blood. The darkness of his skin couldn't conceal the gray tinge of shock. His life force flickered erratically and then flared with a strange, febrile brilliance.

"He's too old to take an injury like that one," Agnes said after a time, putting Alanna's thoughts into words. "He can't have much blood left in him."

"Yes, but I didn't expect him to survive until I got him into the carriage. He must have a tremendous will to live, and there's a strange feel to the energy of his life force, as though sometimes he draws on a source outside himself."

He lay like one already dead for several hours. Alanna had begun to despair of his regaining consciousness when he stirred. She shifted to the edge of the seat beside him to check on him just as he sighed and opened his eyes. They were deep, deep blue eyes, like a summer sky. When she looked into them, she felt as if she were falling down into a well of swirling azure, but she couldn't cry out or look away. Then his eyes shut and the world returned to normal around her.

He spoke in a thin, thready whisper, "So young. Why did you have to be so young?"

Still shaken by the effect of his eyes, his reference to her age irritated Alanna. "I'm twenty-three. I've been the chief healer in this area for seven years."

His eyes opened again, but this time they were just the eyes of an old man, shrewd and amused. "You have spirit, at least. And clear eyes. I could have done worse." His voice was a mere thread of sound, barely audible above the rattle of the wheels. Yet, as she listened to him, Alanna felt that she was alone with him in a pool of silence and the thin thread of his voice was the most important thing in the world.

"You could have done worse than what?"

"Than you." His lips twisted into the vestige of a smile. "I hunted for years for someone to carry it after me. I trained three women, but they died or broke faith. I was old. Perhaps my judgment failed." He sighed and his eyes closed. Alanna thought that he'd lapsed back into unconsciousness, but his voice came again, "Perhaps it fails me now, but I have no choice. Let it be that Jehan, patron of travelers, guided me to you."

His eyes opened again and he stirred on the narrow seat, as though surprised by a sudden thought. "You have green eyes. Cormor told me once that, if I was lucky, I'd find a girl with red hair and green eyes. I'd forgotten."

The memory seemed to strengthen him and he tried to sit up. Alanna pulled out another travel blanket from under her seat and used it as a cushion to make him comfortable.

"Who are you and why were you attacked?" she asked when he was settled.

"Fetch my bag and I'll tell you." His breath came in gasps, as if the effort to sit up had exhausted what little strength remained to him.

Alanna hesitated. His portmanteau was still on the back of the karioth.

"Fetch it," he said. "I need it now."

Alanna leaned out the window and called to Edmer to stop. The karioth seemed to have been expecting this for instead of shying away she came to the coach door and stood quietly while Alanna unstrapped the bag.

Only when Alanna had the bag inside the coach did the mare move away. Alanna signaled the coachman to drive on.

"Open it. There's a package on the top."

She unbuckled the bag noticing as she did so that the leather had been carved or pressed into a design of scales. The straps that held it closed had the appearance of snakes and the buckles were the snakes' heads. It looked old but the leather was strong and supple. It opened easily. As the old man had said, there was a cloth bound package on top and she pulled this out. It was light and felt curiously warm to her touch. She hastened to put it in his lap.

"No. Open it. It will soon be yours. Just hold it where I can touch it."

Alanna started to deny any claim to that strangely warm bundle, but sensed the depth of his will and gave way to him, unwrapping it as he bade her. Inside lay a great, pulsing jewel the size and shape of a goose egg. Deep emerald in color, it had a core of fire which expanded and contracted like the beating of a heart. She took it in her hand. It felt hot, but not painfully so, and she reached out and he entwined their fingers together around the stone. It flared at his touch, the pulses coming more rapidly. Alanna felt energy flow through her, filling her. She looked from the jewel to the man lying on the seat and it was as though the years and pain had rolled away. In the glow of the gem he no longer appeared to be dying, but he shook his head at the wonder in her eyes.

"No," he said, "it can't prevent my death. I'm a man. It has never linked with me as it will with you. It cannot save me. I only hope it will give me time to tell you something of what you must know." His voice was stronger and she no longer had to strain to hear him.

The flaring energy of the jewel had distracted her, but when Alanna caught the intent of his words she exclaimed, "You don't mean to give it to me? It must be valuable. Tell me the names of your heirs and I'll see it's sent to them. I can't take such a gift!"

"You have no choice. I'm dying and you're here. It will be yours." Then, in a softer tone he mused, "Perhaps it's no more than chance, but Cormor sometimes saw strands of the possible futures." He sighed. "It doesn't matter. It will be yours."

"But I don't want it. I don't even know what it is," Alanna protested.

His expression, which had grown distant, focused on her again. "Vyrkarion, the Talisman of Anor. You have wizard talent and training

enough to be a healer, you should recognize one of the living crystals."
His voice rang with pride. "The first of the karionin. Cormor, the last of
the great wizards, gave it to me to hold in trust until I found the one to
bear it after me. I could never use it fully, being a man, but you will."

"No! I'm no wizard. And the living crystals brought destruction to
even the great wizards." Alanna tried to draw her hand away from his,
but he prevented her.

"Stop!" She felt the energy of his anger flare through the jewel where
their hands still intertwined. "It shall be yours." He paused as his anger
subsided and spoke more gently, "You needn't fear that it will harm you.
The process of creation weakened the wizards who made the karionin,
but that wasn't the fault of the crystals. Agnith's madness created the
Wizard's Bane, not Cinkarion. You have talent. You must learn to use
it." He hesitated, then added, "Never flinch from destiny, child. That
changes nothing, only makes it more painful. It's your fate to bear
Vyrkarion, as it was mine to keep it for you."

She took a deep breath and let it go, striving for calm. "I don't want
such a destiny. There must be someone else."

He shook his head. "No one. When I die, and that will be soon now,
it will be yours. Yours until your death and no one will be able to take its
power from you save by your death. Even if it's stolen, it will respond
only to your will until you die. Don't fear it. It's neither good nor evil,
though one may use it for either. Its nature is power. It's a symbiote, alive
in a way, but what intent it may have is Jehan's will. What use you put it
to is up to you." With his free hand he reached out and stroked the side
of her face. "I'm sorry. It's a burden you didn't seek, but perhaps such
power is only safe in the hands of those who don't seek it." He sighed
again and an expression of pain or regret crossed his face. "I can't train
you. You'll have to find another to do that. My apprentice would be best,
or Derwen in Ninkarrak. That's where I was going, to Ninkarrak." His
voice died away.

"At least tell me your name and why those men attacked you."

"What?" He appeared startled by her question, as if the information
was something she ought to know. "I'm Myrriden, apprentice to the
Wizard Agnith in her last days. She was fond of me; sent me to safety
before she called the Wizard's Bane. I've lived in the south, in Belkova
mostly, for the last eight hundred years, kept alive by my duty to
Vyrkarion."

"Then why are you here, in Ilwheirlane?"

"I heard in the month of Anor that Maera had sent a prophecy saying
that 'Vyrkarion must come from the south.' So I set out for Ninkarrak."

"You've ridden all that way? It must be more than seven thousand
kilometers from Belkova to Ilwheirlane by land." Alanna had heard
fantastic tales of the endurance of the horned horses; now she could no

longer doubt their truth. "Why didn't you take a ship? They sail regularly from Lara to Ilwheirlane. Surely it would have been easier and safer."

Myrriden shook his head. "I don't like the sea. My experiences with it have been unpleasant. In recent years I've traveled nowhere that Loyce couldn't take me." He lay back against the pillows and shut his eyes. "I didn't expect to be pursued."

"Who would pursue you? Who were the men who attacked you?"

"Those were no men," he said. "Isklarin, agents of Gandahar. They picked up my trail when I crossed the Gwatar and their Road of Masters. I'd hoped to pass unseen, but their wizards have grown too strong, far too strong. Aavik, the lizard lord himself, follows me. His hirelings sought to kill me."

"Aavik? The ruler of Gandahar? Why would he follow you?"

His eyes opened and focused on her. "How sheltered you've been from the world, not to know the answer to that. Do you know nothing of what is happening in the south? Have you not heard of the taking of Ardagh, Nadrum and Darenje, the conquest of Lamash, the rebuilding of the Road of Masters?" His voice was weak, but Alanna heard anger in it.

"All those things happened before I was born. We have peace with the isklarin now. Their ships trade in our ports. Why would the ruler of Gandahar attack you?"

"Peace! They but bide their time." Myrriden's tone was contemptuous, but his anger had spent the little strength remaining to him and he had to struggle for breath before he could continue. "No, child, Aavik wants to resume the Dragon Wars, see mankind returned to slavery. He moves slowly, picking off the human nations one at a time, hoping our leaders will be blind and not band together to stop him until it's too late. With one of the karionin, he won't need to wait. He's a powerful wizard now; Vyrkarion would make that power almost limitless. He mustn't succeed."

"How can I stop a wizard?"

Even in the glow of the jewel, Alanna could see his ashen pallor. When it came again, his voice was the thin, thready whisper it had been when he first woke. "You must. My death... break trail. Take time to find you. Before they do, find my apprentice... in Ninkarrak. He'll train you..."

Myrriden died.

The great gem flared brilliantly and Alanna dropped it as the heat burned her hand, but as it fell in the old man's lap she saw the light go dark so that what lay on the bed was just an opaque, green stone. She hesitated, but only for a moment, then she picked it up. When she touched it, she felt a wave of energy. The crystal cleared and the flame rose again inside it and began to beat in the same rhythm as her heart.

III

> When he was but a baby
> And his mother made him cry,
> There was a pretty maiden
> Who would comfort him and sigh.
> Sigh, sigh for the Wanderer
> Wherever he may be,
> For he is doomed to exile
> By the shore of Sorrow Sea.

— FROM THE *BALLAD OF AUBREY THE WANDERER* BY ANONYMOUS

Jerevan woke to pain and blindness and the knowledge that Myrriden was dead. The shock of his old master's death was what had roused him. But why had he been unconscious? What was the matter with him?

"Where am I?" he demanded, sensing someone near.

"You're at home, my lord," the familiar voice of Otto, his servant, informed him.

The memory of the battle came back to him. "The isklarin?"

"Dead. You outlasted them, or you wouldn't be here."

"Derwen?"

"Dead."

Jerevan sighed as he accepted his guilt. If he could have linked with Derwen, Derwen would still be alive. But he hadn't been able to control his instinctive reaction to such a linkage. Self-control was something he'd taken pride in, and in this most critical instance his self-control had failed. He deserved his pain. It was a lesson to remind him that he had not progressed as far as he had thought.

"How long have I been unconscious?"

"Two weeks. I was growing concerned."

Jerevan grimaced and brushed a hand across his face. "So long and my head is still killing me. It was a close thing, Otto."

"Yes, my lord."

"If I'd been able to link with Derwen..."

Otto snorted. "And if seralin had wings, they still wouldn't fly. I was with you all the years you fought his curse. There'd never have come a time when you could link with that one."

Jerevan had no response to that. It was true, no matter how much he might wish that it was not. Still, he had another concern now.

"Myrriden is dead. That's what woke me. Vyrkarion has a new bearer. I must find out who. We'll have to take the carriage. You'd better start packing."

"You've only just regained consciousness..." Otto protested.

"That doesn't matter. I'll have to heal on the road."

Thrym paused with his back against the outer wall of the stairwell, holding his breath, concentrating on the sounds made by the guard clumping up the stairs beneath him. Background music from the ballroom echoed in the stone-lined spiral, but his hearing was keen. He sighed with relief as the footsteps shuffled to a stop at the landing below. The guard had not heard him.

Like a shadow Thrym slipped on up the stairs, cursing the thick walls that blocked even his exceptional vision. Four levels up, five. Rad Flickra had supplied him with maps of the lower floors, but had been unable to get information about these levels in time. One more spiral of the staircase and he would reach the floor with the first of the balconies, but there were sounds now of men moving above him. How far up? He abandoned caution and ran up the next circle of stairs. A heavy wooden door led off the landing. He tried the handle, the touch of his fingers as delicate as a lover's, his mind probing the mechanism. It was unlocked.

Almost too easy, he thought, as he opened the door and eased through. He closed it even as the steps of what sounded like a whole patrol of guards clattered down the stairs behind him. The room he had entered was large and unlit, but darkness was no hindrance to Thrym. His sight was not human sight, but the sight of the were-peoples who saw the true nature of things, their inside construction as well as their outer form. As clearly as though the room were brightly lit, he saw the worn carpet, the shelves of dog-eared books, even the contents of the cupboards filled with stuffed animals and toys.

A playroom! He must have entered the private apartment of a member of the court, perhaps even a member of the royal family. A child would be asleep by this time, but there might be others still awake. Any child living in the Black Tower would have attendants.

Thrym crossed the room to the opposite door, a shadow among shadows. The hall beyond the door was lit, although it appeared unoccupied. He should have been able to see better through the door, but something in the Black Tower itself limited vision; he had noticed it before. It was disorienting. He was not used to limits to what he could see. The balcony had to be off one of the rooms in that direction, though, so he would have to chance the hall.

VYRKARION: THE TALISMAN OF ANOR

Thrym stepped into the hall before he realized that it was no longer empty. A woman had emerged from the right hand door on the other side. Small and delicate, the top of her head would fit below his chin, and her skin was the whitest he had ever seen, blood vessels showing through the surface like a faint blue tracery. She had hair the color of cornsilk and her eyes, big and dark, looked like bruises in her pale face. He had never seen anyone appear quite so fragile.

Jehan, he thought, a guard's one thing but I can't hurt this one.

Minta Banes smoothed the wrinkled sheet and tucked it back under the restless form of the sleeping nahar, Aubrey Cinnac, heir to the throne of Ilwheirlane. His bad hip had been bothering him all day and he had taken a long time to fall asleep. She was just straightening, when she heard the music. The melody was faint, but she still hurried to leave her charge's room and close the door behind her.

Although the music had not lasted long, for her to have heard it at all meant that someone had opened the door of the nursery suite. Otherwise noise from the ball could not have penetrated so far. No one should have opened that door at this hour of the night. It only led to the playroom and the apartment she shared with Aubrey. Since no one would come to see the nahar at this hour, nearly midnight, it had to be someone to see her.

Minta shivered. She had not seen her husband in months but there were other men, both guards and lords, who had expressed an interest in her company, and not one of them would she welcome.

She tiptoed across to her other door, the one that opened on the hall to the playroom. It was ajar. She pushed it open and looked out. There had only been a brief burst of music. She hoped whoever had opened the door had gone away, someone who had got the wrong floor, perhaps. It happened; the whole Tower was a warren and people often got lost. She stepped out into the hall.

The man coming through the open playroom door was tall and wore a black domino and a mask that covered the upper half of his face, but Minta relaxed when she saw him. There was a fall of rich lace at his throat and his stockings were of silk with a pattern of hand-embroidered lilies on them. A guest from the masquerade ball. Perhaps he was lost after a few too many drinks. At least, he was not anyone she knew. She leaned back against the door.

He, on the other hand, was obviously startled.

"Who are you?" Minta asked.

Her question seemed to reassure him. "Just a man who wishes to make an unheralded exit, fair lady," he said, approaching her.

"There's no way out of the Tower from here." She frowned. Why had he not retreated when he realized he had come to the wrong place? Strangers were not permitted in the royal apartments.

His eyes narrowed. "On the contrary, for me there's an excellent exit from here." He bowed and in the same movement, the finale to the bow, stepped up to her until their bodies touched and she was pressed against her door. She tried, far too late, to dodge sideways and away, but he gripped her arms, gently but firmly. She could not escape.

"The room you just came out of, does it have a balcony?" His voice was low and urgent.

Minta was surprised to realize that she was not afraid. His hands were strong but he was not hurting her. He had not hurt her even when she struggled. His touch was gentle, almost tender. "Yes," she said, "but it's a long drop down to the foot of the cliffs and there aren't any lower balconies. This room is on the sea side."

"No matter." He smiled and led her back into her room. Once inside with the door shut, he released her. "What's through there?" He pointed at Aubrey's door.

"Nahar Aubrey's room." Minta was suddenly frightened for her charge where she had not feared for herself and she moved sideways to block his door. "If you hurt him, your death will be unpleasant."

"Don't get excited, little one." Thrym grinned and pulled off his mask, revealing mocking amber eyes. "I have no intention of harming anyone." He began to undress.

"What are you doing?" Minta's voice quivered. She knew it would do her no good to scream if he meant to assault her. No one would hear, any more than they would have heard if he had been her husband or Lord Charden.

"Don't worry," he laughed, "I have no desire to take your virtue, or at least," and his eyes swept over her slender form covered only by a nightgown and a thin robe, "not right now."

She felt the heat rise in her cheeks. "Then why are you undressing?"

"I climb better that way." His smile faded. He was down to his pants and she looked away from him, but her eyes found his image in her mirror and she did not look away again as he finished stripping.

His skin was an even bronze color, his body slender, well over medium height and beautifully made. Minta found herself shivering at the sight of him, the long lines of his thighs, the width of his shoulders. But he paid no attention to her. He put all his things into a cloth sack he had unfolded from around his waist and she caught a glimpse of jewelry. He had to be a thief. She knew she should make some effort to escape and warn the guards, but she had no desire to do so. She remembered the firm, gentle grip of his hands and she could see the sleek symmetry of his body. She would hate to see him in chains.

He finished packing his things and turned, his amber eyes finding hers unerringly in the mirror. A lock of dark hair draped his forehead.

VYRKARION: THE TALISMAN OF ANOR

He grinned and grasped her shoulders, turning her around to face him, unconscious of his nudity.

"Do you get any free time?"

His thumbs rubbed sensitive points on her shoulders so that Minta felt an insane desire to press herself against him. She could not remember when a man had handled her as gently before. She felt warm and as safe as she had felt in her father's arms as a child. But the other feelings his hands evoked did not remind her of childhood.

"Sometimes." She felt reckless. "I have Miunesdays off, but I have to be back by eleven."

"What's your name?" He drew her close, his hands moving over her back and shoulders causing tremors inside her.

"Minta." She lowered her head but looked up at him between her lashes. She was hoping he would kiss her.

"Well, pretty Minta, I'd like to kiss your soft, pink lips, but then you might be even more shocked by what I have to do now. So I won't. You see, I'm only half human and, though it's an advantage in my trade, my next trick usually discourages girls like you." He smiled at her, but she sensed bitterness behind the light words.

"If what you're about to see doesn't bother you too much," he continued, "you might meet me next Miunesday at the Inn of the Golden Ingling, at the north end of the harbor. I'll be there by five and stay until nine, but you won't see me if you try to make it a party."

He released her and stepped onto the balcony, putting his sack down near the edge. "You really would be better off not watching this time," he said, turning away from her. Then his whole body began to shift and melt before her eyes.

Minta stifled a scream, pressing her fist into her mouth and biting it, but her eyes did not leave the metamorphosing shape on the balcony. It — she could no longer think of that shifting mass as he — went down on all fours and grew longer. She could see the form of a lizard emerging. She shuddered. He was an isklar, then, one of the lizard folk. And yet, he had called himself half human. The isklarin never referred to themselves as in any way human no matter how mixed their blood. At least, she had been told they didn't.

The form solidified, a sleek lizard with intricately colored patterns on its pebbled skin that looked like scaled plates. It was about one hundred and seventy centimeters from the snout to the base of the tail, and the tail was that long again. But the head disturbed her the most. Its skull was not flat, but domed, disturbingly human. Minta could not help staring. When it looked up and met her eyes, its eyes looked sad. Then it grabbed the sack in its teeth and was gone.

She ran out onto the balcony and looked over the railing. The lizard was already several floors down. Holding the sack in its mouth, it ran down the sheer wall of the Tower as though it were on level ground.

Minta watched until the lizard disappeared into the darkness at the foot of the cliff.

IV

4730, 473RD CYCLE OF THE YEAR OF THE OX
MONTH OF ILFARNAR

> There was a time when wizards ruled the world,
> And in that Golden Age the wizards made
> Eight living crystals to enhance their power
> And guarantee their patterns never fade.
> Anor and Torin first, the two made one,
> Their crystals fused and something more, some part,
> Was torn, and so was born Vyrkarion,
> The Talisman of Anor, from their hearts.
>
> — EXCERPT FROM "ILKARIONIN, THE LIVING CRYSTALS"
> PUBLISHED IN *LEST WE FORGET: A BOOK OF TEACHING RHYMES*
> BY WILTON WIRRAMARETH OF ILWHEIRLANE, 4207

Alanna arrived at the Inn of Three Sulcaths in Tarm on the evening of the ninth day of her journey to Ninkarrak. The inn was a long, rambling brick building overlooking a small lake at the edge of the town. Much of the shore of the lake was surrounded by reeds, but the brief glimpse she had of a milling mass of huge water birds convinced her that the inn's name was grossly inaccurate. The Inn of Three Hundred Sulcaths would have been more apt.

The building was old, the oak panels inside dark with the patina of centuries. As Alanna passed through the public bar to the private parlor she had reserved, a man sitting at a table near the center of the room looked up to meet her glance. His eyes were dark pools in the dimly lit barroom. Gazing into them, she felt the same shock she had felt when Myrriden's eyes first opened, the feeling of sinking into infinite depths. The sensation of vertigo was so overwhelming she stumbled and almost fell. She caught herself on the back of a chair, but she could not tear her eyes away from his. She got an impression of pale hair and tanned skin before he looked away and she was able to flee after the landlord.

Jerevan sat at his table and watched the figure of the woman who now bore Vyrkarion disappear behind the door to a private parlor. The sight of her seared him. Normally he could have extended his vision and watched her even through the door and walls, but this evening he was having trouble just maintaining consciousness. His head ached and his vision, even normal human vision, blurred in and out. The damage done in his recent battle with the isklarin was far from healed. He was still suffering badly from mind burn and the drain of traveling and tracing Vyrkarion had not helped his condition, but he'd had to see for himself.

What? That Myrriden, his first and most important teacher, was dead? He'd known that; he'd felt Myrriden die.

The new bearer? Yes. That had been his reason. He'd needed to see her in person. But now what?

The sight of her had nearly blinded him all over again. She might be untrained, but her aura was bright. She'd be a strong wizard someday, as strong or stronger than he was. So much for Derwen's claim that such strength was rare.

He shook his head. It was rare. He knew that from his own experience. And Derwen was dead. There was no point in scoring off a dead man. He hadn't realized until now how much antipathy he still felt toward Derwen. He'd buried his bitterness instead of dealing with it. Men might be able to afford to do that, wizards could not.

Yet he was a wizard now, the strongest in all the human lands. The others looked to him for leadership. He'd have to work his way through his past resentments and find some way to heal himself of, not only the guilt, but the hatred that had caused that guilt.

But not now. Now he needed to rest and heal. He'd seen the new bearer of Vyrkarion. She was young and bright and too much for him to deal with until his healing was more advanced.

In his present condition, he hurt too much to even think about her. He pushed his chair back from the table and Otto came and helped him up to his room.

Who was he? Why had just seeing him had such an effect on her? Safe in the private parlor, Alanna felt for the Talisman on its chain around her neck, yet concealed by the bodice of her dress. Surely Aavik couldn't have found her so quickly?

Yet the thought of facing the man again when she went up to her room frightened her. She worried about it all evening but, when she finally did go out, he had left. She was thankful for the reprieve, but sensed it was temporary.

The sight of the same man lounging in the doorway of the public bar the next morning when she came down the stairs was, therefore, not unexpected. She swallowed a lump in her throat, however, when she realized that the second coach and four in the courtyard beside her own belonged to him.

Seen in daylight, the stranger appeared broad-shouldered, but lean, and much taller than she had thought him the night before; leaning against the doorframe, he towered over the youth sweeping out the hallway. She thought for a moment that he would speak to her, but he only nodded. His eyes were steel-blue and the light-colored hair was golden, cut in a smooth cap. His clothing looked expensive and in the height of fashion, from the Esterian lace at his throat and cuffs to the silk-lined cloak. He made her think of a sword sheathed in velvet.

Did he know she carried the Talisman? Was that the reason for his apparent interest in her?

She eyed him covertly as her bags were strapped to her coach and had to admit that he was handsome. He had high cheekbones and a jutting chin, a strong face with smooth tan skin taut over prominent bones. His mouth was wide and thin-lipped, yet sensual. She shivered and tore her gaze away.

His carriage followed hers through the morning as they climbed higher and higher into the Croghans, a range of low hills that dissected the coast. She stopped for luncheon at the Falcon's Flight in Thirsk. When his carriage continued on, Alanna thought she must have been mistaken about his interest. She felt relieved and angry with herself for letting her imagination get out of hand. But that evening, when she stopped at the Pied Pony in Harby, she saw him again.

The next morning his coach was again waiting when she was ready to leave, but he still made no attempt to speak to her. As his coach followed hers across the wide fields of the central valley of Ilwheirlane, drab now with the onset of winter, she was torn by both fear and fascination. Was he an agent of Aavik, the wizard-lord of the isklarin, bent on wresting the Talisman away from her? If not, who was he?

His coach continued on when she stopped for lunch at Mosby. She wondered at this, for she had warned Edmer and the grooms not to tell anyone where they intended stopping that night. The order had puzzled them, but she was certain they had obeyed her. Nevertheless, this time she was equally sure that the stranger had not stopped following her.

She had planned on spending the night at the Running Hart just outside of Oswestry, but, as her coach approached that establishment, she signaled Edmer to drive on. "We'll stop at an inn in the center of the town," she called up to him.

"What if there aren't rooms available this late?" he protested.

"Then we'll continue until we find an inn that has room. Drive on."

He did so and a quarter of an hour later drove into the courtyard of the Blue Boar in the middle of downtown Oswestry, a large town which had grown in recent years with the increase in the volume of woolen manufacturing.

As Alanna had never heard of the Blue Boar until she saw its sign, she couldn't think how the stranger could find her there. Yet his emergence from the public room as she entered the inn was again not totally unexpected. Some part of her had sensed from her first sight of him that escaping him wouldn't be simple. He startled her, however, when he greeted her.

"I've been waiting for you," he said. "I'd begun to wonder if you'd changed your plans," he paused and his eyes laughed, "yet again. I've ordered dinner for us both."

She hesitated. Now the time had come to face him, she found that her fear had receded. She could detect nothing threatening in his manner. Perhaps the flash of humor in his eyes, blended with the sarcasm, disarmed her. At any rate, the Blue Boar was a busy posting inn. Surely it was better to face him over dinner within its walls than on some isolated stretch of road.

"My lady doesn't speak to strange men, sir," Agnes interrupted. "How dare you address her in that manner?"

"It's all right, Agnes. He isn't a complete stranger, I suppose. I've known him by sight for several days." Alanna smiled at the absurdity and, catching an answering gleam in his eyes, was again reassured.

"But, my lady..."

"Never mind, Agnes. See to our things." Alanna turned to him. "If you have dinner ordered, then let us dine."

He smiled and she felt the pull of his charm. "After you, my lady."

The landlord showed them to a private parlor with a table set for two. The stranger walked over to the fireplace. His blue coat fit impressively broad shoulders, and his pantaloons did not disguise powerfully muscled legs. Alone with him after the landlord had shut the door, Alanna felt intimidated by his obvious physical strength and the sense of controlled power he emanated.

"You're brave," he said, turning to face her. The firelight glinted in the fine textured gold of his hair.

Her face felt stiff. "May I ask your name and why you've been following me?"

He bowed. "Rayne, Jerevan Rayne, at your service."

"As you know my travel plans, I assume you know my name as well."

He laughed and she again felt an intangible pull, as if some part of him reached out to her and urged her to laugh with him. "Alanna Cairn, the Tamrai of Fell. I read the inn register the first night I saw you."

"That doesn't explain why you followed me, or why you would bother reading the register."

His expression sobered. "Or what business I have inviting you to dinner?"

"That too."

He turned from her and strode across the room. She felt a momentary triumph at having resisted his charm. She sensed his disappointment even as she was again impressed by his strength.

On reaching the window, he said, "You're carrying a certain jewel." He turned to face her. "Do you know its value?"

Alanna's hand went to her breast and her head came up as though he had slapped her. It was the Talisman that interested him! She realized how alone she was, her maid upstairs and Edmer in the servants' accommodations, but she managed to maintain at least an appearance of calm. "What does that matter to you, Master Rayne?"

The dark blue eyes held hers, studying her and then releasing her, and her earlier triumph at having resisted him died. He hadn't been trying.

He shook his head. "Don't be afraid. I mean you no harm." He strode back to the fire. "It recently came to my attention that the Wizard Myrriden was bringing Vyrkarion north. I also discovered that other interests meant to intercept it."

"Other interests?"

He faced her and she was caught by the force of his eyes. "Was Myrriden still alive when you found him?"

"How did you know…?" She checked herself, flushing.

"That you'd found him." His expression mocked her. "You're carrying Vyrkarion. Either he gave it to you, or you took it from his body."

"He gave it to me, but he was dying."

Jerevan went to the bell pull and summoned the landlord. "You can tell me what happened over dinner."

"Why should I?"

He smiled and Alanna saw with an unpleasant shock that the expression on his face was pity. She had been feeling small and afraid, but that realization angered her. She didn't want to be pitied by anyone, but particularly not by this arrogant stranger.

His words, however, expressed not pity but determination. "You'll tell me what I want to know because I won't answer your questions until you've answered mine. You need my information far more than I need yours."

Before she could answer him as she felt he deserved, the landlord knocked and entered with two serving maids carrying the first course of their dinner. It was some minutes before they were again at liberty to speak freely, and by that time Alanna had realized the probable truth of his words.

When the maids left, she told Jerevan of her meeting with Myrriden. She began reluctantly, but his comprehension was so quick, his questions so apt that in the end she told him everything Myrriden said before his death and, in addition, an outline of the events leading up to the meeting of the Town Council in Idris and her petition to the Estahar.

When she finished that part of her story, Jerevan frowned. "I knew, of course, that the eslarin had closed their borders. All Ninkarrak was stunned when the ports of Isin and the great port at Elkova closed to human shipping. But I must admit, I hadn't thought about the consequences to the sylvith crop."

Alanna sighed. "Did they at least tell the merchants why? Can it be related to what Myrriden said about Gandahar and a revival of the Dragon Wars?"

"No," he shook his head. "Eslarin harbors were open to human shipping throughout most of the original Dragon Wars. I can't see them breaking their policy of neutrality to side with Gandahar now. Although what Myrriden said about Aavik is true, you mustn't doubt that."

"My father was a follower of Jehan. He believed that all the races should live in peace, that the age of wars between the were-peoples and humanity ended long ago." Her tone was wistful.

Jerevan smiled. "An admirable vision. As another worshiper of Jehan, I hope that such a time will come. But your father was foolish if he thought we've already achieved that goal. Peace is a dream some of us work toward. It's a long way from being reality. The fighting in Cibata has never stopped."

Alanna wanted to argue but realized that she didn't know enough of current world events. She sighed and turned back to her dinner.

Begun with beef dressed in a sauce made from sylvith pods and a dish of mixed greens, the meal continued with roast sulcath and candied lommas fruit, served with an excellent red wine. Jerevan was an attentive host and Alanna enjoyed herself so well she forgot her earlier fears. "That was delicious. You judged my tastes well," she said, finishing the last scrap on her plate.

He smiled and she experienced again the draw of his powerful sensuality. But it was no longer just a physical attraction she felt. His mind was so quick. She had never before found anyone with whom she could discuss things so easily.

"That was my intent," he said. "Would you like dessert?" His blue gaze felt warm. A faint network of laugh lines radiated from his eyes.

"No, thank you, but I would like another glass of wine. It's superb."

Jerevan refilled her glass and his own. "It's from Sussey, the area around Ruffin. They produce the finest red wines in the world there. It's a beautiful place to visit as well."

Alanna thought wistfully of that sunny, southern isle famous for its music, its fruit, its pearls and its wine. "I've always wanted to travel, but this is the farthest I've ever been from home. What are they like, the dolphin folk? I've never met any of the were-kind."

"The people of Sussey are incredibly open and friendly, but they're not pure-blooded. They're descendants of native ingvalarin and ship-wrecked human sailors."

"The dolphin folk never hated humanity, did they?"

He shook his head, smiling. "No, they're too happy to hate. They have the endless playground of the sea and music I can't begin to describe. They're the most joyous people I've ever known."

A sudden thought made Alanna ask, "Are they all wizards? I mean, if they all have mixed blood, do they have both vision and will?"

Jerevan frowned and his eyes assessed her. "Many do, of course. They're the greatest sailors in the world because most of them have at least some control over wind and wave. And their present ruler wields another jewel like the one you bear with greater power than has been seen since the Age of Wizards. Still, only a few stay with their studies. They have talent, but most of them lack desire."

His words or his attitude gave her the clue. She had sensed his power all evening, but she hadn't put a name to it. Now, she said, "But you don't lack either, do you? Who are you?"

"I told you; my name is Jerevan Rayne."

"But who is Jerevan Rayne, and what is your interest in the Talisman?"

He sighed and his tone was regretful, "Perhaps you'd know me better by my title. I'm the Hetri of Leyburn."

Alanna gasped. Of course, she knew him better by his title, and she was appalled at how much the knowledge hurt. She would never have sat down to dinner with him if she had known his identity. His name was a byword for loose living, vice, and perversion, and had been so for over fifty years. The infamous Hetri of Leyburn, no wonder he appeared handsome: he could take any form he chose. No wonder, too, that she had sensed a basic sensuality in his nature; for nearly a hundred years his time had been ill spent in every form of lecherous indulgence. And above all he was famed for his sadism, particularly with regard to women. Even in Fell she had heard the tales of ladies of rank who had killed themselves after becoming involved with him.

Alanna thought of the dark pull of his sensuality and how quickly she had been drawn to it and shivered. She rose and started to leave.

"Wait!" Jerevan also rose from his seat. "However much my presence may offend you, Tamrai Cairn, don't you think you'd better endure it a little longer? That is, if you still want to know more about Vyrkarion and how I found you."

Alanna hesitated, her hand on the door handle. Her skin crawled at the idea of facing him now that she knew who he was, but he was right; she did need information. In fact, she had a duty to perform and, whatever else the Hetri of Leyburn might be, he was a powerful wizard. In a time when the number and skill of wizards had been declining for centuries, it was said that he alone of humankind could claim to have the full knowledge and power of the wizards of old. She turned back slowly.

"That's better." Jerevan still stood by his chair.

"How did you find me?"

"I have all the books of Anor and Torin, the creators of Vyrkarion, as well as those of Cormor and Belis. I doubt if anyone else alive knows as much about the karionin as I do. I knew the hour Vyrkarion began to move north. I'd have met Myrriden in Lachan, but I was delayed." His hand went to the left side of his face as though feeling for something.

"What would you have done when you found him? Slain him and taken the Talisman?"

"Vyrkarion is of no more use to me than it was to Myrriden. Only a woman can use it fully. And, in case you haven't noticed, I may have followed you and fed you dinner, but I haven't harmed you," he paused and ran a meaningful look down the length of her body, "in any way."

Alanna flushed, but stifled any further response. She walked back to the table. As the Hetri of Leyburn was not noted for his scruples, angering him could prove dangerous. Her hands gripped the back of the chair she had sat in through dinner. "Will Aavik be able to track me as you've done?"

"I doubt it." Jerevan pulled his chair out from the table and sat down. "Vyrkarion protects you from normal farseeing. Only someone trained to know exactly what to look for could have found you. Such information isn't available, as far as I know, in Gandahar."

He paused and Alanna felt heat rising in her cheeks as he studied her. His eyes were no longer warm, as they had been over dinner, but analytical. "Nevertheless, once you reach Ninkarrak it will only be a matter of time before Aavik finds you and from then on, until you're trained, your life will be in constant danger. It's imperative that you begin your training immediately."

He added more gently, "Sit down and finish your wine. There's much more I need to tell you."

Alanna shook her head. "I don't want to hear any more. I've listened to you too long already. I know I need to be trained, but the only thing I need from you is the address where I can find the Wizard Derwen."

Jerevan's eyes narrowed. He leaned back and said, "In his grave. I doubt you'll get information from him there." His lips twisted. "Now will you sit down?"

Alanna sank into the chair, pressing her hands together to keep them from trembling. "Myrriden said that either his apprentice or Derwen would train me. Only he never told me the name of his apprentice."

Jerevan's expression softened. "Derwen died before Myrriden in an assault by wizards from Gandahar. They caught us off guard. I was injured in the conflict myself." His expression was suddenly grim and his hand again went up to feel his left cheek. "That was what kept me from meeting Myrriden."

"Do you know who Myrriden meant when he spoke of his apprentice?"

"He had a number of apprentices over the years, but in this case he almost certainly meant me." Jerevan shifted in his chair, as though he had started to move closer to her and then changed his mind. "The idea of having had me as his apprentice amused him. He often referred to me in that way."

Alanna's hands clenched into fists on the table in front of her. "I can't be trained by you!"

Jerevan grimaced. "There's no one else presently available in Ilwheirlane capable of training you."

"There must be someone else. In any event, do you think I'd take your word that there isn't? Even in Fell your name is infamous."

Jerevan looked amused by her vehemence. "Is it my moral laxity that offends you, or the fear that you might find me attractive?"

Alanna rose again. "How dare you!" She felt cold with the knowledge that he sensed the attraction she had experienced and for a moment she felt again the pull of that deep, controlled sensuality. Then she reminded herself of who and what he was. "If I were to feel attracted by you, I need only remember that your whole appearance is a lie. Before you became a wizard, I've heard you looked quite different, grotesque was the word used, and I'm sure that was a better reflection of your nature." She stalked to the door.

"One moment." Jerevan spoke softly, but the note of command in his voice penetrated her rage and stopped her. When she looked back, the brilliance of his eyes unnerved her. He rose and handed her an engraved piece of cardboard. She resisted the impulse to flinch.

"My card, Tamrai Cairn. I forgive you your impertinence this time. You're ignorant and perhaps I invited it." His eyes stripped her and weighed her, body and soul. He added, "You'll come to me in the end."

Somehow Alanna found the strength to stiffen. "Maera grant I never be reduced to that!"

He bowed and opened the door for her.

V

4730, 473RD CYCLE OF THE YEAR OF THE OX
MONTH OF ILFARNAR

The maiden she was lonely
'Til the maiden met a thief.
The thief he was a charmer;
Would he bring them all to grief?
Grief, grief for the Wanderer
Wherever he may be,
For he is doomed to exile
By the shore of Sorrow Sea.

— FROM THE BALLAD OF AUBREY THE WANDERER BY ANONYMOUS

On the Miunesday after Minta's encounter with the thief, she spent the morning walking in the Royal Park along the cliffs overlooking the Bay of Lanth. The green preserve stretched across the point of land south of the mouth of the River Glyn, isolating the royal compound from the city of Ninkarrak.

In the early afternoon, the harbor drew her. She told herself that she needed a new shawl and walked past the Inn of the Golden Ingling into the market.

The port of Ninkarrak had the largest harbor on Tamar. From the edge of the Royal Park it stretched south for kilometers down the coast. Over two hundred ships could be berthed in the slips and there was anchorage for many times that number. The hills circling the bay sheltered the harbor and ships came there from all over the world.

The market reflected the cosmopolitan nature of the port. Everything that survived shipping could be found in one stall or another. There were goods from Ilwheirlane, too, and street players and mimes mingled with the crowds of shoppers, sightseers and hucksters calling out their wares.

Ironmongers Street displayed ironwork of all kinds from plowshares to chimney pots. Other streets were devoted to other goods: ceramics from the towns of Grede or Finmyth in Ilwheirlane, or from Larsa in Kailane; copperware from Nacaonne; or leather work from Lachan or Pelona. There was even a street dedicated to weapons like dueling pistols and muskets, but Minta preferred more delicate goods.

She could spend hours in Jewelers Row gazing at pearls from Sussey set in gold by the jewelers of Khorat or Mizar, emeralds and amethysts from Nacaonne, sapphires from Amrioth, or diamonds from Jamnagar. In the Street of Perfumes the air was overpowering with the rich, cloying scents of jasmine and anathallia, attar of meldethin and musk. But most of that afternoon she spent in a shop off the Street of Glass watching a glass blower create exquisite figures of birds and beasts. She bought a tiny green dragon with bright red wings and a red tongue, hoping it would bring her luck.

"That's the size they are at birth," the glass blower told her as he took her money.

"Have you really seen one?" Minta eyed the old man curiously. He was small but wiry with a hooked nose and large, precise hands.

"I was from Lamash before it fell and I went to Bayat and learned glass-blowing. Lots of them still live in the southern mountains. Saw a clutch hatch once. They look just like that, right out of the eggs, little grass snakes with blood red wings."

"It's beautiful. I'll treasure it."

"Tell your friends. Lathan the Lamashite on the Street of Glass."

The silk houses and fabric shops were further east, away from the harbor in the more fashionable part of town, but shops in the market sold all kinds of accessories, shawls and capes, gloves, hats or fans. There were shops selling everything Minta could imagine and the sights, sounds and smells fascinated her. Yet, as the afternoon progressed, Minta found herself returning to the region of the Golden Ingling.

Her husband's hands had never been gentle. There had been no reason for the thief to treat her gently. The thief's body, too, had been so beautiful before it changed. Sandor had been heavy and coarse even when she first met him and had only grown grosser with the years. She hated him to touch her. After Sandor, she had thought that she would never want a man.

Yet there was something about the thief. The feel of his hands on her back and shoulders stayed in her mind. So, though she told herself any number of times that she had no intention of going to the Inn of the Golden Ingling at five o'clock, Minta knew all the time that she would.

She entered the tavern half an hour after five. She had been on the street nearby for some time, but at the last moment she had almost left, torn by fear and shyness. She felt that, if she went to meet him, he would take it as an admission that she wanted him, and that terrified her. Yet she did want him, and that terrified her more.

When Minta did go in she was pale and felt more as if she were going to an execution than to a potential lover. The light in the tavern was dim. She froze inside the doorway, waiting for her eyes to adjust, incapable in any case of going farther.

The tavern was not full, but a number of people, mostly men, sat at the tables or in front of the bar. Several gaudily dressed women waited on them. Minta's eyes were beginning to make out faces when the thief materialized out of the dimness beside her.

Thrym had known she was coming. Rad Flickra might call him a fool for making a date with her, but he was not fool enough to walk headlong into a trap. One of Flickra's men had followed Minta from the moment she left the Royal Park and he had watched her himself for the past half hour from behind a curtain in an upstairs window.

He had not believed she would take the final step. She had watched him change. No human woman would want him after seeing that.

"I didn't think you'd come," he said, cursing the unsteadiness of his voice. He put his arm around her and guided her toward a booth at the back.

"I didn't want to." Minta sat on the edge of the seat, looking relieved when he sat opposite rather than beside her. A candle set in a round glass holder threw a fitful light across her face. She looked tense and he wondered again if a troop of guardsmen were not on their way. At least Flickra's man would warn him.

"Why did you then?"

"I didn't mean to, but my feet just came." She smiled.

Some of Thrym's wariness eased, replaced by tension of another kind. He said, "I'll have to kiss them then, those little feet of yours."

Minta shivered. "Why did you invite me?" Her eyes were intent on his face. He saw the strain in her expression even in the inadequate light from the guttering candle.

The question stunned him. He hesitated, trying to put words to something that he had not thought about, only felt. "I wanted to see you again, hold you again. From the moment I touched you in the hall, I wanted to touch more of you. You looked so beautiful, so delicate, like frost flowers in the north that melt when you touch them, but you didn't melt. You made me take fire." He paused. "I thought you felt the same way when you watched me in the mirror, but I was afraid what I did later would spoil it. I'm glad it didn't." He grinned and gathered her hands into his.

"I don't even know your name," Minta protested, trying to pull away.

"Thrym," he said, interlocking their fingers, despite her resistance.

"Just Thrym?"

"Some call me Thrym Isknac, 'lizard-born'." He eyed her face for her reaction, but could see no change. She was uneasy, but not more so than before. "I have no name really but Thrym." He turned her hands in his to stop their fluttering, his thumbs finding her palms and massaging.

Minta stilled and her eyes widened. "Don't," she murmured.

"I must," he said. "Come upstairs. I've taken a room. We won't be disturbed."

She gasped, looking panic stricken. "I can't. It's too quick. I don't know you." Then, "I'm married."

Thrym hesitated. That was the last thing he had expected her to say. If she had claimed to be a virgin, he would have been less shocked. "Isn't it a bit late for you to think about him now? If you loved him, you wouldn't have come."

"Love him?" Minta laughed, "I hate him, but it's still wrong."

Thrym studied her, trying to see inside her to what had brought her. He had some wizard talent, but analyzing emotions was not an aspect that he used often. She shivered under the intensity of his gaze and he felt a wave of fear and uncertainty, but underlying it and mingled with it there was a craving for warmth, and somehow that feeling of warmth was associated with him. He swallowed and fought to calm himself. The feel of her emotions excited him, but she was still afraid and it was suddenly important to him that, when they did make love, she not be afraid. "I could have told you more if we'd gone upstairs, but I'll wait," he said, raising one of her hands to his lips and kissing the palm, "for now."

Minta's eyes widened and her tongue flicked across her lips nervously. Thrym could feel her awareness of him through their linked hands and he continued to caress her, enjoying the little tremors she was helpless to control.

"Why don't you tell me," Thrym said, "about this husband of yours. If you hate him, why did you marry him?"

"I didn't have any choice."

Her obvious dislike of the subject made Thrym anxious to learn more. "Why not?"

"My mother." She paused.

Thrym waited. Finally, she said, "He would've hurt my mother. She's old and we didn't have much after father died. Sandor would've taken what little we had left."

"How could he do that?" Thrym wondered what had caused the look of revulsion on her face when she said her husband's name.

Minta bit her lip. "I don't want to talk about it."

"Why not? You brought the subject up."

She sighed. "He was a soldier assigned to duty with the Shore Guard. He had authority in our village." She paused, then glared at him. "And I was pregnant. Are you satisfied?"

Thrym was alarmed by the degree of his dismay at her confession. "Was your husband the father?"

"Yes."

"Then why didn't you want to marry him? If you were willing to bed with him…" Thrym closed off his awareness as a wave of revulsion almost overpowered him.

"Bed with him? Who said anything about a bed? If you must know, I was pregnant because he lay in wait for me behind my house, stuffed a rag in my mouth, dragged me into the woodshed and raped me." Minta's voice, which had been close to a whisper, rose on the last words and her hands clenched into fists, her whole body rigid with the memory. She swallowed. "I thought he'd leave me alone after that. And he might have done, if he hadn't left his seed in me. A wizard couldn't have done it better in one try."

Thrym fought down his own response to her emotions and the pictures her words evoked and recaptured her hands. "Your mother didn't know?"

"No."

"Why not?" She's so delicate, he thought. My first finger and thumb meet around her wrist. How could anyone treat her so?

Minta swallowed. "My mother did sewing and laundry for the soldiers in the garrison. If Sandor had passed the word, they'd have gone to someone else and she'd have lost her livelihood. She was old. There was nothing she could do."

"But why marry him?"

"He found out I was pregnant. He wanted the baby and he offered my mother money. We were poor and, anyway, my mother's a devout Miunite. She believes men know best. It was better for her never to know the truth. Sandor was even careful not to hurt me then, because of the baby. At least, while we lived in Bury."

"There was no one else you could go to?"

"No." Minta looked up at him with her enormous, dark eyes and he felt as though he were drowning in them. "I don't know why I told you all that."

Thrym's felt his lips twist and he raised one of her hands and kissed it. "Because I want to know all about you. Was your baby a girl or a boy?"

"A boy. He was stillborn."

Minta's voice had not broken, but Thrym felt her pain. He cursed himself for his clumsiness. "Can you tell me about it?"

"I've told you so much, I may as well tell you the rest." She pressed her lips together as though bracing herself. "We only lived in Bury for a month after we were married. Then Sandor was transferred to the Royal Guard. It was a big promotion. He was pleased until we got to Ninkarrak and found out that even married guards have to live in barracks here. There are special apartments for couples, but they aren't very private. Anyway, our second day here he got reprimanded for hitting me. It was just a slap, but I had a black eye and his commander saw it." She shivered and Thrym clenched his teeth to suppress his anger.

"He kept his hands off me for two months, but I could see the pressure building in him. I was so scared it would have made me clumsy even without my pregnancy. I tripped and broke his favorite beer stein. He couldn't hold back his anger any longer. He beat me, I went into premature labor and the baby was born dead." She sighed. "Sandor's commanding officer had him thrown in jail for six months. He lost his promotion and any hope of future advancement, so now he blames me for that, too."

Thrym felt the horror of her story stir the hairs on the back of his neck where bony plates would have risen in a frill ready for battle in his lizard form.

Then Minta smiled. "But I was lucky, really. Nahar Vanith delivered Nahar Aubrey a few hours after I lost my baby, so I was right there to be his wet nurse. I love Aubrey more than I could ever have loved a child of Sandor's and, as I live in the Black Tower now, I hardly ever see him."

They talked for a long time after that. Thrym ordered dinner and they ate and talked and drank and talked until it was time for Minta to leave. He did not ask her a second time to go upstairs with him, although he sensed that by the time they finished eating she would have gone.

He walked her home, his arm resting across her shoulders. They strolled up the hill at the north end of the harbor to the Royal Park, back through the park to the gate of the royal enclosure, stopping just out of sight of the guards. There he kissed her, holding her close in his arms. Her lips were warm and her mouth was sweet when his tongue teased her lips apart. But he left then, saying, "Next week. Same time, same place."

VI

4730, 473RD CYCLE OF THE YEAR OF THE OX
MONTH OF ILFARNAR

> "Of were-folk there are races six;
> Be careful now, don't get them mixed.
> "A gamlar can become a bear,
> And roam the north with thick, white hair.
> He really hasn't any foes,
> He's seven feet from nose to toes.
> "An isklar, when he changes shape,
> Can raise a frill around his nape.
> A lizard, he sheds hair for mail,
> And waves his long, reptilian tail."
>
> — EXCERPT FROM "THE WERE-FOLK"
>
> PUBLISHED IN *A CHILD'S GUIDE TO THE LARIN AND OTHER BEASTLY TAILS*
>
> BY ENOGEN VARASH OF ELEVTHERAI, 4557

Jerevan had not appeared when Alanna left the inn the morning following their confrontation, but his coach caught up with hers about an hour later. He stayed behind her the rest of the four days it took her to reach the capitol. He did not attempt to speak to her again, however, and she assumed that he followed her merely to keep an eye on the Talisman.

She spent her last night on the road in Ayle at the Sleeping Dragon, about fifty kilometers from Ninkarrak. The traffic that close to the capitol was much heavier than any she had seen before. Wagons carrying everything from pig iron to poultry lumbered in steady streams to and from the city. Private carriages and public stages vied for opportunities to pass the slower traffic and periodically, at the sound of a horn, they all pulled aside for the streamlined, dark green coaches with the gold trim that carried the mail. Mixed with the vehicles were an uncountable number of riders and pedestrians. Fortunately, if the posting inns were busier than those she knew in the mountains, they were also more efficient. She was impressed at the sight of ostlers switching whole teams of horses in less than three minutes.

Alanna's first view of Ninkarrak came from the summit of the ridge of hills that circled the Bay of Lanth, broken only by the cut made by the River Glyn. As her coach topped the rise and began its descent, she was awed by the panorama of spires and buildings. It was one thing to read about the population of the capitol, quite another to see it spread out before her. The azure ribbon of the Glyn flowed across the plain to the wrinkled, turquoise expanse of the bay. On both sides of the river and from the edge of the plain to the shore, she detected only a few islands of green amid the vast sea of buildings.

Three hours later Alanna's coach turned into a sweeping drive and drew up in front of her aunt and uncle's elegant home on Ninfal Street.

Una Farquar, Alanna's aunt, was a plump, pretty woman with pink cheeks and a mass of golden ringlets lightly salted with gray. She hugged Alanna and, ignoring the fact that Alanna was half a head taller than she, proceeded to scold her as she would have a daughter. "About time you came to visit, I've been inviting you for years." She pulled back and examined Alanna more closely. "My dear, you look exhausted. How long have you been traveling?"

Alanna grimaced. "Fifteen days."

"I can have your dinner sent up on a tray, if you want to have a bath and go straight to bed?"

"No, that's very kind, Aunt Una, but I'll be fine and I need to talk to Uncle Anin."

"Of course, dear. He's out now but he'll be delighted to see you. He's been looking forward to your arrival, too. This house has been so empty since our boy decided he needed a place of his own."

When Alanna went downstairs for dinner, Anin Farquar rose ponderously to greet her and his hug came close to breaking her ribs. She remembered him as a big man, but he had grown. Alanna's mother, Anin's sister, had been a tall woman, as Alanna was, but Anin was not only nearly two meters in height, he was almost that big around.

Still, she had always found him a keen judge of character with a great deal of common sense. Further, as Chief Customs Officer of the Port of Ninkarrak, she knew he had influence in certain government circles and she hoped he would be able to advise her on how to present her petition. She had to wait until dinner was over and he had retired to his study, however, before she had a chance to be alone with him.

"Uncle Anin, may I speak to you for a moment?"

He looked up from his papers and studied her with kind, but shrewd, eyes. "Thought you had something on your mind. I suppose it has to do with why you moved up your trip." He smiled. "After all these years, I didn't think it could be just an overwhelming desire to see us."

Alanna looked rueful. "You know I've always wanted to come." She crossed the room and sat in the chair in front of his desk.

"I know, Lanna," he said, using the name her mother had called her. He settled back in his chair. "Now, what's bothering you?"

"You'll keep what I tell you confidential?"

He frowned. "Of course, if that's what you want."

"Yes, Uncle, it is." She waited until he nodded agreement before she leaned across his desk and told him everything that had happened to her since word came to Fell that the eslarin had closed their borders.

Anin scowled several times during her narrative and on one occasion seemed about to interrupt, but when she would have stopped, he waved for her to continue. "No, go on. I'll ask questions afterward. You said it was Leyburn in the coach that followed you?"

She did go on, concluding, "I even gave him your address, told him I intended staying here with you and Aunt Una."

Anin linked his hands across his belly. "Leyburn said he was the only one who could train you?"

"Yes!" Indignation sharpened Alanna's voice at the memory. "At least, he said he was the only person presently available in Ilwheirlane. I told him it was out of the question."

Anin's shrewd eyes twinkled at her. "He got under your skin?"

Alanna sat back. "He misled me. But from what I've heard, there's nothing unusual in that, or in behavior a great deal worse. I only hope I never have to see him again."

"Oh, they scare children with tales of the Wizard of Leyburn," Anin said, frowning, "but it's all gossip and viciousness. You're bound to run into him if you let Una drag you around to all the social events. And I can tell you right now she'll never let either of us have any peace if you don't."

"You mean he's received?"

Anin laughed. "Child, he's a relative of the Estahar, eleventh in line for the throne, if I remember correctly, and he's the most powerful wizard the human lands have left. Of course, he's received. It was an honor for him to offer to train you."

Alanna swallowed, unnerved. "But the things he's done. Even in Fell we've heard of him."

Anin leaned forward. "I don't know what you heard in Fell, but you're bound to meet him and, if you're rude to him, you'll be the one to suffer. He has a bad reputation for his dealings with women. I agree that you don't want your name associated with his in that way, so be careful. If you snub him, people will ask why and the answers they come up with aren't likely to please you. What's more, if you want wizards to help with the sylvith fruiting, Leyburn's the man you must deal with, not the Estahar."

Alanna rose. "How can that be? Are there no wizards at court?"

"Only Leyburn now that Derwen's dead."

She turned away and started pacing the room. "You mean there aren't any other wizards in Ninkarrak?"

"Not that many, and none attached to the court. If you want wizards to aid you, you'll have to deal with them directly and Leyburn's their chief. I'm sorry, but that's the way it is."

Anin leaned back in his seat. "You have to understand that the worst crimes laid at Leyburn's door, the rumors of sadism and perversion, are just that, rumors. There's never been any evidence to support them. He's a powerful wizard, probably the most talented since Cormor, and he's eccentric, spends a lot of time in strange places, but most of what's said of him is based on envy and spite."

Alanna turned back to her uncle. "There's a saying in the mountains, 'When you hear thunder you know there was lightning, whether you saw the flash or not.'"

Anin shook his head at the set expression on Alanna's face. "Very well, but remember that his guilt or innocence isn't something you're competent to judge. If you want the aid of enough wizards to fruit all the sylvith trees in the Mallarnes, he's the only man who can help you. You can petition the Estahar, but the most Idrim will do is consult Leyburn for you, which might not be the best way to enlist his aid."

Anin studied her, then looked down at his hands clasped across his stomach. "As to finding another wizard to train you, that will be difficult. There's a wizard I've heard of, a Ramal Guitara from Esterias. He's said to have had some formal training, and he's supposed to have talent. I'll see if I can get an introduction for you."

"Then there is a chance that I can find someone else?" She gripped the edge of his desk.

He shifted in his chair. "A chance, yes, but that's all." He leaned over the desk and placed a hand on one of hers. "If we can't find another wizard soon, you'll have to accept training from Leyburn. You'll have no choice, Lanna. Without training, the Talisman will be your death warrant."

Anin paused. Alanna waited. She felt too numb to speak and she could see that he was debating whether or not to continue. Then he said, "Myrriden was right to warn you of a renewal of the Dragon Wars. If Idrim wasn't a fool and his whole court a bunch of self-serving scoundrels, he'd have realized that the Dragon Wars began again one hundred and fifty-four years ago when Gandahar took Ardagh."

The change of subject surprised her. "But Ardagh was a nest of pirates. Gandahar did the human nations a favor exterminating them."

Anin shook his head. "Your father and I argued the same point. He blinded you to what's happening in the world. He was a brilliant scholar when he kept within his own fields of expertise, but he had no understanding of the were-folk. I hope for all our sakes, child, now that you're carrying the Talisman, you'll reexamine what he taught you."

Alanna bit her lip and said, "Leyburn said the same thing."

"Then you should have listened. Ardagh was a nest of pirates, perhaps, but it was a human nest of pirates and the reason Gandahar took it was anything but altruistic."

"They preyed on all the shipping in the Thallassean Sea."

"Gandahar had no shipping in the Thallassean until after taking Ardagh. The isklarin chose that port because it was nearest to the site of Sikkar, their ancient capitol, and closest to the Valley of the Gwatar, their shortest route into the human lands. You don't think they were doing us a favor when they conquered Darenje and Lamash?"

Alanna hesitated, sensing the truth of her uncle's words. Much as she might regret it, she had recognized her father's inability to face unpleasant facts. "No, but they haven't done anything else since taking Lamash, and that was thirty-eight years ago, before I was born. I know they had reason to hate us once, when we took their lands and when Anor and Torin sank Sikkar. But the Dragon Wars ended thousands of years ago. Why should the Gandaharans hate us now, when most of them have human blood? How can they go on hating humans when they're partly human themselves?"

"The Gandaharans don't think of themselves as part human. They put human children to death as soon as they discover them. Their very word for human, 'malar', means 'blind'." Anin shook his head. "But they don't all hate ûs. The isklarin themselves are divided into two camps, those who worship Kyra the Destroyer and those who worship Jehan. It's the worshipers of Kyra who want to see mankind returned to slavery and all the lands Gandahar once held restored."

"But why now? Why after all these years should the Dragon Wars start up again now?"

"The were-folk didn't dare move openly against us during the Age of Wizards, but there aren't many human wizards in these days, and those who are left are only half trained." He looked down at his desk and played with his papers. "Leyburn told me once that Aavik, the ruler of Gandahar, was a high priest of Kyra before he became Estahar. It's since he came to power that Gandahar has become a real threat to the human lands."

Alanna felt stunned. "You know the Hetri of Leyburn personally?"

"Of course I know him. We've been on the same side of a number of political fences." Anin frowned. "Look, Lanna, I know I promised to keep anything you told me tonight confidential, and I'll hold to that if you insist, but I'd no idea that what you'd have to tell me would be of national concern. I'd like to tell your story, or at least parts of it, to a man I know at court, one of the few men in that mound of maggotry I trust. He might be able to help you."

"What did you call the court?"

Anin sighed. "I forgot, you know nothing of local politics. Idrim's court is just what I said. Idrim himself wasn't too bad when he was young, but he's senile now. And most of his advisors are worse: self-indulgent, dishonest sycophants. Groman Charden, Lanrai of Horgen and Lord Chamberlain, is the worst, a degenerate with a finger in every shady transaction in Ninkarrak. Idrim's old, and he was never strong even in his youth. Nahar Vanith tried to guide him and for a time she kept a rein on the corruption, but since Idrim's conversion to Miune he's taken the notion that he can't trust her judgment. Her brother, Arrel, is a total weakling, but Idrim dotes on him and conditions go from bad to worse."

Alanna pressed her lips together. "Can nothing be done?"

"Nothing I know of. Not while Idrim is Estahar. Corruption at court is no new thing, Lanna. It's always there to one extent or another. A strong ruler clears it out for a time, but it creeps back. And Idrim..." He shrugged.

"If all of humanity is in danger from Gandahar, how can they ignore it? I don't believe it can be as bad as you say or something would be done." Alanna's agitation drove her to her feet and she paced restlessly.

Anin watched her for a moment and said, "Some people would rather not face reality; they fear what they might see. You must have met people like that even in the mountains?"

Alanna shook her head. "We're practical in the hills. Everyone realizes that, if something isn't done by spring, there'll be no harvest next year." She turned to face him. "I don't see how the eslarin, who love all living things, can be so cruel, and with so little explanation."

Anin's eyes narrowed. "They didn't give any explanation to the merchants when they closed the ports. A little is better than nothing. What did they say?"

"It wasn't an explanation," she said, frowning. "But they told Sallus of Lachan that they wouldn't enter human lands again until 'he who should never have been born' was dead."

Anin inhaled sharply. "You're sure of those words, 'he who should never have been born'?"

"Yes. They made no sense to Sallus or anyone in the mountains, but that's what the eslarin said. Do they mean something to you?"

"Agnith's fires! Who'd believe they'd react so drastically?"

Alanna sat down again facing him. "React to what? What do the words mean?"

"I can't tell you now," Anin said, not meeting her eyes. "It's not within my authority. But no one at court has heard those words."

"Surely you're wrong. They were the talk of the borderlands for weeks before I wrote to you."

"They may be known in the Mallarnes, but I haven't heard them before and I'm usually well informed." He looked back up at her. "Will you give me permission to discuss your story with my friend?"

She stood, clenching her hands on the edge of his desk. "If the court is so corrupt, whom do you trust?"

Anin nodded. "Errian Saumer, the Hetri of Colne and Chief Privy Counselor. He's lost favor recently because he's stood by Vanith, as I have, but he's still a canny politician."

Anin hesitated then added, "What I've told you tonight is confidential, too. I'd rather even Una didn't hear that I'm one of Vanith's supporters."

Her eyes widened but she said, "I'll never repeat anything you tell me in confidence, Uncle Anin."

He nodded. "Good. You'll like Errian." He smiled and rocked back in his chair. "There are some who'd say I shouldn't have been as frank with you as I've been, but he won't be one of them. Do I have your permission to tell him your story?"

Alanna sank back into the chair. "Whatever you think best. I never meant my petition from the Council of Idris to be a secret, anyway. But why can't you tell me what the eslarin meant?"

"You'll find out soon enough. I'll get hold of Errian tomorrow and arrange a meeting." Anin smiled at her. "He'll give you better advice than I can as to how to present your petition. If I were you, Lanna, I'd wait until I spoke to him before doing anything else."

"Very well, but time is an important factor. I need to find at least one wizard who was trained, or received training from a wizard trained, at Onchan. Griffith, our local journeyman, said that only a wizard with both the high sight and that background would be familiar with the chromosome patterns of sylvith trees. Another complication," he sighed, "but we've talked enough tonight. Get to bed now, or Una will have my head for tiring you. Don't worry. Things will seem more hopeful when you've had a good night's sleep."

Despite Anin's final words, Alanna retired that night more disturbed than she had been before speaking with him. She had hoped for reassurance. She had wanted to be told that Myrriden's words had been the irrational ravings of an old man, and the Hetri of Leyburn's confirmation of them another instance of his wickedness. Instead, all her worst fears had been confirmed and her confidence regarding the nobility of the leadership in Ninkarrak shaken as well.

Her uncle had even cast doubt on her decision not to be trained by Leyburn. But there she couldn't bow to his judgment. She remembered too well the fascination she had felt from the moment she had first seen Jerevan Rayne. Even her uncle had warned her against him as a man but, if she took training from him, she would not be able to avoid seeing him in that light. Much as she hated to admit it, his physical attraction had been too compelling.

And now it appeared that she would have to beg him for aid for the sake of the people depending on her. At least she had already told him of the situation and the nature of her petition. Perhaps he would see his duty and act to find the wizards needed without further urging on her part. How could she plead with him and still refuse to be trained by him? Alanna shivered.

VII

4730, 473RD CYCLE OF THE YEAR OF THE OX
MONTH OF ILFARNAR

Ma nalor pon va bohedal a valodar
ulen ilvalodarse son emd,
kor quen non marlin du:

Duid marl co nalor pon lo e jente taborun
ful ilkaroth, iltaborun cood:
Va a karoth pon lowe kunle ma a
end a yanod.

"No wizard may prolong the life of another being
beyond that being's natural span,
but for these three exceptions:

"The third exception states that a wizard may make and
honor a contract with one of the karothin that states:
The karoth's lifespan shall not be diminished by
the period spent in service."

— EXCERPTS FROM *THE LAWS*
ISSUED BY THE COUNCIL OF WIZARDS

Rakshe scraped his hoof across the thin coating of ice that sheathed the grass. Soon, he thought, he would have to move the herds down from the high plateau to the river valleys of the south and west. But he sensed that the coming winter would be a harsh one. He wanted to wait as long as possible, so the mares would not over-graze the rich but limited area of the valley country. He took an unsatisfying bite of frozen grass and lifted his head at a disturbance among the kariothin on the northern edge of the herd.

A lesser karoth, one not familiar to him, had been galloping hard, and the news of his arrival was circulating among the mares. Rakshe could see uneasiness spread like ripples radiating across a pond into which a stone has fallen.

"*Who comes, and why?*" he demanded, his mind searching the center of the disturbance for the mind of the newcomer.

VYRKARION: THE TALISMAN OF ANOR

"Your pardon, lord of lords." The mental response was weak, as if the sender was close to passing out from exhaustion. *"I mean no disrespect in coming thus unannounced, but I bear urgent tidings. A great one has made a summoning in the north, one greater than any we have met before. There were none that suited him in the herd of your deputy, Errwan. He ordered that the summons be brought to you directly."*

Rakshe snorted and shook his head, looking out over the vast herd of kariothin. They had all heard the news of the summoning by now. He sensed their distress.

He pawed the ground and snorted, watching the steam of his breath dissipate in the icy air. Many years had passed since one of the gods-that-walk had claimed a steed. *"Show me,"* he ordered the young stallion, who was drawing close to the foot of the hill where Rakshe stood.

The newcomer was a chestnut, but his coat was white with lather and his head hung down, as though he had to watch his feet to keep them steady. His response was slow and at first the picture he sent was blurry. Then it sharpened and Rakshe saw the summoner in his mind. He stiffened and his nostrils flared. Powerful, very powerful, he thought. He sought back through the memories of his ancestors to find a being to compare and found only one. Not a mere user of power, this one, but illormavasha, a god-who-would-die. Rakshe had heard that such a one had been born some thirty years before in Arvonin, but he had doubted the truth of the rumor.

He snorted. But still, to be summoned like a servant. He rose on his hind legs, pawed the air and screamed his rage to the skies. Then he saw that his anger had started the kariothin milling in confusion. He landed.

"Assemble," Rakshe ordered the herd. *"To me,"* he ordered the lesser stallions who served him.

He tossed his head. In the history of his kind, few had dared to summon or sought to master a karoth. The users of power took the services of mares and were grateful. Rakshe thought back. Anor had ridden a karoth, and Cormor, but neither of those stallions had been a herd ruler when they were called to serve. Yet the one who summoned now was not merely a user of power. He was different, illormavasha.

Rakshe sighed, controlling his rage. What fate decreed would be, and he could not deny it. He would go to meet the one who summoned and, if none of the mares or the lesser karothin would do, then Rakshe himself would serve. So be it. It was no shame to serve a god, albeit a mortal one doomed to die. The herds would still be here when he returned.

So, Rakshe, karoth of karothin of all the herds of Akyrion, gave instructions to the lesser stallions who served him, and walked north to meet his master-to-be.

He crossed the high plateau to the base of the mountains, the jagged white giant's teeth that rose, range on range, to the north and east. On the second day, in the early morning with the sun still hiding behind the peaks and casting long shadows, Rakshe met Rhys, the summoner.

The image that the chestnut karoth had shown Rakshe had been accurate, although Rhys was not quite as tall as he had appeared to the lesser stallion. Rakshe guessed that he was about two hundred and ten centimeters, very tall for a man, but only average height for an eslar. Something of the eslarin appeared in the cast of his features, also, but he lacked their fine-boned look and his skin was fair, unlike the nearly black skin of a male eslar. His shoulders were broad and his arms and legs muscular, though his waist and hips were lean. He had none of the epicene slenderness of the eslarin.

Moreover, Rhys dressed like a human peasant in rough boots, woolen breeches and a coarse, homespun shirt unbuttoned at the neck despite the cold. Only one feature of his attire did not fit the plebeian image: the sword strapped to his back. A large, two-handed blade, it held in its hilt a blue jewel like an enormous sapphire the size and shape of a goose egg. Inside the gem was a core of fire that expanded and contracted like the beating of a heart.

Rakshe halted, his feet spread apart and his head high. He studied his summoner. Rhys' black hair hung long and loose to his shoulders. His eyes, slitted vertically like a cat's, or an eslar's, were so deep a blue they seemed violet. The slitted eyes were the final proof, Rakshe thought, that rumor had not lied. Rhys was half eslar and half human, a mixture forbidden by Tarat, the god of the eslarin, since Edain, the first of that mix, had dared to use her power to challenge the gods. The sun was rising behind Rhys' back, but it seemed to Rakshe that the aura of the half-breed's power was brighter than the sunlight.

Rakshe tossed his head and snorted. He had bowed to fate, but he was still angry with the manner of his summoning. *"I have come as you requested, rai."*

"You, then, are the one who will serve me?"

The force of the mind behind the question beat at Rakshe like a physical blow. He braced himself against it, yet even faced with that power he maintained his defiance. *"Was it not your command that I alone should serve you?"*

"I did not summon you. I called as it states in The Laws *it was my right to do when I met the first of your herds in the foothills. My request upset them, and they sent for you. They said that none of them were fit for such an honor."* Rhys shrugged.

Rakshe snorted, thinking of Errwan. Then he looked again at Rhys. He nodded his head, and thought, *"Rai, I was annoyed at first, but now I see that they were right. They feared you too much and, therefore, would not have served you well."*

"You do not fear me?"

VYRKARION: THE TALISMAN OF ANOR

Rakshe considered, measuring the power of the questioner. Rakshe's mind held the memories of his ancestors. His was a line of rulers and he remembered them, and one of those he remembered had served the Wizard Cormor for many years before becoming lead stallion. Cormor, Rakshe thought, is no greater than Rhys, but Cormor was great in the fullness of centuries and this one, with his eslar blood, is still a child and already his mind glows with power. Yet, he holds his mind open to me. Power is not of itself to be feared. Of course, there was always Tarat's curse to be considered, but he would not worry about that now.

"No, rai," Rakshe thought, *"I do not fear you. I will serve you under the conditions set forth to my ancestors by the Council of Wizards for all the years you have need of me, but I shall not fear you."* He lowered his head then and touched the tip of his horn to the ice slick rock at his new master's feet.

"Good. I don't like people who fear me."

Rakshe snorted again, a sound very like laughter. *"Then, rai, you're fated to dislike most of those that you shall meet."*

VIII

4730, 473RD CYCLE OF THE YEAR OF THE OX
MONTH OF ILFARNAR

> "Take two identical boxes. Fill them with different
> substances of equal weight. When the subject touches one
> box, initiate a pleasure response. When the subject touches
> the other box, initiate a pain response. Mix the boxes and
> present again. If, after the first or second repetition, the
> subject discriminates between the two outwardly identical
> boxes, the subject has larin sight…"
>
> — EXCERPT FROM *KAGRESOD GRESACAD*
> "UNDERSTANDING DISCRIMINATION" BY ENKAR HAKIST, ILWHEIRLANE, 3207

The last Miunesday in Ilfarnar was one of those rare summer-like days that occur sometimes in late fall. The sun shone, the sky was a spotless blue, and Thrym had invited Minta to a picnic. She skipped through the gate of the compound.

He was waiting for her in a gig harnessed to a fat chestnut mare. He jumped down barely in time to catch her as she flung herself into his arms. He whirled her around and kissed her.

"Ooh, I'm so happy!" Minta exclaimed. "A whole day, and it's such a beautiful one."

Thrym laughed as he lifted her into the gig and jumped up beside her. "Behave yourself, minx, or we won't get to where I plan to take you."

"And where's that?" Minta felt like a child waiting for a treat. She had seen Thrym three times since their first rendezvous, every day she had off, but they had met at the tavern and he had never been free before five o'clock. Minta wanted to savor every moment of this time together.

"A place I know of. You'll see when we get there." Thrym's expression was indulgent.

Minta turned to look at him, too happy to care where they went. It was the first time she had seen Thrym in daylight. How handsome he is, she thought. Young, too. Why, he doesn't look much older than me. She studied his broad forehead with the shock of wavy, brown hair that tended to fall across it, and the amber eyes. Then she sidled closer to him so that he could put his arm around her.

"I've missed you," she whispered into his shoulder.

He looked down at her and his expression was half amused, half something else she couldn't define. "I've missed you, too." He kissed the tip of her nose.

They left the park by the east gate. The road ran past the great estates of the nobility and a few foreign embassies. Despite having lived in the Tower for six years, Minta had never been that way before and she was impressed by the splendid homes with their sweeping lawns and gardens right in the heart of Ninkarrak. They soon left the main road and turned onto a winding lane that wandered between even larger mansions. Then Thrym pulled up before a closed, wrought iron gate and jumped down to open it.

"Do you have permission to go in here?" Minta asked as he climbed back up beside her and drove the gig through.

"Of a kind." He jumped back down to close the gate behind them.

"What does that mean?"

Thrym frowned. "There's no one living here but one old caretaker and he's told me many times to visit whenever I want. Anyway, at the moment he's in no state to object."

"Why not?"

"Stop worrying, Minta. I wouldn't get you involved in anything illegal. The caretaker's sleeping off a hangover down at the Duka in Farinmalith. I left him there last night blind drunk and I gave instructions that he was to be kept happy today. I didn't want him interrupting us. But even if he does come back, he won't raise a fuss about our using the place."

"What's Farinmalith?"

"Great Jehan! You've lived in Ninkarrak all this time and you've never heard the name of the thieves' town? Farinmalith, the 'roads that lead nowhere,' the Maze, the thieves' quarter, the heart of Ninkarrak. It's where I live," he added, suddenly sober, his eyes assessing her reaction.

She flushed. "I know you're a thief, but I try not to think about it."

"I've noticed."

"What kind of place is the Duka?"

"It's a hotel, not a brothel, if that's what you're thinking," he said. His jaw was clenched and a muscle jerked in his cheek.

Her mouth opened in surprise. "I didn't think that."

Her expression penetrated his anger. He shrugged. "Sorry. I know you don't like what I do. I don't much like it either, but I shouldn't take it out on you." He looked away from her down the drive and gave the mare a slap with the reins across her hindquarters. "Rad Flickra, the owner of the Duka, is a friend of mine. He's an ex-mercenary and still a member of the Mercenaries' Council."

"Is that what you want to do, be a mercenary?" she asked.

"Yes," he said, "that's what I want, but the way things are now it may never happen."

He pulled the horse to a stop in a small courtyard behind the manor house. Then he jumped down and lifted Minta out. She walked around and looked in through the dusty windows while he tended the horse and unpacked the gig.

"Why has the place been abandoned like this?" she asked as he took her hand and led her through what had once been a formal garden and across a field that had once been a lawn. "I thought, when you said there was only a caretaker here, that the owners were away, but it looks as though no one's lived here for years."

Thrym shrugged. "No one has. It belonged to the old Lanrai of Calder, but none of his children lived longer than two or three years. There was something wrong with their blood. Anyway, there's a problem about identifying the heir and so far the executors have been too tight-fisted to consult a competent wizard."

"It's a pity. This must all have been beautiful once," Minta said, stepping carefully to avoid the sharp spines of star thistles that had grown up amid the tangle of grass.

Beyond the overgrown lawn, a narrow path led through some trees still brilliant in their autumn colors to the side of a spring-fed pond. The grass around the pond had been kept short by a flock of geese. Next to the pond stood a round building like a summerhouse, but enclosed, with windows facing the water. One of the geese, a large, gray gander, took exception to their arrival and started honking angrily and flapping his wings.

Minta gasped, "How lovely! It's like a scene from a picture book."

"I hoped you'd like it. Come on, let's put the basket down over here. I bet you haven't even eaten breakfast yet."

Thrym's voice sounded gruff, but Minta sensed he was pleased with her reaction. She smiled. "I haven't. I was too excited."

He gestured theatrically as though to spank her and she dodged, laughing. From another man the gesture would have terrified her, Minta thought, but it hadn't occurred to her that Thrym might hurt her. She was amazed at herself.

Thrym seemed to sense the shift in her mood. "What's the matter?" he asked. Then angrily, "You didn't think I'd hit you, did you?"

"No," Minta said, her eyes meeting his. "I knew you wouldn't. That's what surprised me. How can I know something like that?"

Thrym took her into his arms, hugging her. "Don't fret, Minta. Trust your instincts. I'll not harm you or cause you harm ever, if I can help it."

"Then you'd better feed me." Minta slipped away and sat down by the basket.

Thrym got out a jug of lemonade, a loaf of marin nut bread, and two large lommas fruits. He peeled and cored these with his pocket knife and then hand-fed Minta the slices. The juicy fruit was sweet and tart at the same time. When they finished, he leaned over and licked a drop that had run down her chin. From the drop of juice, his mouth moved up to hers and he pressed her back into the grass.

"Well," he said after a time, when her head was dizzy from his kisses, "have I gone slowly enough for you? Do you know me well enough now for me to take you into that summerhouse? There's a bed there made up ready for us."

"I was afraid you were never going to ask me again."

"No danger of that, but I wanted to wait and make it perfect." Thrym ran his finger down the side of her face. "When I first saw you I thought you beautiful, but I didn't look deeper. I assumed you knew what you were doing. Then, when I found out what your life has been like, I realized you didn't have a clue. So I held off until I could make it special for you, for both of us."

"Oh, Thrym!" Minta hugged him. "It's you that's special, just being with you."

"Hush." He carried her inside.

Quite a long time later, in the drowsy aftermath of their lovemaking, as Minta's fingers explored the dark tangle of hairs on his chest, she asked, "Thrym, isn't there any way I can tell you from a human?"

He frowned, but there was no way she could offend him just then. "I am human, Minta. My parents were citizens of Gandahar, although they both must have been part human, but I was born without were-vision. I only saw the surfaces of things. So when the examiners tested me at nine months, they condemned me to die. My mother had given birth to an earlier child, though, who'd also been condemned. She hadn't been able to bear the thought of losing another, so she arranged for the Varfarin to get me to safety if I failed the tests. They substituted the body of a child that had died of natural causes and smuggled me out of Gandahar."

"What's the Varfarin?"

"An organization; Varfarin means 'the open roads.' Its members are followers of Jehan and they're dedicated to freedom." Thrym shrugged. "At least, that's what I've been told. I don't know much, just what's generally known in Farinmalith and a little that my foster parents told me before they died."

"I've never heard of them before, but I'm grateful to them." Minta hugged him and then leaned back. "Do they rescue a lot of people?"

"I guess so." Thrym wound his fingers through the pale golden strands of her hair and pulled her head back to rest on his shoulder. "They've been around a long time. The Varfarin was founded by Cormor before he joined the Council of Wizards. They free slaves and save refugees from all over, not just Gandahar, but no one knows much about how they operate. The members take a vow of secrecy. They have code words and recognition signals so they'll know each other, but no one else will know them."

Minta nestled closer, but she was still curious. "So no one knows who any of them are?"

Thrym snorted. "They're not as secret as all that, or who could they get to join them? No, a few of their high officials are known, if you ask in the right places. They call them alfarin, 'wanderers,' and the chief wanderer, the Esalfar, is always a wizard. Their current Esalfar is the Hetri of Leyburn."

Minta sat up and turned to Thrym. "The Hetri of Leyburn! But he's Aubrey's tutor."

"Is he?" Thrym pulled her back against him. "Then the boy must be talented. I thought the wizard blood had died out in the royal family, but Leyburn wouldn't bother with anyone who didn't have real talent. They say in Farinmalith he's going to be as powerful as Cormor someday."

"Aubrey is talented," she agreed. "Lord Leyburn's been training him since he was two." She clapped a hand over her mouth. "Thrym, you won't repeat what I just said. It's supposed to be a secret." Her voice was small and scared.

"What do you think I am?" he demanded. "Course, I won't repeat anything you tell me not to. It's kind of an honor for the kid to be taught by Leyburn, but I can see why Vanith would want to keep quiet about it."

Minta sighed. "He really is talented, but I think he studies too hard. With his bad hip, he never gets to play with the other children at court. In fact, he never seems to play at all. He's too solemn for a child his age."

Thrym grinned. "You're too solemn for a child your age." He kissed her, then said, "I think we'd better think about lunch before the ants or the geese carry off the basket."

They dressed and went back outside to sit on the grassy verge. They ate companionably for a time and tossed bits and pieces to the geese who waddled up onto the shore to beg for handouts.

"Where did you go when the Varfarin got you out of Gandahar?" Minta asked.

"Leyburn found a home for me with a family here in Ninkarrak. They'd been retainers of his." Thrym tossed another chunk of marin nut bread and watched the geese squabble over it.

"Did they treat you all right, the people he left you with?"

They sat next to each other, their shoulders touching, and Thrym took her hand and squeezed it. "They were good to me, but they were old and it was hard for them, raising a young boy. When I was nine they were killed in a fire and I was sent to an orphanage." He grimaced at the memory. "It wasn't a pleasant place, but then again, I wasn't an obedient child. When I was eleven I ran away. I've been on my own ever since."

"Thrym, if you were judged to be human, how can you change?"

He looked at her sharply. "Does it bother you?"

Minta felt his tension and realized that he was afraid of her answer. "Oh, no!" She turned and gripped his shoulders, urgent in her need to reassure him. "It doesn't bother me like that. It's just, I want to know all about you, and that's part of you too."

"Oh, Jehan," Thrym hugged her, "you're incredible. Ever since I was a teenager and first learned to shift, every girl who found out treated me like I had the plague. And none of them ever saw me do it. But you..." He broke off and buried his face in her hair.

Minta clung to him, feeling his tension ebb. For the first time in her life she felt strong and sure. Thrym needed her and her love as much, perhaps, as she needed him.

"Well," Minta prompted him after a time, "how did you learn to change?"

Thrym laughed. "Persistent, aren't you? Very well." He settled her in his lap so he could caress her as he talked. "I was about fourteen and I'd made a bit of money working as a courier for Rad. I decided to celebrate and there was a carnival in town. You know, one of the traveling shows that go 'round the country and have all different kinds of acts."

"I've heard of them. I saw a parade once, but I've never been to one."

"No?" Thrym kissed the top of her head. "Well, cheer up. I'll take you to the next one that comes to Ninkarrak."

"Would you?"

"Course, I will. I like them, too." He grinned. "Anyway, one thing every carnival has is a wizard, and the wizard in that carnival was letting children under fifteen see the world through her eyes, one sic per vision. How could I resist? After all, it might have been my birthright. So I went in."

"But wasn't it a fraud? I thought all the carnival people did was trick people into thinking they saw things."

"I don't know about most of them, but this wizard wasn't a fraud. She made me see. I can't explain it to you, Minta, it's like nothing else. One look and I was hooked. I kept going back. I must have gone through her booth more than twenty times during the two days before the carnival left town. The last few times the wizard wouldn't even take payment; she told me to look as long as I wanted. She said that I should try to see that way myself, that I had the talent if I'd just train it. I tried for a year, but I couldn't do it. Then one day I was desperate to know what was in a bag a man was carrying and suddenly I could see right through it, everything in it and everything else around me."

Minta looked puzzled. "Isn't it confusing, being able to see through things? If you can see right through them, how do you know where they are?"

Thrym hugged her. "It isn't like that. I can still see the surfaces and where everything is; I can just see inside as well."

"Oh," Minta said, not really understanding, but anxious to please him. She toyed with one of the buttons on his woolen shirt. "Did having the were-sight make you able to change, just like that?"

"No." Thrym caught her hand. "Not quite, but I am part isklar and I inherited the were-change ability. If I'd never developed the sight, I'd never have known because I couldn't have triggered the change. But having the sight it was inevitable that I'd find this thing in my brain and try to see what it did. It's kind of fun," he said, "and in my lizard form I have the were-sight naturally."

"How old were you then?" Minta ran her fingers across his chest where she had undone the buttons.

"Fifteen, almost sixteen." Thrym trapped her hand again. "Stop that, or I'll have to drag you back inside."

"Would you, really?" she teased, running her other hand down to his waist and tickling him.

"That's it, then." He rose, hefted her over his shoulder and carried her back into the summerhouse.

They whiled away the afternoon in love play and, when the sky began to grow dark, they were surprised because hardly any time seemed to have passed. Neither of them could get enough of touching and being touched.

They took a different route on leaving the estate, crossing Harbor Boulevard. This was the main route the haulers took moving goods from the river docks to the main harbor. It ran northeast to southwest across the city and marked the end of the fashionable, residential area. On the south side of it, Thrym found a tavern where they ate a quiet dinner.

Outside the tavern, before helping her back into the gig, Thrym asked her, "Would you mind if I visited you in the Tower? I don't think I can wait until next week to see you again."

"But you can't. The guards wouldn't let you."

"I won't see any guards if I take the same route I left by the last time."

Minta looked at him in astonishment. "You mean you can climb up the Tower as easily as you went down it?"

Thrym grinned at her expression and also in relief that the idea hadn't horrified her. "Would you mind?"

"Mind! Of course not. I've been dreading not seeing you, too. But you'll have to wait until after nine, so we won't be disturbed."

"It's more likely to be the early hours of the morning, if you don't mind my waking you?"

Minta smiled at him. "I'll mind terribly if you don't."

IX

4730, 473RD CYCLE OF THE YEAR OF THE OX
MONTH OF ILFARNAR

Gabo ba het a illorin.

"Madness is a gift of the gods."

— ESLARIN PROVERB

Rakshe cantered through the tall grass to the top of a low rise over-looking a lake. From that vantage, the village appeared to be only a grove of trees on the shore, but he and Rhys were in Arvonin, the eslarin land of "water plains." Such giant trees in the middle of otherwise open grass and lake country had to be sharakin, eslarin home trees.

While Akyrion was bordered on two sides by eslarin nations and ruled by the half-eslar, half-gamlar baneslarin, Rakshe had rarely encountered the firstborn until this journey with Rhys. He found meeting them on a daily basis, as he had during the past weeks, unsettling. They were, after all, the race that had lifted his own to sentience.

"Well, go on. It will be dark before we get there, if you don't move soon," Rhys thought.

"Would that matter?"

"Not to me. But I've gathered that eslarin are creatures of the sun and prefer to conduct their business by day. I want to cause the minimum amount of disturbance."

Rakshe snorted, but started down the hill. *"Your presence is sufficient disturbance, rai. Once they see you, I don't think they even remember the time of day."*

Instead of laughing, as Rakshe had expected him to do, Rhys frowned and the grip of his legs tightened. *"Why do they fear me so much? Until I came here, I never meant them harm."*

"Which implies that now you do?" Rakshe asked, disturbed by Rhys' sudden change of mood.

"They anger me. They're afraid of me, yet they defy me. It would serve them right if I justified their fears."

Rakshe slowed to a walk as he reached the edge of the grove of home trees and kept his thoughts shielded. His master was capable of violence. He didn't want another comment of his to aggravate the situation.

The sharakin were enormous, every bole more than fifty feet in circumference and some more than twice that. Rakshe imagined that in summer, when the leaves formed a green umbrella overhead, it would be dark beneath them even at noon. Now, with only a few brown leaves clinging to the vast canopy of branches, the light was still dim.

As he entered the grove, five eslarin drifted out of the shadows to block his path, three of them like tall, pale wraiths and the remaining two like part of the shadows themselves, three women and two men. Both sexes were dressed alike in tight fitting, yet flexible garments in shades of brown, gray and green. Rakshe stopped.

"You are not welcome here." The thought came in unison from all five. Powerful telepaths, the eslarin had no spoken language of their own, although they could communicate in Eskh with those less gifted. Rakshe was relieved to sense that, while their thoughts were wary, these eslarin were unafraid.

"I have determined that my mother lives in this village. I wish to see her," Rhys demanded.

"Your conception and birth may not be incidents she wishes to recall."

Rakshe shifted his haunches as he felt their opposition. Still, their reactions were better than the terror and complete denial of Rhys' right to exist that they had encountered in some of the other eslarin home places.

"Her wishes are a matter of indifference to me. Send her out, or I'll burn this village one tree at a time until I find her. You and she had the power to destroy me at my birth, but you did not. Now the power is mine."

"You wish to make us regret our generosity?" This time only one of the five responded, the one on the far right. She was the tallest of the women, and appeared to be the youngest, although age was difficult to determine with eslarin who considered a lifespan of a thousand years as dying in one's prime.

"Generosity or cowardice?" Rhys' thought was sardonic. *"You wanted me dead, but none of you could face getting blood on your hands. You thought my grandfather, being a wizard, would kill me for you."*

"No," she answered, her face as expressionless as all the eslarin faces had been from the beginning. They did not, as Rakshe had learned, display emotion in physical reactions, but in the quality and tone of their thoughts. This eslar's thoughts were indignant. *"No one here has wished you harm. Your father was mad. Yet it wasn't a congenital condition. Gar's madness was the kind the gods send. That was why, when he forced his seed upon me, I nurtured it. I need not have done so. I could have rejected the egg before the chromosome pattern was set. That would not have put blood on my hands."*

The last thought was scathing, but she continued less heatedly, *"Yet I let you grow within me. You were conceived in the month of Cerdana, the time of sowing, in the Year of the Ox, also a time of sowing in its way. I took that as a sign from Maera. It wasn't cowardice that granted you life; but you are right, it wasn't generosity either. We of the House of Anglivar are gene dancers and worshipers of Maera. There was never any question of our slaying you."*

"So you are my mother Sallys." Rakshe felt Rhys' tension in the grip of his legs. "If you didn't wish me dead, then why did you give me to Essitur?"

"I could not have kept you," Sallys thought. *"I had no way to control a wizard child. You would have grown to be as mad and as ungoverned as your father, or Edain, the first of your kind."*

"You didn't consider that Gar's madness might have come from Essitur?"

"Your grandfather is twisted. I saw that when I took you to him. He's made himself sick with ambition and envy, but I knew that he wouldn't physically harm you. He did, after all, succeed in raising you."

"You're not afraid that I might be mad? I have the power to raze this place, and everyone in it."

Rakshe flinched, instinctively stepping away from the outflow of such violent emotion, forgetting for a moment that he carried the source on his back.

Sallys glided forward. Eslarin were rarely clumsy, but Rakshe thought Sallys imbued with a special grace. She had hair the color of moonlight and skin like cream, yet her eyes dominated her face: huge, blue-violet eyes with vertical slits, Rhys' eyes. Her paramount emotion was anger. *"You may carry the madness of Tarat's curse, but you are not mad now. Nor will you destroy anything here, not a single twig. Instead, though you are still a child by our years and the burden may lie heavy upon you, and Tarat's curse heavier yet, you will obey Maera's will and fulfill your destiny."*

Rakshe felt Rhys recoil at the image of his childishness she projected, his anger draining away as wine flows from a bota pierced with a knife. "My destiny?"

"We are all playthings of the gods," she thought, her anger also dissipating. *"Happy is the simple peasant, who doesn't merit their attention. But you were born to a line of rulers in the Year of the Dragon, a time of violence, in the month of Dirga, the season of storms. Even the name I gave you, Rhys, means 'change.' You know what your path must be."*

Aavik Zaikar a Siarral, Estahar of Gandahar, glared at his apprentice, Gatah Ussarra. "What do you mean you can't find Vyrkarion? The old fool died, didn't he? What happened to his belongings?"

Gatah swallowed. "The kindred of Maera in Idris saw to his burial and distributed what was useful among the poor. None of them knew anything about a living crystal. I read them and they told the truth."

"Who found his body?"

"One of the local nobles. The man I questioned thought it was a woman, the tamrai of Fell, but he wasn't certain. I learned from another source that the tamrai left for Ninkarrak that day, but her departure had been planned beforehand. It couldn't have related to Vyrkarion."

Aavik shook his head. "You found no trace of power anywhere around Idris. Therefore, Vyrkarion was no longer there. We may not be able to farsee bearers of the living crystals, but in an area with so little talent being used, you would have felt the disturbance of Vyrkarion's presence. No, it's here in Ninkarrak and, now you've given me a name, I'll find it."

He looked around at the luxurious chamber the Foreign Secretary of Ilwheirlane had offered him as a visiting dignitary, supposedly from Kailane, and smiled. "Ilwheirlane is softer than I had dared to imagine, rotten in its heart. I may not even need Vyrkarion to win all I've dreamt of winning."

Gatah looked frightened. "There are wizards here. The Varfarin..."

"Bah." Aavik's face contorted with rage. "Don't talk to me of the Varfarin. I'll see them all capped, so they can do no more harm. Then I'll watch them tortured one by one."

Aavik enjoyed the way his apprentice flinched at his anger. Gatah wasn't strong, but he was obedient, a useful trait. "But," he said, moderating his voice, "I have another job for you. There's an official in Idrim's government who wishes to help us. He's afraid of some provincial wizard. In return for our promise of aid, he says he can get some of my soldiers admitted to the Royal Guard. But there's a problem. Theolan, the High Priest of Miune, occasionally blesses the troops and when he does he carries the Staff of Miune which enables a skilled bearer to recognize shape-shifters. I want you and however many other of my apprentices you need to arrange for the theft and destruction of the Staff. Do you understand?"

"Yes, rai, I'll see to it."

Some two weeks after Rhys' confrontation with his mother, Rakshe stopped at the edge of a line of skeletal woods and looked across the Lake of Illor. On the far shore lay Castle Valkarn. He snorted. It was noon and snow sifted down from gray clouds. The frozen surface of the lake was blanketed in white, but the ice wouldn't yet be thick enough to bear his weight. He'd have to go around. Rakshe was startled by the pleasure he took in the delay. He'd run long and hard after their search through Arvonin to reach this place before the heavy snows, but he didn't look forward to entering Valkarn.

"Your home, rai," he mocked, hiding his disquiet.

Rakshe felt the grip of Rhys' legs tighten and he galloped out of the woods and along the shore. There was a crust of ice over the thin coating of snow on the ground. Rakshe liked the crunchy feel of it under his hooves. The moisture from his breath condensed in the cold air making streamers of cloud.

From more than a mile away Rakshe sensed Rhys' grandfather, Essitur Cinnac, the younger brother of Idrim VII of Ilwheirlane, waiting for them. The old man knew they were coming, but the heavy iron gate wasn't open to receive them. Rakshe halted before the entry.

"You found it." Essitur spoke from his stand on the parapet above the entryway to the castle. Rakshe knew that the old man's eyes were on the great sword strapped to Rhys' back and the blue jewel in its hilt.

Rhys said, "Yes."

Rakshe studied Essitur. This was the man who had left the court of Ilwheirlane for a primitive fortress in the wilderness, taking along his wife and son, just so he could study wizardry. The karoth found he sympathized with those who had tried to keep Essitur from his studies. The old man's hair was white, worn long and unkempt, as was the full, flowing beard that covered his chest past the point where the parapet cut off Rakshe's view. His eyes were bloodshot but seemed to burn and he still made no move to open the gate. Instead he asked yet another question, "The eslarin gave you no trouble?"

Rakshe felt Rhys shift on his back. "The eslarin would prefer my nonexistence."

"You know they've closed their frontiers to men?"

"I came through Arvonin." Impatience was apparent now in Rhys' voice and Rakshe sidestepped as Rhys' legs tightened around his ribs.

Essitur glared at them and Rakshe suppressed a shudder, wondering if Sallys would be so confident of the rightness of her decision if she saw Rhys' grandfather as he was now.

"You'd better come in," Essitur said finally.

"That was my intent."

Rakshe snorted as the iron gate rose and Rhys' legs gripped him like a vise, urging him forward into Valkarn.

X

Valt ab celod al end illorincen,
Nan a rhesal end e lith,
Ean lot acad tamarin
Ful eanse remin a garth;
Ean lot acad illarin
Ful cer e sar a nith.
Ilad acad larin ba nan a lorin
E jastwe wa sarin.

"In the beginning the Five Gods,
Children of another time and space,
Created all the worlds
With their thoughts of power;
Created all the races
With seed and blood of fire.
Thus all the races are children of the gods
And are joined by blood."

— FROM THE SONG OF CREATION,

ONE OF THE TEACHING SONGS OF JEHAN THE PLAYER

From the day of Alanna's arrival, her aunt was full of plans to entertain her. "I can't give you a ball, my dear, at this time of year. There
simply aren't enough people. And, anyway, I've already planned your
ball for the end of Dirga, right after your presentation, when everyone's
in town. But just a small party with a little dancing to celebrate your
arrival. It will give you a chance to meet everyone who's still here." Una
paused for a moment, frowning. "You do understand?"

"Of course, I understand, Aunt Una. Indeed, I hope you won't put
yourself out on my account. I'm not here for social reasons."

"Nonsense, my dear. Whatever brought you here, you can't hide
yourself away and entertaining is something I enjoy. I never had a
daughter to present," Una said, looking wistful, which silenced any
further protest Alanna might have made, particularly as Anin invited
Errian Saumer, the Hetri of Colne and Chief Privy Counselor to his Royal
Majesty Idrim VII, to the party.

VYRKARION: THE TALISMAN OF ANOR

Colne was a tall, gaunt man, the planes of his face deeply defined and his skin the color and texture of old parchment. His smile was the automatic, worn smile of the lifetime politician, but Alanna thought that his eyes, behind their heavy lids, looked kind. He made himself agreeable to everyone, even dancing one of the country dances with his hostess, but after dinner he retired with Anin to the study.

Alanna was preoccupied during the remainder of the evening and she joined her uncle and his guest in the study as soon as the other guests had left.

"Well, Tamrai Cairn," Colne said when she entered, "I hope you'll forgive my intrusion on your party, but I thought it would draw less comment if I came to you."

"I'm honored, your grace."

"Nonsense," he said gruffly. "Vyrkarion will make you the equal of anyone when you're trained. I've given Anin a letter of introduction to Ramal Guitara, but I doubt he'll do you much good. He may be from Esterias, but I'm pretty sure that he got whatever wizard training he's had in Ravaar."

"But that's a pirate stronghold. How would he get wizard training there?" Alanna asked.

"One of the few places in these days where he could get such training." Colne snorted. "Unfortunately, the core of truth in what they teach is so overlaid with religious mish mash it's almost useless. It's a pity you won't accept Leyburn."

"I'm sorry you feel that way, your grace. I understand that may make it difficult for me to complete my mission with regard to the Council of Idris." Alanna hesitated and bit her lip before continuing. "I did tell the Hetri of Leyburn of the situation in the mountains but, under the circumstances, I'm not sure what good it would do to plead with him, and I'm anxious to put my petition before the Estahar. My uncle says that you're the best person to advise me how to proceed."

"Hm." Colne studied her. "You have made it difficult for yourself, if you won't ask Leyburn. Idrim's just going to tell you that he'll look into it and that will be the end of it."

"Then what would you advise me to do? There are lives at stake." Alanna's voice shook, and she added, "It was my understanding that, at the very least, Idrim could tell me how to contact the Varfarin."

Colne's heavy lids drooped, concealing his eyes. "Why would you want to know that?"

"I've heard that the wizards of the Varfarin are dedicated to saving lives. Surely they could do something to help?"

Colne shrugged. "The Varfarin is an international organization. Most of its members live in Cibata, or in the countries bordering Gandahar. What made you think that you could contact them here in Ninkarrak?"

"The Hetri of Carahel told me before I left Fell that either Idrim or the Wizard Derwen could tell me how to reach them."

"I see."

Alanna saw Colne's eyes meet her uncle's. She said, "But you could tell me, too, couldn't you, Lord Colne?"

The drooping lids raised for a moment and Alanna saw a flash of calculation in his eyes. "Perhaps, but considering the present situation, no. I'm afraid I'm not at liberty to reveal that information."

"There are lives at stake. Are lives in the Mallarnes less important than elsewhere?"

"Alanna! That was uncalled for," Anin exclaimed.

Colne frowned, but said, "I do understand your concern. By what month does the fruiting have to take place?"

Alanna took a deep breath and controlled her temper. "It's usually begun at the end of Ingvash and completed early in Cerdana. There have been years when bad weather delayed it until the end of Cerdana. No later than that, though."

"At least that gives us time to work with." Colne tapped his long, gnarled fingers on the arm of his chair. "I can arrange for you to meet with Idrim and present your petition. It may not do your cause much good, but you'll feel better if you've done it. It is, after all, what you promised the people in Idris you'd do." He looked at her gravely and added, "Believe me, I'm sorry I can't do more."

"Thank you," Alanna said. She was unsure of whether she should feel relief at what he was willing to do, or resentment at what he refused to do.

He grunted. "May I ask what god or gods you worship, Tamrai Cairn?"

Alanna was puzzled by the change of subject. "I trained as a healer in the Sanctuary of Maera at Idris, and my father taught me to revere Jehan." She rather expected him to make the same objection her aunt had made when the question of her religious practices had arisen, and was relieved when neither Colne nor her uncle protested, but instead seemed pleased. Soon after that the Hetri took his leave.

Alanna felt troubled by the meeting, but decided to heed her uncle's advice and wait for Colne to arrange an opportune time for her to present her petition. At least, Colne had supplied her uncle with the name and address of a wizard who might be willing to train her.

It was the first week of Minneth before Anin managed to arrange a meeting for Alanna with the wizard from Esterias. She awaited the day of the appointment impatiently, her emotions regarding it fluctuating between eagerness and trepidation.

Ramal Guitara's lodging was located near the commercial area of the city. The address was obscure and Alanna was glad to have her uncle with her. Without his assistance, she might never have found the shabby building which housed a number of rundown apartments. Inside, there was a strong odor of fried onions and rotting lorsks. Guitara's rooms were on the third floor.

When she had knocked on the door, Alanna braced herself for the attack of vertigo she had experienced on her first two encounters with wizards. The shock that she felt at first eye contact with Guitara, however, was much less than what she had felt in the past. It didn't even make her dizzy.

Guitara was shocked enough for both of them, though, Alanna decided after a moment. He stood in the middle of his doorway, looking dazed and blocking their entrance.

"Who are you?" he demanded. He turned his eyes from Alanna as though it hurt him to look at her and settled them on Anin. "What do you want here?"

"We have an appointment," Anin said. "I made it with you myself. You should also have received a letter of introduction from the Hetri of Colne."

"You said you wished to consult with me. I remember that, yes. And I have a note from the Hetri of Colne promising his favor if I help you, but you told me nothing of having with you a bearer of power," Guitara said angrily, still keeping his eyes on Anin.

"My uncle made the appointment on my behalf," Alanna said. "I need training in wizardry."

Guitara's face contorted in a rictus of horror. "No!" he gasped. "I cannot train one such as you! I have my little power and I can control it. What you carry is from the great ones who are gone, the kindred of Rav. I'm not fit to come near it." He raised his arms as though to shield his face from Alanna. "No! A thousand times no! What you ask is impossible." With a final shudder, he ducked back into his apartment and slammed the door in their faces.

Anin tried to argue with him, shouting through the door for him to reopen it, but Guitara refused. Eventually, they had to leave.

Back in her uncle's home, Alanna said, "There must be some other wizards in Ninkarrak. If there aren't, why haven't the isklarin returned us to slavery long ago?"

Anin ushered her into his study. "There are a few, but not many, and you can't expect one of Leyburn's associates or one of his apprentices to train you when he's claimed that privilege for himself."

"There must be other wizards." She bit her lip in frustration.

"There are minor wizards who owe no allegiance to Leyburn, a few even here in Ninkarrak. Unfortunately, a minor wizard is no good to you. Only a wizard with the high sight can deal with the living crystals. For all their knowledge, none of the wizards of Gandahar have produced even one such stone." He sighed. "I'd heard rumors that Guitara wielded real power but, as you saw, they were exaggerated."

"Then how will I find someone to train me?" Alanna sank down on the chair opposite Anin's desk.

"You still refuse to consider Leyburn?"

She sighed. "I don't know. If I can't find anyone else, I'll have no choice, but I want to exhaust all the other possibilities first."

"Leyburn may eventually designate one of his associates or apprentices to train you," Anin said, looking doubtful. "Your only other hope is to locate a wizard somewhere out of Ninkarrak, probably out of Ilwheirlane. The disadvantage there is that you'll have to go to him."

"I wouldn't mind that. I'd go anywhere. In fact, I'd prefer to have someone unassociated with Leyburn."

Anin frowned. "Very well, I'll see what I can do."

In the country, the month of Minneth was a quiet time given over to preparations for the two great feasts of Sun Day and New Year's Day. In Ninkarrak, however, no season was without social activity. On the night of her first ball, Alanna met so many people that, midway through the evening, their names and faces began to blur. One man, however, stood out.

Her hostess introduced him as Avron Esparda, the Tamrai of Siara, from Kailane. He was a man of medium height and she faced him eye to eye, but he had a distinct air of command. Furthermore, when her eyes met his, she felt the shock she had come to associate with meeting a wizard, and in a much stronger degree than she had felt it on meeting Guitara. She recovered from the sinking sensation and examined him. His black hair grew back from a high forehead and a predatory nose. His skin was dark complexioned and his eyes were a brilliant amber.

"You're a long way from your home, Tamrai Esparda," Alanna remarked, aware that he was examining her as intently as she had studied him. "Do you travel for pleasure or on business?"

His lips twisted in a wry smile. "A little of both, Tamrai Cairn. I find your country fascinating."

"Is this your first visit?"

"Regrettably. However, I hope to be a more frequent visitor in future."

She recognized some implicit suggestion in his words, but, before she could converse with him further, he invited her to join a set for a country dance. She assented and the movements of the dance, requiring the regular changing of partners, made any continued conversation impractical.

Alanna had another partner for the next dance and after that she went down to dinner with a gentleman her aunt introduced.

VYRKARION: THE TALISMAN OF ANOR

She didn't see Esparda again until one of the last dances of the evening. The dance was a shalla, a new dance from Pelona. As the dancers remained with their own partners throughout the movements, it permitted a continuing conversation. Esparda talked of general matters until just before the dance ended when he asked whether he might call on her.

Alanna accepted. She was curious about him. He dressed well, although not in the extreme of fashion, and seemed to be a gentleman, but more than that she felt certain he was a wizard. She hoped he might, when he knew her better, be willing to train her. With her uncle's words and her frustrating experience with Ramal Guitara still fresh in her mind, however, she didn't quite dare to ask him outright. She thought her chances of persuading him might improve if she waited until they became better acquainted.

Esparda paid a morning call the next day, and Alanna's first impression was reinforced. He had a brusque manner and he watched her in a peculiar way, but she felt sure he was a wizard. She almost taxed him with it, but decided to wait for an occasion when Una wasn't present.

Before leaving he invited Alanna and her aunt and uncle to join him at the theater the following week. Una hesitated, but at Alanna's look she said, "Why, yes, Tamrai Esparda. I'll have to confirm with my husband, but I believe we'd be delighted to join you."

"Then I will look forward to seeing you again." He bowed stiffly.

When he had gone, Una questioned her. "I don't say he isn't perfectly all right, my dear, but strange people sometimes come from Kailane. It's so close to Gandahar, you know."

"Lady Thanling introduced us at the ball last night," Alanna said. "I understood her to say that he's staying with Lord Essure, the Foreign Secretary."

"Oh, well, if Essure vouches for him, I suppose he must be all right," Una said, but she looked doubtful.

Nevertheless, Alanna enjoyed the evening with Esparda. The play was a revival of the ancient tragedy, "The Defiance of Edain." Although Alanna was familiar with the story, the play impressed her because she had never before seen a human woman playing Trivana who was beautiful enough for it to be believed that an eslar might love her. Nor had she ever before seen the part of Edain, the child who had been born with all the power of the greatest of the great wizards, played convincingly.

So she watched with fascination as Edain indulged her childish whims and then demanded that all around her worship her as an equal to the gods themselves.

The ending, where Tarat, the creator of the eslarin, slew Edain and forbade any eslar from ever again mating with a human, Alanna found almost an anticlimax. Particularly as the play over-stressed Tarat's final curse, when the god swore that he would impose a terrible punishment on all concerned if his law were ever broken.

Outside the theater, while waiting for Esparda's carriage, Una said, "I wonder why they revived that old story. Couldn't they have done something more cheerful?" Then, as though remembering her host might be offended, she added, "It was well played, of course, but it's as old as the towers."

"They revived it because it's been said the law was broken thirty years ago when a child of mixed blood was born in Arvonin, and earlier this year a prophecy told of a 'god-king' to come from the north," Anin said. "They're trying to capitalize on the rumors."

Una stared at him. "What rumors! Oh, I've heard of the prophecy. Well, everyone has. But I haven't heard anything about a half-breed eslar."

Esparda, who had stiffened at Anin's words, demanded, "Are the rumors true?"

"Oh, yes. They're true."

Esparda's face convulsed as he suppressed some powerful emotion. His reaction made Alanna realize the implications of her uncle's words. "He who should not have been born," she thought and her eyes went to her uncle, but his expression was enigmatic. He was watching Esparda. She realized he'd given Esparda the information deliberately and she wondered why. She also wondered why he'd kept the knowledge of the child's existence from her when she first mentioned the words of the eslarin.

XI

When he was just a young child
His father meant him ill,
And sought to bend and break him
To serve another's will.
Will, will to the Wanderer
Wherever he may be,
Though he is doomed to exile
By the shore of Sorrow Sea.

— FROM *THE BALLAD OF AUBREY THE WANDERER* BY ANONYMOUS

Minta stood in the shadow of the hangings by Aubrey's bed and watched as Nahar Vanith argued with Naharil Thurin, her consort.

"I'll not stand for that slimy worm coming anywhere near my child," Vanith said. She was a tall, handsome woman, strongly built, with shoulders as broad as a man's. Her cheeks were flushed with rage. Minta had never seen her look so angry.

"He's my child, too. You seem to forget that sometimes." Thurin's voice was bland, but his manner implied a threat, and his large, coarse hands clenched and unclenched. He was no taller than Vanith, but where her form was graceful despite her strength, he was burly. Although there was little physical resemblance, something about Thurin reminded Minta of her husband.

She could not leave without passing between the combatants; they faced each other on either side of the door. She glanced at Aubrey, hoping he might have managed to sleep through his father's arrival, but he was wide awake. He met her eyes and put his finger to his lips, gesturing for her to sit beside him.

"Your child," Vanith sneered, "and a lot of attention you pay to him. You don't think I believe that it was your idea to have Gurden Semel tutor Aubrey? No, Thurin, I know you too well. This maliciousness comes from Horgen and that rabid priest."

"You shouldn't speak of His Holiness Lord Theolan, like that. It's disrespectful." Thurin sounded more complacent than disapproving. He reminded Minta of a fat cat with a stolen dish of cream.

"I meant it to be," Vanith snapped. "I'm not a follower of Miune, and I won't stand by and let Aubrey be corrupted."

Minta glanced at Aubrey, surprised to catch him grinning. He saw her concern and gestured again for her to be silent.

"Don't you think you should reconsider before being so outspoken? Your father might think it's you who has a bad influence on the child." Thurin purred.

"I'm still the Heir Apparent. My father can disinherit me, but he can't dictate my actions or beliefs." Vanith paused, then added, "I'd be cautious, if I were you. If I'm disinherited, Arrel will assume my place, and that wouldn't suit you at all."

"True, my dear, but I hardly think anything so drastic as disinheritance is required. Your father, as a devout follower of Miune, believes a wife should be guided by her husband. He's appointed Semel as royal tutor at my request. And you know you can't fight your father." His voice hardened. "My son will be taught by Gurden Semel. He's an able teacher as well as a priest. It's time Aubrey came out of the nursery and into the schoolroom." Thurin's eyes narrowed. "I'm surprised you haven't found a tutor for him before this. If you have, and you've kept it a secret, Semel will discover that fact, and it won't improve your position in Idrim's eyes."

"You fathik! You have it all worked out, you and Horgen. But if I truly thought Aubrey's life was at stake, I'd take him out of Ninkarrak and there's nothing you or Horgen or even my father could do to stop me. Have you considered that?"

He smiled. "But you won't, will you, Vanith? If you leave, you'll break your oath to your father. You'll be renouncing the throne, and you'll never do that."

Minta could almost see the tension in the air between them. She wanted to cry out for them to stop. Then Aubrey caught her wrist in his hand. His touch released her from the scene, setting her apart in a thin shell of calm. She shut her eyes and when she looked back at the couple by the door she saw Vanith looking down.

"Well?"

"No, it's not well," Vanith said, "but send your sniveling priest. Only, get out of my sight now."

Thurin bowed. "Anything to oblige, my dear. Semel will give Aubrey his first lesson tomorrow. Have him ready by ten o'clock." He left, smiling.

Vanith stood watching the door for some moments. Then she whispered, "Go, Minta, and see if he's really gone."

Minta bit her lip. She hadn't realized that Vanith knew she was present, but she got up and went out into the hall. She checked the playroom and her bedroom, but there was no trace of Naharil Thurin. She said so when she reentered Aubrey's room.

Vanith was sitting on the edge of Aubrey's bed holding his hands. Minta had often seen them sit like that, but she had never sensed the significance of the pose before. Now she realized that they were communicating, talking in a way that no one could overhear. She felt a pang of jealousy and then reminded herself that Aubrey was Vanith's child. Still, seeing them like that made her feel lonely.

As though he sensed her emotion, Aubrey looked up at her and smiled. "Come and sit down so we don't have to shout."

Minta hesitated, but Vanith patted the bed beside her. "Come along, Minta, we aren't trying to keep secrets from you. You know them all."

Minta asked, "Will Reverend Semel be able to tell that Aubrey's received training? Will that get you into trouble with the Estahar?"

Aubrey smiled wryly, the adult expression looking odd on his childish features. "Are you really afraid that I won't be able to fool one of Theolan's priests?"

Minta swallowed. She knew that Aubrey was clever, but could he fool a priest? Still, anyone who tried to judge him as one would a normal five-year-old...

"Well, then," Aubrey said, apparently reading the answer in the changing expressions on her face, "we're all quite safe, aren't we?"

The next morning, however, as Minta helped Aubrey to wash and dress, the solemn, set look on his face disturbed her. His limp, too, was worse than usual.

Aubrey had been born with a degenerative disease in his left hip. Because of it, he had been slow in learning to stand and walking was painful for him. When Lord Leyburn first became Aubrey's tutor, he had halted the progress of the disease, but done nothing to repair the damage already done. Minta had been appalled by this, knowing that it was within his power to heal Aubrey entirely.

"It's cruel to leave him in pain when you could cure him," she had protested.

"Nahar Aubrey is a wizard," Lord Leyburn had said. "I've arrested the degeneration, but, as he's a wizard and it's his body, his must be the responsibility for changing any part of it. All I'm entitled to do, and that I can do only because of his age, is prevent further damage."

"He isn't even three years old."

"His age is irrelevant to his talent and his will. He's a wizard. If you doubt me, ask him."

Minta had wept. When Aubrey found her crying he had asked her why.

"Lord Leyburn could have healed your hip."

"He did, Minta. He made it much better."

"He could have made it completely well."

"No." Aubrey had said. "Jerevan wouldn't do a thing like that."

"Why not?"

Minta remembered how Aubrey's face had screwed up as he tried to find words to explain. Then he had said, "I am me. Only I can change me. Jerevan knows if he did that…" He had hesitated, then added, "it would be bad."

She still hadn't understood, but after that she had accepted that it wasn't cruelty on Lord Leyburn's part, but some strange rule that wizards had to live with.

That morning there were dark smudges under Aubrey's eyes showing how little he had slept during the night and, as the time approached for his lesson with Gurden Semel, he grew more and more restless. Yet Minta could see that every movement was painful for him.

Finally, he found a pile of building blocks in a cupboard and set the stage for Semel's arrival. He hadn't played with the blocks for years, but he seemed to get satisfaction that morning from building them up and smashing them down.

Gurden Semel arrived at exactly ten o'clock, just as Aubrey was completing his most elaborate structure yet. Semel was a small man, only a few inches taller than Minta. He had lank black hair and his skin was sallow and marked with the scars of acne.

"I can see you're quite a builder, Nahar Aubrey," Semel said, observing the tower of blocks.

Aubrey looked up and Minta was amazed at the blank, wide-eyed expression on his face. "I like blocks," he said ingenuously. "Who're you?"

"I'm your new teacher, your highness. Do you understand what that means?" Semel's black eyes were inquisitive.

"I 'spose it means you're going to teach me something." The innocent blue gaze took in Minta's rigid stance by the door. "Minta teaches me things all the time."

Minta was flustered as Semel turned to her, but she managed to curtsy. "Nahar Vanith told me you'd be coming. I'll leave you now, but call me if you need anything."

"There's no need for you to leave. I'm sure the Nahar would feel more comfortable if you stayed and helped me get to know him better." Semel's smile revealed pale gums and sharp, irregular teeth.

"If you wish."

"Oh, yes, I think you can be quite helpful." Semel turned back to Aubrey. "Now, your highness, you must tell me what you already know?"

"I know lots of things," Aubrey boasted, adding a last block to the pile. The whole assemblage collapsed. He pouted. "Now look what you made me do."

"I'm sorry, your highness," Semel said, disconcerted, "but you must put away your blocks now and come and learn your lessons. You do know about learning lessons, don't you?"

Aubrey eyed him suspiciously. "Learning lessons is like getting spanked if you're bad, but I haven't been bad. Have I, Minta?" He twisted around to face Minta, demanding her support.

"No, your highness," she soothed, "of course, you haven't."

"This is a different kind of lesson." Semel was thrown off stride. "I'm going to teach you to read and write and do figures, and also how to pay proper homage to your creator."

"I don't like lessons."

Eventually, Semel got Aubrey seated at a table and commenced teaching him to read. Minta, who knew that Aubrey had been reading since the age of three, was awed by his ability to dissemble. Semel finally determined that Aubrey was barely familiar with the alphabet and often mixed up similar letters.

In the same manner, Semel determined that Aubrey had a rudimentary concept of numbers and no knowledge of geography. The lesson ended with his leading Aubrey in a prayer to Miune. "You'll have to learn this prayer by heart, your highness, and say it every morning and night."

"I'm not so good at mem'rizing things," Aubrey said, seeming anxious. "I forget."

"That's all right, your highness. We'll just keep going over it until you remember it. But that's enough for today. You did very well." He patted Aubrey on the head. "I'll be back tomorrow and we can continue where we left off."

When he had gone, Minta hugged Aubrey to her. For once he did nothing to stave off her embrace, but hugged her back. She could feel him trembling with reaction.

He withdrew after a few moments, however, and limped to the door. "I think I'll go to my room now and take a nap." He looked sheepish. "I didn't sleep too well last night, and…"

"That's a wonderful idea," Minta said. "You were so clever, but it must have been awfully hard. I was shaking in my shoes."

Aubrey grinned, her admiration soothing him. "It wasn't that hard. He was so stupid, he expected me to be stupider."

Minta laughed. "Get to bed."

"You will call me when Jerevan comes? I… I need to see him today."

"Of course, I'll wake you for that." Minta was indignant that he would doubt her.

"Thank you, Minta."

When the door had shut behind him, she sank down by the table and cried.

Later that afternoon Vanith returned with Lord Leyburn. Minta curt-sied as they entered. "Aubrey's sleeping, but he told me to wake him as soon as you arrived, your grace."

Jerevan smiled. "I'll go in to him. You tell Vanith how the lesson went." The expression in his eyes was kind and Minta felt warmed. She knew why Aubrey had been so anxious to see the wizard. It was impos-sible to believe, in Lord Leyburn's presence, that there was any problem he couldn't handle.

"Well," Vanith said when Jerevan had gone to wake Aubrey, "so Aubrey was able to fool Semel."

"Oh, yes. He hadn't any idea that Aubrey wasn't just a spoilt child, but Aubrey looked so pale afterward and I know he didn't sleep well last night."

Vanith sighed. "Maybe it will get easier for him. The first lesson had to be the worst. And it won't be for long. Not long at all." Vanith sounded tired, too, Minta realized, tired and strained.

She had always seen Vanith as strong. It worried her to realize that Vanith also had weaknesses. "What do you mean? Won't the lessons go on until Aubrey's grown?"

"No. Nothing could be more unlikely."

"What will stop them?"

"Are you deaf, Minta, that you haven't heard the rumors swarming through the court these last months?" Vanith demanded.

"Oh, your highness, I'm sorry to have upset you on top of everything else. Of course, I've heard rumors, but they don't make sense to me."

Vanith shrugged. "No. Well, I wish they made no sense to me. My father's a weak man and a bad ruler, but I don't wish him dead, nor do I want to die with him."

"Then you believe that a 'god-king' will come out of the north next year?"

"No," Vanith said bitterly, "I don't believe in a 'god-king.' I believe that my cousin, the child the eslarin named Rhys, will come south from his home in Valkarn next spring, and that he'll kill, or try to kill, anyone who stands between him and the throne."

XII

4730, 473RD CYCLE OF THE YEAR OF THE OX
MONTH OF MINNETH

Al ease dao, Miune lot malarin,
Cogazad amne oanse loridom.
Ilad, malarin puat lordom Miune
Al imo ilea oan gorbala e
Hesa ac maidom a larin.

"From his goodness, Miune created men,
Demanding only that they worship him.
Thus, men must worship Miune
Lest he abandon them and give them
To the hatred of the were-peoples."

— FROM "MIUNE'S CREED"

"**S**teal the Staff of the High Priest of Miune! You're mad!" Elath Orm gaped at her companion, then looked around to see if she could have been overheard.

She and Fallon Gavi sat at a table in the back of the Duka's bar and dining room. It was early for a hotel that did most of its business with the denizens of Farinmalith, and most of the other tables were unoccupied. Even Rad Flickra, the owner, had yet to make his appearance. No one was close enough to have heard.

Elath turned back to Fal. He was her partner. They had been together for seven years. He was prone to recklessness, but he was a good man to have beside one in a fight, and fighting had been her profession since the age of seventeen. But times were hard. In the last year or so there hadn't been even a border dispute to interrupt the uneasy peace around the Thallassean. Thousands of mercenaries were out of work. She hadn't yet had to turn to thievery to earn enough money to eat, but both she and Fal knew those who had.

"I tell you it's possible. Anything can be stolen given the right backing and conditions," Fal said, leaning across the table so he wouldn't have to raise his voice. Tall and raw-boned, he was not a handsome man. When Elath had first seen him she had expected him to be awkward, he looked so big and bony. But Fal moved with the grace of a dancer; he was, in fact, a dancer of a sort. In his teens he had been a neophyte in the priesthood of Rav in Ravaar, and among the first to study death dancing when it was introduced there.

She had been nineteen the day they met, with two years experience as a member of Trevi Unith's troop, fighting in the south among the Nine Cities of Anat. She had been proud of her skills, but Fal had taught her how little she knew. Fal had taught her a lot. If only he wouldn't push his luck.

Elath bent closer to Fal and met his eyes. Her voice was a whisper, but she stressed each word, "The Basilica of Miune is a maze swarming with fanatical priests. There isn't an hour, day or night, when the treasures aren't guarded. What's more, the Staff is one of the original three, given to the First Fathers by Miune himself. If they guard anything in that wretched place, they guard that. The idea is absurd."

Fal's eyes shied away from hers. "We wouldn't have to perform the actual theft. He wants to do that himself. All we have to do is break in. Then, when he's inside, we stage a distraction. It's a good plan, I tell you, and he can make it work."

"It doesn't make sense," Elath said. "If your madman can steal the staff once he's inside, why can't he get in by himself, too? Who is he and what's he trying to pull?"

"One hundred thousand riktravin, El! Does it matter who he is for that price? We can retire to the country."

"But how do we get paid after he's been killed? Just because he's crazy enough to want in, doesn't mean he'll make it back out."

"He's willing to pay a quarter of the money in advance. Twenty-five thousand riktravin!" Fal said. "It isn't as though we're turning away other job offers."

Elath's eyes widened. "That much in advance? Who in Maera's name has that much money to throw away just to commit suicide?"

"It won't be suicide for them," Fal insisted.

"There's more than one?" Elath caught his slip.

Fal looked away and Elath grabbed his arm. "Tell me, Fal. I'm not taking a step until I know it all."

Fal studied the pitted and stained surface of the table and then sighed and met Elath's eyes. "I've only met one man but he talks about assistants. His name's Gatah and he's a wizard. I had enough training in Ravaar to know that he's genuine and powerful, not some carnival quack. He said we'd have to get a party of five inside."

"If he's so powerful, why can't he get himself in?" Elath pressed.

Fal shrugged. "I didn't understand that part. He said something about Miune having defenses against his kind. I asked him why Miune defended himself against wizards and he laughed and said, 'Only special wizards.' He wouldn't tell me anything else. Just that they'll be in a trance state."

"I don't like it. The idea gives me the shakes. My uncle's a worshiper of Miune and I've been in that place…"

"We won't be going into the Basilica," Fal insisted. "All we have to do is put them in though a back door and wake them up. Then we stir up a disturbance in front. There's a festival coming up. They want a night when there'll be lots of people around to get in the way of pursuit. All that money, El. We can retire, open an inn in the country. Think of it." He leaned over and took her hands in his. "I don't like the idea of turning thief any more than you, but we're flat broke, both of us, and, if it's a choice between thievery and starvation, I'll take thievery. Anyway, the Basilica of Miune can afford it. What's one big risk if it means never having to take any other risks ever again."

Elath sighed and squeezed his hands in return. "I guess I'll have to meet this Gatah."

Fal grinned. "If we pull it off, we'll be sung about in ballads for a thousand years."

Elath frowned. "As long as they don't know our names."

"You worry too much. You've got to learn to trust your luck."

"I don't mind trusting luck, it's stretching it that worries me."

Alanna and Una sat drinking tea in Una's parlor one Miunesday afternoon when Lady Enora Avlen came to call. Enora was a frail, faded woman with a twittery manner. From the expression on Una's face, Alanna could tell Enora had been expected.

"Oh, dear, I hope you're prepared for a treat," she said as she came in. "I know you have no churches in Fell or Idris to equal the Great Basilica of Miune here."

"Probably not," Alanna admitted, "but I'm a worshiper of Maera."

"But, my dear, you must attend at least one service at the Basilica of Miune now you're in Ninkarrak," Una said. "Lady Avlen and I usually go to the local Basilica because that's more convenient for her. And I haven't wanted to insist you join us because I thought that would be dull for you. We have to sit in the unaccompanied women's section and in the local Basilica that's so far back one can hardly hear the sermons. But today we're going to the Great Basilica and you mustn't miss a chance to see that. I doubt if there's anything to equal it anywhere. It's the most splendid sight and today's a festival day so the service will be especially beautiful." She paused and looked wistful. "We've arranged it all for your sake."

"I'm not a worshiper of Miune," Alanna protested. "You know that. We discussed it when I arrived. I've never been to any of his basilicas."

"Do forgive me," Una said. "I know your father and mother had all those strange ideas, but now you're here you must at least hear the teachings of Miune. The priests will understand your not being familiar with the rituals if we explain you're from the country."

"The festival ceremonies are particularly beautiful," Enora added. "You really must see them."

Thus pressed, Alanna consented to accompany them. The Great Temple District comprised several square kilometers of the city and contained churches dedicated to all five of the high gods, the Lorincen. Priests and a number of wealthy merchants also lived in the district, where all the streets curved in honor of the gods. The Great Basilica of Miune was the largest of the churches, with an immense gold dome that could be seen from anywhere in the southern end of the city. In the lurid light of the setting sun it flamed with the same salmon color as the sky.

The priest at the entry wore a crimson robe edged with gold and jewels. He frowned when Una explained that Alanna was new to Miune's worship, but said only, "Kneel, woman, when in doubt and watch the other women." A young boy acting as usher led them through a complex of small, bejeweled rooms and into the vast sanctuary at the center under the golden dome. Alanna knelt with the rest of the congregation. Another priest, a tall, cadaverous man with thinning, white hair, had just begun to speak.

"We're in luck," Lady Avlen whispered. "That's his holiness, Lord Theolan, the High Priest. He doesn't often perform regular services. He must be here today because of the festival."

As though he had heard Enora's whisper, Theolan turned toward them and Alanna felt his power. This was the man who had converted the Estahar to his religion by sheer force of will. She shivered. Theolan's eyes were black and burning, the eyes of a fanatic.

"The other gods squandered their energies," he said, his voice reverberating through the vast, airy space of the dome. "They created many races. Miune made mankind. As He created one race, that race should worship Him alone. Remember, Miune imparted a piece of His own divine will to us, His children."

The priest took from the altar an ornate staff of some dark, shiny material. He raised it in his large, bony hands and shook it above his head. "By this Staff and the power He has given me, I can protect you from the evil ones who would return us to bondage. But only if we keep faith. If we break our faith, He will abandon us to the wrath and envy of the were-peoples."

The sermon went on and on. Alanna had started to doze when Theolan came to the subject of women.

"And as the divine whore Maera betrayed Miune, so will every woman betray those men foolish enough to believe in them. Never trust the offspring of the Great Whore. Never let a woman have power over you."

He paused. His burning gaze searched the room and for a moment seemed to focus on Alanna. "As for those of you who carry her blood, the blood that changes with the flux of the moon, your blood is tainted; you cannot help the evil that is in you. Thus, it is your duty to be ruled by those men set to guide you and never question their right to authority over you."

Alanna blocked out the rest of his words. She would have risen and left if such an act wouldn't have attracted unwanted attention. The philosophical distaste she had felt for the religion of Miune turned to outright disgust.

Elath waited until a drift of cloud dimmed the face of Ranth, the moon, and then ran as swiftly as she could with her heavy burden across the last stretch of open grass into the bushes at the base of the Great Basilica. She lowered the man she had been carrying to the ground as the cloud passed and checked for any guard who might have seen her, but the grounds appeared peaceful in the moonlight.

She had pulled her long black hair back from her face into a tight braid and brushed the pale skin of her face and hands with soot. In the long sleeved black shirt and pantaloons and soft, black leather boots she could pass for a man. She was tall enough and the loose shirt hid the curves of her breasts. The straight nose and the firm line of her jaw could well have belonged to a handsome boy.

Sinking back into the shadows at the base of the wall, Elath shrugged the pack from her back and withdrew a long, fine cord. Braided of spider's silk, it was almost without weight and as strong or stronger than the steel claw affixed to one end.

Where were Fal and the others?

Ranth dimmed again as a second cloud scudded across its face and two more misshapen shadows crossed the lawn: Fal and Cyrene Delant, each with a wizard slung over one shoulder. Cyrene was another mercenary who had worked with them before.

As Fal reached her side, Elath started to spin the cord.

"Wait," Fal whispered. "The others are coming."

"Let them come. We still need to climb the wall," Elath whispered, but she let the cord go slack.

"I don't want a noise to draw the guards while any of us are still in the open," Fal said.

"What if it's a trick and they betray us?"

Fal snorted, "It's not like you to shy at shadows, El. Why would they betray us? They've already paid the advance to Flickra. If anything happens to us, it won't get them their money back."

A third cloud dimmed the moon and two more dark forms slipped across the grass, Thrym and Flava Narlis, both with their limp burdens.

Flava was another mercenary, a friend of Fal's, but Thrym was a thief Elath had brought in with the idea of benefiting from expert advice. Thrym had been trying to join the Mercenaries Guild for several years and in better times would have succeeded before this.

Elath shivered. None of them would be here if the times were better. She glanced at the unconscious wizard on Fal's back. Gatah, Fal called him. He was small and dark and his eyes were yellow. Something about him made Elath's skin crawl, perhaps the way he had of looking through her as though she wasn't there.

Elath spun the cord again and with a smooth, rippling motion hurled the hook up over an ornate molding that circled the roof. She jerked on the rope, then tried it with her full weight. When it held, she climbed up, hand over hand. The cord swayed and turned but it held. At the top she grasped the edge and pulled herself over.

The surface of the Basilica's roof was plated with copper, green with verdigris and patterned by bird droppings. The spires and minarets reminded her of an ant's view of a forest of distorted and moldy fungi.

Elath tugged on the rope three times and felt the pull on it as Fal and Cyrene climbed up. Then the three of them pulled the limp wizards up one at a time, while Thrym and Flava stayed at the bottom to tie them into the sling they had brought. When the wizards were all on the roof, the others followed.

"That way," Fal whispered when they were all up, consulting the crude map given him by Gatah and pointing to the great, gold dome looming over the lesser growths around it. Elath started to pull up the rope, but Thrym stopped her.

"We may need that for a quick escape. Leave it," he whispered.

Elath nodded, picked up her burden and followed Fal out over the roof. She had to watch her footing. The copper plating tilted crazily between the multitude of towers and was slippery in places with fresh bird droppings. Fortunately, the distance was short to the base of the central dome. Once there, they circled around some forty-five degrees of the dome and then ventured out over the roof again, heading toward a minaret topped by a golden globe. The diagram had looked easy to follow when Fal had shown it to her. The symbol above each of the minarets was unique. The tower Gatah had marked as their goal was smaller than most of the others, and the door into it was as round as the globe above it.

Thrym lowered the limp body of the wizard he had been carrying to the surface of the roof, wedged it with his foot to keep it from sliding, and examined the lock. "A child could pick this," he grunted. He took a tool from his pack, stared at the lock for a moment, put the pick into the keyhole and twisted once. Elath heard a click and the door swung open.

"I don't like it," she whispered. "It's been too easy. If the Basilica is this simple to break into, how have the priests kept their treasures for so long?"

Fal caught her arm and pulled her close. "Maybe all the other thieves had nervous qualms, like you, at the last minute," he murmured into her ear.

Elath pulled away. Fal was too confident; he frightened her. She didn't trust the wizards at all, but there was nothing she could do now but hope for the best.

Fal carried Gatah inside and the others followed, Thrym at the rear as he had paused to replace his lock-pick. The inside was dark. Gatah had assured them that the priests would be too busy with festival duties to maintain their usual guard on these rooms. So far it looked as though he had told the truth.

Elath was lowering the wizard she had carried to the floor when Thrym stopped in the doorway and grunted. He dropped his burden and his hands went to his head. "I've tripped their alarm. They have a guard against shape-changers. They know we're here," he gasped and backed out the door. Elath leapt through it after him. Flava also made it through, diving head first, as the door started to swing shut. Cyrene took too long getting the wizard she had been carrying off her back and the door closed in her face. Elath's last view of Fal was of him shaking the wizards awake, not even trying to escape.

Elath hurled herself against the round portal and tried to pry it open but she could get no purchase on the smooth surface. As she pressed against it, the door began to feel warm, the heat growing until she had to back up to avoid being burned.

"Come on!" Thrym grabbed her arm and pulled her away. "We've got to get out of here. There'll be guards swarming all over this place in a moment."

"Fal and Cyrene..."

"Our getting killed won't save them," Flava said, climbing to his feet. "Which way did we come? This blasted roof all looks the same to me."

"This way," Thrym said, starting out across the roof. "I memorized the tower we came up by." Elath took one more look at the door, which had turned a dull red and was glowing, then followed Thrym.

They made it to the minaret closest to the rope before they heard shouting near the door they had just left. From the roof they could see that the garden was already swarming with guards and priests carrying lanterns.

They slid down the rope in a moment when no one was close and flattened themselves to the ground under the bushes as four guards approached, a priest with them aiming the beam of a lantern up and down the wall.

The guards would spot the rope, Elath realized. Their only hope was surprise. "When the light hits the rope, we attack together. Thrym can take the one holding the lantern," she whispered, drawing her knife from its sheath.

She felt fingers touch her in two signals of assent as she started to crawl. The faint rustling of their passage through the bushes as they took up positions was drowned out by the noise made by the approaching men.

The guards drew closer. Elath saw the light from the lantern pass over her rope, pause, then start to return. She leapt to her feet and launched herself at the man beside the priest holding the lantern. Her knife entered the guard's ribcage before the light could return to the rope. He grunted but had no time to cry out. The lantern holder had also gone down, putting the light out.

As Elath freed her knife and looked around, an arm struck her on the side of the head. She fell, rolling away and pulling the knife with her. Then she was on her feet again, diving for the fifth man, the last one on his feet. He started to turn but went down with the impact of her body and she drove her knife sideways into his throat.

"Put on their clothes," Flava whispered, rolling a body toward the bushes.

Elath pulled at the body of the man she had just killed and dragged him back into the shrubbery. Thrym was hauling the last of the other bodies under cover a few paces to the right of her. She looked out cautiously but no one had noticed the struggle. All the guards she could see were looking away toward the front of the building where one of the priests was shouting.

Elath stripped the guard's body and donned his clothes over her own. In a moment they were all dressed and Thrym, wearing the priest's robes, had relit the lantern. They walked across the garden and only broke into a run when they reached cover on the far side of the road.

Alanna tensed. She heard shouting from behind the altar. Lord Theolan had finished his sermon earlier and left. Two other priests had spoken after him, but more briefly, and then had come the singing of a number of hymns. Alanna knew none of the words and disapproved of the sentiments expressed. So, as she was not singing, she heard the cries from the rear a little before the rest of the congregation.

Four men and a woman burst through a curtained doorway to one side of the altar and ran down the aisle. They were dressed in black and seemed to have blacked their skins as well. One of them was limping and the tall one in the lead had a cut across his forehead. He carried the staff Alanna had seen in the hands of Lord Theolan earlier.

"Stop them," a priest yelled, following them through the doorway, leading a group of guards. "Blasphemers and thieves. Stop them in the name of Miune."

The congregation stirred and several people on the aisle rose and tried to intercept the runners. The first one to block their path was knocked off his feet by the staff, however, and for a moment it looked as though the two leading thieves, the tall man and the woman, might still reach the door before the mass of the audience could react. Then a row of people on the aisle in the back of the room moved to block the exit.

Seeing their escape cut off, the three smaller men at the rear hesitated and the audience fell on them in a pile of bodies.

The tall man slowed long enough to toss the staff to the woman. Then he dove into the people obstructing the door, striking out with his hands and feet, which he used as weapons in a manner Alanna had never seen before, while the woman defended his back. They both fought desperately before the sheer mass of people brought them down.

The congregation was in an uproar, but after a time the milling in the aisle ceased, the wounded were taken away, and the five thieves were dragged to the base of the altar, the woman and one of the smaller men obviously dead. Lord Theolan reappeared and stood beside the podium from which he had spoken earlier. Alanna saw that someone had returned his staff to him, one end of it smeared with blood. She felt queasy at the suddenness of the violence.

"Silence!" Theolan cried. "Return to your seats." There was a brief stir as everyone went back to their original places. Then the huge room quieted, all of the audience turning to face the high priest.

He raised the staff. If his eyes had looked fanatical earlier, now they glowed with madness. "These thieves would have stolen the Staff of Miune. Thus we know they fear its power, so I shall use that power against them. Strip them and bring them to me."

The guards holding the three living prisoners dragged them back to their feet, tore their clothes off and shoved them forward naked in front of Theolan. Alanna felt the audience's tension, almost like hunger, and it frightened her. The thieves looked pathetic in their nudity, defenseless, but there was no pity in Theolan or his congregation.

The tall thief appeared almost unconscious, blood streaming down from the cut on his forehead. Alanna noted that, despite his boniness, he was well muscled. The two shorter men seemed uninjured, but their bodies looked softer. Still, they stared back at Theolan defiantly.

"Foul shape-changers, show your true form," Theolan cried and brought the staff down to strike each of the prisoners before him. The tall man swayed when it struck him, and almost fell down, but there was no other reaction. However, the shorter men screamed in agony under the blows.

The audience echoed the screams as, where the staff hit them, the shorter men's flesh shifted. Alanna stared, nauseated, as first their shoulders and then their whole bodies melted and changed before her eyes. In less than a minute two large lizards crouched where the men had stood.

"So, isklarin filth. You would defile the Basilica of Miune?" Theolan cried. "Then die the death of Miune." He brought the staff down again, and where it struck the lizards they again began to melt, but this time there was no change into a new form. Their bodies liquefied into shapeless blobs on the floor. The blobs twitched and burbled. Alanna gagged, unutterably relieved when their death-throes ended and they lay inert.

Theolan's crazed eyes returned to the semi-conscious man he had struck with the rod first. "So you are not of the spawn of the Destroyer, but a tool of that vileness. You have betrayed your maker," he cried, his voice rising in volume. "You would have stolen the very Staff of Miune and you have sullied it with blood. Blasphemer!" he screamed. "What punishment is great enough for such a crime?"

Alanna looked around and was appalled as the rapt faces of the congregation contorted in frenzy. "Death!" they cried. "Death to the blasphemer!"

"No!" Theolan shrieked, raising the staff. The audience stilled, their eyes fixed on him in adoration. "You shall not die, man, for dying is an end of punishment. You shall live, but you shall live as an example to all of the wrath of Miune."

Theolan paused and the congregation waited, awe-struck. Into the silence, he intoned, "So that you cannot see to covet another's goods, I put out your eyes." He thrust the tip of the staff into the man's right eye. There was a sound like meat sizzling on a hot pan. The prisoner screamed and slumped in the guards' arms, unconscious. Then Theolan thrust the staff into his left eye.

Alanna closed her own eyes, trying to shut out the roar of approval from the crowd around her. Even from halfway across the room, she thought she could smell the odor of burning flesh. She wanted to be sick. She wanted to be anywhere else but in this church where such brutality was cheered by people who called themselves human.

The crowd quieted and she looked up to see Theolan again holding up the staff. When his audience had stilled in expectation, he continued, "Even without sight, such as you might be tempted to steal. So that you may never again touch another's property, I take off your hands." This time he touched the staff to one of the man's arms at the wrist. The skin appeared to grow hard. Then Theolan drew back the staff and gave the arm a sharp rap. The flesh cracked and the hand fell off with a thud. Theolan moved the staff on to the second arm.

Alanna had attained a state of numbness. She no longer even tried to shut the horror out, it was too overwhelming, too dreadful. She simply watched, her mind fixing on details as though to deny the whole. Thus she noticed that the stumps of the thief's arms appeared bloodless, as though the ends had been cauterized.

Theolan returned the staff to the altar and gestured to the guards. "Take him out and throw him in the street." He turned then to the congregation and said, "Now we must sing a hymn of thanks to Miune for guarding us from evil."

Alanna wanted only to go home. She felt sick and appalled, defiled by being, however inadvertently, a witness to such horror. At least the rest of the service was brief.

She was silent as they left, thankful that even Una appeared to be subdued by what they had seen. When they were once again seated in Lady Avlen's carriage, however, Una said reverently, "In all the years I've worshiped Miune, I've never before seen the Staff used. You were fortunate to see such a miracle, Alanna. You should take it as a sign of Miune's blessing."

Alanna stared at her, shocked beyond speech.

"Yes. Why I've never felt the power of Miune so strongly before," Enora agreed. "We really must make the effort to come to the Great Basilica more often."

"You call that butchery a miracle?" Alanna found her voice, and then controlled herself with an effort. "I accompanied you out of politeness and perhaps a trace of curiosity. But never, under any circumstances, could you get me to submit to that again. I'm a worshiper of Maera and Jehan. What you term 'a miracle', I'd describe as the criminal acts of a madman."

Lady Avlen gasped. "But you saw what the isklarin would have done? How the Staff protected us? Jehan is the creator of the werepeoples. You can't worship the god of our enemies."

"His followers worship him as the God of Tamar and all its different peoples. He's the Player, the Minstrel, whose goal is to give pleasure and peace to everyone, no matter their race."

"That sounds all very well, Alanna, but when you've learned more about the world, you're bound to change your mind," Una said. "I'm extremely disappointed that you can take that attitude after witnessing such a miracle."

It was nearly dawn before Elath found Fal. He was unconscious and she and Thrym had to carry him back to Farinmalith, to the bleak attic room they shared while waiting for better times. It was obvious that he had been kicked and beaten by departing members of the congregation even after his mutilation. There were cuts and bruises all over his body.

"Do you think he'll live," she asked Thrym after they had bathed him and put him to bed.

"Not if the gods are merciful."

XIII

4730, 473RD CYCLE OF THE YEAR OF THE OX
MONTH OF MINNETH

> *Shemin co a maje onin;*
> *Ilnalor gres ilamvalod jer.*
> *Maje onin ba matanalad.*

> "Fools speak of straight lines;
> The wizard knows the universe curves.
> Straight lines are illusion."

— FROM THE WRITINGS OF THE WIZARD CORMOR

"Everyone will be at the grand ball Idrim's giving in honor of Sun Day," Una said. "And really, you aren't on their list yet; you haven't been presented. I mean, I arranged for you to be presented in Dirga, before the ball I'm giving for you. But you can't miss Sun Day." Una looked horrified at the thought. "So I went to Lady Avlen. She's a lady-in-waiting to Nahar Vanith, you know. And she's a real friend. Despite that scene you made after visiting the Basilica, she said she'd see what she could do, and I just received a note from her. They've put you on the guest list. Isn't that wonderful?"

"Yes, Aunt Una, that's marvelous. Thank you very much!" Alanna exclaimed, for once in agreement with her aunt.

Since her meeting with the Hetri of Colne, she had expected daily to be summoned before Idrim to present her petition. So far, no such summons had arrived and she was worried. She wanted to see the Estahar and make up her own mind about him and his court. She knew the Privy Council wasn't in session during Minneth, but the high officers of state would surely be present at the royal ball. She intended to see them and, if possible, plead her case.

Arriving at the ball, Alanna found the sheer size of Ninkarrak awesome. The Black Tower had given the city its name from the time of the rule of Gandahar when the city had been called Ninkarrakova, city of the Black Tower. It loomed above her head many times taller than even an eslarin home tree and, as it was built into the sheer cliffs overlooking the bay, she knew it also descended more than fifty meters into the solid granite of the headland. The monolithic black stones fitted together so perfectly that it was difficult to insert a fingernail between the blocks.

She couldn't imagine how it had been built without wizardry, yet it had existed long before men had come to Tamar. The isklarin claimed that it had been built by the gods.

The ballroom was equally as impressive. When Alanna and the Farquars were announced, she felt dwarfed by the vast room large enough to hold an entire manor house beneath its vaulted ceiling. Several hundred crystal chandeliers illuminated the scene. Large windows in the curving outer wall allowed a panoramic view of the bay, dark and jeweled with the twinkling lights of the ships in the harbor. The other walls were paneled with the silver-gray of sylvith wood and hung with tapestries, and the royal family held court from a dais positioned midway down the wall to her left.

Even after her conversation with her uncle, Alanna had expected Idrim, a descendant of Vydarga the Red, to be a nearly godlike figure. All her life she had heard tales and read histories of the wizard-kings of Ilwheirlane. Nothing her uncle could have said would have prepared her for the reality of an ancient, bent man with rheumy eyes and a bald head. She searched for any trace of nobility in either his appearance or manner and found none. Age might have brought on his physical disabilities, but age alone wasn't responsible for his querulous voice or the weakness apparent in his jaw and mouth.

She turned from Idrim to the people who shared the dais with him, two men and a woman. The woman was, of course, Nahar Vanith, the Heir Apparent. Her face, with its hooked, bony nose and hawklike eyes bespeaking a pride in keeping with her lineage, reassured Alanna. Thus, it startled her to realize that the Heir Apparent was in the seat farthest from Idrim, lowest in precedence. Such a seating arrangement was a public insult.

The man at the Estahar's right had to be Nahar Arrel, Vanith's brother, but his looks were even more disappointing than his father's. Although younger than Vanith, Arrel looked older, his face marked by dissipation. He had the same weak chin and loose, thick-lipped mouth as Idrim, but where his father was gaunt, Arrel was plump and his sand-colored hair hung in oily strands around a sallow face.

The last figure on the dais sat between Idrim and Vanith and had to be Naharil Thurin, Vanith's consort. Sitting, he appeared to be over medium height and burly, with a blunt, heavy-featured face. Alanna had heard that Vanith's marriage had been one of political expediency, but, while Thurin could not be described as a handsome man, he at least displayed none of the weakness apparent in Vanith's father and brother.

She was still studying the royal family when Lord Colne greeted her, "Good evening, Tamrai Cairn. How are you enjoying Ninkarrak?"

"Lord Colne, I'm so glad to see you again," Alanna said. "I'm enjoying my stay very much."

"I heard what happened with Guitara. I'm sorry."

Alanna grimaced. "The very thought of dealing with me terrified the man."

"A pity," Colne said, "but I suspected his reaction might be something like that, if he got his training in Ravaar. They worship Rav there, and all the holders of the karionin are looked on as lesser deities."

Alanna's eyes were again drawn to the royal dais. "I've been anxious to hear from you. Have you arranged the interview you promised?"

Colne's lips twisted in a half smile. "Yes. You can present your petition to Idrim on the morning of the third Maerasday in Iskkaar. I apologize for the delay. Most of the court officials are off duty this time of year."

He studied her face for a moment and added, "I saw you looking at Nahar Vanith. This would be a good time for you to meet her, if you like?"

"I'd like nothing better."

Taking her arm, Colne led her to the end of the dais where Vanith sat with a thin grouping of courtiers about her.

"Your highness, I'd like to introduce you to Alanna Cairn, Tamrai of Fell," Colne said when he had Vanith's attention. "I mentioned the bearer of a petition to the Estahar from the Mallarnes region, if you remember."

"I'm pleased to make your acquaintance, Tamrai Cairn. I'm always happy when Errian presents me with a new face." Vanith smiled, her angular features softening.

"I'm honored, your highness," Alanna responded with her deepest curtsy.

Vanith questioned her in some detail about the sylvith crop and the exact repercussions to be expected if the fruiting did not take place the following spring. Alanna was impressed by the Nahar's quick grasp of the problem and its ramifications. However, when she started to explain how the Kindred of Maera would help to preserve the present crop, Vanith cut her off. After that they spoke on neutral topics, Vanith asking about her home in Fell and how she was enjoying Ninkarrak.

Alanna didn't know what to make of Vanith's sudden change in attitude or the subtle signals she exchanged with Lord Colne. Then Vanith said, "You must visit me, Tamrai Cairn. You're presenting your petition on the third Maerasday in Iskkaar, I understand. I'm giving a small luncheon that day. You'll enjoy meeting my other guests." Vanith's gray eyes were intent, watching her.

"I'm overwhelmed, your highness. Of course, I'd be delighted to attend."

After that someone else came up to speak with Vanith and Alanna withdrew, Lord Colne still securely by her side.

"You told her that I carry the Talisman?"

"Yes. It was my duty to tell Idrim and Vanith." He paused, eyeing her shrewdly. "And it's to your advantage that they know. The knowledge that some day you might be able to aid them will add weight to any request you make now. I asked that they spread the information no further. Idrim's weak, but he'll keep his word. Vanith has talent of her own and might be of assistance to you. Also, at the luncheon you'll meet her son, Nahar Aubrey."

"Surely he's still a baby?"

"He's five, almost six. He'll surprise you."

"My uncle said something about him the other day, that the future of Ilwheirlane rested with him, but I thought that was mere extravagance. How much can one tell of such a young child?"

Colne's hooded eyes studied her before he said, "I presume he also warned you not to spread that information?"

Alanna's eyes narrowed. "Why yes, but I assumed…"

"That I already knew anything your uncle might say." Colne nodded. "In this case, that's true. But you have to watch your words here in Ninkarrak." He looked around the room and Alanna realized that they stood quite some distance from anyone else. He said quietly, "Aubrey has been Leyburn's pupil since the age of two. Other than Leyburn himself, there's been no such talent discovered since Cormor." He again checked the area around them. "I'm telling you this in confidence. It's not to be mentioned to anyone else, not even your uncle."

Alanna's eyes widened, but she kept her voice down. "Vanith lets Leyburn teach her child?"

He snorted. "Aubrey could be in no better hands. You shouldn't judge Leyburn on the basis of rumor. Think about it." Colne took her arm to lead her back to her aunt.

Alanna swallowed, disturbed, but she was saved from having to respond when they were accosted by an ill-favored man stuffed like wadding into a green velvet suit. Alanna noted with disgust that his bulging clothes were stained with spots of grease and that the lace of his cravat was dirty.

"Introduce me to your young friend, Colne. I can't remember when I've seen you with a prettier bird in tow," the foul man said, reaching out with a stubby finger to caress Alanna's cheek. She flinched, then held herself still. Beneath his heavy perfume she smelt the sour odor of his unwashed body.

Colne's lips tightened. "Of course, Horgen. This is Alanna Cairn, Tamrai of Fell. Tamrai Cairn, may I present Groman Charden, Lanrai of Horgen and Lord Chamberlain of Ilwheirlane."

Alanna curtsied, attempting to conceal her distaste. She remembered Anin speaking derogatively of the Lord Chamberlain but, as with the

Estahar, she had still been unprepared for the actuality. She set aside all thought of presenting her petition on her own to anyone in Idrim's court.

Lord Horgen ogled her. "I see I must pay more attention to the newcomers among us. Colne has stolen a march on me, but he can't expect to keep the advantage now I've seen the prize." He licked his lips.

She controlled her revulsion and said, "Lord Colne was just returning me to my aunt. If you'll excuse us, Lord Horgen."

Colne followed her. Out of Horgen's hearing, he said, "His seeing you in my company was unfortunate. He'll watch you now."

"He wouldn't really...," she hesitated, "approach me?"

"No. He merely wanted to get your reaction." He paused and went on, "He likes to manipulate people, particularly if he can make them suffer in the process."

"He's horrible. How could a man like that attain a position of such responsibility?"

"Don't underestimate him. He's risen to his present position because he has a genius for finding people's weaknesses, and taking advantage of them. Be wary of him."

"I shall be," she said as they reached her aunt, "and thank you, Lord Colne, for your kindness."

"No need to thank me. The pleasure was mine." He turned and re-crossed the room to Vanith's side.

When it was time for dinner, Alanna accepted an invitation to sit down with Captain Erryl Redat whom she had met earlier in the month. A tall, burly man with bristling red side-whiskers, he commanded a ship in the Royal Navy and was currently tied to port while his ship was refitted. He invited her to come aboard any time in the next few weeks to see it and took her to dine at a table occupied by a group of fellow officers and their partners.

The officers told exciting tales of places they had visited and battles they had fought all over the world. The Royal Navy's main concern, they said, was the suppression of piracy. And the most fearsome of all pirates were the linlarin who sailed with letters of mark from their rulers in Senanga, Mankoya or Gatukai and attacked all human shipping ruthlessly.

"I thought we were at peace with the tiger folk," Alanna said, after a particularly bloody tale.

The others laughed. Erryl explained, "There's no such thing as peace with men as far as any of the linlarin nations are concerned. All the current peace means is that the war is scaled down for a time. They fight at the level of guerrilla bands instead of armies, and raids of one or two ships instead of fleets, but the tiger folk can't conceive of a real peace with humans."

"The Estahar of Senanga not only issues letters of mark," Captain Garlis added, "he pays a bounty for every human ship sunk, no matter what the prize aboard. The ahars of Mankoya and Gatukai have similar policies."

The conversation upset Alanna, reminding her of another that she preferred to forget, when the Wizard of Leyburn had said, "The fighting in Cibata has never stopped." She was still thinking of those words when, as though her mind had summoned him, Jerevan himself appeared before her.

"May I have this dance, Tamrai Cairn?"

She hadn't known he was present, so there was no way she could have braced herself for the meeting. The dance just starting was the shalla. She would have preferred almost any other. She didn't want to be near him, but she remembered her uncle's warning.

"Certainly, your grace," she said, feigning a calm she was far from feeling.

"I know you don't want to speak to me but I have to speak with you," Jerevan said as soon as he had her on the dance floor.

"On the contrary," Alanna said, recognizing a golden opportunity. The Wizard of Leyburn could help all the people of the mountains, if he wished. "I'm glad of the chance to speak to you. My uncle tells me that, if wizards are to go to the Mallarnes next spring, it must be by your will. I remember explaining the problem that night at the Blue Boar."

"Yes. So you did."

"What do you intend to do?" Alanna couldn't help the anxiety that lent a faint tremor to her voice.

Jerevan frowned. "I'm not sure. What I'd like to do, and what I may be able to do are two different things. There's a shortage of wizards in Ilwheirlane right now."

"I take it that means you don't intend to do anything," she said. "I should have known what to expect."

"That's not what I said, nor what I meant."

"No? Then what did you mean? Do you, or do you not, intend to send wizards to the Mallarnes in the spring?"

"I don't know," Jerevan said. "There are too many other factors to be considered."

"What other factors?"

"I can't tell you. At least, not here and now."

"Then when?"

"I don't know that either." He shook his head. "As soon as I can. As soon as I know all the answers myself. Look, let's leave this for now. We need to discuss your training."

"There's nothing further to discuss, your grace."

Jerevan hesitated, then he said, "You seem to have a devoted admirer in Tamrai Esparda."

"I don't see that that's any affair of yours."

"As the highest ranking wizard in the human lands, anything you do is my affair, Alanna, until you're sufficiently trained to control and protect what you wear."

"I haven't given you leave to use my name, your grace." She had to grit her teeth to keep from saying more.

"I know you haven't, Alanna, but that's not going to stop me." His smile mocked her.

Alanna glared. "Very well, say what you have to say."

"What do you know of Esparda?"

The question caught her off balance, but she recovered. "Just that he's a gentleman, unlike others I can think of."

"Nothing else?"

Alanna looked away from him, but admitted in a less defiant tone, "Well, I think he's a wizard. I've been hoping he'd admit it so I could ask him to train me."

Jerevan's grip on her tightened. She looked up at him in alarm. "Oh! Now I suppose you'll do something to stop him."

But his expression puzzled her. He looked torn between exasperation and a dawning amusement. "You really think he'd make a better instructor than I would?"

She swallowed. "Yes!"

His expression was suddenly grave. "If I were to warn you to beware of Esparda, what would you say?"

"I'd say you were trying to stop me from finding anyone else to train me."

"Why would I do that?"

"Because you want the Talisman's power."

"Very well, Alanna. If that's how you see things, have it your way, and see where that takes you." He sounded tired.

She looked up at him, feeling an involuntary thrill as her eyes met his heavy blue gaze. He didn't look tired. His features appeared as perfect as she remembered them, but a thin white line crossed his face from the edge of his left eye to his chin. It looked like an old scar, but she felt sure she hadn't seen it when she had dined with him at the Blue Boar.

Her eyes narrowed as she tried to remember. No. She was certain there had been no scars on his face.

Jerevan seemed to sense her thoughts, as his hand went up to his cheek to feel the scar in a gesture Alanna recognized his having made several times that night in Oswestry. "I'd forgotten it. It was an ugly wound when we first met, so I veiled my face in illusion." He grimaced. "Your accusations were quite justified, as it happened. I couldn't, under the circumstances, protest that I don't normally use my talents to alter my appearance."

"I thought you could take any form. Why not just alter yourself to a state without wounds?"

"You make it sound so easy," he laughed, "and I could have done it, too, if I hadn't had the wounds in the first place. Aavik's associates were strong, and they outnumbered us three to two and Derwen was old and failing in his skills. They almost killed me and they did kill Derwen. Altering the form of matter takes energy. I was in a coma for over a week after the battle. I only came to when I felt Myrriden die. It was all I could do to ride in a carriage and trace Vyrkarion. The reason I waited so long to talk to you was that I couldn't even have held that minor illusion for the length of our talk those first two days. In the state I was in, just finding you exhausted me."

"I thought you were playing cat and mouse."

"I was sure you'd think up some devious motive for my behavior."

"Couldn't you make it disappear now? Surely you've recovered by this time?"

He shook his head, smiling wryly. "As a matter of fact I haven't fully recovered. And I have other calls on my energy. Keeping track of you, for instance."

"I don't need anyone, much less you, keeping track of me."

"I wish that were true. Then, maybe, I could pander to my vanity." He grinned.

She stiffened but recognized the futility of arguing with him further. The dance was ending and she insisted that he return her to her aunt.

Esparda came up to her a few minutes later. "I didn't know you were acquainted with the hetri of Leyburn, Tamrai Cairn?"

"He's an acquaintance, and not an agreeable one."

"Yes. He has a bad reputation and I feel it is well deserved," Esparda said. "He visited my country once some years ago. The things he did, they were not what one likes to think about."

"If he broke your laws, why was nothing done to stop him?"

"He is powerful," Esparda said, "which makes it difficult to deal with him." He looked pensive, then said, "I have an interest in your country's history. I wonder if you would accompany me to the histor- ical museum. Have you anything planned for the day before New Year's Eve?"

Alanna, still incensed by her conversation with Jerevan, said, "Why, no. And I haven't seen the museum yet, either. The idea sounds delightful." Esparda returned her to her aunt then, but she noticed that he left the ball immediately thereafter.

Jerevan watched from a corner of the ballroom well back from the dance floor as Alanna danced with Aavik. Colne, standing beside him, said, "You didn't tell her who he is?"

Jerevan shook his head without taking his eyes off Alanna. There was no one else close and he knew the music would drown their voices. "I don't think she'd have believed me if I had, and she might have told him of the accusation. I couldn't take that risk. I hadn't realized my reputation was so dreadful among the common people around the countryside until I met Alanna."

"There was that scandal and you're away so much," Colne said. "You haven't been very social in recent years."

"And I'm a wizard, Errian, don't forget that. To the common people, that alone is enough to damn me, never mind the rest."

"She'll be a wizard too, now."

"A strong one. But she's so damned young and naive. I can't remember ever being that young, even before Derwen cursed me."

Errian smiled wryly. "You don't truly regret becoming a wizard do you?"

Jerevan shook his head and turned back to face his friend. "Not usually, not any more. But being a human wizard with the world the way it is today is no joyride. There are too few of us, and too many isklarin and linlarin trying to bag us like trophies for sport."

The look of shock on Colne's face stopped him, and he realized just how bitter he had sounded. No, by Jehan, just how bitter he was. Alanna was beautiful, bright and young and she looked on him as an ancient monster. And she was right to look at him so. He'd seen too much and done too much. His innocence had been lost in a childhood he hardly remembered. The youth of his body was a lie, when his mind was full of horrors he couldn't have imagined when he'd been Alanna's age.

Colne's expression changed to concern. "I'd forgotten you were a prisoner of the linlarin. Their breeding programs are an abomination."

"At least I was spared that," Jerevan said wryly. "Sorry, I'm not good company tonight."

Errian smiled and his eyes were warm. "Nonsense, Jere, but you're carrying too much on your shoulders. Get some rest."

Alanna didn't see the hetri of Leyburn again. As far as she could tell, Jerevan might have come just for the one dance he had danced with her and then left.

His behavior hadn't been quite so singular, however, as Alanna discovered the next day when Lady Avlen came to call. This time Enora had not been expected and, while Una greeted her friend warmly, she also regarded her with a trace of wariness. The emotion coloring the faded cheeks was rampant curiosity and Enora was bent on discussing the previous evening at length.

"I was never so surprised in my life as when Leyburn asked Alanna to dance," she said the minute she sat down.

"Yes," agreed Una, looking flustered. "It surprised me, too. I hadn't known they'd met."

"And he danced with her first," Enora said. "You know he only danced with five other women before he left, all of them young and beautiful. You'd think he'd be ashamed after what happened to his last," she paused, looking arch, "companion. But he's always been that way, brazen, and no one dares deny him."

Alanna excused herself. Leyburn's name and the obvious aim of Enora's gossip distressed her. Also, she felt guilty. She had accepted the invitation from Esparda in a mood of defiance, and she was regretting it. She had no interest in him except as a tutor in wizardry and it had occurred to her, after accepting his invitation, that agreeing to spend a good part of a day alone with him might mislead him.

As it happened, she was granted an opportunity to avoid that situation the following day. Erryl Redat called to invite her to see his ship and, on learning of her previous plans, said that, as he had never seen the museum either, would she mind if they made up a party. Alanna was delighted with this solution.

Esparda was not. He arrived just after Erryl and his guests, Captain Varno Garlis and his wife Janea, and, on being told that the others would accompany them, looked annoyed.

"I thought I was to have you to myself."

"Captain Redat was so eager, and I thought it would be more fun to see the museum with a party. I'm sorry you're offended."

"Not offended," he said with a touch of dry amusement, "merely disappointed."

Despite this doubtful beginning, Alanna enjoyed the trip. Seeing how people had lived in the distant past fascinated her and she studied the museum's exhibits in detail. She was particularly struck by a display of clothing styles from the beginning of the human era to the present.

"Poor things," she remarked, looking at the rough wool and leather garments that had been the standard human garb during the early years of the Dragon Wars. "They must have fried in the summer time."

"Yes, and I bet that wool felt scratchy. I can't see you in a suit like that, dear," Janea said, looking at her husband.

There was a model of a soldier of Vydarga's time dressed in thin leather sandals, a skirt of leather strips hung from a waistband, and a bronze breastplate and arm-bands. Looking at it, Erryl said, "Jehan, they must have been brave, going into battle half naked like that."

Captain Garlis grinned. "I don't know. It might have needed more courage to wear the wool."

Alanna laughed with the others but, glancing at Esparda, she was startled to see an expression of anger on his face. It was gone in a moment, but it disturbed her.

She challenged him a little later, before a display of artifacts created by the great wizards. "Don't you consider the contributions of the great wizards important, Tamrai Esparda?"

"On the contrary, Tamrai Cairn, I find their contributions quite overwhelming."

She was bothered again by the impression that his words were subject to more than one interpretation, but shrugged the impression off. He was unusually silent for the rest of the tour.

The following day was the last of the mathedin, the days between Sun Day and the New Year called "not days" because they were not included in the fifty weeks of the Tamarian year. Una held an open house with a vast buffet and all day long people came and went. Alanna sensed a tension beneath the gaiety, however. The following day would be the first day of the Year of the Dragon. The world was about to change and they all feared what the changes might bring.

Book II

THE YEAR
OF THE DRAGON

Theocan a Gand ba end a ganod
e rhysin lotwe wa ganod.

"The Year of the Dragon is a time of violence
and the changes caused by violence."

— FROM *THE BOOK OF YEARS*

XIV

4731, 474TH CYCLE OF THE YEAR OF THE DRAGON
MONTH OF ISKKAAR

Malarin la caunen a ren;
Larin la abcanin a ren;
Eslarin la acad.
Kunalorin la qua larin,
Ilnalor la qua eslarin.

"Men see the surface of things;
see the insides of things;
Eslarin see all.
Journeymen see as the larin,
The wizard sees as the eslarin."

— FROM *THE BASICS OF WIZARDRY*
BY THE WIZARD ANOR

Alanna didn't see Esparda again until the morning of the first Kyras-day of the new year, when she met him while riding with Erryl and Captain Garlis in the Royal Park.

"Been out of town?" Erryl asked.

Esparda eyed the captain sharply, but said, "Yes. I had business to attend to."

"I hope your affairs prospered," Alanna said, reining her horse in as he had grown restive positioned between Erryl's and Esparda's horses. The chestnut gelding was fresh and fought the rein, tossing his head to get the bit in his mouth.

"No! They did not," Esparda said. He held his horse back as well, so that he and Alanna were left side by side and somewhat behind the other two riders.

"I'm sorry," she said, controlling her mount and turning back to Esparda. She thought she heard anger in his voice, and he did look more severe than usual.

"Will you accompany me tomorrow to see the ship museum by the harbor?" he asked.

"Well…" Alanna tried to think of an excuse and at the same time steady the chestnut which, sensing her agitation, started to dance again. She suddenly felt uneasy at the idea of being alone with Esparda. "I'd have to check with my aunt. I believe she has an engagement she wants me to attend with her."

Esparda eyed the growing distance between Alanna and himself and the other two riders, and said, "I have a particular reason for asking. I know of the jewel you wear."

"Oh!" Her mind leapt. Was he going to admit that he was a wizard?

As though reading her thoughts, he said, "Yes. I am a wizard. I knew that you guessed this from our first meeting, but I was reluctant to speak of it."

"Because you didn't want to take me on as an apprentice?" Alanna stroked the chestnut's neck and suppressed her earlier doubts. If he were willing to teach her, she could put up with a few oddities in his manners.

Esparda seemed amused by the question. "I might be willing to train you. There are conditions I would have to make, however, and I cannot discuss them here. Will you come with me tomorrow? Alone this time."

"Of course." Then, remembering her earlier excuse, Alanna added, "I'm sure my aunt will understand."

His expression told her that he understood perfectly, but all he said was, "Then I shall pick you up at ten o'clock. Until tomorrow." He bowed in the saddle and rode off.

Esparda's coach pulled up in front of the house on Ninfal Street at precisely ten the following morning. Alanna hardly kept him waiting long enough for his coachman to get down and open the door for her, she was so eager. It surprised her that he had chosen a coach, even with only two horses. For the short distance to the harbor, she would have expected him to have driven a lighter vehicle, a phaeton or a curricle.

She was concentrating on her arguments to persuade him to take her on as an apprentice, however. She had been going over and over these in her mind and she felt confident that she would be able to overcome any reservations he might have.

"I've been looking forward to this," Alanna said as soon as she was seated.

Esparda seemed taken aback by her eagerness. He said gravely, but with that underlying irony that so often disturbed her, "I can assure you that I have looked forward to it also."

"Then you're willing to train me?"

"If you meet my conditions."

"What are they? I assure you I'll cooperate every way I can."

"Really!" Esparda eyed her in a manner quite different to his previous treatment of her.

Alanna flushed, but controlled the angry words that rose to her lips. "You mock me, Tamrai Esparda, but you know very well what I meant. Please tell me what your conditions are, so that I can respond to them."

"You will know them presently."

Unable to elicit any further response from him, she sat back in her seat and looked out the window. She was still unfamiliar with the city, but she realized as soon as they crossed one of the bridges across the Glyn that they were headed north rather than south, the direction they would have taken to reach the harbor.

"We aren't going to see the ship museum?"

"No."

She felt no alarm at first. After all, she hadn't come to see the museum, but to persuade Esparda to teach her wizardry. If he wanted to hold their conversation somewhere else, that was fine with her. However, the terseness of his reply disturbed her.

"Where are we going?"

"That, too, you will find out presently." There was a coldness to his expression that she hadn't seen before.

"I insist that you tell me now, or take me home."

"You are not in a position to insist on anything."

"Why are you doing this?" she demanded, sudden fear making her voice unsteady.

"Come now, you're not a child. You're carrying something of value that I want." He smiled but there was no warmth in the expression, only satisfaction. "If you cooperate, I'll let you live and use Vyrkarion through you, train you, as it were. If you resist, I'll kill you and find another more amenable bearer. You understand? Those are my conditions."

"I see." Alanna sank back into her seat, clasping her hands together to conceal their trembling.

She noticed for the first time that the inside door handles of the coach had been removed and the locks reworked so they would open only to a key. In her excitement she had overlooked this when she got in or it might have alerted her to Esparda's purpose. The coach would have to stop sometime, though, and when it did she would be on the look out for any opportunity to get away. As there was nothing else she could think of to do, she watched their route through the window.

They drove for several hours, heading north out of the city by the coast road. At first the traffic was heavy, but when they left the city proper it thinned and the buildings on either side of the road grew farther and farther apart.

The first stretch of road where no buildings could be seen was within sight of the bay to their left across a barren stretch of rocks and dunes partially covered by coarse grass. A small copse of trees lay on their right, between two fields strewn with the rank remains of harvested cabbages. As they drew abreast of the trees, there was a sound like a thunderbolt and the coach lurched to a halt. Another explosion next to Alanna blew one of the doors half off. Her ears rang, as though her head were full of clanging cymbals. She was thrown against the opposite side of the coach

ALAMEDA FREE LIBRARY

and felt a splinter strike her arm. Esparda had also been thrown and she lay part way across him, her ears ringing, dizziness threatening to overwhelm her. But the door was hanging askew. She managed to roll over and get her feet underneath her, ignoring the cacophony that filled her head. Then, with her eyes fixed on the drunkenly swinging door, she half leapt, half dove through the opening.

She landed awkwardly near the side of the road and scrambled for the shelter of the ditch. Then, with just her head above the level of the road, she looked back at the coach. Three riders blocked its progress. One of the riders held a blazing sphere of light. She blinked at the brightness, but felt the energy of that fierce, miniature sun even with her eyes shut.

While she watched, her ears still ringing, the riders moved off the road. The coach horses, who had been rearing in their traces, bolted. The coachman was slumped sideways, unconscious or dead, and the vehicle jerked into motion once more.

As the coach drew level with the riders, Esparda knocked the broken door out of the way and braced himself in the doorway. He also held a bright ball of light. Streamers of flame lanced out between the two brilliant spheres. Even from her concealed position, Alanna felt the energy of that battle. Time stretched. She sensed nothing but the twin lances of light growing longer as the coach drew away and the nova of energy where they met and fought.

Just when Alanna feared her mind would break from the pressure, one of the streamers began to give way. There was another tremendous explosion of light and sound.

When she could see again, the coach was disappearing in the distance. The weaker lance, the one that had given way, had come from Esparda and Alanna wondered if he were dead.

Alanna's ears still rang and blood trickled down from a splinter embedded in her arm and from a graze she had taken on her elbow when she landed in the road. Mud caked her skirt and she felt dizzy from the backlash of the energy used in the combat.

Through eyes still watering from the flash, she saw that the rider who had held the original ball of light was doubled over in his saddle. She couldn't see his face. A stockily built man with a dour countenance held the reins of the unconscious wizard's horse, and the third rider was coming in her direction. She struggled to her feet and faced him, wondering what to do, but, before she could take any action, she recognized Erryl Redat.

"Can you take my hand and get up behind me, Tamrai Cairn?"

His voice came to her as though from a distance, but she was relieved to hear anything other than the ringing. "Yes, I think so. How did you know what happened?" Blinking away the tears from her still smarting

ALAMEDA FREE LIBRARY

eyes, she inserted her foot into the stirrup he freed for her and swung up behind him.

"We'd best get out of here," the stocky man said, joining them, the reins of the wizard's horse in his hand. "The master's done, and if that one isn't," he nodded in the direction the coach had taken, "we won't have any defense when he gets back."

"Yes, you're right. There's no time for explanations now. Let's go," Erryl said, reining his horse back toward the trees.

Alanna clung to him as the horse jumped the ditch and entered the small wood between the cabbage fields. They rode cross country, avoiding buildings and crossing roads only when no traffic was visible. Alanna was too shaken and weary to take in much, but it seemed to her that they were heading generally east and south, so she assumed that they were circling the outskirts of Ninkarrak.

As she sat behind Erryl, it was difficult for her to see the other riders, but when at last they stopped at a small farmhouse, she saw that the wizard was still unconscious.

"Will he be all right?"

"I hope so," Erryl said.

They dismounted and Erryl helped the other man lift the wizard out of his saddle. Alanna gasped when she saw that the unconscious man was the Hetri of Leyburn.

"What's he doing here?"

"Rescuing you," said the stocky man, "which you wouldn't have needed, if you had any sense."

Alanna stood stricken. The truth of the stocky man's accusation mortified her.

"I'm sorry," she said, following the men as they carried the hetri into the farmhouse and laid him on a low couch in the front room. "Can I help him? I am a healer."

They ignored her as Jerevan stirred at that moment and raised his hand to his head. "Jehan, what hit me?"

"Can I get you anything, your grace?" the stocky man asked.

"Yes, Otto. A new head," Jerevan said, struggling to sit up. "I hope I wasn't out as long this time as I was the last time I took on an isklarin wizard?"

"No, your grace, we just arrived at the rendezvous," Otto said, helping him to sit.

Once in a sitting position, Jerevan peered about blearily. "What happened?" He rubbed his forehead. "Did we get her?"

"Yes, she's here," Otto said.

Alanna stepped closer to him. "Thank you for rescuing me. Believe me, I'm very grateful."

"But would rather be grateful to almost anyone else." Jerevan brushed a hand over his eyes and squinted in her direction.

Alanna flushed. She knew she had sounded grudging and she hadn't meant to. "I'm sorry if it sounded that way. I truly am grateful." His presence and his weakened condition disturbed her.

Jerevan grimaced, his eyes finally focusing on her. "Don't worry. You'll get over it."

Before Alanna had an opportunity to retort, he turned to Erryl. "Is the coach ready? We need to get out of here before he traces us."

"I'll see to the coach now," Erryl responded, as he might to a commanding officer, and left the room.

"Otto, get me something for this head. And pray to Jehan I hurt him as much as he hurt me. I think I did." He frowned with the effort of remembering.

"Yes, your grace. Right away."

When Otto left the room, Alanna said, "His lance gave way just before the explosion. I saw it."

"What do you mean? What lance?"

"That's what it looked like to me, two lances of light. It hurt me to watch, but I know that the one from the coach dimmed and then there was an explosion that almost blinded me."

He nodded. "Vyrkarion has sensitized you, but then you had training when you studied with the Kindred of Maera. You're further along than I thought you'd be anyway, and that's lucky." He rubbed the back of his neck. "If you read the energies right, I knocked him out at least. I wish I could believe I killed him, but I don't think I had enough energy left for that."

"What did you mean by implying that I'd recover from my gratitude?" Alanna asked. "I hope I don't have so short a memory. I also want to apologize for not heeding your warning. I behaved irresponsibly."

"Prettily said, but before your humility chokes you, I'd better tell you that you won't be going back to your uncle's tonight. I imagine that will restore your spirit."

"You're not taking me home?"

"Precisely, my dear Alanna," he said. "You've escaped from Aavik and are now my prisoner. From the malik pen to the griffin's lair, so to speak."

"Aavik! What does Tamrai Esparda have to do with Aavik?"

He looked startled and then he laughed, "Jehan, he kidnaped you and still didn't tell you who he was. Oh, that's rich. And you berated me because I gave you my name and not my title." He roared with laughter and then clutched his head. "Oh, that hurts," he groaned, but he was still chuckling when Otto came in bearing a decanter of brandy and a snifter.

Alanna felt the world sway around her. She clutched the back of a chair. She had no doubt that Jerevan was telling her the truth. His words explained all the things she had found strange about Esparda, the little inconsistencies she'd put down to his being a wizard. His being Aavik even made clear the meanings of some of his statements which had sounded cryptic at the time.

Otto poured brandy into the snifter, handed it to Jerevan and retired.

Jerevan drank, his laughter subsiding. He studied Alanna then said, "Don't look so woebegone. I'm not kidnaping you permanently, at least not yet, and not ever if you're sensible. I've just arranged for you to spend a few weeks somewhere where you'll be safe. Right now, if I returned you home, you'd be a staked seral, and I'm not in any shape to stand off more wizards tonight."

"Then you aren't going to use me as... as Aavik threatened to?" She hesitated on the name, still finding the truth of it mortifying.

Jerevan shrugged. "I don't know how he threatened to use you, but I shouldn't think so." He drank more of the brandy and sighed, "That's better. The drums are fading."

Otto returned and said, "The coach is ready, your grace, and the riding horses have been unsaddled and put in the paddock. The Captain says he'll come back for them tomorrow."

"Very well, Otto. Tell Erryl we'll be right there." He looked at Alanna. "Are you ready to go quietly, or do I have to use force?"

"Where are you taking me?"

"A house I own in the hills east of the city. It's not a residence I advertise, so I don't think Aavik will find it, at least not for a while. I've already sent a message to your uncle telling him what happened and that you'll be staying with me."

"My uncle will know where I am?"

"Not the location, Aavik might read it from him. But the company, yes. He's going to tell your aunt that you've been injured in a coach accident, but not badly hurt, and that you'll be restored to her before long." Jerevan rose, holding onto the arm of the couch with one hand. "And, Alanna, you'll be able to return to your uncle's at some point, if you agree to being trained by me starting tomorrow morning."

"You said I'd be a staked seral if I went home," Alanna said, "but I really wouldn't be. I've learned my lesson. I'd never go near Tamrai Esparda or... or Aavik again."

Jerevan answered her with the same weary patience she had heard used by parents to a dull child, "Aavik won't try to kidnap you again. He'll kill you. He tried kidnaping because he didn't think anyone had recognized him and it was convenient for you to hold Vyrkarion until he got it back to Gandahar, to the bearer of his choice. He'd have killed you as soon as he got you there. If he told you otherwise, it was just to keep you cooperative." He swirled the brandy and drank it down. Then he set the glass on the table and held out his arm to her. "Are you ready to go?"

She took it, knowing she had no choice, and walked beside him to the waiting coach and four, with Erryl perched in the driver's seat and Otto beside him.

"How did you know he'd kidnaped me?"

Jerevan sighed. "I've watched you, or had you watched, ever since you arrived in Ninkarrak. I knew about your date with Aavik and made preparations for it. My main fear was that he might be stronger than I am, but there was no backup available. He wasn't, so here you are."

"Why didn't you warn me?"

Jerevan's expression turned ironic. "I tried, if you will recall the night of the ball, but you didn't want to listen?"

"I meant again, about the kidnaping."

"What would you have done, Alanna? Taken my word, or faced him with my accusation?"

"Faced him with it," she admitted.

"Then he'd have killed you."

Alanna sank back in the coach seat feeling miserable. And the worst of it was that she was now going to have to accept training from the Wizard of Leyburn.

She glanced at him. He was lying back in the seat with his eyes closed, so she took the opportunity to study him. There was no sign of age or dissipation in his features. He appeared to be in his early thirties, his face smooth and tanned, but with lines of decision deeply graven. His wide, thin-lipped mouth was set with a faint twist that could have been due to pain and yet looked sensual. She sighed. He had a strong face. Not the face of a man who shirked responsibilities, much less of a man dedicated to perversion. Yet what can his appearance indicate, she asked herself, when he can take any form he chooses? She turned back to the view from the coach window.

Heavy clouds gathered in the west and the sun, setting through them, fired them with orange flame. Alanna read from the sun's position that the coach was heading northeast. They left the coastal plain and began winding through the low hills that ringed the bay. She was tired, but her mind kept going over what had happened. A sudden thought made her blurt out, "How could you have been watching me? I never saw anyone following me. Surely I'd have known."

Jerevan opened his eyes. "I had men watching your house. Whenever you left, or anyone not belonging to the household entered, I was notified. After that, I used my crystal." He pulled a clear jewel from his pocket and showed it to her. It was about the size of a hen's egg. "Using it to focus my mind, I can farsee any place within, say, eight hundred kilometers, although the detail diminishes with the distance. When I was unable to watch you, I had Erryl take over."

"Erryl's a wizard?"

"No. Only a journeyman. He's never been able to attain the high sight, but he can mind speak a fair distance and use a crystal for far-seeing in a several kilometer radius."

"Could Aavik watch me the same way?"

"No." Jerevan frowned. "I told you when we first met that Vyrkarion protects you from most farseeing. Aavik doesn't know what to look for, or he'd have snatched you up off the street long before now. But you're a blind spot to him, unless he's actually looking at you."

"Will I be able to farsee as you do?"

"Some day. It's not difficult, but it'll take time for you to learn to concentrate to the degree necessary."

It occurred to her that, watching her with his wizard sight, her clothes were no barrier to his vision. She flushed.

"They never have been," he said, reading her thoughts. "For that matter, neither is your skin, but blood vessels don't excite me. My vision shouldn't bother you; you don't have anything to be ashamed of. To the contrary, you're very beautiful."

Alanna controlled herself with an effort and remained silent. He was simply confirming something obvious to him; it was childish of her to resent his abilities. She leaned back on her side of the seat and tried to sleep.

Snow started to fall before the sun left the sky and night descended without even the light of the stars. Several hours later the coach reached its destination. All Alanna could tell about the house was that it was large. The butler who opened the door for them greeted Jerevan as though he were expected, saying, "I'll notify the chef that you've arrived, your grace. I believe dinner will be ready in half an hour."

"Very good, Malling. We'll be in the yellow saloon. And we'd like some tea right away."

"Certainly, your grace." Jerevan escorted her to an elegant room with primrose silk curtains against cream walls and one wall papered with a pattern of golden flowers. At the end of the room, an array of bottles and glasses sat on a tray. Jerevan went straight to this and poured himself a brandy. "Wine, Alanna? I recommend the Aliaga, or would you prefer to wait for the tea?"

"The tea will be fine."

She sat in a gilt legged chair. Within moments a servant came and placed a tea tray on the small table by the chair. There were two cups, and she looked up at Jerevan.

"Yes, I'd like a cup, too," he said, answering her unspoken question. "Heavy on the sugar. It's good for shock."

VYRKARION: THE TALISMAN OF ANOR

Alanna poured for him and then for herself, adding more sugar to her own cup than was her usual preference. She had certainly undergone some shocks of her own. In fact, after the various stresses of the day she felt drained. She still feared Jerevan's power to attract her, but knew she'd have to face it. She had to be trained. Her kidnaping by Aavik demonstrated that beyond any possibility of doubt. And she'd have to accept Jerevan as her teacher. She'd found no one else, and time had run out.

Jerevan was silent, lost in thoughts of his own. Unhappy ones too, Alanna reflected, for his eyes were narrowed and his jaw set. He hardly seemed aware of her presence.

She finished her tea and asked if she could be shown to a room to clean up before dinner. He glanced at her abstractedly, said, "Yes, of course, ask Malling," and went back to studying his cup. Alanna didn't know whether to be relieved at his lack of attention, or annoyed by it.

Malling took her upstairs and showed her to a room carpeted in tones of blue and rose with a matching floral print on the curtains and bedspread. His face was expressionless, but she could tell from the careful way he avoided looking at her that her appearance shocked him. As he opened the door of her room and ushered her in, he said, " I'll send one of the chambermaids up to assist you to dress. I believe you have time to change before dinner."

"Thank you, Malling." She smiled, his manner was so reassuring after the high drama of the day.

One look in the mirror, though, drove every other thought from her head. Her fall from the coach and the long ride had brought her hair down in a mad tangle. A great smear of mud crossed her cheek, and her dress, which hadn't been designed for riding, was not only muddy and crumpled, but torn as well. Her hat had disappeared.

She had just stripped off the dress when the chambermaid arrived with a bowl of hot water. "What can I do with this?" Alanna asked, holding up the tattered remnants.

The maid eyed the remains. "Can I get you out another dress, my lady?"

"I don't have anything else with me."

The maid looked startled. "Begging your pardon, my lady, but, while the master said your trunks wouldn't be here until tomorrow, he brought a case of your things this morning."

Alanna gaped at the girl, but recovered. If Jerevan had supplied her with a wardrobe to make her stay appear as normal as possible, she wasn't about to spoil the effect of his efforts any more than she already had. "Oh, good. I wasn't sure they'd arrived. Yes, by all means get me out another dress. And a clean slip," she added, fingering the soiled one she was wearing.

She gave herself a quick sponge bath and then sent for more water and washed and redid her hair, running a comb through the tangles ruthlessly. The maid helped her to dress. Alanna wasn't surprised to find that the gown she chose fit, although it wasn't one of her own. She was beginning to appreciate Jerevan's thoroughness. Made of a dull gold satin, the dress had a much lower neckline than she was accustomed to wearing. Alanna almost told the maid to choose another, as the Talisman wouldn't fit inside a bodice cut that low. Then she remembered that with Jerevan there was no need to conceal the jewel.

She descended the stairs just as Malling announced dinner. She was pleased with her appearance, aware of the way the low cut gown displayed her figure, and the way the green jewel at her breast brought out the green of her eyes. Jerevan, entering the hall from the saloon, stopped dead at the sight of her.

"Magnificent!" he said and smiled. "A remarkable improvement for so short a time."

Dinner was a quiet meal. Both she and Jerevan were too tired to make idle conversation. She did ask at one point, "Captain Redat accompanied me to the historical museum to prevent Aavik from kidnaping me, didn't he?"

"You're learning."

Later, as Alanna peeled a cotulume, she asked, "How great was the danger that Aavik might be more powerful than you are?"

Jerevan selected a marin nut from the bowl of fruit and nuts in the middle of the table and rolled it between his fingers. "About fifty-fifty. He's had a lot more experience, but I'm a fast learner."

"How could he have had more experience?"

Jerevan's blue eyes laughed. "How old do you think he is?"

"He looked in his mid-thirties," Alanna said, puzzled. Then, "Oh, you mean, like you, he's made himself look young. How old is he?"

Her words took the amusement from his face. "No, Alanna, that's not what I meant. Neither of us have ever made ourselves look young, we just haven't aged. That's one of the first things you'll learn." He sighed. "But, yes, I meant that he's older than I am. I'm not sure of his exact age, but he took the throne of Gandahar some two hundred years ago."

She shook her head. "How could he be so old and not show any sign of it? How can you?"

Jerevan cracked the nut he was still holding in his hand and extracted the nut meat. "A wizard with command of the high sight only ages if he gets careless or if he wishes to do so. Does my age horrify you, Alanna?"

"I don't understand how wizards can live so long and still look young. When I read in the history books that Anor and Torin and the others lived hundreds of years, I always thought of them as looking their age. And Myrriden looked like an old man." She studied him, sensing that her words disturbed him. The knowledge reassured her. He was sensitive to something. Perhaps he had other weaknesses. He was still human, despite his power and his reputation.

"Myrriden wasn't really a powerful wizard, nor did he have any particular desire for a long life. His partial linkage to Vyrkarion kept him alive, but he never worked at maintaining himself other than to prevent decay or disease. That was his personal choice. Wizards usually end up looking the age at which they feel comfortable. Myself, I wouldn't feel right as an ancient," he said, his eyes mocking. "You might respect me more, but think what a nuisance the long, gray beard would be."

She stiffened, wanting to answer the challenge in his eyes, but caught herself. She couldn't afford to spar with him. She had to make sure their relationship stayed solely that of master to pupil. She took a deep breath and said the words she'd reconciled herself to saying, "That night at the Blue Boar, you said I'd come to you in the end. Well, you've won. After today, I would have done so."

She waited for an expression of satisfaction or triumph, but instead he looked weary. "That's something."

"Is that all you have to say?"

He shrugged. "If you expected me to be in raptures over the prospect of having you as an apprentice, Alanna, think again. I'll start your training because I'm the only person available who's capable of doing so, but I'm not expecting to enjoy the experience." He rose and started to leave the room. In the doorway he paused. "Good night. Your lessons start in the morning."

XV

4731, 474TH CYCLE OF THE YEAR OF THE DRAGON
MONTH OF ISKKAAR

Iskkaar and Minneth linking in the north,
Brought forth Belkarion, the Heart of Snow,
And found it thought, like other living things,
Except its thoughts were adamantine and slow.
Then Redri and Cerdana joined to bear
Golden Kaikarion, the Harvest Stone,
And Rav and Sugra copulated to
Create the Eye of Rav, Ninkarion.
Yet as the karionin waxed in might,
So did the strength of those who gave them birth
As slowly wane. Thus did the wizards learn
The price of power and creation's worth.

— EXCERPT FROM "ILKARIONIN, THE LIVING CRYSTALS,"
PUBLISHED IN *LEST WE FORGET: A BOOK OF TEACHING RHYMES*
BY WILTON WIRRAMARETH OF ILWHEIRLANE, 4207

W hen Alanna finished her breakfast the next morning, Malling informed her that Jerevan wished to see her in his study. This proved to be a large room at the back of the house. Books covered three of the walls, mounted in floor-to-ceiling shelves, except for the space taken by a handsome marble fireplace. Windows made up the entire fourth wall. Jerevan stood by a lommaswood desk, gazing out at a terrace and a snow covered slope stretching down to a frozen lake. He turned as she entered.

"All braced to face the griffin?"

Alanna colored. "I don't think of you as a griffin exactly."

He laughed. "I won't ask what you do think of me. It wouldn't get your first lesson off to a good start." He sobered. "First, you must take off Vyrkarion. I can't work with you while you're wearing it."

Her hand went to her breast. "Why? I'd have thought it would help?"

"It will help you when you're practicing, but you can't wear it when I'm demonstrating something to you." He paused and studied her. "Do you know what Vyrkarion's purpose is? What it does for the wizard, or wizards, using it?"

"Not precisely. I've heard that the living crystals are like magnifying glasses, they amplify power as a magnifying glass amplifies an image."

He nodded. "True, as far as it goes, but the crystal I showed you yesterday is an amplifier. Vyrkarion is much more. To begin with, Vyrkarion is sentient. It's designed to take two minds and link them with itself. That's why, with only one mind using it, it has little more power than a regular crystal. Somehow — and even Anor and Torin weren't sure why — the tripartate entity is much more powerful than the individual parts. It can also stand greater amplification."

He broke off and came around the desk. "The problem is," he said, putting his hands on her shoulders. "I don't think you're ready to have your mind linked with mine."

She started to pull away from his touch, but as the meaning of his words penetrated she froze. "No!"

"Precisely. So you'd better take it off."

Shaken, she reached down and pulled the Talisman out of the bodice of her dress. As she took it in her hand, she saw its golden core pulsing. She studied the glow as it grew brighter. It was fascinating. She felt as though she were being drawn inside its radiance.

Jerevan took one look at it and released her, jerking his hands away. The glow faded back to its normal level. Her eyes went from the jewel to his face. She felt dazed. "What happened?"

He looked pale. "I'd no idea the pull would be so strong. It isn't safe for me to touch you when you have your attention focused on it."

She put the Talisman down on his desk, feeling let down as the attraction faded. "What's it like, the linkage?"

"I don't know." His voice was soft. "It's the wizards' marriage rite."

"What do you mean?"

He turned away and walked to the window. "What I said. I have no idea what a deep linkage is like. Anor and Torin developed the technique. They began linking through an ordinary crystal. It gave them a great deal of additional power. That was how they were able to sink Sikkar long before they created Vyrkarion, by forming a deep linkage together and then linking in a group of minds with them. But a linkage established through one of the karionin can't be broken. It's binding. The legends say that Anor and Torin loved each other before they linked minds. But afterward, the creation of such a linkage was considered a wedding ceremony. Wizards don't attempt it unless they're prepared to spend their lives together. There haven't been that many successful matings. To speak to someone who knows what it's like, you'd have to go to either Akyrion or Sussey. Belkarion and Lyskarion are the only karionin fully linked to wizards at this time."

"What happened to the unsuccessful ones?"

He turned to face her, looking startled. "What?"

"You said there haven't been many successful matings. That implies unsuccessful ones."

His eyes narrowed. "Several attempts to create karionin failed, and one or both of the wizards died. For instance, every attempt where the wizards were the same sex. Apparently, a deep linkage requires sexual polarity. That may relate to the fact that each of the karionin bonds only to one sex, male or female."

Alanna felt sure there was something else she should ask, something that would explain why the subject of unsuccessful linkages disturbed him. But she couldn't think, she was still too shaken by the memory of the attraction she had felt.

"So, shall we begin?"

Alanna nodded and he led her to a chair. Placing a table in front of her, he brought two candlesticks from the mantle over the fireplace and lit one. "You're a healer and you saw the flow of energies when I fought with Aavik. Look for the flow of energy in the flame the same way you'd feel for the life force of a patient. When you see the energies with your mind, duplicate them over the second candle. Watch while I do it."

He reached across the table and took her hands. The moment he touched her she saw the candle flame, not as a tongue of light, but as a complex flow of gases and energy. Even the candle itself, caught in the strange double vision, became granular, many tiny particles bound within in a form. She felt dizzy and shut her eyes. That eliminated the feeling of seeing double, but the strange vision held until Jerevan released her. When the world came back to normal, she saw that the second candle was burning.

"What happened?" she asked.

"I showed you what you must learn to see."

"I'll never be able to see like that."

"Yes, you will," Jerevan said. "I'll leave you now so my presence won't distract you. Try shutting your eyes, as you did while I demonstrated. The vision will come, like drawing a curtain, but don't worry if it doesn't come right away. Even ready as you are, it takes time. You won't be able to hold it long, either. That comes with practice."

He left then, and she tried to recapture the vision she had seen through his eyes. She tried until she wanted to tear her hair, but nothing happened.

At noon, he fetched her for lunch, but afterward he returned her to the study. Then he demonstrated a second time before leaving her alone until dinnertime. By then her head ached from concentration and she had little appetite. She retired early.

Upstairs, Alanna was astounded to find Agnes waiting in her room.

"What has that man done to you, my lady?" Agnes asked.

"Agnes, what are you doing here? How did you get here?"

"Your aunt said to pack a trunk for you, seeing as how you'd been injured and had to stay in the country for a spell. I said, wherever that trunk goes, I go, my place being with my mistress. And here I am."

"Oh, Agnes." Alanna hugged her.

"That Captain Redat drove me here, but seeing the state you're in, my lady, all I can say is that we should be leaving right now."

"I can't." Alanna turned away and went to the window. "I need to learn to use the Talisman, the jewel the old man gave me."

"Why you'd want to use one of them stones left around by the old wizards I don't know." She followed her mistress to the window and began undoing Alanna's dress.

"Truthfully, nor do I, but I don't seem to have a choice."

"Well, my lady, no good is like to come of it." She finished removing the dress and carried it to the cupboard, saying over her shoulder, "I was never so shocked in my life as I was when I found out whose house this is."

"I know, but he's the only man who can train me. And he did save my life. Tamrai Esparda tried to kidnap me."

"Seems to me, he's kidnaped you himself."

"Well, not exactly."

Agnes said, "I don't understand at all, but I suppose you know your business best."

Despite Agnes' doubts, Alanna went to bed that night feeling better for having an ally and familiar face near her.

The next morning, however, was a repeat of the previous one. That afternoon, though, Jerevan said , "You look as though you could do with some fresh air. Would you like to go riding?"

Her eyes lit up at the prospect. "I'd love to."

Jerevan had two horses saddled and brought round for them, a bay stallion for him and a chestnut mare for her.

"I thought wizards rode kariothin," Alanna said as they crossed the park, the horses' hooves crunching the thin crust of snow.

"I do, sometimes, but I'd never keep Valla here just to be available for an occasional ride. She's in the northwest with her herd. If I need her, I summon her. It takes her about ten days to reach me. Less, if I call her from Leyburn."

She eyed him curiously. "Have you been to Akyrion, seen the gamlarin and the baneslarin?"

He smiled. "Yes. I've visited, but there are few pure-blooded gamlarin left. The baneslarin are a proud people. I like them."

She looked away, surprised to find herself liking him. He wasn't behaving at all as she had expected. Far from being amorous, he was polite and avoided touching her whenever possible. She told herself that she should be relieved, and surveyed the countryside.

The area around Tormar House, as Jerevan told her the estate was called, consisted of rolling hills and stands of hardwoods: chestnuts, julan, and beech trees. An icy wind had blown the open stretches clear of snow, but filled the hollows with deep drifts. Alanna enjoyed the ride despite the cold. She was sorry when it was over, for then Jerevan returned her to the study and frustration.

A week passed and Alanna grew desperate as she made no progress. Her daily rides with Jerevan were the only times she could relax.

"This is the hardest part of any wizard's training," he said one afternoon. "It isn't unusual for even a promising apprentice to take months before achieving a breakthrough, especially one starting after the age of twelve."

She gasped.

"It shouldn't take that long for you, though," he said, grinning in response to her look of horror. "You've been sensitized by Vyrkarion, and by the training you took at the Sanctuary of Maera. It will happen any time now."

"I hope so. I'm supposed to present my petition to the Estahar and have lunch with Nahar Vanith on Maerasday, a week from tomorrow."

"I've arranged for your audience to be delayed until your training has reached a more advanced level. I hope that you'll be able to return to your uncle's house then, as well. I sent for several of my associates some time ago. It's taking a long time for them to reach Ninkarrak, but enough of them should be here soon to supply a guard for you."

"If you'll have enough wizards to guard me, can't you send some of them to the Mallarnes?"

His hands tightened on the stallion's reins. "Believe me, if I can, I will. I don't like the thought of starvation among the hill peoples any more than you do."

"Do you know the sylvith patterns?"

"Yes," he said. "Myrriden wasn't trained at Onchan, but Marion, another of the wizards who helped to train me, was. Derwen's apprentices know them, too."

"Then, if I'm willing to stay your prisoner, can't you send the ones you planned to have guarding me?"

"You're prepared to prolong your captivity?"

"Don't mock me, Jerevan." She used his name for the first time.

He frowned. "I know better than you what's at stake and I'll do what I can to supply wizards to the Mallarnes for the fruiting. You have to learn to trust me."

She looked away, avoiding his eyes.

Near the end of the second week the candle went out of focus and she saw the flow of gases and the lines of force she had previously seen only through Jerevan. She cried out and the vision slipped away.

When Jerevan entered the room, she was trembling with reaction. "I did it!" she said, her eyes shining.

"Good," he said. "Now do it again."

"I don't know if I can."

"Don't think about it. Do it."

She tried, but nothing happened. She stared at him, frustrated. "I can't."

"Yes you can. Take my hands." He held them out and she took them, bringing the vision back into focus.

"There. You did it."

The image dissolved. "I was just looking through you."

"No. You expected to see the flow of energy when you took my hands, so your mind brought it into focus. I wasn't looking."

"Oh!" Alanna focused again. This time managing on her own, but only for an instant. Her head hurt.

Jerevan anticipated this, for he said, "That's enough for today. You'll have a headache soon, if you don't have one already. That's normal the first time. Go up to your room and rest. You'll also be very tired."

She no sooner got to her room than Agnes arrived with a cordial for her to drink. Alanna realized with vague gratitude that Jerevan must have sent the medicine. She drank it and, despite the pain, fell asleep moments after her head touched her pillow.

The next morning her head still ached, but it was a dull pain rather than the stabbing knives of the previous day. Agnes helped her to dress and she went down to breakfast.

As soon as she had eaten, Jerevan took her back to the study.

"My head still hurts," she protested.

"I know, but it's like a muscle. You have to exercise it until you work the soreness out and get accustomed to the higher level of use."

"You mean I'll go through this every time I learn something new?"

Amusement lit his eyes. "The pain shouldn't be quite as severe in future, but to some extent, yes."

"You went through this?"

A grim expression crossed his face. "I went through worse. I didn't have Vyrkarion to help and I studied under rather difficult circumstances."

Alanna felt guilty for reminding him of whatever had caused his reaction, but Jerevan recovered. He told her about Vydarga the Red, the first wizard, saying, "He taught, 'What can be seen, can be altered; what can be fully seen, can be duplicated.' Even nearly five thousand years later, those words are still the foundation upon which all wizardry is based."

Three days later, in the middle of her third week at Tormar House, Alanna duplicated the candle flame. Afterward, though her head ached, she believed for the first time that she could become a wizard.

By dinner time her headache eased, leaving only a vague discomfort, not enough to keep her from feeling more light-hearted than she had felt since finding Myrriden.

After Malling served the malleen soup, a rich concoction made from leaves of the malleen tree and heavy cream, and filled their glasses with a dry white wine from Krydani, Jerevan toasted Alanna, "To my most promising apprentice."

"Would you have said that if I didn't bear the Talisman?"

Jerevan studied her. "I don't lie, Alanna, or say things just for effect, whatever the occasion. It's difficult to say what your potential was before you took up Vyrkarion, but when the College of Wizards was open in Onchan you wouldn't have left the Sanctuary of Maera without notice of your talent being sent there."

"There were no wizards available when I studied in Idris, not even a journeyman, only healers."

"The problem of our times," he said. "Still, that reminds me." He turned to Malling. "Please bring me *The Laws*. It's on my desk in the study." Malling nodded and departed.

"*The Laws*?"

"You took an oath, didn't you, when you studied healing?"

"Of course. All healers take it." She grinned. "Let me guess, there's an oath for wizards, too?"

He shrugged. "More than one, I'm afraid. Before I can teach you anything that will enable you to affect others, you'll have to swear to all the laws set by the Council of Wizards."

"I thought the Council died in the Wizard's Bane."

"Most of the Council members died, but the laws and the oaths survive. One oath you must swear to states that you, in turn, will not train others without first obtaining their oaths." The butler returned with a large, leather bound book. "Thank you, Malling." Jerevan handed it over to Alanna.

When the main course had been served and Malling had withdrawn, Alanna said, "Jerevan, tell me about the living crystals."

"What do you want to know?"

"Oh, everything. There was a poem, 'Ilkarionin,' I was given to help me remember them when I was a child, but I've forgotten most of it."

"Yes," Jerevan said, "you should know the histories of the karionin. You know Vyrkarion's?"

She nodded. "I looked it up. It was the first, made by Anor and Torin. After they died it was stolen and used against the Council in the wizards' final battle, when they created the Bane. Its bearers died with the rest, except Cormor and Belis and Myrriden, of course." She looked at him, but he nodded for her to continue. "When Cormor went back after the battle and collected all the crystals, he gave the Talisman to Myrriden."

"Very good. Only one mistake. Cormor didn't collect all the karionin. One of them, Belkarion, was never there, and he couldn't find Cinkarion, Agnith's crystal. It wasn't found until some eighty years ago. Also, he left Ninkarion in the Bane."

"Because it had been used for evil?"

"No! Rav's use of Ninkarion couldn't make Ninkarion evil. Like all the karionin, it's a focus, an amplifier, but also a living entity. The karionin have volition, by Jehan's will. They may do evil things by the will of their bearers, but they aren't evil themselves."

"Myrriden told me that it was neither good nor evil, but could be used for either. Yet, as a child I had the impression that the crystals caused the deaths of the wizards who made them?"

He nodded. "The creation of the karionin took something from their creators. The wizards who made them declined in vitality afterward. Iskkaar and Minneth faded away. Torin and Anor allowed themselves to die, as in the end Cormor and Belis did. Rav went mad. Only his will kept him alive so long. Redri and Agnith were near death and mad by the time of the final battle. Even Lindeth and Ingvash were weak."

"But wouldn't using one have the same effect?"

He shook his head. "No. It was the process of creation that sapped them. Others using the karionin are strengthened like Myrriden. And he had only a partial linkage."

"Its power frightens me," Alanna said, admitting to Jerevan what she hadn't previously admitted to herself. His hand reached out to rest on hers, and she added, "I'm afraid of the responsibility. Who am I to carry a thing of such power that its use can change reality?"

Jerevan's answered her in almost the same words Myrriden had used, "A girl with clear eyes untainted by ambition or greed."

Alanna shook her head. She felt filled with ambitions and desires and her desires felt particularly dangerous. They both fell silent for a time, Alanna lost in reverie, the only sound the howling of wind in the eaves.

When Malling returned to clear away their dinner, Jerevan said, "Set the drink tray in my study, Malling, and that will be all for tonight."

"Very well, your grace."

In the past, Alanna had excused herself after dinner and retired to her room, but this evening she followed Jerevan to his study.

The room looked different at night with burgundy velvet curtains drawn across the windows. A fire blazed in the hearth and the room felt cozy with the flames flickering on the leather and gilt bindings of the thousands of books, despite the storm still growling outside.

"Join me?" Jerevan asked, holding up a bottle of brandy. "It's from Esterias, the region around Deaan where they make the very best."

"Yes, I'd like some. My father used to drink it. There was a merchant who lived in Idris; he went to Esterias every year to bring back brandy and lace."

Jerevan poured them each a small amount. When they sat down near the fire, Alanna's mind went back to their earlier discussion. "If Cormor didn't leave the Eye of Rav in the Bane because it was evil, why did he leave it?"

"I think he felt that it belonged to Rav's apprentices, and that one of them should claim it."

"I've heard it said that Rav was the embodiment of evil, but all I remember about him is that two wizards fought over the right to link with him."

Jerevan leaned back in his chair, his head resting against the padded back. "Mehdi and Sugra fought, but it wasn't simply a matter of gaining Rav's favor. Rav was breaking the laws of the Council, training wizards from Gandahar in the art of using crystals to focus power. He also taught some of their children the high sight. Mehdi found out. She was one of the older wizards and she remembered the Dragon Wars. She would have betrayed Rav to the Council, but Sugra killed her first. Sugra was young and believed in Rav."

"But why would Rav break his oath?"

"No one knows for sure." He shook his head. "Cormor believed that Rav was part isklar, one of the children born without were-sight in Gandahar whose parents smuggled him out to Kailane. That happened to many children, but Cormor thought that, in Rav's case, his parents stayed in contact with him even after he went to Onchan. If that's true, it would explain a great deal."

"My family took me to Onchan for the summer once," Alanna said, swirling the amber liquid in her glass. "I saw the College of Wizards, but it was abandoned. What happened to it? Why are there so few wizards left today?"

"A number of factors, but Rav did a lot to make wizardry unpopular. There've always been tales of wizards doing horrible things to people, but most of them are semi-legendary, like the stories of the Garden of Leila. Rav performed experiments using human subjects and left the subjects around to prove the truth of the tales. People said that what one wizard does, others probably do, too. Parents refused to allow their children to be tested. With fewer and fewer students, eventually the College died." Jerevan sighed. "It doesn't take much to shake people's confidence in something they don't understand to begin with."

They sat in silence for a time, watching the flames and sipping the velvet fire of the Esterian brandy. Finally, Alanna asked, "Did one of Rav's apprentices claim the Eye?"

"Yes. He was insufficiently trained to deal with the poisons of the Bane, but he lived long enough to set up a priesthood in Ravaar."

"And they still train wizards there," she said, remembering Ramal Guitara.

"Yes, but not very good ones. So far no one trained there has attained the high sight dependably." He grinned. "I heard about your meeting with Guitara."

She flushed. "I behaved foolishly."

He studied her downcast features. "Yes, but I placed you in a difficult situation that night at the Blue Boar."

She looked up and her eyes met his. "You knew how I felt." The words were an accusation.

"Yes," he sighed, "but the attraction between us is a two-sided coin, Alanna. I felt the same way."

Her eyes narrowed. "But you're…" She hesitated.

"An ancient, jaded roue, incapable of real feelings," he said, filling the silence. "Isn't that what you were going to say?"

"No," she looked down at her hands, clenched into fists, and relaxed them. "That wasn't what I was thinking."

"Wasn't it?"

"No!" She looked up and met his eyes. "That's what I thought then, the night at the Blue Boar, but that's not how I see you now."

This time he was the first to look away. He let out a deep breath. "It's time we cleared the air. I admit I handled our meeting badly. I should have told you who I was from the beginning, and I should have tamped down the attraction between us until we had a chance to get acquainted. But I wasn't thinking clearly." He swirled the brandy in his glass. "I'd climbed out of what had nearly been my deathbed and dragged myself halfway across the country to meet you. I wasn't at my brightest." He looked up at her again. "I took one look at you in that dingy bar, your life force burning brighter than the crystal at your breast, and all I wanted to do was warm myself."

"I felt bewitched."

He smiled and nodded. "So did I, Alanna. But I didn't cast any spells."

She straightened in the chair and her chin rose. "I promised myself when you brought me here that I wouldn't let our relationship be anything other than master and student." She stared at him. "I can't risk changing that."

He sighed and his eyes went back to the fire. "I wasn't expecting you to. I just wanted you to hear my point of view." In the silence she heard a log crackling. Then he sat up and drained the last of his brandy. "It's late. Time to say good night." He rose and took her hands, pulling her up.

The grip of his hands felt warm. She allowed herself to be drawn to her feet, but her breath caught as her body came up against his. She could feel the heat of him, see the pulse in the hollow of his throat. Her eyes shifted up to meet his. The moment stretched. Despite her earlier words, she wanted him to kiss her. He wanted her, she could see it in the warmth of his eyes, feel it in the beat of his heart, but he drew back and released her.

"Good night, Alanna."

She climbed the stairs, torn by conflicting emotions. What was the point in keeping him at arm's length, if he really did care for her. Despite herself, she desired him. But she was angry at herself for that weakness. While one part of her could argue that his age didn't matter when he looked and acted young, and his reputation didn't matter, when he showed her nothing but consideration; another voice warned her that she couldn't trust him. There had to be some basis for the rumors surrounding him and, until he explained them to her, she couldn't afford to lower her defenses.

The next day Jerevan told her to examine her hand with her new sight. He showed her the patterns made by the capillaries distributing blood to every cell. He showed her the differences between the cells: muscle cells, nerve cells, blood cells, even the epidermal layers and the cells that made up the hair follicles. She found them all confusing, particularly as she could only hold the sight for a few seconds at a time.

That night she claimed to be too tired to continue their conversation. She avoided joining Jerevan in his study in the evenings that followed, also. She was too disturbed by her feelings about him.

Jerevan stared into the fire and sipped his brandy, telling himself that he was glad that Alanna had avoided a repeat of that too intimate after-dinner conversation. He wasn't ready for any deeper relationship between them than master and pupil, any more than she was. His history with regard to relationships wasn't good, and with his background a relationship with the bearer of one of the karionin would be madness.

There could be no secrets in a full mindlink and there were things in his past that he wanted no one else to see, certainly no one as young and untouched as Alanna. With the Wizard Marion that hadn't mattered. She'd been there with him all through his struggles with Derwen's curse. She'd seen him when he came back from being a prisoner in Ravaar. She'd cursed him for being a fool, yet she'd loved him despite it all. But Marion had been neither young, nor innocent. She'd worn a cap herself as a prisoner in Senanga. She'd understood pain and what it could do to the mind.

And she'd died in Senanga. Jerevan closed his eyes to keep in his tears. It had been almost sixty years since her death; one would think the pain would lessen with time, but it didn't. No, he could be nothing more to Alanna than her teacher.

And yet he couldn't deny the desire he felt for his young apprentice. He hadn't felt such an instant attraction for anyone since the first time he met Marion, before he'd even become a wizard. And he'd always suspected that Marion had deliberately enchanted him that night. Now, he knew, the attraction was completely natural, and mutual, and that made it all the more dangerous.

And, if he was going to think of dangers, there was Vyrkarion. There was no question about what the living crystal wanted, it wanted him to link with Alanna. He'd known that since the moment he touched her when he started her training. Vyrkarion had almost forced the linkage then.

And if Vyrkarion's power was needed, as the prophecy had predicted? What then? How could Alanna, completely untrained, utilize the power of the karion?

He shook his head and took another swallow of his brandy. If only he didn't carry so much personal baggage. If he could just be the man he had been before Derwen cursed him, then he could think of nothing he'd like more than to link with Alanna, but not even a wizard could alter reality that much.

Alanna didn't manage to see her hand to Jerevan's satisfaction until another week passed and it was close to the end of Iskkaar.

"Now you have to examine and memorize every part of your body," he said. "Eventually, you'll examine yourself daily and maintain yourself in the form you've memorized. If a single cell dies or changes, you'll know to treat it right away."

Her eyes widened. "I'll never be able to remember every cell in my body."

He grinned. "Perhaps not, although you'll be surprised what you learn to remember after a few years training. But what you can't remember, Vyrkarion will. That's a crystal's second major purpose, to retain patterns. When you learn to communicate with Vyrkarion, you'll be able to use it in place of your own memory. Vyrkarion never forgets. Some day you'll even learn to understand the patterns Anor and Torin used."

Several days later, when she had again performed the examination of her hand to his satisfaction, he drew a needle from a package in his pocket. "Now I'm going to prick you."

"What!" She stared at the needle, which seemed alarmingly large and sharp. Her jaw clenched.

He sighed with exasperation. "You've got to learn to trust me, Alanna. I'll prick myself first, to show you what I want you to do. It's just a sewing needle. I'm sure you've hurt yourself more seriously with an embroidery needle. The idea is for you to heal the wound. Watch."

He drove the needle into the heel of his hand. When he removed it, blood welled up from the puncture. Then the blood retreated; the wound closing to just a fading, pink dot.

She stared at him. "I can't do that."

"You can see the way your blood flows in the capillaries. You can see the cells in your skin. Examine them closely before I prick you. You've been able to see the life force for years. Now you can see the details of the flesh. Remember, what you can see you can alter. What you can remember, you can duplicate. When I prick you, the pattern of the cells in your skin will change. Change it back to the way you see it now."

She swallowed, but brought her hand up. She knew her fear was irrational. Her only explanation was the edginess she always felt when he was present, a side-effect of her awareness of him.

"Examine your palm, Alanna. You have to concentrate."

She jerked and brought her attention back to her hand. The prick he made was tiny, much smaller than the puncture in his own palm, but she still found it difficult to heal. The blood and cells made a more complicated pattern than the gases of the candle flame and were harder to manipulate. Her training in healing helped, but her inner sight faded at critical moments and it would be minutes before she could get it back. It took her the rest of the day to close the pinprick, remove the scab that formed because of her slowness and heal the damaged cells. Her head was more painful than her hand had been when she finished.

XVI

4731, 474TH CYCLE OF THE YEAR OF THE DRAGON
MONTH OF ISKKAAR

> They held him in the Tower,
> A prisoner of him made,
> So that he could not send for
> Those who might give him aid.
> Aid, aid for the Wanderer
> Wherever he may be,
> Though he is doomed to exile
> By the shore of Sorrow Sea.
>
> — FROM *THE BALLAD OF AUBREY THE WANDERER* BY ANONYMOUS

"Sorry, miss, but I've got orders not to let Nahar Aubrey out of the Tower." The guard looked young. Minta thought he couldn't be older than eighteen, and his fair skin was flushed with embarrassment, but he stood firmly in front of the entryway.

"Who gave the order?" Minta demanded. "I'm sure Nahar Vanith will want to know why her son is being kept a prisoner."

The guard swallowed and his skin flushed a darker shade of red, but didn't step aside. "The order came from the boy's father, Naharil Thurin, on behalf of His Majesty. The boy isn't a prisoner. He's being kept safe from those who might try to kill him."

"Assassins in the royal compound?"

The guard stiffened. "It's not my duty to question my orders, miss, just to obey them. Now, take the boy back upstairs. It's for his own safety. These are unsettled times."

Minta took Aubrey's hand, "It looks like we're not going to get that walk I promised you." She feared Aubrey might protest, but he nodded and turned to limp back up the stairs.

When they'd returned to the nursery, she said, "Aubrey, I'm going to leave you here for a few minutes. I've got to tell your mother about what the guard said. Will you be all right?"

"I'll be fine."

"I won't be long." She hated to leave him but she knew Vanith would want to know what had happened.

"It's all right. I'm not upset," Aubrey said. "I've been expecting something like this."

She hugged him. "You may not be upset, but I am. How dare they make you a prisoner in your own home?"

Minta hurried to Vanith's apartment on the floor above. Lady Avlen was on duty in the antechamber.

"Why, Minta dear, whatever is the matter, you're so flushed?"

"Is her highness in her rooms?"

"Why, yes, dear, but she's resting. I really don't think I should disturb her now. You know how high strung she is. It's so hard for her to get any rest. I understand how she feels, because I'm that way myself. I just live on my nerves."

"I must see her. It's urgent."

"Oh dear, is something the matter with Nahar Aubrey? You should have said so at once." Lady Avlen's lips pursed with concern.

"No, there's nothing the matter with him, but it's about him that I have to see her," Minta said.

Lady Avlen drew herself up like a ruffled pigeon. "Well, if there's nothing wrong with him, you shouldn't imply there is. You had me quite upset. I told you before that the Nahar is resting. You'll have to come back later."

"I'm not resting any longer, Enora," Vanith said, coming out of her bedroom. "As it's urgent, I'll see Minta now. Please see that we aren't disturbed." She turned to Minta, "Come in."

When Vanith closed the door behind them, she brushed her hand across her face and Minta was shocked by the bruised look around her eyes. "What is it, Minta? It must be important, or you wouldn't have left Aubrey."

"I was going to take Aubrey for a walk in the park," Minta said, biting her lip and trying to find words to express her indignation. "He's been shut in so much since his lessons started, I thought the fresh air would do him good. But when we got downstairs, the guard wouldn't let Aubrey out of the Tower. He said that Naharil Thurin, with the Estahar's authority, ordered that Aubrey be kept inside. He said it was for Aubrey's own good, that it was dangerous for him outside."

"You went straight back to the nursery?"

"Yes. I didn't like to leave him but I thought you ought to hear right away."

"Thank you, Minta." Vanith put a hand up and rubbed her eyes again as though they ached. "It's all moving so much more swiftly than I'd anticipated." She sighed. "If only Jere were here, or I could get a message to him. Thurin, may he burn in Agnith's fires, had my father change all my guards last week. Now there isn't anyone I can trust to carry a message. They're all loyal followers of Miune and under Horgen's finger." Vanith paced across the room, then turned back to Minta. "Get back to Aubrey now. It would be a good idea if he's never left alone in future."

"They wouldn't harm him, would they?"

Vanith paused and shut her eyes. "I don't think so, not yet. He's more valuable to them alive than dead. At least, I hope so. But they'll want to separate him from me. If only I knew Horgen's plans."

Minta started to leave, then turned back. "Would it make a difference if you could get a message to Lord Leyburn?" Minta chewed on her lip, then said, "I know someone who could take a message for you."

"Who?" Vanith's voice sharpened. "It can't be one of the guards. However willing he might seem to be, he'd be bound to report it."

Minta avoided Vanith's eyes. "Please don't ask me anything more. I just know someone who'd take a message."

Vanith took Minta by the shoulders. "It might mean all our lives. I have to know. Who is it?"

Minta shook her head, but Vanith took her chin and forced it up. As Minta's eyes met Vanith's, she felt as if she were sinking into a deep well. Vanith's eyes were enormous, gray-blue whirlpools, and she was drowning in them. When she was on the point of passing out, Vanith released her.

"So, you have a lover. I thought so, but there have been so many other things to think about."

"I'm sorry." Minta sank down on a chair and started to cry.

Vanith looked surprised. "Why be sorry? I'm happy for you."

Minta looked up at her with eyes wide. "I've been meeting him in secret. I've even had him in my room."

"That's impossible," Vanith said, her eyes narrowing. "How did he get in? How did he get by the guards?"

Minta looked stricken. "I thought you saw it all in my mind."

Vanith shook her head. "My talent isn't that strong. All I saw was that you had a lover and that you trusted him." She stood over Minta. "Come, you must tell me the rest now. How does your lover come to your room? I'd have said there was no way to pass the guards."

"He's a thief," Minta said. She began to cry again.

"All right, Minta, he's a thief, but how does he get to your room?"

"He's part isklar." Minta sniffed, trying to wipe her eyes. "He just walks up the wall of the Tower when it's dark and comes in by the balcony."

"An isklar! Are you sure he isn't an agent of Aavik?"

"He can't be," Minta said. "He thinks of himself as human. He was born in Gandahar, but he was one of the condemned children. The Varfarin rescued him. He didn't develop the sight until he was in his teens."

"All right, Minta. Are you willing to let me meet him, with Aubrey?"

Minta tried to swallow and coughed. "He doesn't come every night, just when he isn't working."

"How often?"

"Two, sometimes three, nights a week."

"This is Maerasday. When did you last see him?"

"He came Tamarsday night."

"So you can reasonably expect him tonight or tomorrow night?"

"Yes," Minta said reluctantly.

"Will you introduce me to him when he comes?"

"Yes."

That night Minta prayed that Thrym would come. She tossed and turned for hours, listening for the sound of his step on the balcony, but it never came. The dawn was gray and dreary. She spent Jehansday trying to appear normal to Aubrey, whose pale face also showed signs of missed sleep.

Vanith visited them in the afternoon after Aubrey's lesson with Semel. She looked searchingly at Minta, but said nothing. Aubrey went to bed early and it hurt Minta to see how the strain was telling on him.

She went to bed determined to wait for Thrym, but she soon fell into an exhausted sleep.

Thrym slipped into Minta's bed and let his hands caress the silken warmth of her body, loving the way she turned to him, welcomed him, even when half asleep.

"Oh, Thrym," she moaned, clutching him tighter as she woke. He tried to sooth her but there was a desperation in her lovemaking that frightened him.

Even afterward, when she normally snuggled against him and fell asleep, she clung to him.

"What's the matter?" he asked.

She hugged him and he could feel her body trembling. "I'm so glad you came tonight," she murmured. "I've been going out of my mind. There's something I have to tell you."

"What is it?"

"Aubrey's been made a prisoner. Naharil Thurin won't even let him out to walk in the park. Vanith wants to reach Lord Leyburn, but he's out of town and there's no one she can trust to send with a message." Minta paused.

Thrym knew how much she loved Aubrey, but her anxiety seemed out of proportion. "That's too bad," he said, "but what's got you so upset? They haven't threatened you, have they?"

"I told Vanith about you."

Thrym felt as though he had been kicked in his guts. "You what!" His whole body tensed as he listened for the sound of guards. "I trusted you," he whispered, sick with the pain. He pulled himself off her and rolled away.

"No! Wait, Thrym!" Minta grabbed his arm. "Vanith won't betray you to the guards. Listen, please listen to me. I knew you'd be angry, but you've got to listen. Vanith needs you, and Aubrey needs you, too. He's a prisoner. They need your help to carry a message. Vanith wants to meet you."

"I just bet she does." He jerked his arm free and got out of the bed.

"You should listen to Minta, and not jump to conclusions," a voice said from the shadows.

Thrym crouched and whirled, prepared for combat. A small boy struck a match and lit the lamp near the door. When the wick caught, the boy turned to him. *"Minta loves you. She didn't mean to betray you."*

Thrym shook his head, swallowing. He had not often experienced the mind speech. Even amid his fear and the sickness he felt at Minta's betrayal, Thrym admired the boy's composure. He had to be Nahar Aubrey.

"Yes. I am Aubrey Cinnac." The boy smiled. *"And you are not in danger."*

Thrym felt the truth in the child's mind and some of the shock and fear drained out of him. He straightened.

"Minta merely hinted that she could find someone to carry a message. My mother forced the rest out of her, but none of us mean you harm. To the contrary, we need your help."

Thrym took a deep breath and let it out slowly, seeing Aubrey's image of Minta in tears and remembering how she clung to him earlier. "I understand, rai. I reacted in haste," he said. He bowed in the manner due to royalty.

"I'm no one's master, Thrym, not even my own." Aubrey grinned. "If my mother is going to meet you, don't you think you should dress?"

Thrym started, realizing that he was naked. He flushed and turned to the bed to put on his clothes. "Only one other person's ever used the mind speech with me. I catch surface thoughts sometimes when I concentrate, but I don't have much practice."

"Why didn't you contact another wizard? There are many who would have helped you."

"I've lived by thievery since I was eleven. It's all I know. What sympathy would a wizard have with a thief?" Thrym finished putting on his clothes and turned back to the child.

Aubrey eyed him up and down. "Aren't you forgetting that you're at least a journeyman yourself?"

"Not a very good one. What use is it to me? Wizardry can't put food on the table or clothes on my back."

"It could, if you were skilled enough."

Thrym looked down at his feet. "I've never liked the idea of it. I'd rather go along as I am. I don't want to play games with other wizards."

"It's good to be afraid, but you have to learn to control your fear."

Thrym stared, realizing that the boy had done more than simply speak to him with the mind speech. *"Get out of my mind!"*

"I'm not reading your thoughts now. I saw enough when I first touched you." Aubrey tilted his head. *"If you want to make it fair, look at me. My mind's open and you do know how."*

Thrym stiffened. The boy was daring him! He reached out.

Power and warmth. Order and disorder. Thrym shook his head, never having imagined a will so strong, or accompanied by so much... What was the emotion that filled Aubrey? Passion? Compassion? Neither really described what he felt. Yet, despite the power, the boy was a child and still had the simplicity of childhood. There was also fear.

"The power scares you, too," Thrym said.

"Of course."

"You're braver than I." Thrym shifted his feet, uneasy with what he saw in the child's mind.

"No. I've had more training," Aubrey said. "The first thing the Wizard of Leyburn taught me was that we should all be afraid, but we should rule our fear, not let it rule us."

"Your talent is much greater than mine."

"Yes. But so is my responsibility."

Thrym studied the boy. Then he grinned, knowing that what he was going to propose was outrageous, but he didn't care. If he was going to be manipulated, he would do some manipulating of his own. "Very well. I'll do what you want. Carry your messages, or anything else. And not just now, but from now on. Then, whatever I do, it will be your responsibility, rai." Thrym's grin expanded and he stressed the last word. He was tired of being a thief, of having to sneak around to see Minta. If this boy wizard wanted favors done for him, he could give Thrym a formal position as his liege.

There was a long silence. Aubrey looked stiff and solemn and Thrym wondered if he might have pushed too far. The boy actually looked as though he had grown older in just the last moments. But at last Aubrey sighed and nodded. "Very well. I need your service, so I accept your terms. Kneel."

Thrym hesitated, wondering if he was really doing the right thing. Aubrey's service would bind him for life. Then he remembered the clarity of the child's mind, the warmth. He sank down on his knees.

Minta stared at the man on his knees before the child, sensing some ritual taking place between them on a level beyond her power to grasp. She wasn't sure whether it made her happy or jealous. She only knew that the sight of them like that affected her deeply. Their rapport ended when Aubrey gave Thrym his hand and Thrym kissed it.

"Now you're my servant, Thrym. My will shall bind you for the rest of your life," Aubrey said.

"So be it," Thrym answered.

Aubrey turned to Minta and smiled, as if he understood her mixed emotions. "I think my mother is waiting."

Minta jumped up, grabbed a robe and ran from the room.

When she reached Vanith's rooms there was no lady-in-waiting on duty. Vanith herself came to the door. When Minta looked surprised, Vanith said, "It's best that our meeting have no witnesses." Then, "I thought you'd send Aubrey to fetch me. Who's with him?"

"Just Thrym," Minta said. "Aubrey told me to come for you. I think he wanted to be alone with Thrym for a while."

Vanith looked vexed, but she accompanied Minta down the stairs to the nursery without saying anything further.

Aubrey and Thrym were both sitting on Minta's bed when she and Vanith entered. Thrym was telling Aubrey a story about the Farinmalith.

Vanith said, "So you're Minta's midnight visitor. She thinks well of you." Thrym rose and bowed, a flush rising in his cheeks at her words. He looked to Aubrey for support.

"Don't tease him, Mother. He's agreed to come into my service, a rather thankless and dangerous occupation."

Vanith's eyes narrowed. "What do you mean?"

"I mean that I've taken his oath. He's now bound as my liege," Aubrey said. "I'm sorry, if it offends you, but it was our wish and it's done."

Vanith's eyes widened. "I'm only surprised. Your decision was very sudden." She hesitated. "He will take a message to Lord Leyburn then?"

"Yes, your highness. I'll take the message." Thrym grinned at Minta. "And run any other errands you happen to think of. It'll give me an excuse to come by more often."

Minta flushed but his impudence relieved her. She had been afraid that what happened earlier might have changed him.

"That will be sufficient for now," Vanith said. "I have the message here." She pulled a sealed envelope from the sleeve of her gown and handed it to him. "It needs to be taken to Tormor House in the hills to the east of the city, just north of the village of Cooslip." She paused, then added, "That address is a private one. It is not to be released to others."

Thrym nodded. "I won't repeat it."

Aubrey rose and said, "Come, Mother. Now that's taken care of, I think we've disturbed enough of Thrym and Minta's rest."

Vanith hesitated. "Don't I get to at least talk to your new liege?"

"Don't you trust me?" Aubrey eyed his mother with a challenge in his eyes.

Vanith's face stiffened. "Of course I trust you. I just want to talk to someone who can come so close to you so quickly." She glanced at Thrym.

"But I need to talk to you," Aubrey said and led Vanith from the room.

Minta studied Thrym. His eyes followed Aubrey until the Nahar left the room and she couldn't understand the expression on his face. He turned to her when they had gone, suddenly defensive.

"I'm sorry, Minta. I should have trusted you, but I've got out of the habit of trusting people."

She went to him and put her arms around him. "That's all right. I knew you'd be angry." Minta sat on the bed and pulled Thrym down beside her. "What happened between you and Aubrey?"

He shut his eyes and sighed. "You heard. I swore an oath to serve him."

"Why?"

Thrym shrugged. "I can't put it into words. It doesn't fit." He shook his head. "He's going to be one of the great wizards, yet he's still a child and has a child's fear and a child's warmth. I know now why the Eskh word for wizard is nalor, child-god. He's powerful, yet he needs people, needs me. Before I met you, no one ever needed me." He hugged Minta. "And he understood my fear of using my will, even though my power is so little compared to his. I can't explain any more than that." He laughed. "And anyway, I'm tired of being a thief. I wanted to join the Mercenaries' Guild, but being liege to Nahar Aubrey is an even greater rise in status."

"Then I'm glad," she said, helping him to undress again. "It means we'll be together."

"Yes," he said, pulling her close, "so it does."

XVII

4731, 474th Cycle of the Year of the Dragon
Months of Iskkaar and Dirga
Edain: Summon the people so that
they may bow down before me,
and worship me.
Trivana: But, child, that will anger
the gods. They are the only
beings entitled to worship.
Edain: Nonsense. The gods are all
old. Why should I care for
them?

— Act III, Scene 7, Lines 7 - 15,
from *The Defiance of Edain*

Rakshe saw his master emerge from Valkarn and galloped through the lush grass of the meadow to meet him. The grass was tall and fragrant, spotted with wild flowers, argerium and sweet clover, but beyond the meadow and the castle the northern winter banked snow in drifts as tall as a man. Used to wintering in sheltered lowland valleys, Rakshe hadn't liked the snow, so Rhys built a dome of force with his mind and created summer.

Rhys broke into a run as Rakshe approached him, leaping through the long grass as gracefully as the karoth, and Rakshe swerved away from him, playing a game of which they had both grown fond. So they played tag through the meadow, startling the butterflies, and the weak winter sun shone on them and the north wind licked at the dome but could not come in. When they tired of the game, Rhys formed a brush from the air with his will and curried the karoth, knowing that Rakshe liked the feel of the bristles against his skin.

"You are happy?"

"Like a colt. It's strange after so many years to have no more responsibility," Rakshe replied, leaning into the soothing brush, relaxed but aware, feeling for Rhys' mood.

"Ah, responsibility. A word. I don't know its meaning. Yet it seems I'll soon have to learn," Rhys thought, a frown creasing his broad forehead.

"Then we go south with the spring, rai?"

There was a pause before Rhys answered. Rakshe heard crickets chirping and a soft breeze teased the ends of his mane, a gentle echo of the fierce gale outside.

"*Have I a choice? You heard my mother, and my grandfather is worse. He reminds me constantly of the prophecy. The vision came to one of the Kindred of Maera, he harps, therefore it must be Maera's will.*" Rhys' frown was more marked and anger colored his thoughts.

"*The future is not fixed until it has become the past, rai. You know that.*" Rakshe's tail swished like a banner of black silk. He'd come a long way toward understanding his master, but he didn't yet know enough to influence Rhys.

"*You would have me defy the gods?*"

"*What angers one god may please another,*" Rakshe thought, trying to gauge his master's mood. His major problem was Rhys' lack of practice in discussing anything. His master had been raised in seclusion. Aside from a few servants chosen for their meekness, the only sentient being with whom Rhys had been able communicate had been his grandfather, until he met Rakshe. The karoth was just beginning to understand what such total isolation meant. Coming from a herd culture, even the thought of it horrified him.

"*Would you have me break my oath, beast?*" The brush dissolved into the air from which it had come, and Rhys slapped the karoth on his rump with a force that stung.

"*I'm your servant, rai. I'd see you happy.*"

"*Ha. You're bored without your herds of kariothin and seek to herd me. Be wary, I'm not so easy to lead.*" Yet Rhys' tone was no longer angry and he reached out to scratch a sensitive spot by Rakshe's ear.

"*I understand, rai.*" Rakshe bowed his head, reflecting that, despite his upbringing, Rhys possessed a shrewd mind. He'd have to tread warily, but that increased the challenge.

Rhys laughed.

On a day when swirling snow dimmed the skies above his warm meadow, Rakshe again asked, "*Rai, have you made your decision?*" Rhys was grooming him, as had become his habit after their play.

"*You would see me unsheathe the Sword of Cormor on Ilwheirlane, and spread destruction before me? You are bloodthirsty, friend.*"

"*I'd see you ride south, rai, away from this place. I have not suggested anything further,*" Rakshe thought, upset by the edginess of his master's mood.

"*Then watch yourself, beast.*" There was anger in Rhys' thought. "*You must learn to be careful. I'm no mare of your herd to be nipped into place.*"

Rhys paused and the brush vanished. Something in his stance altered, as though his anger spurred some deeper decision. "*As you and my grandfather are so anxious for me to take this throne, I think I'll start the process early. We'll leave today.*"

Rakshe tossed his head in distress. *"This is the height of the season of storms, rai. Why not wait until the weather is better?"*

"Don't you like storms, Rakshe? I do. I like their wildness and their freedom." Rhys laughed, but not with humor. *"I'm tired of being pent within castle walls with only you and my grandfather for company. How can I learn anything that way? If my fate is to rule Ilwheirlane, then let me go out to meet it. And if the weather is stormy, so much the better. It matches my mood."*

Rhys rode Rakshe out of the Vale of Valkarn on the first day of Dirga, named for the Wizard Dirga, mistress of storms. No longer did he shield either Rakshe or himself from the elements. A blizzard swirled around them and Rhys exulted in its fury. Black clouds covered the sky and turned day into night. The wind shrieked down from the icy wastes of the north and brought snow in blinding sheets. Rhys was angry and his anger found expression in the violence of the tempest, his mind reaching out not to calm but to intensify, so that the storm became a reflection of his rage.

Rakshe knew that Rhys' resentment wasn't directed at him, but, struggling through the snow and sleet, that knowledge was small comfort. He resolved yet again to be careful when he tried to influence his master.

They traveled east through the mountains to Jevac Lessar, the Eastern Ocean. Rhys had decided he wanted an army to follow him and only on the coast could he find trained men, for only Ilwheirlane's coasts were fortified. Ilwheirlane's land borders abutted neighboring human nations or lands controlled by the eslarin or the baneslarin, and neither of those peoples fought wars. Linlarin pirates frequently raided the seacoasts, however, and every village had its lookout tower and Shore Guard and every major harbor had its fort and guardians.

On the sixth day of Dirga, Rhys rode Rakshe out of the storm and up to the gate of the fort at Aire, the northernmost harbor in Ilwheirlane. Then he held up the sword that had been sheathed across his back and said to the guard, "Summon your commander."

The guard stared at Rhys like a rabbit mesmerized by a malik. Then he went dumbly to do as he had been told. Rakshe pitied him. No untrained human mind could withstand the will of his master.

When the commander came forth, Rhys said, "Know man, that I am Rhys Cinnac, true Estahar of Ilwheirlane. I hold the Sword of Cormor, which bears in its hilt Cyrkarion, as proof of my claim. From this day forth you are mine and shall obey me. Open the gate and summon your men so that they may also become mine."

All was done as he commanded.

XVIII

4731, 474TH CYCLE OF THE YEAR OF THE DRAGON
MONTH OF DIRGA

Ac resal a ilgand, co kujalne
bores less pail a ser.

"To learn from a dragon, speak softly
and carry a lot of meat."

— ESLARIN PROVERB

The first day of Dirga dawned clear and cold. Alanna sensed a stillness in the air presaging a storm, but Jerevan assured her it wouldn't arrive until evening. "There's a carnival in the village nearby and we could both do with a day off. It's on the way to Ninkarrak so it'll only be here today and tomorrow."

"A carnival," Alanna exclaimed. "How marvelous! I haven't been to one for ages. They don't often get to Fell. But isn't this the wrong time of year?"

"It's unusual for carnivals to tour Ilwheirlane in the winter," Jerevan said, "but there's a festival planned this summer in Ninkarrak. I expect a number of touring companies will be arriving early." He grinned. "There'll be shelter. Cooslip has a covered market."

Alanna felt her spirits rise. Jerevan had been away for two days earlier in the week, and afterward he'd seemed preoccupied. He didn't confide in her, but she was glad to see him more relaxed. When the groom brought round a team of bays hitched to a sleigh with sides carved in the shapes of two black swans, she laughed aloud.

The snow ran off the runners of the sleigh like spun sugar and the horses' breath formed twin geysers of steam. The air was still under the cobalt arch of the sky and so cold it tingled in Alanna's lungs. The team was fresh, but Jerevan controlled them easily, his long fingers slender even encased in leather gloves. Alanna reflected that his hands had to be strong.

It suddenly struck her how little she knew of him. All the things she had thought she knew didn't relate to the man sitting beside her. She often gave him cause for anger but he never lost his temper. She'd never seen him act in a cruel manner. His staff were fiercely loyal, or so Agnes told her, and most of them had known him all their lives. They wouldn't be so devoted if he weren't a good master.

How had he earned his reputation for sadism and perversion? Was he so fine an actor that he could hide the evil portion of his nature for weeks, even months, to overcome her reservations? To what purpose? Her training was already in his hands. She'd been forced to trust him for that. Why should he care for anything more? But, of course, there was a reason. The Talisman was designed to be used by two wizards linked together. She looked again at his steady hands on the reins and then at his face. She wanted to trust him.

As though sensing her scrutiny, he turned and smiled, his blue eyes warm. "Relax, this is a day for enjoying ourselves, not thinking deep thoughts."

She couldn't help her answering smile. He was right, she would enjoy the moment and, for a day, forget about the future.

The carnival occupied a vaulted building on the edge of the village. The snow on the field outside had been trampled to a hard icy surface, slippery in the shade and slushy in the sunny spots, but the treacherous footing hadn't discouraged anyone. Although it was still early, the area was already crowded with gigs and wagons and even a few other sleighs. Two large tents had been set up along the edge of the building, one housing the animals and the other advertising the carnival wizard.

Jerevan pulled the sleigh up at the edge of the field and gave the reins to one of the men waiting to attend to the horses, flipping him a coin. Then he jumped out and turned to help Alanna down. When she hesitated, he lifted her and lowered her to the ground. She felt the strength of his arms and the mist of his breath against her cheek and pulled away, knowing that, with his wizard sense, he couldn't help but be aware of the effect his closeness had on her.

Inside the market building, booths were everywhere with their pennants flying. At first she was self-conscious walking beside him, her hand barely touching his arm as he guided her through the crowd, but as they wandered through the fair, she relaxed. They watched a puppet show and an act where two dogs danced together on their hind legs. Then Jerevan threw hoops at models of famous people to win her an elegant doll with a porcelain head and the robes of a nahar.

"Isn't it cheating when you can put the hoop anywhere you want with your will?"

"It would be if I'd used my talent rather than natural skill, but the barker would have caught me." Jerevan nodded at the thin man with protuberant eyes who had taken his coins when he bought his chance with the hoops.

"How?"

"Most carnival people have some wizard training, Alanna. It's a part of their profession." His blue gaze was intent. "Did you think I'd cheat just to win you a doll?"

She felt herself flush. "No, I didn't think that."

Jerevan smiled, his eyes lighting with laughter. "That's good, because I intend to win you several more prizes, my lady."

After he won her the prize, Alanna found herself gripping Jerevan's arm, like a child amid wonders. There was a man with a brilliantly colored bird that talked when spoken to, and an enormous animal the size of a small mountain with a tail coming out of its head that could lift things.

While observing a troop of acrobats from Kandorra perform, Alanna said, "Most of them have feather crests and look like the hailarin dancers I saw at the ballet, but they're taller and less delicate. That one over there even has hair. If they're not hailarin, what are they?"

Jerevan smiled. "Half-breeds, part hailarin and part human. Many of the hailarin in Kandorra are of mixed parentage. Only the Dancers' Guild still insists on its members being pure-blooded. And actually that's illegal here in Ilwheirlane, only Idrim has refused to enforce the Act of Toleration."

They watched high wire walkers, fire eaters and mimes, and listened to minstrels. Toward the end of the afternoon, Jerevan took her back outside to the large tent where barkers announced the wizard's show. They sat down near the front and Alanna noticed strange symbols painted all over the inside.

The wizard wore a long, purple robe embroidered with the same symbols when he came on stage. She thought that, despite his bright trappings, he seemed rather nondescript. He stood just over medium height with disordered blond hair and a crystal like the one Jerevan wore on a golden chain around his neck. That surprised Alanna, because nothing else about him looked genuine and she had assumed that, as a carnival wizard, he must be a fraud.

The lights dimmed yet the carnival wizard stood out. It startled Alanna to realize that he was outlined by a faint aura.

"Good afternoon, ladies and gentlemen. My name is Ashe. I am, as you can see, a wizard, and my aim is to entertain you."

She watched idly at first, more aware of the man sitting beside her than she was of the objects on the stage that the wizard made appear and disappear. Yet, as the tension of the crowd grew, she watched with more interest.

Then the wizard said, "But that's enough of childish things. You want to ask questions of Lord Thevrai, don't you?"

"Yes!" the crowd shouted.

"Then you shall." He threw something to the ground at his feet and there was an explosion of light and color. Alanna blinked and when she could see again the wizard had vanished. A view of a valley lined with mountains took his place. Snow capped the mountains, but the valley itself looked green and lush.

The wizard's voice came, disembodied, from the air, "This is the Vale of Elgandrach in Zamarga. Here lives one of the oldest of the worms of the earth. Sometimes he answers questions for those who ask him politely. Do any of you have questions?"

An excited but awed murmur of assent came from the audience and the viewpoint of the vision changed, moving toward the far end of the valley. A cave lay at the base of a cliff.

As they seemed to approach, a nightmarish creature emerged from the cave. A head like a giant snake's rose above a massive serpentine body that extended out of sight into the cave. On its back, about seven meters behind its head, there were what looked like vestigial wings, but surely, thought Alanna, that beast could never have been meant to fly. It was enormous, endless, as coil after snake-like coil emerged from the cave, each coil thicker around than the height of a grown man.

The disembodied voice spoke again, "Meet Lord Thevrai, Sky Lord and Dragon Ruler, one of the eldest of the worms of the earth. Once, in his youth, he could fly, but that was many thousands of years ago in the springtime of the world."

The voice rose in volume and the wizard appeared in the glowing scene, standing before the dragon's head. "How old are you, Lord Thevrai?"

The dragon stirred, the great coils shifting until he towered above the puny figure of the wizard. Then a voice like the clashing of cymbals said, "Years beyond measure, wizard, as you well know. I was born when the gods still walked the world and even the mountains were young." There was no anger in the voice, only a dry amusement, as though this were a ritual that they had played out many times before.

"You have an audience, Lord Thevrai. Will you answer their questions?"

"For the usual price," the dragon's voice rang through the tent, "and those that I can answer. I'm old, but not omniscient."

The wizard disappeared from the scene and his voice came again, disembodied, in the tent, "Who has the first question to put to Lord Thevrai?"

"Ask him what the harvest will be like next year," someone shouted.

"Lord Thevrai cannot foresee the future," the wizard said.

"Who stole my watch that my grandfather gave me?" another voice called out of the audience.

"Come and stand before Lord Thevrai and he shall answer you."

A man rose in the audience and then, as though transported, he materialized within the vision, standing in front of the dragon. As he restated his question, another scene appeared in the air inside the first scene that still held the man and the dragon. This new image was apparently visible to both the audience and the occupants of the original vision. It showed the man who was standing before the dragon in different clothes and in another place. After a moment another, smaller man bumped into him and, clearly apparent to the audience, picked his pocket.

"Jehan, if that isn't Pele Griff," the man standing in front of the dragon shouted. Moments later he was transported back to his seat and the wizard's voice asked for another question.

Several more people asked about stolen or missing articles and had the thefts or objects shown to them. Then someone in the audience cried out, "We've heard that the Dragon Banner has risen again in the west. Is that true?"

The hard, ringing tones of the dragon cried out, "Behold the Valley of the Gwatar and the Road of Masters."

The scene within a scene, which had shown the succession of petty thefts and missing items, expanded to show a river valley, the hills around it parched and golden in the sun. A road paved with great blocks of stone ran down the length of the valley next to the river. Wide enough for twenty men to ride abreast, it supported rank after rank of the mounted troops of Gandahar, soldiers riding the great scaled lizard-birds called maliks. The dragon's voice came harsh on their ears, "They marched so to Lamash last fall, one hundred thousand strong. In the spring they plan to attack Belkova and the city states of the Valley of the Ranaodh."

There was silence in the tent as the vision faded. The dragon spoke once more, "Enough." The vision of the Vale of Elgandrach also faded, until only the wizard was left on the stage.

Ashe smiled. "As Lord Thevrai has said, enough. Thank you ladies and gentlemen." He bowed and walked off the stage. There was an overwhelming round of applause as the audience threw off the numbness the visions induced.

Alanna would have left with the rest, but Jerevan stopped her. He waited until most of the crowd left and then guided her up onto the stage and through the curtain to the back of the tent. They found the wizard in a small curtained area to one side, removing his stage makeup. Jerevan motioned for Alanna to have a seat and she sat down cautiously on a rickety chair.

"That last scene was effective, Ashe. What month was it?" Jerevan asked.

"Redri. I was there. I reported what you've just seen to the Council of Kovarain in Lara, but I don't think they'll muster much opposition. Too busy arguing about who'll pay for it, if they have to hire mercenaries." Ashe snorted. "I wish old Kennar Larkin were still Kovarai of Lara. His grandson's a fool."

He turned then and looked at Alanna. She felt the familiar, dizzy sensation of first contact with a wizard and a strong one. She drew a breath and tried to steady herself. "It was real then?"

"Of course." Ashe cleaned his face of makeup, revealing a dark tan, and removed his embroidered robe. Under it he wore plain cord riding breeches and a linen shirt. Without the ornamental trappings, he looked like anyone she might meet in the street. Except for the contrast of his tan with his pale hair, he was in no way remarkable.

Jerevan said, "Ashe, you haven't met my new apprentice, Alanna Cairn, Tamrai of Fell. Alanna, this is the Wizard Ashe, one of the strongest wizards I know, and one of the best teachers. If he'd been in Ilwheirlane when you arrived in Ninkarrak, you'd be his pupil now."

"I'm pleased to meet you," Alanna said. "I never expected to meet a real wizard at a carnival."

Ashe looked sharply at Jerevan, but laughed, the dark face splitting to reveal flashing white teeth, "I wasn't born a nobleman. I have my living to earn and why not in a carnival? It keeps me in practice. Also, as you saw, it's a useful way of spreading information, if I wish to."

"Have you been watching the north?" Jerevan asked.

"Yes," Ashe frowned. "I don't like the feel of it."

"No. There's too much anger," Jerevan agreed.

"What do you mean?" Alanna asked, looking at Jerevan.

He returned her gaze, one eyebrow arched. "It's too complicated to explain now. We'll discuss it this evening." He turned back to Ashe. "I'll need you soon. You'll stay nearby?"

"I've got an engagement in Ninkarrak all next month. I can prolong it until summer, if I must," Ashe said. "There'll be work then with the fair."

Jerevan frowned. "It's important Ashe. There's a crisis coming. This storm may precipitate it."

"You think I can't feel what's coming?" Ashe demanded, his eyes narrowing. "It's not something I want to challenge. I'm not sure anyone should."

"Idiot," Jerevan said, his face breaking into a smile. "Did you really think I'd ask you to fight that?"

Ashe's face relaxed. "Sorry." He tilted his head. "But you've always supported Vanith?"

"I still do," Jerevan said, "but she and I both agree I have another duty in this case. Those who'll accompany her do so on their own."

Ashe nodded. "What can I do then?"

Jerevan looked at both Ashe and Alanna, as if weighing them, then turned back to Ashe. "You can help me steal a counter from the board."

Ashe's face lit with understanding. "The child, Inanda spoke of a child."

Alanna looked back and forth between them. "What are you talking about? What crisis? What child?"

Jerevan said, "You'll know this evening, Alanna."

"Why not now?"

"Because Ashe has a schedule and we're holding him up."

She was about to protest again when she realized that this wasn't the time or place to argue with him. She sat back and listened, hoping to pick up further information on her own.

"Will Magra be coming back from Cibata?" Ashe asked.

"Yes, Magra, Rainal and Kindric. It'll leave us short-handed there, but that can't be helped and at least Cibata has a good crop of journeymen."

"What about Vitry and Basel? I passed them in Zamarga last month. Did you send for them, too?"

"I sent for as many wizards as could be spared without stripping our operations bare, if they had any chance of getting here before summer," Jerevan said, frowning.

Ashe looked distressed and seemed about to say something more, but Jerevan interrupted, "It's time we headed back, or we'll be caught in the storm. Congratulations, by the way: It's amazing how much Thevrai picked up, and your performance has improved, too."

"I give Thevrai my routes these days so he'll know what areas to watch. I also let him do more of the spiel. His voice is more impressive than mine." Ashe turned to Alanna. "A pleasure to meet you, Tamrai Cairn. I hope I'll see you again."

"Thank you. I hope so too," she said, rising. "I enjoyed your show. I've never seen anything like it. Was the dragon real, too?"

Ashe grinned. "He won't be pleased to hear you ask. He's vain. But vision is as much a curse as a gift by the time a dragon reaches Thevrai's age. He's clairvoyant over vast distances and, once he's experienced something, he never forgets it. Somewhere in his memory he has events recorded all the way back to when the gods walked the world."

"I'd heard of elder dragons being wise, but doesn't the sheer volume of memory confuse them."

Ashe nodded. "That's it exactly. After a time the memories flow together and get jumbled so they don't make much sense. He's great with recent history, though, anything within the last ten thousand years. Unfortunately, he's expensive." Ashe broke off and looked at Jerevan. "That reminds me. I'll need some more young bullocks, and they have to be fat. He's picky in his old age."

Jerevan laughed. "I'll contact the ranch in Pelona, but you're too soft with our venerable worm. You have to learn to bargain. He pretends he's forgotten or confused, but I don't entirely believe him. For the right price I imagine you could get him to remember back to the time when the towers were built."

Ashe shrugged. "Maybe you're right. I wouldn't want to try. I did him a favor once and he asked me what I'd like to know. I told him I wanted to see the truth about Vydarga." He broke off and grinned. "Nobody warned me about dragon enthusiasm. It seems the old snake took a fancy to Vydarga and watched every moment of his waking life from the time he was fifteen and first learned to see. What's more, generous ol' Thevrai was willing to let me see it all. Speeded up, of course, but even then it would have taken years. As it was, I was there for three weeks and we'd just covered the first slave rebellions and the declaration of freedom for Ilwheirlane. I swear I could write the definitive biography of Vydarga's early years."

Jerevan roared with laughter. "Jehan, that must have been quite a favor. You'll have to tell me what it was some time. I have a few questions I wouldn't mind having answered myself, but I'll remember to be specific about the timing."

Ashe grinned. "If any of them are about Vydarga, remember I'm the world's leading expert." He turned to Alanna, "It was a pleasure meeting you." His voice altered to a stage whisper, "I wish you luck." He nodded at Jerevan. "I've heard he eats apprentices for breakfast, but don't let that armor plating of his fool you, inside he's as tender as a hungry malik."

Jerevan grinned and punched him on the shoulder. "Mock my authority will you? Just wait and see what I have in store for you."

When they got back outside the tent, the swan sleigh awaited them. Jerevan helped her in and took the reins from the attendant. The western horizon glowed with brilliant salmon-colored clouds as they left and it was full dark by the time they arrived at Tormar House, the moon and stars obscured by the coming storm.

They didn't talk much during dinner, but when Malling cleared the main course away and left them with a platter of fruit and cheese, Alanna said, "There was something you were going to tell me, wasn't there?"

Jerevan nodded. "Yes. In fact, there's a great deal I need to tell you. I'm just not sure how to go about it."

"Why don't you start with why you never told me that you were Esalfar of the Varfarin."

He grinned. "I thought you'd realize that after the meeting with Ashe. Actually, I didn't tell you because I wanted to see how long it took you to figure it out for yourself." One eyebrow arched as he took in her outrage. He helped himself to a cotulume and began to separate the segments.

Alanna stared at him, striving for control. It was several moments before she felt in sufficient command of herself to speak. "All right," she said finally, "why do you want me angry?"

He laughed. "I don't, not really. I just told you the truth. You should have realized I was Esalfar long ago."

"Lord Colne refused to tell me."

"That in itself should have identified me," Jerevan said. "Who else would Errian have tried to protect? He knew you were prejudiced against me. He didn't think giving you my name in another context would help. Particularly as you were bound to meet Aavik and might be indiscreet."

Alanna looked down, unable to meet his eyes.

Jerevan sighed. "I suppose the best way to start is to tell you about another of the karionin."

"Which one?"

"Cyrkarion." He looked down at the cotulume sections on his plate and began to spread one with cheese. "Cyrkarion was Cormor's own crystal. Before he died, he took it north into Akyrion and hid it. He told Elgan, his grandson, that no one would find it except the one for whom it was meant. Cormor was the most powerful of all the great wizards. He saw as the eslarin see, all the spectra of energy even to the level of the spinning particles that make up matter itself, and he held that sight naturally all his waking hours, often for days at a time. The Council of Wizards only required a wizard to be able to hold the high sight for twelve hours to be classified as a great wizard."

He paused and ate one of the cotulume sections, his eyes reflective, then continued, "Some have also said of Cormor that he could see the future, or some of the possible futures, not as the sibyls perceive it, but as the gods do." He offered a cotulume segment to Alanna.

She shook her head. "So Cyrkarion is hidden in Akyrion?"

"No, not since last year."

"Who found it?"

His eyes met hers. "Rhys Cinnac walked into the mountains of Akyrion last summer and found Cyrkarion as easily as though a trail had been blazed for him." Jerevan paused. "You've asked several times what crisis was coming. I know my lack of answers has irritated you, but until this morning there's been a question as to what form the crisis would take."

"Who is Rhys Cinnac? And what happened this morning?" She realized that she was gripping the carved arms of her chair.

"Rhys Cinnac is the grandson of Essitur, Idrim's younger brother. This morning he left Valkarn, his home. Even now he's riding toward Aire."

"The god-king from the north," she said, swallowing the lump that rose to fill her throat.

He nodded. "Yes. He's coming, Alanna. Until the time he left Valkarn, there was doubt. Even after the prophecy, no one knew for sure what he'd do. But this storm is of his making. All of northern Ilwheirlane is engulfed in a blizzard, and he's riding through it."

"What do you think will happen?"

Jerevan sighed. "I don't know. No one has any idea how he thinks, what he wants. Except that, right now, he's angry and his anger is deadly. But if he wants the position of Estahar, there's no one capable of stopping him. Nor do I think we should. The court needs cleaning out, and Rhys Cinnac would certainly do that."

"You saw this by farseeing?"

"Some of it." He leaned back in his chair. "For the rest, everyone at court has known of Rhys' birth for the last thirty years. The eslarin reported it to everyone in his family."

Alanna gasped. "He's the baneslar? Rhys Cinnac is 'he who should never have been born'?"

"Yes." Jerevan nodded. "Essitur's son Gar suffered from bouts of madness, but his father trained him as a wizard anyway. During one of his fits, he raped an eslar and deliberately implanted his seed."

Alanna shook her head. "No. I don't believe it. No one could force pregnancy on an eslar."

Jerevan's brow arched. "True. But Sallys al Anithal took Gar's madness to be the will of Maera."

Alanna sighed, running her finger along the design of carved wood in the arm of her chair. "So all the time he stayed in the background with his grandfather, the eslarin ignored his existence. But when a prophecy announced that he'd rule Ilwheirlane, they panicked and closed their borders."

"Precisely," he said. "If they do business with men this year, they'll do business with one whom Tarat has cursed."

She shut her eyes. "You don't know what kind of person he is? Whether he truly is another Edain?"

"No. With his eslar blood he's really still a child and his actions have been unpredictable." Jerevan ran a hand through his hair. "It doesn't help that, from what we've been able to establish, Essitur, his grandfather, is nearly as demented as Gar was."

"But you're not planning to try to stop Rhys?"

"No," Jerevan said. "I'm Esalfar of the Varfarin. If I fight him, I set the Varfarin against him. Both Vanith and I agree that such a course would be madness. On the other hand, there are individual members of the Varfarin who will stand by Vanith and Idrim. They know it may come to a battle. We're hoping, however, that some kind of bargain can be struck."

Alanna pushed her plate away, remembering her meeting with Vanith, the woman's strength and her pride.

"Come," Jerevan said, getting up and coming around the table to her side, "it's time we got some rest. It's been a long day."

"Yes." Alanna let him pull her to her feet. The warmth of his hands was reassuring, but tonight there was no passion in his eyes. He looked weary, and it occurred to her that he'd spent a large part of the day far-seeing, despite his other activities.

He nodded. "Yes. I'm tired, too tired to even think about the other issues between us tonight." He kissed her on the forehead and released her. She was surprised at how much comfort such a gentle caress gave her.

The next morning Alanna went back to work with new energy, despite the violent storm that raged outside. Jerevan seemed amused by her intensity.

"Ease up, Alanna. The single hardest learning step may be behind you, but you've a long road ahead of you before you'll be a real wizard. I've been studying for roughly three quarters of a century and I'm not yet fully trained. Cormor was one hundred when he qualified as a member of the Council, and he was the youngest ever to so qualify. What's more, he started his training at the age of six. I have decades of study ahead of me before I reach his level of skill."

"Then how can you possibly teach me enough to let me to go home in just a few weeks?"

He laughed. "You don't need to know much to call for help. I never expected to turn you into a wizard in so short a time. I only need to teach you enough to enable you to erect a barrier and call me if you're attacked. Actually, Vyrkarion will almost erect the barrier for you. What I have to teach you is how to call for help with your mind if you need it."

He spent the whole day with her, trying to teach her to sense his sending, to "see" the energy of his thoughts with her mind. "It's simply a different form of energy," he told her. "If you can sense the life force in your body and the movement of gases and energy in a flame, then you can learn to sense the energy of a mind directed at you, and learn to direct your own mental energy outward."

Later, he said, "You can see the sunlight, the different colors have different wavelengths. The energy of the mind is just a different wavelength in the spectrum of energies."

Alanna strove to stretch herself to new limits of sensitivity, but the closest she got was a feeling of irritation, like an itch inside her head, whenever Jerevan said he was sending to her.

He told her that was a good sign, but she was depressed that night at dinner. The storm that prevented their afternoon ride did nothing to lighten her mood.

"Cheer up," Jerevan said as they finished their meal. "Imagine if you hadn't been sensitized by Vyrkarion and hadn't had a healer's training. You couldn't have expected to reach your present level of expertise for over a year."

"Did it take you that long?"

"No," he grimaced, "but I was a child when I learned mind speech. It was my later training that was difficult. I, too, was an adult before I started serious study."

"What made you do it? I mean, why did you want to become a wizard?" Something in Jerevan's expression made Alanna pause, and she finished, "I'm sorry. I didn't mean to pry."

Jerevan's expression was grim, but he shook his head. "You're not prying. You have a right to know my motives." Yet he hesitated, either gathering his thoughts or choosing how to phrase them.

"I didn't want to be a wizard," he said at last. "I'm related to the House of Cinnac, though, so I was examined for talent at birth. I showed exceptional promise and Derwen pleaded with my parents to be allowed to train me. My mother was a worshiper of Miune and opposed to wizardry. My father, respecting her beliefs, refused. The law required that I be trained as a healer, as you were taught, but he forbade anyone to instruct me further. Derwen cheated a little and sent a wizard to teach me healing, so I was actually close to being a Healer First Class before my training stopped, but it was stopped when I was five."

Jerevan paused. "My father died when I was nineteen. Derwen came to me then and asked me to become his apprentice, but I'd just inherited the hetrion and the study of wizardry was the last thing from my mind. I refused."

He picked up a marin nut from the bowl in the center of the table. "Derwen renewed his plea three years later, after my mother died. I refused again, even though that time he warned me that I'd regret it. He was old. He'd never been a great wizard and he knew his powers were failing. Cormor made him responsible for finding someone with real talent to succeed him, and he took that responsibility seriously. He was desperate and I was a vain and foolish young man."

Jerevan broke off and the shell of the nut in his hand cracked with a snap. His eyes revealed the memory of pain. The long, slender fingers unclenched and Alanna saw that the nut had been crushed. What memories could still disturb him so much after all this time?

Jerevan recalled himself with an effort, discarding the crumbled nut and wiping his hands. He continued more lightly, "He cursed me. I had to study wizardry to undo the effect of the curse. It was unpleasant and gave me an unparalleled motive for intensive study. You remarked at our first meeting that rumor said that I was grotesque before I became a wizard. For once, rumor was correct, but what you see now is my natural form, Alanna."

She bit her lip. "I'm sorry. I said a lot of things that night that I now regret."

Alanna wanted to ask him about the basis for the other rumors regarding him, but remembered the expression on his face when she'd asked him why he had become a wizard and held her tongue. If he wanted her to know, he'd tell her, but she shrank from causing him such pain twice in one night.

Instead, she said, "If you aren't planning to fight Rhys, what are you planning?"

He smiled. "I've been waiting for you to ask that. But, Alanna, it isn't simply a matter of what I'm planning, not anymore; it's what we're going to do, you and I. Whatever we do from now on, we'll do together."

Her eyes widened. "Then what will we be doing?"

"We're going to save the child."

Alanna's brow furrowed. "You spoke of a child with Ashe, the child of the prophecy, but the prophecy never said what child?"

"I know of only one child whose fate could be critical to Ilwheirlane, and that child is Aubrey Cinnac." He looked up and met her eyes. "Inanda spoke of Vyrkarion coming out of the south in the same breath as she said that the child had to be saved, or the coming age would be an age of chaos. Vyrkarion will be needed to save Aubrey." His eyes rose to meet hers. "You must learn quickly, Alanna."

"You told me just this morning that I can't begin to learn enough to aid you, not for years," she said, stunned.

"There is a way."

Alanna stared at him, knowing what he was going to say, terrified that he would say it. The silence stretched and she realized that he was waiting for her response. He didn't have to say anything more; he knew she understood. "I could link with you," she said. "That is what you mean, isn't it?"

Jerevan nodded. "It's been between us since we met. We might as well discuss it outright. A linkage would advance your training and enable me to use your will and the power of Vyrkarion to enhance my own strength."

"But once formed, it can't be broken."

He rose and walked around the table to stand by her chair. When she made no move, he drew her to her feet, pulling her up against his body. Then he kissed her. His lips felt warm and firm; her lips parted beneath them. He tasted good. Her hands rose to let her fingers explore the thick springiness of his hair and the smooth, hard muscles of his back through his shirt. His kiss was as sweet as she had feared it would be, so sweet she drowned in the feel of it, until the Talisman grew hot, burning her breast and bringing her back to reality.

Jerevan must have felt it, too, for he released her, his breathing as uneven as hers. Their eyes met. "I do desire you. The attraction between us is strong and Vyrkarion wants us to link," he said, "but your reservations are valid. There are no secrets in such a linkage and my past contains much that cannot help but disgust you."

Alanna stared at him, shaken. "You could have forced the linkage. I couldn't have stopped you, not just now and not when you first started my training."

"Yes. I could have, but I won't. I'll never link with you, Alanna, until you tell me that you are absolutely sure that such a link is what you want. You have my word."

She wanted to draw the Talisman out and go back into his arms, linking with him forever. Yet, she also wanted to run away from him and everything a relationship with him might mean. The rumors she'd heard about him were obviously untrue, but what was true?

Jerevan had lived a whole lifetime she knew nothing about. If she linked with him, never mind his talk of things that would disgust her and all the rumors, wouldn't she lose herself in his much greater experience?

"I can't," she said, shaking her head. She backed away from him. "Not yet." She turned and ran to her room.

XIX

4731, 474th Cycle of the Year of the Dragon
Month of Dirga
And while he was a prisoner,
It was a time of strife,
When wicked men conspired
And sought to end his life.
Life, life for the Wanderer
Wherever he may be,
Though he is doomed to exile
By the shore of Sorrow Sea.

— FROM *THE BALLAD OF AUBREY THE WANDERER* BY ANONYMOUS

Minta was on her way down to the kitchen when she saw Lord Horgen on the stairwell below her. She pulled back on the landing and flattened herself against the wall, hoping he was on his way down rather than up. She had no desire to be mauled by him or slobbered over in the dim privacy of the stairwell.

When she heard his steps descending, she sighed with relief and peeked over the railing in time to see him go through the door to Naharil Thurin's apartment two floors below. She crept down the stairs after him, thinking to get past and down to the kitchen before he emerged.

When she reached the landing outside the Naharil's rooms, however, she saw that the door was slightly ajar. A clot of mud had lodged in the sill preventing it from closing. She stared at the gap, remembering what Vanith said about knowing Lord Horgen's plans. Then, not allowing herself to think what might happen if Horgen were to emerge, she put her ear to the crack. Silence. She opened the door wider and peeked inside.

The antechamber was laid out like Vanith's and it was unoccupied. Minta stepped inside. Two doors led out of the room, aside from the one by which she had just entered. She knew that, if the layout were the same as Vanith's, the right one would open onto a hall leading to Thurin's study and sitting room, and the left one would lead directly to his bedroom.

She tiptoed to the left door and opened it a crack. The room beyond was a well lit hall. She saw a section of the sitting room and heard Thurin's voice raised in anger. She closed the door as Horgen crossed her field of vision, relieved that he was facing the other way. Her breath came in short gasps and she looked with longing at the exit to the stairwell, but she tiptoed back across the anteroom to the other door.

While there was little illumination in the room beyond, it was clearly Thurin's bedroom. Leaving the door to the anteroom open, she slipped inside. The curtains were drawn and no lamp had been lit, but she could see a line of light under the door that connected the bedroom with the sitting room. She could also hear the murmur of voices. She crossed the room and pressed her ear against the door.

Horgen's voice was raised in anger. "Don't be a fool," he said and then his voice lowered into an indistinguishable jumble.

Minta took the door handle and twisted it. When she had turned it as far as it would go she eased the door back until it was open a crack.

"You're a madman," she heard Horgen say. "You don't stand a chance of staying alive if Rhys takes over, no matter how many waivers of right to inherit you sign."

"I'll hand the boy over to him," Thurin said. "That will prove my good faith. His claim's better than mine anyway, with the boy dead."

Minta crouched behind the door and shut her eyes. She didn't dare try to look at them. All she could do was listen, and hope that Thurin needed nothing from his bedroom.

"Nonsense," Horgen said. "You know the chances of his letting you live are minuscule, and even if, by some miracle, he doesn't kill you, there's no hope of your being allowed to remain in Ninkarrak. If Rhys takes the throne of Ilwheirlane, your best chance is being exiled to your own estates or, more likely, out of the country. With your tastes, I think you'd find that difficult."

"Well, what better idea can you come up with? You weren't so smug and superior yourself a few months ago." Thurin sounded like a sulky child.

"That was before I had the good fortune to meet someone who can actually do something about Rhys." Minta heard satisfaction in Horgen's voice.

"Impossible! You know as well as I do there isn't a wizard in the human lands with a chance of challenging him, not even my precious cousin Leyburn."

"Who said anything about the human lands."

"What do you mean?"

"I mean," Horgen said, "that the best wizards aren't found in the human lands any longer. I've made contact with an agent of Aavik. He told me that, for a price, he could assemble enough wizards to destroy even Rhys."

"Who's Aavik?" Thurin asked. "And what kind of price?"

"Come now, use what few wits you have. Aavik is the Estahar of Gandahar. Don't you pay attention to anything but the gratification of your senses?"

"You're a fine one to talk."

"At least I use my intelligence."

"By that I suppose you're implying I don't," Thurin said, "but who thought of imprisoning the brat. Why, Vanith could have taken him out of here at any time, if I hadn't seen to it."

"I've already told you my opinion of that ill-considered action. You've all but notified Vanith in writing of your intentions." Horgen paused, and Minta heard a sound like glasses clinking together and then the sound of liquid being poured. "But that's irrelevant. What matters now is stopping Rhys, and we can only do that if we can meet Aavik's terms."

"How do you know you can trust him?"

"I don't trust him, but it's to his advantage as much as ours to dispose of Rhys. The last thing he wants is a strong wizard ruling Ilwheirlane."

"Why doesn't he stop Rhys by himself then, if he can? Why does he need to deal with us?" Minta flattened herself against the wall as Thurin's voice came from just the other side of the door. She heard his shoes scuff the carpet as he turned back to face Horgen.

"Even Aavik doesn't dare face Rhys without one of the living crystals. The agent I spoke to said that Rhys has Cyrkarion and any other wizard, or group of wizards, who attempt to oppose him would have to have a living crystal of their own for there to be any likelihood of success."

"So, what good is that!" Thurin exclaimed. "We have less chance of coming up with a wizard stone than he does."

"Ah, but that's just it. We do have a way of getting a crystal for Aavik. There's one here in Ninkarrak, and what makes it better, it's being carried by an untrained woman. I've even met her. Pretty thing, but haughty."

Minta shivered at the leering tone in Horgen's voice. She wished she could leave, but they hadn't said anything definite about their plans. She tried to control her breathing.

"How did you find that out?" Thurin asked. "It doesn't sound likely to me."

"Aavik's agent told me. Aavik apparently attempted to kidnap the woman, after verifying that she has the crystal, but Leyburn interfered."

"I don't like it," Thurin said. "If Leyburn's guarding her, what chance will we have to get near her, much less get the stone from her?"

"That's where we have an edge over Aavik," Horgen chuckled. "He's failed once, and his agent admits that he doesn't know where Leyburn's keeping the girl now, but I know where he's going to bring her soon."

"Where's that?"

"Here, to the Tower. Vanith wants to meet her, and she's bound to bring the Talisman with her for a royal audience."

"The Talisman?" Thurin sounded confused.

"Yes, the Talisman of Anor. We have to deliver the crystal to Aavik, preferably with the girl still living. Then he'll be able to face Rhys. His agent says he has eleven strong wizards with him now and more on the way. When Aavik and one of his agents form a linkage with the stone, they'll be powerful enough to overcome even Rhys with the Sword of Cormor."

"Does Theolan know you've been dealing with the isklarin?"

"Of course not!" Horgen said. "For Miune's sake, don't say anything to him about this. He'd have a fit and damn us all."

"So you don't dare tell Idrim, either. How's he going to feel if his precious throne gets saved by a bunch of lizards?"

"He won't be around to feel anything," Horgen said. "Aavik will make sure that Rhys finishes off Idrim, Vanith and that little snake Arrel before he meets his own end. That will make you the boy's Regent and me your advisor."

"What if Theolan finds out?"

"How could he, unless one of us tells him? Aavik assures me that Theolan's staff will soon be neutralized and the Gandaharan troops will all be properly uniformed as Royal Guards. In the confusion of mustering the army, I've been able to assign any posts I want."

"You mean there are isklarin soldiers here, too, not just wizards?"

"Aavik brought troops, yes. After all, if Rhys succeeds in taking the throne, the whole balance of power around the Thallassean would be upset." Horgen added, "You don't believe all that nonsense Theolan preaches about the malice of the were-peoples, do you?"

"No..."

"Well, forget it. Aavik's interests and ours coincide right now."

"But how do you know you're going to be able to deliver the stone? What will Aavik do if you don't? I don't like it. It scares me, dealing with were-folk. And how do you know Leyburn plans to bring this woman to meet Vanith? If Aavik didn't tell you that, how did you find out?"

"One of my men heard Vanith issue the invitation when Colne introduced them back at the Sun Day ball. The date was set several weeks ago. It wasn't kept then, but if Vanith wants to meet the girl, they're bound to arrange another meeting soon."

"That sounds a bit uncertain. How do you know they haven't already met?"

"They couldn't have. I've had agents watching Vanith for months and she hasn't slipped away from them once. No, I'm certain the meeting is still in the future."

"What do I get out of this? Why bring me in, if you could hand over the girl yourself? I don't want to kowtow to Aavik any more than I want to kowtow to Rhys," Thurin protested.

"Don't worry," Horgen sneered, "Aavik knows he can't conquer Ilwheirlane. All he wants is custody of the boy until he's grown. During that time, he's willing to let you be Regent."

"So he wants the boy, does he? Then it's just as well I stopped Vanith from leaving with him, isn't it?"

"I keep telling you, Vanith wouldn't have taken him anywhere, you fool," Horgen said. "And if she wanted to take him, do you think your idiot guards could stop her? Remember, she may not be powerful, but she is a wizard. She could walk right by them with the boy, if she wanted to."

"Then why hasn't she?"

"Because she's still Heir Apparent. She'll stand by her oath to her father to the end. She's stupid, but she isn't a coward. When Idrim rides north with the army to meet Rhys, Vanith will be by his side and she'll make no move to have Aubrey taken to safety until after she and Idrim have left."

"How do you know?"

"I understand how she thinks and how you think, your highness," Horgen said, "so don't think you'll be able to get rid of me once you're Regent. You'll continue to do what I tell you to, or some of your personal habits will be made public, and, if that happens, you know the Privy Council will appoint someone else."

"You're no frost flower yourself."

"The difference between us, your highness, is that I'm a thorough man and can prove what I say."

There was a silence of some moments and Minta pictured the two of them glaring at each other. She was afraid to leave without the cover of their voices to hide any sound she might make.

"All right, what do you want me to do?" Thurin asked.

"Aavik wants to have at least one of his men at every entry and exit of the Tower to intercept the girl when she tries to enter. Being wizards, they'll also serve the purpose of guaranteeing that the boy stays where he is. Even the least of them is stronger than Vanith," Horgen said.

Minta was afraid to wait longer. While they were still talking, she tiptoed back across Thurin's bedroom and through the door into the antechamber, closing it behind her. She opened the door onto the stairwell landing, slipped through and closed it, dislodging the mud so that it closed all the way. Then she ran for Vanith's chambers.

She was trembling when she reached them and knocked on the door. Lady Elriggan was on duty and seemed surprised by Minta's appearance, but she admitted her at once.

"I'll see if Her Highness will see you. Have a seat for a moment," she said.

Minta sank into the chair, trying to control her shivering.

Lady Elriggan reemerged from Vanith's room immediately. "Go right in, Minta."

Minta went in and closed the door behind her. Then she fell to her knees at Vanith's feet, sobbing.

"What is it, Minta?"

"They're going to guard the Tower with wizards. Naharil Thurin is going to sell Aubrey to Aavik. Oh, it was awful."

It took Vanith some time to make sense of Minta's disjointed narrative, but then she said, "You were very brave, Minta. I'm grateful for what you did, and thankful they didn't catch you."

"Oh, your highness, I was so scared, I thought I'd faint and they'd find me."

Vanith stroked Minta's hair and said, "I must get another message to Jerevan, warning him of the wizards on guard. He won't be able to bring Tamrai Cairn to see me now. I'll have to visit her, and for that he'll need to bring her to town. I can't go beyond Ninkarrak without my guards reporting my activities."

"Lord Horgen said he had men watching you all the time, that they've been watching you for months," Minta protested.

"Yes. I've known about them. I wasn't sure whose men they were, but I knew I was being watched," Vanith said. "If I need to, I can lose them for a few hours without their knowing it."

Minta wiped her eyes. "Tomorrow's Miunesday. I can tell Thrym tomorrow evening," she said. "I can even carry a message for him to give to Lord Leyburn."

"Yes." Vanith paused, considering. "That would be best."

"Oh!" Minta looked distracted. "I was just going down to the kitchen to fetch milk and some of the chef's meldarcanin when I saw Lord Horgen. Aubrey will wonder where I've got to."

"Who's with him?"

"Lena, the nursemaid. We were playing a game of the fathik and the hens and I'd lost a round, so I went for the refreshments," Minta said.

"Well, that's all right." Vanith smiled. "I'll see that refreshments are sent up to you. Why don't you just go back and rejoin your game. I'll come this evening after Lena has gone and we'll put together a message."

"Very well, your highness."

Miunesday dawned bright and cold. In the early afternoon, Minta walked down the hill from the park to the northern end of the harbor. It was too early to go to the Golden Ingling, so she decided to eat her lunch on a bench by one of the piers. She loved watching the ships with their colorful sails and exotic cargoes.

The ship docked in the slip in front of her was a huge four-masted bark, part of Ilwheirlane's merchant marine with a cargo from Nacaonne. The stevedores were unloading boxes of copperware, crates of plantains, kwaluccas, and mangoes and planks of a rich, dark wood.

Two piers down she saw an old fashioned galleon, stately but clumsy compared to more modern ships. She was wondering where it came from when she saw Lord Horgen mount the gangplank. A dark, saturnine man met him at the top and ushered him along the deck and into a cabin. Minta rose and started toward the market. Before she had gone far, however, she looked back and memorized the name of the ship, *Ilfargand*, the "Migrating Dragon." Then she hurried to get out of sight. She had no desire for Horgen to see her and think she was spying on him. The irony made her shiver.

When she met Thrym at the Golden Ingling, she told him all she had overheard and what she had seen that morning.

"The *Ilfargand*, you said?"

"Yes. It's a galleon in a slip at the north end of the harbor."

"I know the ship." Thrym nodded. "It's supposed to be from Kailane. The captain's been hiring in Farinmalith. He must have taken on over two hundred mercenaries."

"What would a ship captain from Kailane want with mercenaries?"

"That's what a number of people have been wondering but, if he's working for Aavik, I can guess," Thrym said. "Look, I was going to take you dancing tonight. A friend of mine's giving a private ball, and I thought you'd enjoy it, but now I want to see someone else first. Do you mind?"

"Of course not," she said. "I'm not dressed for a ball, and I've never liked dancing."

He frowned. "Your dress won't matter at this ball, and as for not liking to dance, you've just never danced with me." He drained the last of his ale and took her by the hand. "We'd better hurry."

By the time they reached the southern end of the market, the sun had set. The shops looked smaller and the goods less fine. Bars and cheap hotels lined the streets. Minta pressed closer to Thrym when a garishly dressed woman called out, "Want some variety, lesska?"

The streets narrowed and, though lamps still lit some corners, they grew less frequent. Minta had never gone in this direction, but she knew they were entering the Maze, what Thrym called the heart of Ninkarrak, Farinmalith.

"I wouldn't normally take you here, but I'll need to borrow a horse if I'm to take Vanith's message out to Leyburn, and my friend will appreciate knowing what you told me about the *Ilfargand*."

"What are you going to tell him?"

"That Aavik's behind the hiring. He was thinking of signing up himself, but thought the contract sounded scaly. I want to catch him before he changes his mind. He may also be able to tell me the names of some of the people already hired."

"Why do you want to know that?"

Thrym hesitated, then said, "It might come in useful. Leyburn's sure to want to know as much as possible about Aavik's activities."

"You think your friend will loan you a horse in return for the information."

Thrym laughed. "No. I think he'll lend me a horse because he's a friend. Just as I'll get the information to him as soon as possible because I know it'll make a difference to him."

It was dark when they stopped in front of a dilapidated wooden building at the end of a narrow cul-de-sac. Thrym rapped at the door in a complicated pattern. Minta looked, but she could see no light coming from the windows.

"Are you sure he's in? There aren't any lights," she said, looking over her shoulder at the alley behind them and trying to shake off the feeling of being watched. The darkness didn't conceal the dirt and decay. The twisting little lanes were too narrow, the buildings too close together; they pressed in on her, making it hard to breathe.

"Shh, he's coming. People in Farinmalith like privacy," Thrym whispered.

They waited and Minta began to shiver; she wasn't sure whether from cold or nervousness.

The door opened smoothly, without any of the creaks or groans Minta would have expected from its decrepit appearance. The man who ushered them in was also out of keeping with the exterior of his house. For one thing, he was enormous, well over two meters tall, Minta estimated, and his shoulders seemed as broad as those of any other two men. Thrym was tall and well built, but next to this man he looked like a child.

"Thrym," the giant said when the door closed behind them, "what're you doing here at this hour? I'd heard you were going to Flickra's ball." He glanced at Minta.

The entryway was dark, but Minta could see light coming from an open doorway toward the back. The floor was carpeted.

"Minta, this is Varl Ganna. Varl, meet Minta. We are going to the ball, but I wanted to talk to you first. I heard something that might interest you, and I need to borrow your horse tomorrow." He paused and asked, "You haven't signed with Satig yet, have you?"

The giant frowned. "I told you, I don't like the sound of it. There's too much he isn't saying. It's good to meet you," he added, nodding at Minta and ushering them into the lighted room at the back. "Why, do you have another job?"

Minta was surprised to see that the room was well furnished with sturdy, comfortable furniture. Heavy, black curtains covered all the windows, which explained the lack of light reaching the street. Varl

Ganna looked even bigger when Minta could see him clearly, and none of his size was accounted for by fat. His biceps were as thick around as the muscles of most men's thighs. His hair was long, hanging to his shoulders, and pure white.

"No. Just more information about that one," Thrym said, pulling Minta down beside him on the large, well-padded couch. "Satig's working for Aavik of Gandahar. What's more, Aavik's in Ninkarrak."

"How do you know?" Varl scowled. "If it's true, he's going to have a lot of unhappy mercenaries. Lorval would never have signed up for the isklarin. He's from Lamash."

"It's true. I can't tell you yet how I know, but from the evidence, I'm sure of it."

Varl slammed a fist into his other palm. "Agnith's fires! How would he dare such a thing?"

Thrym grinned. "You know the isklarin. Men are malarin. It probably never occurred to Aavik that anyone might find out."

Varl grinned back, "You lizards are an arrogant bunch of bastards. If you're right, though, it'll mean a Council meeting. Will you be able to testify to the source of your information before the Council?"

"I think so. I'll know tomorrow for sure. That is, if I can borrow your horse?"

"You know you can have him any time. He's more your horse than mine, anyway. He's not up to my weight," the giant added. "Would you like some wine before you go?"

"Not tonight. Don't have time. Was Flava going to the ball?" Thrym asked.

"Yes, I think so," Varl said. "He's been doing some work for Flickra. You'd better tell Flickra, too, while you're there. And tell him I'll meet him at the Corriden tomorrow afternoon, three o'clock."

"I'd planned to tell him anyway, but I'll give him your message. We'd better be going, though. I have to teach Minta that dancing's not so bad, if you've got the right partner." He put his arm around her, laughing as she flushed under both men's scrutiny.

"I envy you such an arduous labor." Varl grinned. "Yes, with so much work before you, you'd better get an early start."

Thrym rose, pulling Minta up with him. Then he clasped hands with the giant. "Depending on how things go, I may know someone in need of men some day soon."

Varl's eyes met Thrym's and Minta sensed the tension between them. Finally, Varl said, "I'll wait then. I need a rest anyway, but not more than two months. After that, I'll need a job or face starvation. There's a lot of me to feed."

"Thanks," Thrym said.

VYRKARION: THE TALISMAN OF ANOR

They arrived at the Duka about half an hour later. From the outside it was a handsome stone building with the symbol of a trident in gold on the awning in front. The music coming from it was loud enough to be heard for several blocks, and Minta saw groups of revelers entering and leaving in a steady stream. She also saw what Thrym meant by saying that her dress wouldn't matter. The revelers wore everything from actual rags to the most elaborate ball gowns Minta had ever seen, even at court. Thrym whispered, "Told you so," as he guided her through the throng to the ballroom.

Any receiving line that might have existed had long since broken up. There was no longer even a doorman on duty to announce the late arrivals. Thrym led her to a large table at the back of the room occupied by two men and a woman. The woman was beautiful, Minta thought, eyeing the jet black hair that contrasted so strikingly with the smooth, fair skin. The man next to her was big and blond and looked drunk. The other man sat across from the woman and her companion. Small and wiry with a thin, vulpine face and a thatch of graying, rust-colored hair, he eyed them curiously as they neared the table.

"Flickra," Thrym said, speaking to the smaller man who had watched them approach, "I want you to meet Minta. Minta, this is Rad Flickra, your host tonight." He lowered his voice and said, "I have information for you, and a message from Varl Ganna."

The vulpine man's eyes narrowed, and his glance darted across the table. "Not here. Mingle. We'll meet in the back room."

Thrym nodded. "Flava should know, too, and Elath since she's here."

Flickra's eyes went to the woman across the table from him. She was talking to the other man and hadn't appeared to notice Thrym and Minta's arrival but, when Flickra looked her way, she looked up immediately. Minta saw Flickra wink at her, a flutter of one eyelid that would have been imperceptible from a greater distance. Minta's eyes went back to the black haired woman in time to see the almost invisible signal returned. Even the man next to her, seeing her in profile, couldn't have noticed.

Flickra grinned at Thrym. "She'll be there, but it better be good. Elath's got a valar tonight." He looked at Minta and added, "She won't like the competition, either."

Thrym's voice hardened. "The information's worth it, and Minta's with me."

Flickra grinned. "No offense meant."

Thrym nodded. "None taken. Come on, Minta. You still haven't had a chance to learn what dancing's all about."

He helped her off with her coat and led her onto the floor. The dance was a shalla, a dance she hated because it had given Sandor an excuse to paw her in public. Yet this evening, with Thrym's arm at her waist, his hand clasping her's and his warm amber gaze devouring her, the whole act of dancing took on an entirely new meaning for her. She felt light-footed and beautiful. His firm hands guided her through the steps and Minta found it easy to let her body follow where he led. She felt as though she were floating, lost in the stately rhythms of the music and the warmth of his touch.

The next dance was a country dance and, though she was parted physically from Thrym at times by the movements, their eyes stayed linked. She couldn't have said whether they'd been dancing for minutes or hours when he led her off the floor. She only knew she didn't want to stop.

Thrym grinned at her. "I know. I don't want to stop, either, but I've got a meeting to attend. And you have to be back at the Tower by eleven. It's after nine now."

He took her into another room where platters of food were laid out, both hot and cold. They helped themselves, then Thrym took their plates and guided her out through a back door. They went down a narrow corridor and up some stairs to another hall. Thrym handed her the plates and knocked on the third door.

It was opened by a man Minta hadn't seen before. Behind him she saw Flickra and the woman, Elath, sitting at a round table playing cards.

"Hello, Flava," Thrym said. "Hoped I'd find you here tonight."

Flava was a pale-skinned, sandy-haired man of medium height. Minta thought him nondescript until he grinned in response to Thrym's greeting and his face took on a puckish air.

"No one's hanged you yet?" Flava asked, shutting the door behind them.

"Have to catch me first," Thrym said.

When they were all seated at the table, Elath said, "So what's the emergency? Had a live one, but he probably won't wait, so it better be good."

"How's Fal, Elath?" Thrym asked and Minta heard concern in his voice.

An expression Minta couldn't recognize flashed across Elath's face. Then she shrugged. "As usual."

Thrym grimaced. "Sorry." He glanced at Flickra, who shook his head.

Minta wondered at Thrym's hesitation, but he continued, "I wanted to warn you to be careful of Satig. He's hiring for Aavik of Gandahar. What's more, it's probable that Aavik himself is in Ninkarrak right now."

There was a moment of stunned silence. Then Flickra said, "How do you come to know this, Thrym? It's not that I doubt you, but my sources are usually good and I've heard nothing."

Thrym said, "I can't tell you my source, now. I'll have to clear it with him first. The point is he overheard a conversation between a man who'd talked with an agent of Aavik's and another man. The first man was quite clear in saying that Aavik and eleven other wizards of Gandahar are currently in Ninkarrak. He was planning to meet with Aavik's agent again, and this morning my source saw him board the galleon *Ilfargand*."

"What does the girl have to do with this?" Elath asked. This close to her, Minta saw that she had eyes like sapphires. She looked arrogant, almost regal, with her head held high, and her tall, slender body displayed by the low-cut gown.

"My name is Minta. I'm a friend of Thrym's. He wanted to take me dancing tonight," Minta said.

Flickra glanced at Thrym oddly. "So you're developing your own sources. I'll have to keep an eye on you." He hesitated, frowning. "What did Varl have to say? I take it he hadn't signed with Satig when you told him?"

"No. He'd been leery before I spoke to him. He said Lorval signed, though."

There was another silence at the table. Then Flava laughed. "That'll be a short contract, if what you say is true. Lorval would forfeit all he has not to fight in that camp."

Flickra's sharp face looked pinched. He said, "He's not the only one. I can think of more than a dozen who've signed with equally good reasons to hate the isklarin. I assume that Varl will call a Council meeting. When does he want it?"

"Three o'clock at the Corriden."

"Will you be there?"

The question came from Elath. Minta was surprised by the sharpness of the tone.

Thrym frowned. "I hope to be back by then. I have an errand to run in the morning."

Elath's brows knit. "Having made the accusation, you'd better be there to justify it. If you're not, the whole meeting will be chaos. I hadn't told Flickra, yet, but I signed with Satig this morning."

The others stiffened. Thrym said, "What do you plan to do? Tell him of my accusations?"

Elath bit her lip. "No, not yet. If you're right, my contract is void. I insist on a Rav clause. I think Lorval does, too." She paused, then added bitterly, "But a lot of the men don't, especially when they're as hungry as we've all been this year, and Satig didn't want to put one in for me. I should have known something was wrong, from the way he argued about it."

"What'll you do, Elath?" Flickra's voice was hard.

"If you prove what you've said at the Council meeting, I'm out of a contract and no danger. If you can't prove it, I'll demand Council truce of half an hour, and notify Satig of the accusation."

Flickra nodded and Thrym said, "That's fair. I should've asked if any of you had signed a contract recently."

There was a slight relaxation of tension, but the atmosphere was still strained. Flickra said, "That's all we can do tonight then." He eyed Thrym and added, "Don't be late tomorrow."

Thrym nodded and rose. "Come on, Minta. It's time I took you home."

XX

Win saiven hesav nith,
kor niles hesavetwe wa maidom.

"Many foods feed fire,
but the hottest are fed by hatred."

— ESLARIN PROVERB

Alanna and Jerevan were finishing breakfast when Malling announced the stranger, a tall, dark man with an air of cocky self-confidence. He was plainly dressed in boots, cord pants and a brown leather jerkin.

Jerevan greeted him with a frown. "Thrym, what brings you here?"

Thrym glanced pointedly at Malling and Alanna. "I have a message for you, to be delivered in private."

"That's all right. Alanna will hear whatever you have to say, anyway, so you may as well tell her at the same time you tell me." He gestured for Thrym to sit down. "Will you have something to eat?"

Thrym looked at the sideboard and accepted eagerly. "Thank you, your grace. It's a long ride out here for someone as little used to horses as me. I'm starved."

"Fine. Malling, will you set another place."

When Malling left, Jerevan turned to Thrym. "What's happened?"

Thrym pulled a folded piece of paper from inside his jerkin and handed it to Jerevan. "Not all of it's in the note, though. Minta saw something else yesterday morning when she was down by the harbor waiting to deliver that to me."

Jerevan scanned the note. "Horgen's made a deal with Aavik. How cozy for them. What would Theolan think?" He looked up. "What could Minta add to this?"

"She saw Horgen board the *Ilfargand*, a ship supposedly out of Kailane. The captain, Satig, has been hiring in Farinmalith. I figured that meant Satig was working for Aavik, too, so last night I notified four members of the Mercenary Council. It seems Satig has been reluctant to add Rav clauses to his contracts. If he is working for Aavik, there's likely to be a mercenary uprising."

"Jehan! You put a tiger in the malik pen if you told them that," Jerevan exclaimed, then broke off as Malling returned with Thrym's plate and set a place for him at the table.

When Malling left again and Thrym was helping himself at the sideboard, Alanna said, "I don't understand. What's a Rav clause, and why would the mercenaries revolt? I understand their not wanting to work for the isklarin, but can't they just quit?"

"Who'd hire them afterward?" Thrym asked, coming back to the table.

"Thrym's right," Jerevan said. "A mercenary is bound by his contract. If he walks out on it, he can't be hired legitimately again. The only exceptions are, if the contract is declared to have been negotiated fraudulently by his governing Council, or if his would-be employer is willing to take a forfeit in lieu of his services, either a cash payment or someone willing to take his place."

"I see, but what's a Rav clause?"

Jerevan grinned. "You remember the Wizard Rav, don't you, and how I told you he was training the isklarin secretly?"

"Yes…"

"A Rav clause says that the contract is void if the apparent employer is a front for anyone from whom the mercenary wouldn't otherwise have accepted employment, as for instance, an isklar. The clause must list the employers to whom the mercenary would take exception, and Gandahar usually tops the list. Once a contract is declared void, the mercenary is free to take other employment."

"So if there were no Rav clauses in the contracts the mercenaries would be bound to fight for the isklarin, even if they don't want to?" she asked.

"That's right," Thrym said, looking up from his food, "unless they can get their Council to declare the contracts fraudulent. That's what the Council meeting will be about this afternoon." He looked at Jerevan. "I need to prove that Satig's working for Aavik, and I don't have proof."

"Tarat's furies!" Jerevan said. "I didn't want to alert him to how much I know."

"You don't need to appear personally."

Jerevan sighed. "No. If proof's to be given, it had best come from me. At least the upset among his mercenaries may distract him." He studied Thrym, who looked anxious. "All right. I'll come and testify before your Council that Aavik's been in Ninkarrak since the end of Ilfarnar, and that he arrived off the *Ilfargand*. Will that convince them, do you think?"

Thrym stared at him. "It flaming well ought to. It convinces me. You mean you've known he's been here for months and you haven't told anyone?"

"To the contrary," Jerevan said, "I told a number of people: Idrim, Vanith, Aubrey, Colne, my associates and apprentices, all I could reach." He counted them off on his fingers. "I even told Alanna's uncle, the Chief Customs Officer of the port."

Alanna looked up, startled, but he didn't elaborate and she didn't want to question him when they weren't alone.

"Couldn't you get rid of him?" Thrym asked.

"How? I'm one man. Admittedly, I've established that I'm stronger than Aavik by himself, but he arrived with over a dozen well trained wizards with him. I, on the other hand, can call on two other wizards and three half-trained apprentices, all that are currently in Ninkarrak."

Thrym looked disconcerted. "The army..." he hesitated.

"Precisely. The army is under Horgen's thumb and will do nothing until Idrim takes it north to face Rhys. And from what this note indicates, it's been infiltrated by Gandaharan troops in any case," Jerevan added in a tone of disgust.

Thrym looked down at the food on his plate, which seemed to have lost its flavor for he pushed it out of the way. "Can't you do anything?"

Jerevan smiled. "I can attend your Council meeting this afternoon. Isn't that enough?"

Thrym eyed him uncertainly. "I suppose. It'll solve my problem with Minta, anyway."

"You took her with you to Farinmalith when you alerted the Council?"

"I didn't have time to take her anywhere else after she delivered the message. It shouldn't have mattered," Thrym said, "but Elath Orm, one of the Council members, saw Minta and knew she was with me. I think she suspected that some of my information came from Minta, and she'd signed up with Satig yesterday morning. Elath believed my story, but she requires proof to break her contract. She insisted on a Rav clause. She said she'd hold her tongue until after the Council meeting. If it's proved that Satig's working for Aavik, then she'll be out of a contract and have no reason to report what I said. If it isn't proved, though, she'll report to Satig."

"I see your problem, but my testimony should clear Minta of involvement whether I convince the Council or not. And I'm fairly certain I can be convincing, one way or another." His jaw clenched.

Alanna, watching him, was suddenly reminded of the feel of his lips against hers. A new tension had stretched between them since the night he'd kissed her. He hadn't kissed her again or said anything more to persuade her but she knew now that he did want the link.

Jerevan hadn't let the new awareness between them interfere with her training, however. She could receive mental images now, although he told her that he had to do the equivalent of shouting at her to get her to hear him. True mind speech was still beyond her as, so far, she'd only mastered a few of the images and tended to get confused between even the ones she was supposed to have learned. She'd also begun to learn to send, although the distance she could be heard from was still limited to her immediate surroundings.

"Get Agnes to help you pack your things, Alanna," Jerevan said, interrupting her wandering thoughts.

"What? Where are we going?"

His eyebrow arched. "You weren't listening. We're going back to town. I have a meeting to attend and I'd prefer you to be nearby. You can stay with Lady Farlon, a cousin of mine."

"I can't go back to my uncle's?"

"Aavik's men are still watching your uncle's."

"I'll get ready then," she said rising and leaving the room, conscious of Thrym's curious eyes watching her.

When she came down about half an hour later, Thrym had left and Jerevan was pacing.

"Are your bags packed?"

"Agnes is finishing them," Alanna said. She'd never seen Jerevan so agitated. "What's the matter?"

"I don't like it. Everything's happening too soon. Rhys won't be here for months, yet the court's behaving as though he's expected tomorrow. Aavik's playing with them, exciting them. He must be, to have them stirred up like this." He turned to Malling who had come from the back of the house. "Malling, Tamrai Cairn's luggage and mine can follow with her maid in the coach. We'll be leaving immediately. I've told Otto to bring round my curricle."

"Very good, your grace."

"Will Aavik's interference affect your plans?" Alanna asked, as he opened the door for her and ushered her out.

"I don't know. There's nothing I can alter, unless I can persuade Vanith to change her mind and allow me to take Aubrey to safety now. And that's unlikely. She won't disobey her father while he's Estahar and she's oath bound to him. And he's rejected any suggestion of sending Aubrey to safety. I've argued with both of them, but they're both adamant and Aubrey won't leave without Vanith's consent."

They arrived at Lady Farlon's just before noon and were fortunate enough to find her at home. The butler who answered the door ushered them into her sitting room. Witha Farlon was a tall, fashionable widow. Her face was more handsome than beautiful and her once dark brown hair sported a generous sprinkling of gray, but her skin was still smooth. Alanna couldn't guess her age; she could have been anywhere from her mid-thirties to mid-fifties.

When the introductions were complete, Witha said, "Jere, my dear, where have you been? The town's been so dull. Everyone's left for the season. Even Lord Essure departed for parts unknown."

Jerevan's eyes narrowed. "Lord Essure left town? When? Where did he go?"

Witha pouted. "You haven't changed. You never do. You can't even greet me without a cross-examination." She turned to Alanna, "Please sit down, Tamrai Cairn. Can I offer you some refreshment?"

Alanna sat down on one of the delicate, gilt legged chairs and looked inquiringly at Jerevan.

He was eyeing his hostess with grim amusement. "Come on, Witha, you only mentioned it because you knew I'd be interested."

Witha laughed. "Suspected, perhaps. But I can't answer your question. No one knows where Essure went. He disappeared."

"When?"

"Last week. He ate dinner at his club on Maerasday and played some cards afterward. Lord Garven told me he left there just after midnight, and no one's seen him since. His servants say that some of his clothes are missing and the horse he usually rode, but if he packed and left that night he didn't ask for assistance and he didn't mention his plans to anyone."

"What happened to his house guest, the gentleman from Kailane?"

"Isn't it funny you should ask that? I was almost sure it would be one of your first questions." Witha's eyes were full of mischief.

"Then you should have an answer ready."

She shook her head. "You're too impatient, Jere. You should learn to take things easy, slow down a bit. After all, at your age, life should take on a leisurely pace."

Alanna almost laughed aloud at the expression that crossed Jerevan's face. He was gritting his teeth. And Witha's eyes danced.

"Witha, are you going to tell me, or am I going to wring your neck?"

Witha stiffened, but her eyes still laughed. "You wouldn't dare."

"Don't put me to the test," Jerevan said, but Alanna noted that he was having trouble keeping a straight face himself.

"I suppose it isn't really funny, but I can never resist teasing you," Witha said, sobering. "Tamrai Esparda moved in with the Lanrai of Horgen the following day. Lord Essure's other guests, having less exalted connections, are staying at the Dolphin's Rest."

"I suppose it was to be expected," Jerevan said.

"What does it mean?" Alanna asked. "Why would Lord Essure disappear?"

"He wouldn't, of his own volition," Jerevan said grimly. "He must have discovered the identity of his guest, and been disposed of to keep the information from spreading."

Jerevan left after lunch and Witha took Alanna upstairs to her room and then gave her a tour of the house, during which Alanna found herself undergoing an exacting examination. Witha wanted to know everything about her and, particularly, her relationship with Jerevan. Alanna had the uncomfortable sensation that Witha gleaned as much information from what she didn't say as from what she did.

When they finally sat down for afternoon tea in the sitting room, Witha said, "It's amazing. Actually living with him for more than a month and you're not in love with him."

Alanna felt the heat rise in her cheeks. "Surely, you don't expect everyone to love your cousin? No one's irresistible."

Witha grinned. "He comes close. I loved him myself when I was younger. In my teens I used to dream of growing up and marrying him, but I have no talent for wizardry." Her grin faded and she looked wistful. "There was a woman I knew. Her name was Marath, but you may have heard of her as Lady Trevan. She was beautiful and had a bit of wizard talent. Jerevan met her at my come-out ball. That was thirty years ago, not long after he'd started going into society again."

She paused as a maid brought in the tea tray and a platter of small, iced cakes. Alanna wondered what had kept him out of society, but was afraid to ask for fear of ending Witha's confidences.

Finally she said, "I thought he broke his curse some fifty years ago."

"Yes," Witha acknowledged, "but he spent years after that traveling all over Tamar reorganizing the Varfarin."

Witha hesitated, then said, "Looking back, I suppose it was natural he'd be susceptible. He'd ignored women for years after Marion died, and Marath was phenomenally beautiful."

She paused again and concentrated on pouring the tea.

"Who was Marion? I've never heard that name connected to him," Alanna asked sharply.

Witha eyed her knowingly. "No. You wouldn't have. The rumors only cover events that happened here in Ilwheirlane, and only comparatively recent ones at that. The Wizard Marion was the love of his youth. She helped train him in wizardry and she stayed with him during all the years he suffered from Derwen's curse. She died in Cibata, some rescue mission into Senanga, and Jerevan has always blamed himself for not being strong enough to save her."

Witha shook her head and looked down at the cups. "Jerevan has a real problem with responsibility. Do you take cream or sugar?"

"Neither," Alanna said, "just plain." She waited for Witha to continue, but Witha seemed to be concentrating on the tea tray. Finally, Alanna asked, "Marion was a wizard?"

Witha looked up as though surprised. Then she smiled. "I thought you weren't interested in him."

Alanna didn't know what to say. She knew by the warmth of her face that her cheeks were scarlet.

Witha let out a trill of mirth, but sobered and said, "No, I'm sorry. I shouldn't tease you. Of course, I'll tell you about Marion and Marath. Someone better. Jere doesn't have enough sense."

She handed Alanna a cup of tea. "You've heard of Lady Trevan and the dreadful rumors about Jere. I don't suppose anyone with ears in all of Ilwheirlane hasn't," she added, with a trace of bitter humor.

Alanna nodded, and looked down at her teacup. "Yes."

"Marion was much older than Jerevan. I don't think their relationship would have led to a permanent linkage, to marriage, but they were very close and then she died. He was devastated."

"But then he met Lady Trevan?"

"Yes. I tried to warn him that Marath wasn't what she seemed, but he thought I was jealous. Which I was, of course," Witha added. "Anyway, he was very taken with her, even talked of marrying her. She did have some talent after all, only journeyman level, but he may have thought she could learn more and I believe she reminded him of Marion. There was a strong physical resemblance. Fortunately, Marath was already married and her husband wasn't willing to be nice about a divorce."

Alanna frowned, looking down at her cup. "He doesn't seem the type to poach."

Witha smiled at her. "He isn't, but she set out to catch him. She told him her husband abused her, and Jerevan really was quite naive. Perhaps his isolation while dealing with the curse was to blame."

"What was the curse?" Alanna asked. "I've heard it made him grotesque, but I've never heard precisely what it was."

Witha drew a deep breath. "It did more than make him grotesque; it made life unbearable for him and it took him almost thirty years to break it. But he'll have to tell you about that. I can't. It all took place before I was born."

Alanna sighed. "I can't see myself asking him about it."

Witha's brows drew together. "No. I suppose not, but there really isn't much I can tell you. I know Derwen was trying to persuade Jerevan to study wizardry, but Jerevan wasn't interested. Then, apparently, Jerevan made some comment about Derwen's girth, he was a pudgy little man, and Derwen retaliated by cursing Jerevan so he'd have to eat enough to keep his stomach nearly full, or else he's go into convulsions or pass out. And Jerevan couldn't break the curse until he became a stronger wizard than Derwen, so he had to study wizardry."

"So Jerevan got fat? That was all?" Alanna asked astonished.

Witha looked at her. "Well there's fat, and then there's fat," she said. "I think Jerevan got to be pretty huge and couldn't do much for himself or get around well at all."

"Oh," Alanna said, remembering her own reactions to meeting extremely overweight people. "I can see that it would tend to isolate him."

"Precisely," Witha said. "At any rate, Marath persuaded Jere to take her to live at Leyburn despite her husband. They petitioned Idrim, and she probably would have received her freedom, but before that could happen she had a bad fall from her horse. She always was a rotten rider."

"But what started all the rumors?"

"Marath. She was clever and vicious. When she set out to ruin his reputation, she did so with a vengeance."

"Why? You said she loved him?"

Witha frowned. "No. I said I loved him. Marath never loved anyone but herself." She paused and sipped her tea. "As to why, well, I told you she had a fall from a horse. It was a nasty one. She hit her face against a rock and her cheek was badly torn. Jerevan wasn't at Leyburn at the time and the local healer could only close the cut and stop the bleeding. Marath had never developed her talent much and didn't even own a crystal. She might be able to remove a pimple or smooth a wrinkle, but she had no real ability to heal herself and was left with an ugly scar across one side of her face. Of course, at first she wasn't too worried. She knew Jerevan loved her and she knew he was a wizard. She was sure he'd remove the scar for her as soon as he returned."

"He refused?" Alanna asked, startled.

"No, of course not, but you're rushing me," Witha said, taking another sip of tea. "It wasn't her demand to have the scar removed that caused the problem; it was what she said when she asked. She'd been kept waiting for weeks with what she considered a massive disfigurement and she made it plain to him that she expected better service in future; that, in fact, she expected him to keep her young and beautiful all his life, and a wizard's life is a long time."

"If he loved her, wouldn't he want to anyway?"

"No," Witha said. "It's against their laws. I thought you were his apprentice? Haven't you read about the laws of the Council yet?"

"No. He gave me the book and told me to study it, but I haven't gotten very far," Alanna said. "He did tell me I'd have to learn the laws and swear my oath before the next stage of my training could begin, but I don't think I realized their full importance."

"I see. Then you'll have to take my word for it that the thought of maintaining Marath forever never occurred to Jerevan and was something he couldn't do. He told her so." Witha grimaced. "She was furious. She came back to Ninkarrak in an absolute rage. I think she had some idea of making him change his mind at first but, when he didn't come after her, she started telling stories about things she said she'd seen at Leyburn. Over the years the stories grew." Witha's voice died away. Her eyes seemed to be studying the design on the carpet.

Alanna took one of the iced cakes. When Witha didn't seem inclined to continue, she said, "The stories I heard in Fell said that she killed herself because of him."

Witha looked up. "Did they? I'm not surprised. Marath tried hard enough to blame Jerevan for everything. You see, her husband took her back after Jerevan, but when he found her with a another lover a year later, he was livid and swore she'd never have the opportunity to humiliate him again." She broke off and refilled both their cups from the teapot.

Alanna sipped her tea and waited.

Witha grinned, but her tone was delicately malicious, "Marath loved Ninkarrak and being in the center of things. Her husband told her that he was returning to his estates in Balt, which is about as far north as you can go and still be in Ilwheirlane. Then he sold his town house and informed her that she could come with him or he'd get the divorce she'd been so anxious for the year before."

"How unkind of him."

Witha laughed. "Of course, she stayed in Ninkarrak. Lord Eglen was her lover at the time and he set her up as his mistress. He already had a wife and several children, so there was no question of his marrying her. It was quite a comedown, but I suppose she found it preferable to being virtually imprisoned in the far north with a husband determined to be strict with her." Witha sipped her tea. "I'm not sure that I blame her, under the circumstances."

"No," Alanna agreed, "not if he really would have been strict with her."

"Oh, I think he would have been. He didn't like her much by then. But Marath still had her beauty, and there were always men willing to give her whatever she wanted. Her arrangement with Eglen didn't last long; she was too demanding. But when he tired of her, she had no trouble finding a whole series of others."

Alanna took another one of the cakes and nibbled it. "How enterprising of her."

Witha eyed Alanna and laughed. "Wasn't it? But age eventually caught up with her. She'd been thirty when she met Jere and, as I told you, she never developed the little talent she had. By the time she was fifty her looks were going and men were harder to find. She went to Leyburn just before she killed herself. I don't know what was said between them, but I suppose she pled with him one last time to restore her lost beauty." Witha paused and sipped her tea.

"And he refused," Alanna said.

Witha looked as though she were about to protest, but checked herself. "Yes. At any rate, she returned to Ninkarrak in a towering rage. Would you like some more tea?"

"No, thank you," Alanna said, "I still have plenty." She took a sip. "This is such a civilized custom. I've missed it over the past weeks."

Witha pouted. "Aren't you the tiniest bit curious as to what happened next?"

"Of course I am," Alanna said, smiling. "But I have confidence that you have every intention of telling me."

"Jere tells me I'm too obvious." Witha grimaced. "Where was I?"

"Marath had just returned to Ninkarrak. Did she have a lover at the time?"

"Oh, yes," Witha said, "and he was furious when she took off to visit Jere. Anyway, they broke up about two weeks after she got back. And that was when she killed herself."

"Then why, in Maera's name, was Jerevan blamed?"

"Marath sent letters to everyone she knew just before she died. In them, she related the atrocities that Jere supposedly perpetrated at Leyburn when she first ran away with him." Witha's voice hardened. "She must have been involved in some peculiar practices in those last years; the details she supplied in the letters were horrifying. She went on to say that he'd used and abused her for years and blackmailed her with her involvement in the earlier acts. She finished by saying that she'd done his bidding all that time because he'd promised to restore her beauty, but when she'd gone to claim her reward, he'd spurned her, so there was nothing left for her to do but take her own life."

"Wasn't there something he could have done to disprove the charges?"

"What charges? The letters were terribly convincing and a great many people believed them, but there was no proof to any of it, just her word against his and she was dead. No charges were ever filed."

"I see."

"That was what made it so terrible," Witha said. "If he'd been charged, he might have been able to prove his innocence. As it was, he never had the opportunity to present his side of the story."

"What a pathetic creature she must have been," Alanna said, saddened by the story but relieved to have at least one of the gaping holes in her knowledge of Jerevan filled in. She stared down at the tea leaves in the bottom of her empty cup.

"More tea?" Witha held up the pot.

Alanna looked up. "Thank you." She held out her cup. "But what about the other women who've been rumored to have died because of him?"

Witha smiled as though she was pleased with Alanna's question. But her tone was cynical, "He was involved with a lot of women during the years after his affair with Marath, and he may have been a bit ruthless with some of them. He was badly disillusioned. But the real problem was that, after Marath, it became something of a fashion to have been toyed with by Jere." Witha sighed. "I know for a fact that at least one of the women who complained of his cruelty never did more than stand up with him at a few dances."

"A fashion?"

Witha chuckled. "I can tell you haven't spent long in our great capitol. You'd be amazed at the lengths some people will go to when they want to be considered the vogue. Take Pantera Gree, for instance."

"Wasn't she an actress?" Alanna asked.

"Yes. But she was very stylish. She was also a highly neurotic woman. Jerevan was fascinated by her for a period of about a month, but he never gave her any right to accuse him of being unfaithful when he stopped seeing her. Moreover, I don't believe for one moment that she really meant to kill herself. All she wanted was more attention."

Alanna smiled. "You're shockingly partisan."

"I don't deny it. I'm proud of it," Witha said with a toss of her head, "but I've interfered enough. You're probably tired and would like to freshen up before dinner."

Alanna was grateful for the excuse to retire. She liked Witha, but found her company a little overwhelming, and she had a great deal of food for thought.

Jerevan was late getting back. He came in as they were finishing their dinner, and Alanna thought he looked tired, worse than she had seen him look since the day of her kidnaping. There were lines of strain around his mouth and eyes.

"Jere, what in the world kept you? My chef wouldn't let us wait any longer. He's a tyrant, but a genius, so I have to put up with him. Sit down and I'll have a place set for you," Witha said, all in one breath.

Jerevan smiled, but shook his head. "I ate in Farinmalith with the Council. I'll just join you in a glass of wine."

"At least have some fruit and cheese. That's all we're having for dessert anyway," Witha insisted, waving to the maid who was serving them to bring Jerevan a plate.

"All right." He sat down and poured himself some wine from the decanter on the table. After he tasted it he saluted Witha. "I can always depend on the drink in this house."

"Yes," Witha said, "but can we depend on you to tell us what you were up to today?" She nodded as the maid finished distributing plates and deposited a bowl of fruit on the table next to a cheese board. "That will be all, thank you, Elvie."

"Didn't Alanna tell you that I attended a meeting in Farinmalith?" Jerevan asked, glancing at Alanna, when the maid left.

"Yes. But that was all she told me. What happened? Why did they need to consult with you?"

"They wanted proof that Aavik's in Ninkarrak, and that he's involved in the hiring of mercenaries."

Witha gaped at him. "Aavik's been hiring mercenaries in Farinmalith? I should think they'd have spat in his face. Half the mercenaries in Ilwheirlane come from Lamash, don't they?"

"He was using a front man, the captain of a ship supposedly from Kailane. He was also discouraging Rav clauses."

Witha choked. Then she said, wide-eyed, "I gather the meeting was a heated one?"

Jerevan laughed. "You could say that. Particularly when I told them what I think he wants them for." He helped himself to an apple and cut a slice of the soft, Teruelian cheese.

"What does he want them for?"

"I believe my words were, 'for the purpose of interfering with the internal politics of Ilwheirlane,'" he said.

Alanna found herself envying Witha her easy familiarity with Jerevan. Even though he still looked tired, she could see that, under Witha's handling, he was relaxing in a way he never did with Alanna. She knew she ought be glad that Witha was able to ease his tension, but was shocked to realize that she was far from glad; that, in fact, she was jealous.

"Did the Council declare the contracts void?" she asked, afraid of where her thoughts were taking her.

Jerevan raised an eyebrow at the sharpness of her tone, but said, "Eventually. They argued a lot first. Their main objection seemed to be that they didn't think it could be true, because he wouldn't dare to do such a thing. It took me a while to disabuse them of that notion."

"What will you do now?" Witha asked.

"I'm not sure," Jerevan said. "If Aavik has eleven wizards with him, there's not much we can do until a few more of my associates show up. Unfortunately, several of the strongest were in Cibata and, as I can't farsend that distance or spare a wizard, I had to depend on a ship to take my message."

He paused and sipped more of his wine. "At least I know it reached them. I've heard from three wizards who are on their way and should reach us soon. As for the rest," he glanced at Alanna, "it will depend. I believe that most of my associates are stronger and better trained than Aavik's, but there are fewer of us. I'll have to talk with Vanith again."

Alanna swallowed the last of her wine. "There's no chance then, that you'll be able to spare one or two to aid with the fruiting in the Mallarnes?"

Jerevan shook his head. "I didn't say that, Alanna. There are several wizards who were in the far west when I summoned them. I told them that, if it didn't mean too much delay, they were to detour through the Mallarnes and help with the fruiting in both Ilwheirlane and Lachan. I won't know for weeks yet whether they'll be there in time, or what help they can give."

"Why didn't you tell me before? Why did you let me go on thinking you wouldn't do anything?"

"I can't help what you think, Alanna. I never said that I wouldn't try to assist the mountain people. In fact, I remember telling you on several occasions that I'd do what I could. I still don't know what that will amount to."

Witha had watched them both with interest, but now she said, "If you don't mind someone interrupting a private fight, why don't we find more comfortable seats in my sitting room."

"Thanks, Witha, but I'd better go. I have several more things to do tonight." He looked at Alanna. "I've taught you all I can until you've taken the Oath of Council. I suggest you study *The Laws*. You should be ready to take the oath before the end of the month. I'll come by next week and answer any questions you may have."

"Will I still be able to have my meeting with Idrim and Vanith?"

"It's impossible for you to appear at court now. Horgen would be bound to find out."

"Then I won't get to meet Aubrey?"

"No. It would be too dangerous to try and smuggle you into the Tower, nearly as dangerous as trying to get Aubrey out. I'll try to arrange another meeting for you with Vanith." He hesitated. "I told you that three wizards are coming from Cibata. I want one of them, the Wizard Magra, to become your constant companion."

"When I have her with me, will I be able to go back to my uncle's?"

"I doubt it. A lot will depend on Aavik. If he diverts most of his wizards to the Tower, it might be possible. Magra is powerful, nearly as strong as Ashe. And like Ashe, if she'd been available when you arrived, I'd have entrusted your training to her. As it is, you'll be safe in her company if you don't take unnecessary risks." He paused, studying her. "I won't need to see you every day from now on. You have to practice the skills you've learned before I teach you anything else, even after you've taken your oath. And that you can do on your own or with Magra's aid."

"Are you saying that Magra will continue my training?"

Jerevan seemed to catch the emotion in her voice, but not the reason for it. "Don't worry. You'll find it easier to work with her than with me. You'll be able to use Vyrkarion in your training sessions."

"Is she taking over my training permanently?" Alanna demanded, angry that he would break the news to her this way and in front of Witha.

Jerevan was startled by her question, but a warm look entered his eyes. "No, Alanna. She's only going to act as a bodyguard and help you practice for a time. You're my apprentice now and will remain so. But until Aavik leaves Ninkarrak or Rhys arrives with his army, I won't have much time to spend with you."

Alanna let out a deep breath, appalled by the intensity of her relief.

"He's begun his march, has he?" Witha asked.

"Yes. He moved out of Aire this morning," Jerevan said, rising. "He has all the units of the Shore Guard from the whole northeast coast marching with him. As all but the officers of the Shore Guard are part-time volunteers, it makes me wonder who'll be doing the planting come spring."

Alanna also rose and followed him to the door. "How long will it take for him to reach Ninkarrak?"

Jerevan turned back to face her. "The Shore Guard isn't mounted and they aren't used to marching. Most of them have never left their home villages before this. So they aren't making much speed. Two months at the present rate, maybe less as they grow accustomed. A lot depends on whether he stays on the coast or moves inland."

"And Aavik and all his wizards couldn't face him, not even if they had the Talisman?" Alanna's fingers toyed with the crystal.

"To the contrary, they might be able to stop him, if they had Vyrkarion and there were enough of them. But we aren't going to let them have Vyrkarion." He rubbed his left cheek. "We have to deal with Rhys ourselves. Although I can't go myself, a number of the wizards of the Varfarin will ride north with Idrim and Vanith to face him."

"What are their chances of stopping him?"

"Of stopping him outright, almost nonexistent. Of coming to some sort of agreement with him, we don't know." Jerevan put his hands on her shoulders, meeting her eyes. "Rhys was born at the highest stage that a wizard can reach. He draws his strength directly from the ambient energy around him. I'm years away from achieving that ability. Not all the great wizards did. Moreover, Rhys has Cyrkarion. The wizards who'll go north to face him don't plan on trying to destroy him. We only want to come to terms."

XXI

4731, 474TH CYCLE OF THE YEAR OF THE DRAGON
MONTH OF INGVASH

> Yet even as a little child
> The Wanderer, he had power,
> And he could gather men to him
> To serve him in his Tower.
> Power, power to the Wanderer
> Wherever he may be,
> Though he is doomed to exile
> By the shore of Sorrow Sea.

— FROM *THE BALLAD OF AUBREY THE WANDERER* BY ANONYMOUS

"You must let us get Aubrey out of here, Vanith," Jerevan said. "Every day's delay, it gets more dangerous."

"I'm sorry, Jere. You're a dear friend and I know what you say is true, but I can't allow Aubrey to leave now. My father may not be a good ruler, but he is Estahar of Ilwheirlane and I am oath bound to obey him." The strong bones of her face stood out, emphasizing the gaunt hollows under her cheekbones, the lines of stress. Minta thought that Vanith had aged ten years in the past month.

She stood by Aubrey's bedroom window, holding his hand and wishing that Lord Leyburn and Vanith would agree. It frightened her when they argued.

"There's nothing I can say or do to make you change your mind?" Jerevan asked.

"No." She shook her head. "Jehan knows, I want Aubrey safe. And when I've left with the army, I trust you to do whatever you see fit to do to secure his safety. But my father insists that Aubrey stay here, in the Tower." Vanith sighed. "He wanted Aubrey to ride with us. I had to argue that Aubrey's too frail, because of his hip, to ride so far. Even then, it took Thurin's support to make him change his mind."

Jerevan frowned. "Why would he want Aubrey with the army?"

"My father doesn't believe that Rhys will slay him outright." Vanith grimaced. "And who knows, he may be right. He says that, as he's old, he's willing to retire. And as I'm a woman, I'm unfit to reign in any case." Her jaw clenched and a muscle in her cheek twitched. "He means to buy his own life by granting Rhys the Regency throughout

Aubrey's minority. He can't see, or doesn't care, how that would endanger Aubrey. He wanted to have Aubrey present, to be handed over like a piece of trade goods."

"Jehan!" Jerevan swore. "I knew he was a fool, but that's madness."

Vanith laughed. "To such has the House of Cinnac fallen. Believe me, I understand why even the gods conspire against us. But I won't break my oath. If I must die, then I must, but I'll die with honor." Vanith turned away from Jerevan and stood beside Minta, gazing out the window at the angry sea crashing on the rocks below.

Jerevan sighed. "I was afraid that would be your answer, but I had to try. And it isn't Rhys I'm concerned about with regard to Aubrey's safety. Jehan knows how many wizards Aavik will have here by the time you leave, Vanith. There was another ship in port from Kailane today and two more earlier this week. Anin, the Customs officer I told you of, tells me that all of them had inconsistencies in their papers, but Horgen personally ordered them cleared despite the Harbor Master's objections."

"You think they're from Gandahar?" Vanith asked. Minta followed the nahar's eyes and saw spume rise above the rocks where the waves struck the shore.

"I'm sure they are. And who knows how many other ships in port are sailing under false papers that weren't caught at inspection time? I had Anin ask that all shipping out of Kailane be given an extra thorough examination, but I'm willing to bet that's not the only registration Aavik's using." Jerevan paced restlessly across the room.

"At least he's been blocked from hiring forces here," Vanith said, "thanks to you, Minta."

Minta colored. "It was Thrym and Lord Leyburn, your highness. I didn't do anything. I wouldn't know how. And, anyway, Thrym says that not all the men broke their contracts, even knowing they'd been hired by Gandahar."

"Not everyone understands what it would mean if the isklarin win," Vanith said. "The time of slavery is legend, not memory. How can common mercenaries comprehend what that yoke was like?"

"I'm hiring my own men in Farinmalith and the Lamashrak, but I have to be discreet," Jerevan said. "I don't want Aavik to get wind of it, or Horgen. There's a law against maintaining a private army in Ilwheirlane and, while it used not to apply to the Varfarin, Horgen might argue that our privileges are void now Idrim has been converted to Miune."

"Yes. Thrym told us he was helping you find mercenaries," Aubrey said, "but I don't see why you think we'll need to fight." He glanced at his mother, then said, "If we have to flee, Thrym can smuggle me out of the Tower the same way he comes in."

"True, but Aavik's wizards will know you're missing within minutes. We know he has soldiers as well as wizards on those ships and I'll wager they won't be far away. We can get you out of the Tower, but getting you out of Ilwheirlane without a fight will be more difficult." Jerevan's voice was grim.

"How does Aavik dare bring a military force here? I know what Lord Horgen said, but I still can't believe it," Minta protested.

"Who's to stop him?" Vanith asked. "There are always sailors moving on and off ships. There's no way to prove that his men are a military force until he uses them as such. Even if we made accusations, do you think anyone at court is going to worry about the isklarin with Rhys to the north?"

"What are you planning to do about the Gandaharan troops in the Royal Guard?" Jerevan asked.

"Nothing until we're out of Ninkarrak. Then I'll leak the information to a priest and have him test the purity of the army." Vanith smiled. "My father can think of it as a religious purge to reinforce the righteousness of our cause. I'm not worried about the isklarin. They have no reason to turn on us before we face Rhys. It's only afterward that we need fear them and I'll deal with them first."

Jerevan frowned. "That's true, but I don't like the idea of so many of them close to you and Idrim. What would happen if Theolan detected one? He has enough talent to tell an isklar from a man when he's carrying that staff of his. He could force a crisis before you're ready for it."

"Theolan might be able to detect a common isklarin soldier, but he wouldn't know a wizard unless he touched one with the staff, and the troops won't be coming into the Tower or entering a basilica. Aavik and Horgen know of the staff. I'm sure they'll take precautions." She laughed. "It's ironic that I should be concerned about the thoroughness of their plotting. Jehan, but it would be almost worth my death to know that Rhys has swept this court clean." She turned to Aubrey. "Remember that, my son. If I do die, don't hate your cousin because of it. My fate was decreed by the gods and he's but the instrument, not the cause. Love or hate him for what he does to Ilwheirlane."

Aubrey ran to Vanith and embraced her. "I'll remember, mother. Jerevan has shown me his aura. I'll judge him for what he is, and for what he becomes, but I don't want you to die."

"When does Idrim intend to march?" The sharpness of Jerevan's tone made Vanith turn to him. "Do you know?"

"Rhys has been moving down the coast, making roughly twenty-five kilometers a day. He should reach the southern end of Lleyndale before the end of the month. We'll know then whether he's going to turn inland there and come down the central valley, or continue down the coast. We'll leave as soon as we hear." Vanith bowed her head. "That's all I know. I wouldn't know that but for Errian. I'm no longer entitled to attend Privy Council sessions."

"That's better than nothing. It gives us a time estimate." He studied Vanith, then said, "If you truly don't want to know our plans, you'd better go now. I'll promise not to remove Aubrey until you've left. But we need to discuss strategy."

Vanith nodded, her eyes full of pain. "Thank you. I have at least been blessed in having good friends. If it weren't for you, and my faith in you, I'd have been forced to compromise my honor as well."

Jerevan nodded. "I understand, your highness. Whatever happens when you meet Rhys, your son shall be safe. You have my word."

Minta thought that Vanith's eyes looked unusually bright, but the nahar only nodded and left the room.

Elath stepped through the worn wooden door of the Corriden and looked around the shabby meeting hall. Some forty people were assembled, drinking beer or mead and talking desultorily. She knew most of them but made no attempt to join anyone. She had arrived late deliberately, and not just because she didn't like to leave Fal alone longer than necessary. She was tired of men who kept asking if she were ready to take on a new partner. And the women were worse; she could see the pity in their eyes.

Varl Ganna, the white-haired giant who had sponsored Thrym as a member of the Guild, nodded to her. He stood alone also, his difference isolating him. She remembered Fal explaining Varl's unusual size and coloring to her when they first worked together several years before. Varl was half gamlar, his mother having been one of the rare pure-blooded bear people. His human blood made him a maverick among his mother's people, even though he inherited both were-vision and the ability to shape-shift into a bear. He had felt restless and confined in his home village, so he had left to become a mercenary as his father had been.

Elath supposed that their vision and shape-change ability were the links that drew Varl and Thrym together. Certainly, while Varl's great size and strength had led to his making a name for himself as a mercenary, he wasn't close to any of the other men.

She shifted restlessly as she saw red-headed Fianna spot her and start to approach. She often partnered with Fianna when Fal went off on one of his trips, but she didn't want to talk to her now. She turned her head away and edged closer to the door, hoping that Fianna would take the hint.

Thrym chose that moment to arrive and greet Varl. Elath gave a sigh of relief, noting that his entrance had distracted Fianna. She'd timed her own arrival just right.

"About time you got here," Varl said, slapping Thrym on the back. "The troops are restless. Everyone's on edge since the confrontation with Satig and your employer has been as vague about his intent as Satig was. I'm a bit on edge myself, for that matter, so I hope you're going to tell us all what we've been hired for."

"Sorry, Varl. I won't be able to tell anyone that," Thrym said. "I'd better get that straightened out quickly." He crossed the room and mounted a podium at the front of the hall. Then he held up his arms for silence.

"Varl tells me you're here tonight to learn what you've been hired to do, but I can't tell you that yet," Thrym said.

Elath joined in a united groan of protest.

"Wait a minute." Thrym held his hands up again and the audience quieted. "I can give you an approximate date. We'll need you by the last week of Ingvash and we want to know how many of you have sailing experience."

"What good's that? We want to know what we're going to be asked to do," someone shouted.

"Be patient," Thrym said. He waited while the muttering died down. "I'd tell you if I could, but your employer's plans aren't complete yet. Even he doesn't know precisely what you'll be doing, but it won't be anything you'll disapprove of. Remember, we insisted that all your contracts have Rav clauses and none of you listed the Varfarin."

"I heard we'd be called on to fight wizards," someone in the back called out.

"A Rav clause won't protect us from being asked to do something illegal and it's illegal to assemble an army inside the borders of Ilwheirlane," Flava called out. Sometimes he looked just like a fresh-faced country boy, Elath thought, and then his expression would change and you would remember that his sideline was assassination. But why was he heckling Thrym? Flickra had always seemed to like Thrym, and Flava was Flickra's man. She tucked the question away in her mind and turned back to the podium.

"Are you assembled as an army? I thought you were all down here for a party. Haven't we supplied enough ale?" Thrym asked.

"You can never supply this crew with enough ale," Fianna shouted. The red-head was obviously in an aggressive mood, and Elath remembered that Fianna had also signed with Satig.

"Look," Thrym continued, "all I can tell you now is that most of you will be on a ship out of Ilwheirlane by the end of the month. Is that reassurance enough?"

"It will have to be, if that's all you're going to tell us," Varl said. "But why have us come here tonight?"

"Because I want information. It's not really part of your job, but the Hetri of Leyburn suspects that Gandaharan troops have been coming ashore lately, and not just sailors. He wants to know if any of you have noticed an increase in the number of strangers around town, and, if so, where they gather and what they seem to be doing." Thrym looked around at the assemblage which had grown silent. "Well?"

Elath swallowed, thinking of the crowded bars and the unusual mass of people in the market and around the harbor.

"Saw ya girl ta night of the ball, so ya might not ha noticed," a thin, dark-haired man called out. Elath thought his accent was Zamargan. "But ya got ta stand in line for a 'arlot these days. Ev'ry flophouse in ta city's been full since ta middle of Iskkaar."

"We thought they were here for the summer fair," another man called out. There were a few nervous laughs.

"Where do they come from, then?" someone else asked.

"Who's been hiring?" Flava asked, and then nodded at Thrym, "Aside from the Wizard of Leyburn."

"I-if Aavik's b-brought his own troops, why'd he w-want us as well?" a gangly young man asked.

"Grow up, Iggy. You can never have too many men in a fight," a thin, dark man said, "and we're malik fodder to the isklarin."

"So you want us to keep an eye on his lizard majesty's troops, do you?" Flava grinned. "You going to pay us scale?"

"Ain't that more in yer line, Thrym? Ya can wriggle right up next ta 'em," the thin, dark-haired man gibed.

Elath grinned and most of the others laughed or shouted further comments. Thrym smiled good-naturedly and then raised his hands to quiet them.

"Just let me know anything you happen to observe. And, yes, his grace will pay for information. I also want to know how many men didn't take advantage of the Council's ruling and retained their contracts with Satig?"

"I'll tell you that free of charge," Flava said. "Nearly three hundred signed contracts before the Council meeting and only one hundred eighty-three had them dissolved."

"So count about a hundred mercenaries. How many would you estimate off the ships?" Thrym asked.

Elath turned to Flava, who was frowning. As Flickra's agent, he'd know, if anyone did.

"Hard to say," Flava said after a moment. "They don't assemble in any one place, they're all over, but I'd guess two thousand."

"Aw, Gandahar can't have landed two thousand soldiers without someone getting leery," Fianna objected.

"Don't bet on it, sister. Way this town's been run lately, it's a wonder Aavik hasn't landed his whole army and navy combined. That's what happened in Lamash. They just moved in. One day we were at peace;

next day, no country." Elath saw that it was Lorval, a burly, gray-haired veteran, speaking.

"You should know, eh. How'd you get out?" Fianna asked.

"Lived on a farm outside Kappar. Saw the city go up in flames and lit out. Went through the hills to Rahoul, down the coast. Found out later I made it out of Rahoul just a day before they landed there, too. By then I was in Lara, arranging to come here. I was just a kid, but I've never forgotten. At least here they don't have their maliks with them."

The other mercenaries were silent. Elath had heard Lorval's story, and others like it, before, and knew that everyone else present had, too; half the mercenaries in Ilwheirlane came from Lamash, or were children of those who'd fled Lamash. The story wasn't new, but it still shook her. It was one thing to hear it when the nearest isklarin were on the other side of the Thallassean; quite another when the city was filled with armed troops and no one in authority was doing anything about it.

"It's not going to happen here, Lorval. Even if Idrim can't do anything about the Gandaharan troops, the lord in the north can." Thrym's voice broke the uneasy silence that followed the old man's words.

"W-what makes him b-better than Aavik? He's half eslar." It was the gangly young man called Iggy.

Flava said, "And sure as the heat of Agnith's fires the eslarin want to claim him; that's why they so conveniently closed all their ports."

"He's a descendant of Vydarga. He may have eslar blood, but it's men he'll rule," Thrym said.

"So the Wizard of Leyburn sides with the lord in the north." Flava eyed Thrym. "What about the little Nahar, how does he feel about his cousin?"

"Nahar Aubrey's too young to rule, and knows it. All he wants is his life and a chance to grow up away from here. He won't contest his cousin's rule."

"You know his mind so well?" Elath spoke for the first time.

"I serve him," Thrym said.

"The Nahar, not the wizard?" Flava asked.

"Their interests in this are the same. The wizard hired you."

"To get the boy out of Ilwheirlane," Flava said, nodding as though he'd just received confirmation of something he already suspected. "That's what we've been hired for, isn't it?"

"I can't tell you what you were hired for," Thrym said. "But one of the Varfarin's major purposes has always been the welfare of children, wherever they are. On the other hand, you needn't worry about storming the Tower or anything like that."

"That's good enough for me," Flava said.

Elath joined with the others in echoing him.

XXII

4731, 474TH CYCLE OF THE YEAR OF THE DRAGON
MONTH OF INGVASH

> *Garm a nalor ba imolo. Win ren adeva, kor amne nalor et illorin*
> *po malo va qua oa bat ma. Ilgarth puat hartwe wa hadin.*
> "The anger of a wizard is fearsome. Many things kill, but
> only a wizard or the gods can unmake a life as though it
> never were. Such power must be ruled by laws."
> — EXTRACT FROM *THE LAWS* ISSUED
>   BY THE COUNCIL OF WIZARDS

Alanna studied the rules of the Council of Wizards intensively in the days that followed. Staying with Witha, as Magra had not arrived and Jerevan was busy, she had no opportunity to leave the house. Practicing what she had learned of wizardry gave her a headache if she continued for too long at a stretch. Studying was her only alternative and, after two weeks of doing nothing but practice or study, she knew *The Laws* backwards and forwards.

Worse than the inactivity, was finding out how much she missed Jerevan. When she received a note requesting her company for dinner, Alanna was hard put to conceal her excitement.

"Why do we have to go out?" Alanna asked when Jerevan arrived. "Wouldn't we be better off eating in privacy here?"

"I want you to meet two other wizards who've just arrived in Ninkarrak and I don't want Witha to hear everything we say. I trust her discretion, but there's some knowledge to which only wizards are entitled."

"I see." Alanna tried hard to suppress her disappointment at not having Jerevan to herself.

The restaurant was located in the southeastern part of the city, close to the Lamashrak, a sprawling district where many of the refugees from Lamash had settled. It was called Gwalis, the Yellow Cat, and a carving of that small beast, similar to the ones that ran wild in the hills of Zamarga, hung above the door.

Inside the atmosphere was dark and smoky from the cheap oil used in the lanterns but, as well as tables dotted about the floor, there were private booths in the back, and the smell of the food was spicy and appetizing. Jerevan guided her to a corner booth already occupied by a beautiful blonde woman and a tall, gaunt man whose clothes looked shabby beside those of his companion.

"Vitry, Basel, may I present Alanna Cairn, Tamrai of Fell, and my newest apprentice. Alanna, I'd like you to meet the Wizard Vitry," Jerevan gestured toward the woman, "and the Wizard Basel." Jerevan waited while Alanna seated herself opposite the others in the booth and then slid in beside her.

Alanna felt the swift mental evaluation that the two wizards made of her but it no longer caused her dizziness or discomfort now that she recognized it for what it was. She was not yet able to respond in the same way, however.

"I'm glad to meet you, Tamrai Cairn," Vitry said, smiling. "It's always good to learn of another comrade in these days, isn't it Basel." She turned to her companion.

Alanna looked at the man for the first time and was startled to see that his eyes were covered with the opaque, white tissue of cataracts. He turned to her and she realized that, despite the opacity of his eyes, he could still see.

She thought she'd managed to conceal her reaction, but he smiled at her. "Don't be embarrassed. Remember, any deformity in a wizard is a kind of affectation." He shrugged. "Without the cataracts I'd never have learned to see, so they're a part of me, and most wizards don't try to change themselves. We wear illusions or we shape-shift, if we have the strength, but we rarely tamper with our true forms."

There was something in the way he spoke of changing his form that piqued Alanna's curiosity. "Why not, if you have the power?"

Vitry answered, her expression wry. "There was once a plain wizard called Arlyn…"

"Don't make a joke of it, Vitry," Basel said.

"Why not? It happened a long time ago; you should be over it by now." Vitry sounded angry. She turned to Alanna. "Arlyn was a fellow student when Basel began studying wizardry. She was plain, almost ugly. When she became a wizard, she set out to make herself the most beautiful woman in the world. Her great ambition. The problem was, she couldn't make up her mind what form was most beautiful. She kept changing herself until she couldn't remember what her original form had been and, as she always paid attention only to her face and body, she never noticed that her mind was aging until she was so senile she couldn't remember any form at all. Toward the end she mirrored whomever she was with and one day the person she was with died so Arlyn died too, and good riddance."

"That's easy for you to say, Vitry, you were born beautiful," Basel said. "You can't understand her pain."

"No, I can't. What's more, I don't want to and I'm tired of having you refer to her as though she were a martyr. There've been many plain wizards over the years, and no one else ever died as she did. Ugliness is no guarantee of virtue, Basel. Arlyn was selfish, vain and stupid."

"That's enough, you two. How did you find Zamarga?" Jerevan interrupted.

"It was a profitable journey." Vitry sounded relieved at the interruption. "We gathered quite a bit of news on the way. The market for mercenaries should improve soon. The south is finally arming for war. Khorat signed a treaty with Mahran and Ravaar's turning out real soldiers."

"One of the priests there, Kymor Dag, spent several years in Isin," Basel added. "They say he mastered the high sight and studied gene dancing. What's more, when he returned to Ravaar fifteen years ago, he brought with him a man who's been teaching a new form of hand to hand combat to their militant priests. They call it death dancing. It took a while to catch on, but now its revolutionizing their whole system. Apparently, it's a modification of techniques the eslarin developed in their hospitals for treating violent patients. The training stresses mental discipline and utilizes eslar medical knowledge of the body's nerve centers. Some of their fighters are incredibly skilled. We saw a demonstration where one trainee beat two professional wrestlers with ease. Combined with even a small amount of wizard talent, their mercenaries will soon be a dangerous force."

Vitry broke in, "We also have a surprise for you, but we won't tell you about it now. We should be answering Alanna's questions."

The dinner passed quickly after that, with most of the conversation centered around the laws of Council and the reasons for them. They were finishing their wine when Basel said, "We heard in Ravaar that Saranith's taken her third soul, another cousin of the Estahar of Senanga. With him dead, she commands the whole fleet and only the Estahar, Kaya, and his children stand between her and the throne."

Vitry grimaced. "I suppose I should be glad Basel doesn't wear rubies in his eyes."

"What do you mean?" Alanna asked.

Vitry looked surprised. "That's what Saranith does. She has two great big faceted rubies instead of eyeballs. The effect is supposed to be striking."

"Saranith," Alanna said, "the name sounds familiar, but I can't place it. How does she take souls and why would she wear jewels instead of eyes?"

Vitry hesitated and glanced at Jerevan. "You haven't told her about Saranith?"

"No," Jerevan said. "But now you've introduced the subject, you may as well tell her the rest."

Vitry frowned. "Saranith's a linlar, a cousin of the Estahar of Senanga, but her mother was a human slave. She was told when she was a child that linlarin wizards can't normally develop the high sight. They see with their own were-vision so their inner eye doesn't develop. That's true of all the larin." Vitry paused and looked at Basel.

"Blinding often encourages the development of the inner eye, as in my case," Basel continued for her. "Since the time of Rav many of the ruling families of Gandahar have blindfolded young children known to have talent to stimulate the development of higher levels of vision. The royal families of Senanga and Gatukai have recently started doing the same. They've even sent a few of their more talented children to Gandahar for training. Saranith was an extraordinarily ambitious child. When she was twelve she put out her own eyes with a poker."

Alanna gasped, "How horrible!"

"It served its purpose," Vitry said. "She's by far the strongest of all the linlarin wizards. She could restore her eyes easily enough if she wished. Instead, she wears rubies in the sockets. As she's the bearer of Cinkarion, if she ever finds a wizard who can survive linking with her, together they'll match any other power on Tamar."

"She's the bearer of Cinkarion? Why don't the wizards she links with survive?" Alanna asked.

"No one knows for sure," Basel said. "We only know that to date three men have tried, two of them talented wizards, and the linkage destroyed them all. Of course, the two wizards held superior positions that she wanted and were cousins whom she may have disliked."

Alanna was silent as Jerevan drove her back to his cousin's home later that night. Finally, she said, "You didn't like it when they mentioned Saranith?"

"No."

They left the well-lighted, main boulevards, crowded even at that late hour, and wound through the narrow lanes that served the great estates to the east of the Royal Park. These streets were unlit and almost deserted and Jerevan pulled the horses over to the side and drew them to a halt. The day had been warm for Ingvash, a hint of the coming spring in the air, but Alanna shivered.

"You're cold?" Jerevan drew out his crystal. "I'll warm us both."

Even as he spoke she felt enveloped in a sphere of warm air, as though the open carriage had developed a roof and walls and been filled with air heated by a glowing hearth.

"I wasn't really cold," she said, uncomfortable in the heat while wearing her sable coat.

"Then you don't need that coat," he replied, helping her to remove it.

She relinquished the coat, aware that her pulse rate had increased. His golden hair was silvered by the moonlight. His eyes were dark shadows, but she felt the heat of his gaze as clearly as she felt the hot air around her.

"You know what I want, don't you?"

She stared at him, stirred by the intensity of his tone, but unsure what she should do.

He took her hands. "Alanna, you feel the same attraction I feel. Admit it."

She tried to pull away, but his hands tightened. "Answer me— or are you afraid to?"

"You know what I feel. You don't need me to say it."

He relaxed slightly and drew her close to him, letting go of one of her hands to put his arm around her. "Then I'll say it. I love you. I've had to watch myself constantly to keep from touching you, pressuring you. But I've wanted to touch you, and hold you, and make love to you. And I know you've felt at least some of the same attraction." His hand stroked her side and she felt its warmth through her dress.

Her breathing was irregular and her skin tingled along the path his hand traced. "You want the Talisman as much as you want me," she said, striving for control.

"You don't really believe that." His voice was soft and compelling. "Oh, I don't deny I want your help, the use of your strength, but, if that were all that was between us, I'd reject such a linkage myself. There's no privacy in it, we'd drive each other mad. But despite my own fears, I find I want you linked so close to me that no distance can separate us." He turned her until she faced him, then bent to kiss her. His lips were gentle on hers and the flare of passion she felt was irresistible.

Only after Jerevan drew back and set her apart from him did she recognize the heat of the Talisman at her breast. His breathing was ragged and a pulse beat strongly in his temple. "Every time I touch you it gets harder to stop, but even a touch is dangerous while you wear Vyrkarion."

His words sobered Alanna. She drew a deep breath, horrified to find herself trembling and aware that, once again, if he'd continued to hold her in his arms, she'd have linked with him then and there, no matter what the consequences might have been. Worse, she was sorry for the reprieve. "I do want to link with you, Jerevan," she said, "but I'm afraid. I'm afraid of losing myself in the linkage. You're so much stronger than I am. And now I know about Saranith, know the linkage can destroy, and I..."

"I knew that talk about Saranith would upset you," Jerevan said. "That's why I stopped here tonight, after telling you I wouldn't pressure you." With his finger he turned her face until he could meet her eyes. "She isn't relevant to us, Alanna."

Alanna gathered together the shreds of her control. "But it's true that a linkage can destroy the weaker wizard?"

He stiffened. "You don't think I'd hurt you?"

She looked away from him. "My talent is infinitely inferior to yours."

"No! Your training is inferior but your talent, your will, is strong." Jerevan paused and touched her hand, just a brush of his fingertip. "All Saranith has proved is that it's possible for a strong wizard linked to one of the karionin to use that linkage to kill someone weaker. Except for the first time, there's every reason to believe that what she's done she's done deliberately, a kind of formal murder where the reward to a survivor would be so great that her victims volunteer despite the danger. What she does has never been done before, but it's Saranith's linkage with Cinkarion, not her strength or her training or her experience, that gives her the power to destroy minds. You're the bearer of Vyrkarion. It's linked to you and would protect you. And you're not weak, Alanna, only untrained."

She grimaced. "You must think me an awful coward."

"No." He shook his head, smiling wryly. "I think you're honest and too desirable for my comfort. But you don't have to make up your mind now, or ever, if it comes to that. I won't pressure you again."

Alanna looked down into her lap. Her mind went back to the moment she first started her training, when the Talisman had almost drawn her into rapport with him. She remembered the warmth of the feeling, the fascination. "How close would the link be, Jerevan? How closely would we be bound?"

"I don't know. Errin Anifi and his mate Elise, the bearers of Lyskarion, are very close, but they knew each other as children. I've known wizards linked through lesser foci, like the crystal I carry. I've been linked to other wizards myself as you will be when you take your oath. But those are surface linkages; they aren't deep or permanent. All I know is that it will be as profoundly binding for me as it will be for you. And that, despite my training, I'll be as new to it as you."

XXIII

4731, 474TH CYCLE OF THE YEAR OF THE DRAGON
MONTH OF INGVASH

> Attar: Never again shall the blood of
> malarin mingle with the blood of
> my children. Such mating brings
> forth monsters.
> — ACT IV, SCENE 5, LINES 43 - 47,
>   FROM *THE DEFIANCE OF EDAIN*

S oldiers marched behind Rhys. Rakshe felt their minds like little points of warmth and life against the cool background of no-life. He sensed his master's mind reaching back and feeling for them, and he sensed his master's pleasure, as he often did in these days.

There was a wizard approaching, however. One that Rakshe recognized from the mental warning he had received some days ago from a karioth of his herd. The wizard's mind burned brighter and warmer than the minds of the soldiers.

"Rai, there is one who comes. Can you feel? He is south of us, but near."

Rhys and his army had left Beng that morning and were progressing along the dirt track that led out of Asherdale to Dorimer where it joined a spur of the Great Northeastern Road. A storm three days before had left the road snow-covered with patches of ice.

"Many come to meet me," Rhys thought.

"This is not one who comes to serve you, rai. This is one of those like you, but lesser, a candle to your sun."

Rhys laughed. He was accustomed to the adulation of those around him, but Rakshe was usually more acerbic. *"There are no others like me,"* he said, *"not in all the world."*

He expected Rakshe to agree, but Rakshe hesitated and Rhys detected a note of alarm in his thought.

"Then tell me, Rakshe, who is my equal in power?"

"Rai, there is no one now living your equal, but there is one, the master of he who is coming, who will be your equal in the fullness of time." Rakshe spoke carefully, not wishing to anger Rhys.

Rhys' thought showed that he understood how tactful Rakshe was being. *"Do you fear my anger, Rakshe? Rather, I would welcome such a one. I'm lonely, and the minds that follow me, they are the minds of dogs begging for favors."*

"*I do not fear you, rai, but I'm your servant. It's my nature to be bound to you.*" Rakshe was surprised by his master's mood.

"*I sense this wizard. He has no power, not even that which my grandfather can wield. Why do you warn me of him?*" There was a note of irritation in Rhys' thought. Rakshe wondered if his master had indeed hoped for another mind his equal.

"*He's but a servant, as I am. It's the master of whom I bade you to take note.*" Rakshe shivered in the cold wind that blew from the north. Storm clouds loomed overhead.

"*You expected this one. You've been keeping secrets from me.*" Rhys laughed, but the sound was harsh. "*I wonder why.*"

"*Merely that this wizard might come before you at a propitious hour, rai. He's the rider of a mare of my herd.*" Rakshe stepped carefully to avoid the icy places in the uneven track.

"*What does he want?*"

"*A moment of your time, rai. He wants to deliver a message and ask a favor.*" Rakshe was uneasy. His inability to read his master's mood disturbed him more than the cold weather and the treacherous trail.

"*What message and what favor?*" There was anger in Rhys' thought.

"*You should ask him, rai, not me.*"

"*But I'd prefer to hear it from you.*"

"*I don't know the details, rai.*"

"*But you do know the essence?*"

"*Not really, rai,*" Rakshe protested, "*just what I have already told you.*"

"*Then take me to this hedge wizard now.*"

With his master's mind as a goad, Rakshe left the trail and the column of plodding soldiers and galloped through the snow across the hills. At some points he lunged through drifts that rose to his chest, but he did not slow until they approached the lone karioth rider on a trail that would intercept the one Rakshe had left in about an hour's normal riding time.

The karioth halted at Rhys' approach, and both mount and rider waited. The clouds thickened overhead to a heavy, gray darkness. It still amazed Rakshe how the weather in these days reflected his master's mood.

"*Well, hedge wizard! You have a message for me?*"

Rakshe came to a halt some three meters in front of the waiting wizard.

The wizard bowed in the saddle. He was a small, chunky figure on the back of his sleek, brown steed. "*I am the Wizard Kulin,*" he thought. "*I've come on behalf of the Varfarin.*"

"*I know that much already. Say what you have to say, wizard.*"

"*My master, the Wizard Jerevan, Esalfar of the Varfarin, sends you greetings.*"

The storm clouds had not dispersed and the wind was, if anything, colder. "*Well, go on,*" Rhys demanded. "*You didn't come all this way merely to say hello.*"

"No, rai. My master wants to inform you that there are several thousand Gandaharan troops now in Ninkarrak and members of Idrim's government have turned to the isklarin in an attempt to defeat you." Kulin hesitated, and Rakshe could sense his nervousness.

"I am aware of the situation in Ninkarrak, as I am aware of all that passes in Ilwheirlane."

"My master also wants to assure you that he personally will not interfere with your assumption of power, and that the Varfarin will take no part in the coming conflict."

"However, he does not speak for all the members of the Varfarin. But I am not to hold it against the organization if some of the members choose to challenge me," Rhys mocked. "You see how quickly I'm learning your human politics."

Kulin swallowed. "I have come in peace."

Rhys laughed. "You have come in fear! Go back to your master and tell him to send me something better than you, if he wishes to deal with me in future."

"I will so inform him, rai." Kulin bowed a second time and the karioth he rode turned to leave.

"Wait!" Rhys demanded. "What form was my favor to take?"

Kulin hesitated, then thought, "Merely, rai, that the privileges of the Varfarin remain undisturbed. It has been traditional for millennia that the throne of Ilwheirlane support us."

"As I am to be a ruler of malarin, I am to concern myself with the fate of malarin all over Tamar? Is that what your master wants from me?"

Kulin stared at Rhys like a rabbit stares at a malik about to eat it. He was obviously unable to answer such a loaded question. The sky darkened to black and the wind rose, swirling in angry gusts.

Rakshe thought, "Remember, rai, he is but the servant."

Rhys snorted, then laughed, and suddenly the sky lightened and wind died down.

"Very well, Rakshe, as you are so concerned for him. You tell the hedge wizard that I grant no favors to servants, or to anyone who will not face me himself."

"Yes, rai."

"And Rakshe, you'll tell me the next time you hear from one of your herd?"

"Yes, rai." Rakshe bowed his head again, all too aware of the cold wind at his back.

Elath crossed to the narrow window and looked down at the street. No sign yet of Thrym. She could hear Fal struggling to attach his hook to the stub of his arm and she clenched her fists to keep herself from trying to help.

"Got it," Fal said.

Elath turned back and watched as Fal hooked a cup and scooped it full of hot soup from the kettle on the hearth.

"At least I don't have a problem with burned fingers anymore," he said, crossing the room to the table and sitting down. In their small room he moved confidently, knowing the location of every object.

"Thrym said he was going to talk to the Wizard of Leyburn, the one who's hiring, about healing you," Elath said.

Fal turned his head in her direction. No scars marked his face but there were only empty sockets where his eyeballs had once been. His face, always bony, now looked skeletal. "No wizard will defy Miune. You know that, El."

"The wizards don't worship Miune. One of them might do it," she insisted.

"Defy a god for the sake of a thief? Don't be a fool. I'm a cripple and I'll stay a cripple until I end it." Fal brought the cup up to his lips, blew on the hot liquid and drank. Then he said, "I want to live long enough to know the isklarin are out of Ninkarrak. I want to hear that the worship of Miune has ceased to be the state religion. Then I'll die happy."

Elath turned back to the window. "What about me?"

"You've already found a new partner."

She shook her head. Then, realizing that he couldn't see her, she said, "I'm working with Fianna on the job for the wizard, but it isn't any kind of permanent arrangement."

"What about Drusan?"

Elath spun round and marched over to table, banging her hands down on the table in front of him so he couldn't help but hear. "It was one job, Fal. We needed money. Drusan had an inside connection and needed a partner. Flickra introduced us at the ball. We acted as guards for a special convoy of goods, killed or disabled the crew that had been hired to steal it, split the money for the job and that was that. I never had any intention of taking that drunk as a permanent partner. I certainly didn't bed him."

"You'd have been better off if you had. I'm of no more use to you."

Elath stiffened. "That's the first I've heard that Theolan cut off more than your hands."

Fal shifted in his chair. "You know what I mean."

Elath sighed and walked around the table to where she could put her hands on his shoulders. She rubbed the tense muscles of his neck and upper back. "Don't give up, Fal. I need you."

Fal lurched to his feet and his arm, going out to push back the table, knocked the cup loose. It fell with a clatter, splashing soup all down the legs of his pants. He swore and backed away from the table, knocking down the chair. Then he stood still, swaying slightly and turning his head.

Elath bit her lip, but said, "You have your back to the window and the table's about two feet away to your right."

Fal turned and walked to the bed. "You'll have to help me get these wet pants off," he said. "I need picking up after like a baby."

She went to him and helped him change his clothes. They had just finished when there was a knock on the door.

Elath unlatched the door and opened it. Thrym came in, glancing quickly at Fal. "How're you doing?"

"Elath is coping as usual," Fal said.

"What have you heard?" Elath asked.

Thrym's eyes went to Fal and then back to Elath. He shook his head, but said, "Idrim leaves soon to meet the lord in the north. We're to be ready to leave the same night. There'll be a ship at pier thirty-five. Everyone should be aboard by sunset."

Elath looked away from him. Her hands clenched and she stalked over to the window. Fal's head turned as he listened to the sound of her steps. "You've told Elath that the wizard wouldn't help me, haven't you, Thrym? I told her he wouldn't."

Thrym looked at Elath and shrugged. "He didn't say he wouldn't help. He said he couldn't at the moment. Breaking a form imposed by the Staff would take more energy than he can spare right now."

Elath smiled. "Then he'll heal Fal if we just wait a while?"

Thrym frowned, disturbed by the interpretation Elath put on his words. "He didn't say that. He said he thought the punishment sounded too extreme and that, when the current crisis has passed, he'd be willing to hear all the details and then decide. But he also said he didn't know when he'd be back in Ninkarrak."

Fal laughed. "He just didn't want to say no right out."

Thrym shook his head and then, realizing that Fal couldn't see him, he said, "No. He'd have said no fast enough, if that's what he meant. But there's a lot going on right now. He made a suggestion, though. He said you should make your request of the new Estahar when he enters the city."

XXIV

*Ya cosar ya hanawe wa hadin
a Ilcorril a Nalorin.*

"I swear that I shall be guided by the laws
of the Council of Wizards."

— BEGINNING OF THE OATH TAKEN BY WIZARDS BEFORE THEY CAN ADVANCE BEYOND
THE FIRST LEVEL OF TRAINING.

Alanna was in her room practicing when a maid came to her door
and said that Lord Leyburn had arrived and she was wanted in
the sitting room. She went down expecting to see only Jerevan and was
surprised to see a beautiful, black-haired, green-eyed woman at his side.
She felt an instant, violent dislike.

Jerevan introduced Alanna, then said, "Alanna, I want you to meet
the Wizard Magra. She's to be your companion for the next few weeks."

Alanna thought he looked less strained than he had the last time she
saw him. She said stiffly to the woman, "I'm glad to meet you, Magra."

"And these two gentlemen are the Wizards Kindric and Garth,"
Jerevan added, gesturing to two men Alanna had missed when she
entered the room. They stood together by the door, the Wizard Kindric
a slender, blond man, several centimeters shorter than the dark, burly
Garth.

Magra grinned, her face lighting up with gamin charm. "I'm glad to
meet you, too, but if we're going to spend every moment together for
weeks, you'll probably be wishing me in Agnith's fires before long."

Alanna smiled reluctantly, startled to note that the black cap covering
Magra's head wasn't hair, but feathers. "You won't be wishing the same
of me?"

"Oh, probably, but I'm older and have more patience," Magra said
with grin.

Alanna felt herself warm to the slight, exquisite woman and tried to
analyze the antagonism she'd felt at first. Then she realized that it hadn't
been Magra personally she'd felt hostility toward, but Magra's presence
with Jerevan. Alanna had grown accustomed to having his attention, to

being with him. During the last weeks she'd missed that daily contact and the sight of him with Magra had been a shock.

At least, when we're linked I'll no longer feel so jealous, she thought. Her heart trusted Jerevan; so must she. She'd soon take her oath as a wizard with all the responsibility that oath entailed, yet she had doubted her own instincts. That was foolish.

Alanna smiled. "Would you like refreshments?"

"No. We don't have time," Jerevan said. "I've ordered all the wizards in Ninkarrak who are also bound by Council vows to assemble at my home as witnesses. You'll take your oath today. This may be the last opportunity for years to have so many wizards present for such a ceremony."

Jerevan drove them to his own estate east of the Royal Park. Alanna hadn't seen his home in Ninkarrak before and was impressed by it, and even more impressed by its interior. The rooms were filled with treasures from all over the world.

Three women and four men waited for them in a spacious salon. Alanna was relieved to recognize some of them. She remembered the Wizard Ashe, standing with two other men by the window, from the carnival Jerevan had taken her to, and she remembered Vitry and Basel, seated together on a couch, from the dinner earlier in the month.

Magra, who'd been beside her, suddenly darted forward to embrace one of the women by the fireplace. "Dinara, it's so good to see you. Jehan, but it must be nearly fifteen years."

"Sixteen! It was the Year of the Dolphin, down in Lara." Dinara laughed. Nearly as short as Magra, she was more solidly built. She had a mop of bright red hair framing a face that was covered with freckles. "You've been in Cibata, I hear."

"All right, I need everyone's attention," Jerevan said. "This is Alanna Cairn, the Tamrai of Fell and my apprentice. Alanna, I want you to meet the wizards who will be witnesses to your oath taking. Kindric, Garth and Magra you've just met. The woman Magra's clutching is Dinara and Dinara's companion is the Wizard Tana."

The tall woman standing next to Dinara by the fireplace, her long brown hair confined in braids, nodded.

Jerevan waved to the couple on the couch. "Vitry and Basel you've met." He turned toward the window. "And Ashe you've also met. The two men beside him are Kulin and Rainal." Kulin was short, stocky and brown-haired. Rainal was taller with black hair, blue-green eyes and a rakish air. "They're all gathered here to witness your oath. Are you ready?"

"As I'll ever be," Alanna murmured. Even knowing the reason for it, the sense of evaluation from all those wizards at once made her tremble.

"You told me that your father taught you to revere Jehan. Are you prepared to swear in his name?"

"Yes. I understand from the laws of Council that he's the patron god of wizards. I'll be bound by my oath in his name."

"Does anyone here know of any reason why I shouldn't take the oath of this woman?" Jerevan looked around the room at a circle of solemn faces. There was silence.

"*Then we shall link minds.*" Jerevan thought.

Alanna heard his announcement, but the reality took her unaware. She felt as though she were suddenly standing naked on a vast stage with a multitude of eyes looking into her brain.

"*Will you, Alanna, honor your oath given in the name of Jehan.*"

"*Yes.*"

"*Then give your oath, and we shall witness.*"

"I swear that I shall be guided by the laws of the Council of Wizards," Alanna began.

"*What is the first law?*"

"*I will not use the knowledge I gain from my training to act against the interests of the Council, the Varfarin, or my master.*"

"*The second law?*"

"*I will not teach, or transmit in any way, the knowledge I gain from my training to any being who has interests opposed to those of the Council, the Varfarin, or my master.*"

"*The third law?*"

The ceremony continued as Alanna swore to each one of the complex laws with all of the wizards present in rapport to witness her sincerity. Her grasp of word images in the mind speech often failed her and she had to speak the oaths aloud, but she pledged to them all in the linkage. When she had sworn to the last one there was silence for a moment. Then Jerevan thought, "*You have witnessed this woman's oath?*"

The assembled wizards replied as one, "*We have.*"

"*Do you accept her as an apprentice with all the rights and responsibilities that entails?*"

"*We do.*"

The tension that had held them all as she swore to the detailed codes of conduct dissolved. Magra came up to her and kissed her on the cheek. "Well, that's over. How do you feel?"

"Exhausted," Alanna admitted, already feeling the ache in her head from the long period of mental strain.

"How well I remember," Vitry commented. "I went home and slept for a full day."

"I'm afraid we don't have time for Alanna to do that," Jerevan said and something in his voice drew the attention of the others. "Idrim's army is mustering and will leave before another week has passed. The day after it leaves we act. There are twelve of us. I know that Aavik claimed to have eleven wizards with him last month and I suspect he has closer to twenty-five or thirty now. There's a simple method available for getting Aubrey out of the Tower, but getting him away is another matter."

"Would a good distraction be useful?" Vitry asked. "If so, Basel and I might be of assistance."

Jerevan looked at her and frowned. "Now that I think of it, you did mention a surprise. A distraction is exactly what we need. Otherwise, Aavik's wizards will see us when we take Aubrey and be after us with a small army. What have you got?"

Vitry smiled, and Alanna was impressed by the innate sensuality of that expression. "Something that will knock out all farsensing for a hundred kilometers and it should last for three to six hours. Can you guess what it is?"

"This isn't the time for guessing games, Vitry, but I'd say from what you've described that you captured a female firedrake ready for her mating flight. It won't work, though. There won't be any males this far north."

"You didn't let me finish," Vitry pouted. "Basel and I have a female and a male, and the female's been ready to fly for eight months. I've been holding her neutral, thinking I'd take her to Kailane this summer. The gannithin colony in the Sarakians was wiped out a thousand years ago. I wanted to restock them. Basel brought the male." She turned to look at the tall man with the blind, white eyes, sitting beside her and Alanna was surprised by the warmth of her expression. She had considered Vitry superficial, being more impressed by Basel, but now she realized that Vitry's feelings ran deeper than she liked to reveal.

"How much notice do you need? When you stop neutralizing her, how long before she flies?" Ashe asked.

"About twenty-four hours. I can't be exact. If I stop neutralizing her at about nine in the evening though, she's bound to fly sometime the next night. They prefer to do their mating flights at night."

"It sounds like the most effective distraction we're likely to discover," Jerevan said. "We'll just have to hope their song doesn't hurt us as much as it hurts the isklarin."

"You have to remember not to look outside yourself and you'll be all right," Basel said. "I'll have to restore my eyes until they've gone, or I'll be really blind."

"Isn't there a danger of fires?" Ashe asked.

Basel shook his head. "Not with only one male, especially this time of year when it's cold. She'll fly southwest out over the bay, as that's the direction of her homeland. Even if the female takes a dislike to the male, they'll be too far away by the time he catches her to cause any problems."

"Then it sounds like we're not likely to find anything better," Ashe said.

"Let's take it as settled," Kindric added, and there was a chorus of agreement.

Otto carried in a tray of bread, cold meats and cheeses and Jerevan told the wizards to help themselves.

"All right, everyone," he said, "we have our distraction and I have a way to get Aubrey out of the Tower. As soon as we've had something to eat we'll discuss how we get out of Ilwheirlane."

The meeting broke up just after four o'clock. Alanna, Jerevan, Magra and Kindric arrived back at Lady Farlon's house as the shadows were lengthening. All the houses in the neighborhood were set well apart in large gardens and vehicles usually parked behind them, so Alanna noticed the closed coach drawn up on the opposite side of the street as a rarity despite her headache and the haze of exhaustion. When they pulled into Witha's drive, she saw the driver, who had been leaning back in his seat taking a swig from a pocket flask, sit up. He said something to someone inside the coach and a face appeared at the window. For a moment she thought the face was Aavik's, then she realized there was only a slight resemblance. This man was darker and wore his hair differently but, as Jerevan pulled his horses to a stop in the drive, the other coach began to move toward them.

Alanna grabbed Jerevan's arm. "Who are they?"

"Don't worry. I see them. I was afraid they'd find you if you stayed in Ninkarrak too long."

Alanna watched the approach of the other vehicle with horror, but Magra, Jerevan and Kindric appeared calm.

The coach pulled up beside Jerevan's open carriage and stopped, allowing three figures to jump down from it, the man she had seen through the coach window and two women. The coachman also descended from his perch to stand beside them. The two men and the taller woman were dark-haired and dark-eyed. The smaller woman had sand-colored hair and the same amber eyes as Aavik. They all had fixed, expressionless faces but aside from that none of them looked particularly alike. These are isklarin, Alanna thought, but they look so human.

Jerevan, Kindric and Magra jumped down so that the seven figures faced each other as though preparing for some game. Alanna would have followed, but Jerevan waved her back. She hesitated. Then Otto took the reins of the horses and gestured for her to get down on the side of the coach closest to the house. She did so carefully, wanting to help but afraid that anything she did might interfere. When she was safely down, Otto led the horses away.

"You've found reinforcements," the tall, dark isklar woman said. "Aavik was afraid you would if we took too long finding her."

Jerevan said nothing. Alanna, watching from the entryway, could feel the tension.

The blonde isklar farthest from the one who had spoken drew a crystal from her pocket and held it up before her. It began to glow until it was too bright to look at directly, like the fiery globes that Jerevan and Aavik had dueled with when Jerevan rescued her.

As though that were a signal, the other wizards also drew out their crystals. Alanna had to look away from the brightness and shut her eyes, but even with her eyes shut she saw the hard fires of focused energy.

The blonde woman began the attack. Alanna flinched as a fierce shaft of flame lashed out at Jerevan. It never reached him. His own crystal flared and the energies met and coruscated. As one, Magra and Kindric sent lances of force at the isklar woman who had attacked first and then turned to meet the attacks of two of the other three isklarin. The short lances of fire from Magra and Kindric struck the single woman locked in battle with Jerevan. When the flames reached her, her figure blazed with fire. For a moment she was a pillar of light, then the fourth isklar stepped forward and a bridge of light formed, linking him with his beleaguered companion. Her lance, which had failed when she had been forced to defend herself, flared brilliantly.

Magra and Kindric looked to be evenly matched in their contests, but Jerevan was now facing two wizards. The energies were blinding, but to Alanna's horrified eyes the power of the linked wizards seemed to be stronger. She clasped the Talisman at her breast. It felt hot against her skin.

She found herself willing her strength into Jerevan, but the distance across the driveway seemed as wide as an abyss. She took one step and then another. Jerevan's lance was definitely paler now than the lance from the linked wizards opposing him. Alanna covered the rest of the distance between her and Jerevan in a half run, but having reached his side she didn't know what to do. Jerevan's attention was entirely on his crystal and the battle he was fighting through it. How could she help him without distracting him? Might not her attempt to link with him now cause more harm than good? She didn't know, but the Talisman felt hot against her chest, as though urging her to act, and as she hesitated by his side Jerevan's lance seemed to flicker.

Alanna shrugged off her doubts and fears. She had to do something. She took the Talisman in her right hand and brought it up to her face. It pulsed with green flame and for the first time since she'd taken it from Myrriden she felt its presence buoying her up. Then with her left hand she grasped Jerevan's right arm just above his wrist.

Pain. She was in a whirlpool of spinning pain. No, it was a funnel, the eye of a tornado, embedded inside her, sucking at her, draining her. She forced her eyes open and saw an arc of green light between the Talisman and Jerevan's crystal. His lance was now a mixture of white and green and it was the lance of the two linked isklarin which was failing.

Alanna gritted her teeth as the whirlpool tore at the energy inside her, and watched as the isklarin lance became a shield of fire in an attempt to hold off Jerevan's attack. For a moment it seemed they might succeed. Then the dual shield flickered and an arc of light went from the two already linked to the tall isklar woman facing Kindric, joining them. Energy flared out like a nova from the explosion of force caused by their linkage.

Alanna screamed as the blaze of flame engulfed Kindric and billowed out to lick at Jerevan and herself, although she was partially sheltered by Jerevan's body. When the fire retreated, she could hardly see through the dazzle spots in front of her eyes, but she thought Kindric had fallen. Yet the isklarin had formed the linkage out of desperation. After that first tremendous burst of force the triple linkage was erratic, flickering, coruscating, making sight even more confusing to Alanna's already dazzled eyes. The three linked isklarin and Jerevan and herself all seemed to be enclosed together in a tent of flame. Then Jerevan swung the green and white lance one more time and the fires collapsed as the three isklarin fell to the ground.

The coachman, seeing himself the only survivor, broke off his attack against Magra, shielded himself and leaped onto one of the coach horses. Coach and horses started down the drive. Only Jerevan, Magra and Alanna were left standing. Magra knelt down by Kindric, but Alanna wasn't capable of moving. She felt as if all her nerve endings had been scraped raw with only a thin film of green insulating them. And the film was fading. Her hand still clenched Jerevan's wrist. She couldn't make the muscles work to let go. And close as she was to him, she could hardly see him around the flaming suns that filled her vision. Finally, by concentrating on each finger one at a time, she managed to let go of his arm and turn to face him. His feet were spread apart, and his eyes were shut. He was very pale, his skin covered with sweat despite the cold air. She realized that she must not look much better.

"Jerevan, are you all right?"

"I… I will be," he said, his voice unsteady, "but what about you. You could have been killed."

"I thought you were going to be. I couldn't just stand there and watch." The last of the green insulation dissipated. As her heart pumped, she felt blood pulsing against the thin, painful membranes in her head. The agony was intense and growing with each heartbeat.

She put her hand out to touch his arm, gently this time, but his hand caught hers and gripped. "I'm afraid I can't see anything," he said. "Did the flash get you as well?"

"Only a little. I've got some dazzle spots, but I can see."

"Then you'll have to guide me. Have they gone?"

Magra came up to them and Alanna saw that she, too, was pale and beaded with sweat. "They've gone, Jere, but Kindric's badly hurt."

"The isklarin?"

"The three here are dead. The coachman got away. How are you and Alanna?"

"I'll be all right," Jerevan said. "I just got a bit singed in the backlash when they linked. Alanna can see. Also, she's just undergone her first linkage under combat conditions. It's a miracle she's still standing."

Magra nodded. "I'll take care of Kindric. And I'll tell Otto and Witha to help you both to bed. Do you think you can make it inside?"

"One way or another," Jerevan said.

Magra nodded and turned away.

"Can you walk?" Jerevan asked.

Alanna didn't dare move her head to nod. Then she realized that Jerevan wouldn't be able to see her nod in any event. That meant she'd have to speak, but that would hurt, too. "I-I don't know," she croaked. She tried to take a step, but the pain in her head billowed out and she fell into blackness.

Alanna woke the next morning to a blinding headache. She didn't want to open her eyes, but somehow she could sense Jerevan waiting for her. She forced her lids to open, then closed them immediately as light stabbed into her brain. *"Here, let me help you,"* she felt Jerevan's thought inside her. It was strange, she didn't have to strain to understand him as she had before; it was as though she were thinking to herself, except the taste of the thoughts was Jerevan's, not hers.

She felt something shift inside her head and the headache became more bearable. She tried opening her eyes again, and this time was able to keep them open. Jerevan sat in a chair beside her bed. "What happened?" she asked.

"Don't you remember? You linked with me." Jerevan smiled. His eyes were dark blue flames.

Memory of the isklarin attack flooded through her. She'd thought Jerevan was going to be killed. "The isklarin, the battle, what happened?"

"We won, but you were injured. I drew from you too quickly. Without Vyrkarion, the force of the energy involved would have torn your mind apart and killed you. I think we must have been facing some of Aavik's best wizards, and they were not only strong, but skilled in the use of linkages. I owe you my life, and Kindric's as well. We'd both have been killed by that triple linkage, if you hadn't backed me with Vyrkarion."

"We're linked?" She'd been so afraid of linking with him, and now they were linked and she hadn't even been aware of it. Just being able to receive his thoughts as though she were thinking them, surely that wasn't all there was to a linkage?

"*There is a link between us, but it isn't fully open.*" He ran his finger down the side of her face. "*In the heat of battle, all I did was draw energy from you. That type of link can be handled by an ordinary crystal and usually only lasts while energy is actually being exchanged. With Vyrkarion, the link stayed open after the energy exchange terminated, but it hasn't expanded.*"

"So what do we do now?" She wasn't sure what she felt, and her head hurt.

"*First of all, we take a day's rest until you're feeling better and we've both re-couped some of the energy we expended. I thought we'd go to Tormor House where there won't be the danger of another attack. I've done nearly everything I have to do here in town, anyway.*"

"That sounds wonderful. My head aches worse than it did the first day I saw the flame," she said.

"*That's not surprising.*" Jerevan smiled wryly. "*The energy paths in your brain expanded to handle the load. Vyrkarion wouldn't let them break, but you went through changes that should normally have taken nearly ten years of training.*"

"What kind of changes?"

Jerevan shook his head. "*It's hard to explain, but wizard training reshapes a wizard's brain. It usually happens slowly over years as new pathways to handle energy are created and expand. But you just started your training. You only had rudimentary pathways, nothing capable of handling the volume of energy needed for combat. An ordinary apprentice doing what you did would simply have been destroyed and had his or her brain burned out, but Vyrkarion wouldn't let that happen to you. It reinforced your brain paths.*"

She frowned. "My head hurts, but I don't feel any different."

"*You may not feel different now, but you should find your training much easier from now on.*"

"Then the changes aren't harmful?"

"*To the contrary,*" Jerevan thought.

"Then what do we do when we've rested?"

"*When we're more rested, we get to complete the linkage.*"

The next day she took a long ride while Jerevan attended to business and met with people. The fresh air cleared her head of the last traces of the previous day's headache. By three o'clock in the afternoon, when Alanna knocked on the door to Jerevan's study, she was feeling much closer to human.

"Come in," he said in response to her knock.

She opened the door and stepped inside.

He rose from his desk and came to greet her. "You're feeling all right now?"

"I'm fine." She smiled. She had no more doubts, only anticipation.

"Then I think it's time for someplace private," he said. His voice was husky and there was a brightness in his eyes that excited her. He took her hand and they walked upstairs to his bedroom.

There she went into his arms as though that was the natural place for her to be. She could sense his exultation, her own spirits rising to match his. He lifted her up and whirled her around him in sheer exuberance. She was amazed by the flaring sensation of joy and laughed despite her dizziness. They both collapsed, still laughing, on the bed with Vyrkarion flaming.

"Now, Alanna. Look into Vyrkarion now," he said, taking one of her hands in his, the other one holding her close against him.

"Just like that?" she asked, swallowing. The Talisman felt hot where it rested against her skin. "No instructions? No other preparation?"

"Just like that. There's no way to prepare for linkage. All we have to do is look into Vyrkarion while we're touching each other."

She lifted the flaming crystal with her free hand. Her eyes met Jerevan's for a fleeting moment but the Talisman drew her, pulling her gaze down.

"Look into it."

Even without his words, she couldn't have kept her eyes away from it then, the tug of the jewel was too strong. She focused on a swirling green well. Then she fell into that well, down and down and down into the rich, green depths that rang with the faint sound of crystal chimes. She wasn't aware at what moment she knew she was no longer alone, just at some point there were two minds caught in the infinite green whirl, two minds that intertwined so that after a time she wasn't sure which thoughts were hers and which were that other mind's, and after that it ceased to matter.

She floated in a green limbo. It was warm and dark, peaceful and safe with only a faint hint of music like distant bells. At first, she had no sense of identity, only an awareness of comfort and peace. Slowly her relaxation gave way to a feeling of curiosity. It was dark. Where was she? Who was she? Alanna, she was Alanna Cairn. She opened her eyes.

Jerevan. Jerevan was looking at her with a strange expression on his face. Then she realized that she was also looking at herself, and her expression was equally strange. "I'm seeing with your eyes," they said in unison.

Alanna tried to orient herself, but the attempt made her dizzy and even more confused. She was lying on Jerevan's bed. Her bed? Jerevan lay beside her leaning over her, or was she leaning over herself?

"*Alanna.*" Her name startled her, coming into her mind as if she had thought it.

"Jerevan? What's happening to me?"

She felt a surge of power as Jerevan did something and then she was back in herself again.

"*I think it will be easier to handle this way.*"

Jerevan's mind had spoken, she realized. He'd manipulated something, but, despite the fact that she'd experienced the action as though she were performing it, she couldn't comprehend what he'd done.

She was in her own head, and yet, faintly, she was still aware of him and of all that he was seeing and feeling. It was like a focus, she thought. Now she was focused in herself, but if she wished she could stretch out and move her focus into him. His awareness was still present in her mind like a peripheral vision. Being focused in herself, however, she was suddenly aware of the feel of his body lying next to hers. She felt his awareness like an echo of her own.

"*Alanna.*" His hand ran up her arm caressing her but it was her hand, too, and he felt the touch of his fingers as she felt the feel of her skin.

She raised her hand and ran it through the golden strands of his hair, feeling the tingle of her fingers on his scalp from his awareness as clearly as she felt the luxuriance of his hair. The double sensations were too delicious to resist. Their clothes interfered with their explorations so they discarded them. It didn't matter who undid which button, every feel and touch was communal. They were two parts of one organism.

Naked, they explored each other and themselves, for every discovery was dual. They found the places that tickled and aroused. The self-involved creature that had been Alanna and Jerevan was enraptured by the way it fit together to gratify itself. Time ceased to have meaning, there was only steadily spiraling sensation, pleasure that went beyond pleasure to ecstasy and a final, total explosion of the senses.

"*Are you all right?*"

Alanna stirred, the question impinging on her from inside herself and from a vast distance away. Of course, she was all right. Why should she doubt it?

She felt Jerevan's smile as though it were she who flexed the muscles in his face. Jerevan thought, "*You lost consciousness.*"

"I overloaded on pleasure." She stretched. "*Jerevan?*"

"*Yes.*"

"*What happened? Was it real?*"

"*Very real!*" She felt his laughter.

"*Your thoughts feel like my own, as though they're coming from inside me. I know I thought they felt like that yesterday, but this is more intense. Now, I can hardly tell your thoughts from mine.*"

"*It's the same for me. We're two parts of one being. Separate parts, but parts that fit together so well.*"

She felt the warmth of that thought, the intimacy of it, and just thinking about what had happened between them made her blush. "*Will it always be like this between us?" she* asked, seeing herself through his eyes, sprawled on his bed in abandoned disarray.

"I think so. I hope so!"

She forced herself to open her eyes and look at him. He was lying beside her, relaxed, his eyes open and watching her. "I never dreamed the linkage would feel like that," she said aloud, aware that spoken words were unnecessary between them now, but striving for some return to normality.

He smiled, his face alight with appreciation, "Nor did I. It's an aspect of linkage that has to be experienced to be believed."

Remembering what lay ahead of them, she was suddenly anxious. "It's the other aspects we need to explore though, isn't it?"

"Not now." He pulled her back into his arms.

XXV

4731, 474th Cycle of the Year of the Dragon
Month of Ingvash
The isklarin beset him,
Slew those he held most dear,
And all who sought to free him,
They felt the utmost fear.
Fear, fear for the Wanderer
Wherever he may be,
For he is doomed to exile
By the shore of Sorrow Sea.

— FROM *THE BALLAD OF AUBREY THE WANDERER* BY ANONYMOUS

M inta was tired and worried. It was Theosday. Miunesday and Theosday were the days Semel had off, so Aubrey would normally have slept late and so would she.

Not today. Lord Leyburn wanted to meet with Aubrey and Aubrey desperately wanted to see him. They hadn't managed to meet in over a month, since the security around Aubrey tightened. A guard was stationed outside Aubrey's room now, and only Minta, the two maids, Vanith, and Naharil Thurin were allowed past.

So Aubrey would have to be smuggled up to Vanith's rooms for the meeting. Vanith's apartment was one floor up and off the same stairwell, so they only had a single guard to get by, but the plan still frightened Minta.

When the time came for them to leave, Minta arranged the covers on Aubrey's bed to look like he was sleeping in it and then nodded to Aubrey. He was not strong enough yet to hold an illusion, but he could project his vision of the scene to Lord Leyburn. Aubrey had assured her that Lord Leyburn was an expert illusionist. Still, Minta couldn't understand how he'd be able to project a lifelike image, even after Aubrey had gone.

Then an image of Aubrey appeared in the bed, chest rising and falling as though it were breathing, yet Aubrey was standing beside her. Even though she'd expected it, she gasped.

"Don't be frightened, Minta. It's just an illusion."

Aubrey's small, warm fingers found hers and he squeezed her hand. "Will you be all right?"

"Yes." She pressed her lips together and nodded firmly. Then she helped him into the cupboard by the door and closed it. Only after she reassured herself that everything looked normal, did she step into the hall to speak to the guard.

"I just can't reach to put these boxes away, and Naharil Thurin always complains if the room's a mess. Though how he can expect anyone to keep a child's room as neat as a certhob's lair amazes me. Children are the messiest..."

"What is it you want me to do?" the guard interrupted.

Minta opened the door wide and pointed, lowering her voice so the guard wouldn't wonder why Aubrey didn't wake. "Just put those boxes on the shelf in the closet there. I can't reach that high, but you're so tall. There's nothing like having the help of a tall, strong man."

The guard stepped into the room. "These boxes?"

Minta nodded.

The guard lifted the pile of boxes Minta had prepared and carried them into the closet.

Minta tapped the cupboard and followed the guard. "No. Not that shelf. The next one. Yes, that's right. No, that one goes on the other shelf. You'll have to move those other things aside. Oh, dear. I just can't think who put them there," she said, all in an anxious half-whisper.

When the guard came out he crossed the room to the bed and looked down at the illusion. Minta knew the image was lifelike, but having the guard stand over it increased her nervousness. Then the guard grinned and whispered, "The little tyke sleeps pretty sound?"

"Oh, yes," she whispered back. "He's tired. He had a bad night, so I gave him some of his medicine."

"Leg gives him trouble, does it? Tough luck on the kid, being crippled like that."

Minta bit her lip and nodded. Wondering if Aubrey had reached the stairwell yet, she smiled at the guard and walked toward the door. "Nahar Vanith wants to talk to me this morning, to discuss his progress. If he wakes, will you have me called? I'll be in her apartment."

The guard followed. "I can't leave my post, miss, but I can see a message is sent to you when the guard comes by. That's about every twenty minutes. Will that do?"

Minta stepped out into the hall. "Oh, yes. That'll be fine. Nahar Aubrey won't be any trouble; he's very good. I don't think he'll wake, though. And I'll be back soon."

The guard followed her, closing the door behind him.

"Take your time, miss. He looks like he'll sleep for hours yet."

Minta smiled and hurried away. They'd done it. The guard thought he'd just seen Aubrey sleeping, so he wasn't likely to check on him again.

When she reached Vanith's apartment, Lord Leyburn himself opened the door for her. He looked different to her somehow, pale, as though he were under a strain, but also serene. Still, his voice was as reassuring as ever, "The guard wasn't suspicious?"

"No. I nearly died when he went right over to look at the illusion, but he only commented on how soundly Aubrey sleeps."

Vanith embraced her. "You must have been terrified."

"Good work," Jerevan said, "but we've still got to get Aubrey back down there." He turned to Vanith. "You're definitely leaving tomorrow morning?"

"Yes. At long last I'm going to meet my cousin. I must admit that, aside from everything else, I'm curious. I even managed to arrange a private showing of "The Defiance of Edain." I know Rhys was curt with your emissary, but there's still no saying that he won't let us all retire peaceably."

"You'll have enough support with Vitry, Basel and the others to considerably inconvenience him in any event. That should persuade him to negotiate some sort of terms. From what Kulin saw of him, though, you'd do best to take an aggressive stand. He doesn't respect caution."

Vanith laughed. "Couldn't you have found someone better than Kulin to confront him?"

Jerevan sighed. "Kulin was handy. I admit it was a miscalculation on my part."

Vanith nodded. "My stand won't be a pretense. If we can't negotiate, we will fight. We might even find a weakness. He is, after all, still young." She shrugged. "At any rate, I couldn't have stood much more of this waiting." She turned to Minta. "I'm going to leave you now with Lord Leyburn. You're to obey him as you would me."

She bent down and hugged Aubrey, who hugged her back convulsively. "Remember what I've taught you, Aubrey. My fate is in Jehan's and Maera's hands. I'll come back to you if I can. If I can't, remember that I love you very much, and that I'm very proud of you." She hugged him again. Then she stood and left the room.

Jerevan turned to Minta. "Will Aubrey have lessons as usual tomorrow?"

"Of course."

"Will you be able to get out of the Tower tomorrow evening?"

She nodded. "I'll leave as soon as Aubrey's lessons are over. The maids might notice I'm missing, but they know I have a lover. They'll think I've sneaked out to meet him, taking advantage of Vanith's absence. They won't tell the guards."

"Will you be able to take any of Aubrey's things with you?"

"I don't know. Not much, or the guards at the gate would notice."

"I want you to meet us at the harbor by nine o'clock. You're to board the *Morning Star* at pier thirty-five. All right?"

Minta bit her lower lip. "The *Morning Star*, pier thirty-five. And I'll bring what I can of Aubrey's things."

"Yes. Aubrey, you're not to try farseeing anything tomorrow night. Sometime after dark you'll hear and feel a tremendous noise. Don't try to sense what it is. Just keep everything shut down."

Aubrey looked wary. "What will it be?"

"Two of the wizards I sent for brought a pair of firedrakes with them ready to fly. We're not sure exactly what hour but sometime tomorrow night, probably after midnight, the female will start her mating song. That will be the signal for Thrym to climb the Tower for you. We hope to get you down and into a boat before Aavik's wizards sense you've gone. Without the firedrakes, they'd know the minute you left and we wouldn't stand a chance of getting you away."

Aubrey looked upset. "Aren't firedrakes dangerous? I mean, I've heard they can cause dreadful fires. I don't want anyone hurt."

"It's rival males fighting for the female that cause the fires, Aubrey, and we'll only be flying one male. At any rate, we've got to take that risk."

Aubrey's eyes fixed on Jerevan. "There's no time to think of an alternative?"

"No. Not now."

The following morning, the ordered ranks of the Royal Guard filled the courtyard in front of the Tower, the sun glinting off the high polish of their weapons and accouterments. Most of the army was mustered to the east of Ninkarrak, but the Royal Guard was to march through the city with Idrim at its head. There had been signs of unrest during the previous week, and Idrim felt that the sight of him leading his troops would inspire confidence.

Vanith turned to Minta as they emerged from the Tower. "I may not see you or my son again, Minta," she said. Her face was pale, but her eyes were steady and there was an air of calm about her. "If I don't come back, take care of him for me." She hugged Minta and went down to join her father at the head of the troops.

Minta followed her part way down the stair to a point of vantage where she could see the whole courtyard. She had promised to report the scene in detail to Aubrey and she drank it in with eager eyes. She thought the soldiers looked splendid in their hunter green uniforms with shining gold trim. Even the sight of Sandor glaring at her from the ranks couldn't disturb her pleasure. Surely, she thought, Vanith will find a way to defeat Rhys.

She stepped aside as Lord Theolan and a group of lesser priests, vivid in scarlet and gold, brushed by her to bless the troops. Theolan's tall, gaunt form and cadaverous face always made her feel uneasy, but her father and mother had been worshipers of Miune and she felt it only right that the god bless the army and its cause.

It wasn't until the priests reached the bottom of the staircase that she felt a flicker of unease. Hadn't Vanith said something about Theolan's staff and the isklarin?

Vanith mounted her horse and took her place in the procession. As Heir Apparent she should have ridden by her father's side, but instead she was positioned several places back, a minor slight after so many others, but her jaw clenched with anger.

She urged her restive horse into place and stroked his neck, reaching out with her mind to calm him. He was a stallion and didn't like the presence of so many other horses around him. The smell of the mares excited him too. Concentrating on the horse, she hardly noticed the stir at the edge of the courtyard.

Then she heard Theolan's voice ring out, "Stop! Stop! There are isklarin among us." She turned in the saddle and saw him raise a glowing staff. "Your majesty," he cried, waving the staff and running up to Idrim's horse. "You are betrayed, sire! Miune's Staff shows that you are surrounded by your enemies, the lizard filth have penetrated even to the courtyard of the Black Tower."

Vanith swore under her breath and looked around for Horgen.

He stood near the foot of the stairs holding his staff of office as Lord Chamberlain. Even as Vanith located him he called out, "Nonsense, Theolan, you're hysterical. Perhaps there are some half-breeds in the audience, but his majesty's troops are all loyal men."

Theolan turned and raised the staff, pointing it at Horgen. The strange glow that surrounded it changed color and flickered, but didn't die away. "You!" Theolan screamed. "You're the betrayer!" A wind from the bay caught Theolan's scarlet robe and it flapped around his skeletal form. Vanith thought he looked like some emaciated, gory vulture about to take off and fly at Horgen, but he turned back to the Estahar. "He's betrayed you, sire. He's consorted with the isklarin against you. He's blasphemed against Miune!"

"Agnith's fires," Vanith swore under her breath, but she raised her voice and ordered, "Stand aside, priest. If there are isklarin among the guard, then the whole army will be examined when we're outside the city. This isn't the time or the place." If only she had the wizards with her now.

Theolan ignored her. "Your majesty, you must let me purge your forces of this pestilence, slay the reptile scourge, or all that we've built will be destroyed."

Vanith spurred her horse through the crowd toward her father. If he'd just control the priest, something might still be saved.

"Nonsense, Theolan. You forget yourself," Idrim said. "We're just about to ride out to meet Rhys. None of his forces can have reached Ninkarrak yet."

"Not the forces of Rhys, the usurper, but those of Aavik, the scaled one, the beast lord, ride with you now, waiting for your fall." Theolan pointed again at Horgen. "That man, your trusted advisor, one I thought loyal to the faith of Miune, has betrayed us all."

"Your majesty, I've no idea what his holiness is referring to. I've always been your most loyal supporter," Horgen said, moving down the stair a few steps to confront Theolan.

Theolan turned back toward Horgen and raised the shining, golden staff. "Betrayer! Fiend!"

Vanith was closer to Idrim but several guardsmen still blocked her way to his side. "Have the priest arrested, father," she demanded. "He's disturbing the peace."

Idrim turned to her, querulous and bewildered. "Arrest Theolan?"

Vanith swallowed her irritation. "Yes, father. We have to get the army out of Ninkarrak. If there are traitors among the troops, this isn't the place to test them."

Idrim looked around the crowded courtyard, as though seeing it for the first time. "Traitors?"

Vanith bit her lip. Her father didn't understand what was happening. "Theolan thinks there are isklarin among the troops. Tell him you'll have the whole army purged when we get outside the city. But stop him from creating any more of a scene now."

Theolan heard her and turned, pointing the staff toward her. "Whore," he cried, but the glow in the staff went out when it was directed at her. He stared at the staff and shook it, then pointed it at her again.

"I'm not your enemy in this, Theolan," Vanith said. "We'll let you examine the troops outside the city. But let us go now."

Theolan stared at her, his eyes wild, then he turned back to Idrim. "Traitors are all around you, your majesty. I must purge them with the Staff."

Idrim frowned and turned to Horgen, standing at the foot of the stairs some three meters away, watching while Vanith argued with her father. "How can there be isklarin among my Royal Guard?"

"It's impossible, your majesty," Horgen said, raising his voice to be heard above the shocked murmuring of the troops. "Theolan's Staff must be malfunctioning. It's time to start the procession."

"Blasphemer!" Theolan shouted. He suddenly raised the staff and charged at Horgen, waving it over his head like a quarterstaff.

Then, before Theolan could reach Horgen, one of the guards at the foot of the stair stepped between them, drawing his sword, and ran it through the priest. Theolan cried out as the sword pierced him, "Show your true nature, monster." Even though mortally wounded, he found the strength to strike the guard with the glowing staff before he fell. As the staff touched the guard, the guard's form melted and changed, as Vanith had once seen Thrym's do when he left the Tower, except that at the end of the change she saw that the lizard was dead.

Cries of horror filled the air and suddenly half the Royal Guard appeared to go mad as they attacked the rest. Vanith cried out, "Stop. To your places." But only the human troops responded and that made them easier targets.

"Defend yourselves," she cried then, and spurred her horse toward her father. But guardsmen still blocked her way, and the guardsmen were Gandaharan soldiers. They'd moved with practiced coordination the moment the first isklar drew his sword. Idrim was surrounded.

Vanith drew her sword and rode into them. She hacked one isklar's head off and sliced through another's arm before two more closed in behind her. She tried to turn, but one of them grasped her arm from the rear. Then the other ran her through.

Minta screamed as Vanith fell.

The scene was a nightmare, but she couldn't shut it out. She watched as Idrim, disarmed and helpless, tried to escape after witnessing his daughter's death, hauling back on his horse's mouth so it reared. One of the guardsmen drove his sword into the horse's chest and it went down, taking Idrim with it. Minta couldn't see whether he was killed or not.

One of the lesser priests who had accompanied Theolan caught up the golden staff and started to brandish it, seemingly at random. The other priests also began to strike out with their staffs, and here and there about the courtyard the bodies of lizards began to join the bodies of men.

Minta clutched the head of one of the black marble griffins that lined the stair. The pain of its ruby eye digging into her hand distracted her from the carnage below. She started to back away, retreating up the steps into the Tower, but she couldn't tear her eyes from the battle. She saw Arrel cut down as he tried to escape and she saw three men and their horses crushed as the western portcullis came down on them, closing one side of the courtyard. It was impossible to tell who was fighting whom.

Suddenly Horgen shouted, "Get Idrim into the Tower. To the other gate! Guard the gates, you fools! Make sure none of them get away or we'll have the whole army down on us."

She made out the figure of the Estahar then, bloody but still conscious near the foot of the steps. Figures dressed in the uniform of his Royal Guard surrounded him but they were obviously holding him prisoner rather than defending him. One of them gestured and they dragged the monarch toward Horgen.

Minta ducked and ran up the steps, heading for Aubrey's room, but before she reached the entrance she was grabbed from behind.

"Don't kill her," Horgen's voice called from behind her, "she's the little Nahar's nurse. We may need her."

She was jerked around to face the courtyard again. The Estahar was being forced up the steps in the middle of what seemed to be a disciplined troop of men. There were bodies all over. The human troops hadn't had a chance, Minta thought. They couldn't tell friend from foe, but the Gandaharans with their mind touch had no such trouble.

Vanith was dead. So were Theolan and the priests who'd followed him. She saw Nahar Arrel's body. He hadn't even died well, she thought. Then she saw that Sandor was also among the slain. She was a widow. Somehow, under the circumstances, she wasn't able to rejoice in that.

She turned her head, trying to see who had survived. Naharil Thurin was safe, of course, talking with Lord Horgen. The two iron portcullises leading out of the courtyard to the compound were both down. Another battalion of troops were assembled in the Royal Park. They'd been intended to add to the display made by the parade, but she didn't think any human member of the guard had escaped to warn them. The guardsmen crushed under one of the gates had been the closest to getting away.

Minta wondered what the officers of the army outside would think when Idrim didn't come and they saw that fighting had broken out among the Royal Guard. Undoubtedly Lord Horgen would think up a story to tell them. It amazed her how completely the Gandaharans had infiltrated that elite corps. Lord Horgen must have been busy during the past months.

"Take her up to the nursery." Horgen's voice intruded on her thoughts. "Put her in with Nahar Aubrey. Her presence should calm him. The boy's been imprisoned in his room for some time now, so the condition of prisoner shouldn't be strange. What difference will it make to him who his jailers are?" Horgen laughed. "And as for you," he added, chucking Minta under the chin, "you won't have Vanith to stand interference for you any longer." He eyed her up and down, and then gestured to the guard. "Take her away."

Minta felt tears streaming down her face. How would Aubrey escape? For that matter, how would she escape? The Tower had become an armed isklarin camp. How could even Thrym and Lord Leyburn rescue them now. Her thoughts dissolved into despair.

XXVI

4731, 474TH CYCLE OF THE YEAR OF THE DRAGON
MONTH OF INGVASH

> Then wizards fought to rescue him,
> To see that he went free;
> The Varfarin in Ilwheirlane
> Who ever thought to see?
> Free, free the Wanderer
> Wherever he may be,
> Though he is doomed to exile
> By the shore of Sorrow Sea.

> — FROM *THE BALLAD OF AUBREY THE WANDERER* BY ANONYMOUS

"So while there are nearly fifteen thousand loyal human troops camped outside the city and another two thousand in the Royal Park, the Tower and the Royal Compound have been taken over by the isklarin," Rainal said from the doorway as he finished his description of the morning's debacle.

Alanna looked around her at Jerevan and the other wizards who had witnessed her oath, assembled for a final meeting before the rescue. The company looked dazed by the extent of the catastrophe and she found herself evaluating their reactions based on knowledge that was Jerevan's, not her own.

After the incredible intimacy of her linkage with Jerevan, Alanna had spent the following days trying to adjust to a new perception of reality. While she hardly saw Jerevan except at night, she was aware of where he was and what he was doing at all times, like a kind of double vision. She could also mind-speak with him wherever he was with ease, but she still shied away from using that form of communication. It was too intimate. It startled her every time a thought of his emerged in her mind as though it were a thought of hers she had just remembered.

"*It's as though you're inside me,*" she protested at one point.

"*I am; and you're inside me,*" he told her.

But she rejected that unity whenever she could, clinging to physical speech and her own identity, even though she realized that, by doing so, she was neglecting the opportunity to advance her training. It was all too new and strange. But over the last two days she'd also been getting flashes of his memories, particularly when she saw people he knew as well as he knew the assembled wizards.

Tana, standing next to Dinara near the window and as far from the men as she could get, Alanna felt Jerevan note, was the first to break the silence when Rainal finished. "Do the army's commanders realize that Idrim's a prisoner? Do they mean to invade the Tower?"

Vitry laughed, a tinkling sound full of amusement. She reclined on the couch, her head resting against Basel's shoulder. "Men appointed by Horgen? You're jesting. I'm sure they're all sitting around twiddling their thumbs and making nervous noises."

"Vitry's right. I stopped by the camp before I came here and they have no idea what's going on," Rainal said. "Horgen tried to cover up the whole mess with a story about rebels loyal to Rhys in the Royal Guard. Fortunately, the priests had transformed several of the isklarin and Horgen slipped up over disposal of the bodies. Now he's talking about an alliance between Rhys and Gandahar and the danger of widespread infiltration of the rest of the army, swearing that it isn't safe for Idrim to come out of the Tower until the army's been purged. The commanders know something's wrong with Horgen's story, but they don't know what to do. What's more, they really don't dare do anything while Idrim and Aubrey are prisoners. They're patrolling the Park, though, which will make it more difficult to reach the Tower."

"We planned a sea approach, anyway. The army in the Park shouldn't make that much difference," Magra said from the chair next to Ashe's by the fireplace. Alanna saw a flash of them together in a jungle. "Or do the isklarin have patrols, too?"

"Can you doubt it?" Rainal grimaced. "They're patrolling the Compound and the shoreline near the Tower. And every patrol I saw included at least one wizard."

"What will we do?" Dinara asked. She looked upset and Tana put an arm around her to sooth her. Alanna saw them both amid a strange garden full of beautiful but twisted plants.

"We go ahead as planned." Jerevan said. "We'll have to make provision for smuggling Minta out of the Tower as well as Aubrey, but otherwise we change our plans as little as possible."

"Why don't we put it off... a few days, at least," Kulin said, sounding breathless. He was standing by the fireplace, toying with one of the pokers. His hands were sweaty. Alanna had rarely heard him speak before and she was surprised by the tension in his voice until she saw in her mind the picture of a young boy being brutally whipped.

"Because Vitry stopped neutralizing the firedrake last night, didn't you Vitry?" asked Basel, looking down at the top of her head. He sounded resigned, but he was smiling with wry amusement. He looked strange to Alanna with brown eyes instead of the white cataracts.

"Yes," Vitry drawled, stretching. "And it's too late to do anything about it now except neutralize her totally. But if I do that, she won't make a mating flight for a decade at least."

"So it's tonight. At least there's no way they can be expecting us," Ashe said. Alanna saw another flash of him against a background of snow capped mountains.

After that the meeting broke up and Jerevan told the others to go back to wherever they were staying and rest for the remainder of the day.

It was a dark night, the breeze off the bay cool and smelling of brine. Thrym saw Ranth, a thin sliver, low in the sky and setting. He pulled on his oar and thought of Minta trapped in the Tower with Gandaharan troops who wouldn't care if she lived or died. He was rowing ashore with eighteen mercenaries and wizards in one of two boats from the *Morning Star*. The ship had anchored offshore about a kilometer to the south, as close as Lord Leyburn dared bring her lest her nearness raise suspicions. It was a calm night; the waves lapping the shore were only centimeters high. They beached the boats off a point of rock at the foot of the cliffs, below the place where the bonfire was built at Year's End. Dinara and Garth, with eight hand-picked mercenaries, stayed to guard the boats.

Thrym, Alanna, Jerevan, Ashe and four of the mercenaries crept through the boulders and along the scrap of beach close to the foot of the Tower. Seen from the edge of the sea near its base, it was a single priapic erection, enormous and black, rooted in the salt wrack of the shore.

Thrym stripped off his shoes and the dark, long sleeved shirt and black pants that were the uniform for everyone taking part in the operation. Naked, he left his clothes by a rock and, holding his knife un-sheathed in his mouth, he shifted. Then he crawled though the heaped boulders to the edge of the cleared area at the foot of Tower. It felt strange coming this way under these circumstances. He'd done this so many times, always looking forward to the joy of being in Minta's arms. If they'd hurt her... No. He mustn't think of that. Concentrate on the job.

When would the firedrakes fly? Waiting was hard. He sensed the unease of the mercenaries they'd left further back. Everything was ready, everyone in position. Jerevan was just behind him, also in lizard form. It was well after midnight, and still there was no sign of the keening that Vitry had described as the audible part of the firedrakes' mating song. It had to come soon; every minute now increased the risk of something going wrong.

He studied the base of the Tower. He couldn't see any guards, but he never had seen any on this side. Strange that the Gandaharans would share that same blind spot in their defenses. They should know better.

Thrym stiffened. He could hear something. It was more a vibration than a sound, a faint humming that grew louder and louder. He looked up and saw a single flaming form rise into the sky. He started to climb.

Up and up he went, his were-senses shut down so he climbed almost blind. He'd made the climb so many times before that didn't matter. Then he was over the rail and onto the balcony. He shifted, took the knife in his hand and waited for Jerevan to join him. Another large lizard reached the balcony. Thrym opened the pack on Jerevan's back and took out the harnesses. Their plans called for Jerevan to wait on the balcony, as it would cost him too much energy to shape-shift more than twice in such a short period of time.

The balcony door was closed. Thrym pressed his ear to the glass, but no sound came from within. It wasn't locked. He turned the handle and opened it carefully. There was no one inside.

He tiptoed across Minta's room to Aubrey's door and focused his sight through the wood. A low murmur of voices came through, but he couldn't make out what was being said. Minta and Aubrey were both in the room, however and someone else was standing in front of the door. He eased the heavy wooden panel open a crack. A guard stood with his back to the door. Stupid, Thrym thought, and opened it wider to give himself room to stab.

A shout came from another guard on the other side of the room. The first guard started to turn and Thrym's knife glanced off a rib.

Minta and Aubrey had been playing a game on the floor, but when the second guard shouted, Minta threw herself at his legs, tripping him. As he went down she jumped on his back and hit him with the wooden board the game had been arranged on.

Thrym knocked the first guard's arm aside as the man tried to aim his musket and the bullet ricocheted off the stone ceiling into the curtains on the far wall. Then Thrym brought his knife up for a second thrust, this time angling it under the guard's breast bone and into his heart. The Gandaharan collapsed on the floor just as the second guard managed to regain his feet, Minta clinging to one arm.

Thrym swallowed, his knife, slippery with blood, clenched in his hand. He didn't dare aim for the Gandaharan's body for fear of hitting Minta and the guard was already bringing up his musket. Thrym threw, using all his talent to guide the blade. It struck the guard truly, going through his right eye into his brain. He went over backwards like a felled tree.

Minta ran into Thrym's arms. "Thank Jehan you're here. I knew you'd manage to rescue us somehow."

"We don't have much time. Where are the rest of the guards?"

"The stairwell's guarded, but the doors are shut. They won't have heard anything. Someone checks on us every half hour, but he just left."

Thrym handed one of the harnesses to Aubrey. "Aubrey, your ride's on the balcony. Put on the harness and get out there."

He helped Minta into hers as quickly as his fingers would buckle the straps.

"Who came with you?" Minta asked.

"Lord Leyburn," Thrym said, pulling Minta behind him out to the balcony. Aubrey was wearing his harness but Thrym checked it to be safe and attached the harness to Jerevan, showing Minta how to buckle it. Jerevan started down the Tower with Aubrey and Thrym shifted and waited while Minta attached her harness to him. Then he, too, started down.

Alanna crouched amid the tumble of rocks near the Tower's base, watching the female firedrake circling in the clear, starry sky. She was beautiful, and so deadly. More than thirty feet long, an enormous winged lizard outlined in fire, the firedrake hen rose in the sky directly above the Tower, spiraling higher and higher, her great wings streaming sparks as she beat the air, forcing herself up. The flames changed color, now yellow, now red, blue or green, constantly shifting and reflecting off her iridescent skin. The humming vibration seemed to fluctuate with the colors of the flame. The effect was fascinating, almost hypnotic, and Alanna had to tear her eyes away. Vitry and Basel would release the male soon. They'd planned to give the female a fifteen minute head start and nearly that much time must have passed.

"We've got them!" Jerevan's thought emerged in Alanna's mind, filled with elation. *"Aubrey and Minta are both down. We're coming now."*

Only a moment later, a second firedrake ascended into the sky, pursuing the first. The wail of the female rose in volume until Alanna was almost deafened. Then it was echoed by screaming bursts of sound from the male. The male was not just outlined in flame, he was all flame, a raging conflagration flaring across the heavens. Jerevan had warned her not to attempt to use any sense except her normal vision and the mental link they now shared, which seemed in some way to be shielded by Vyrkarion. She thought now that, if the energy of the firedrakes bombarded all the senses as devastatingly as they did the eyes and ears, it would be a long while before the isklarin wizards would be back to normal.

Alanna felt Jerevan climbing across the sea wrack at the foot of the Tower, but he was hampered by the dazzle spots that plagued her vision as well. Still, crouching, stiff and cold, among jagged boulders still damp from the earlier high tide, she wished he'd hurry. Then she was startled as a small form crawled over the rocks and settled down beside her. A child. Varl, the enormous, half-gamlar mercenary, tensed then relaxed seeing the boy they'd come to rescue.

"Hello. I'm Aubrey. You're carrying Vyrkarion, so you must be Alanna. I'm glad to meet you," he whispered.

She strained to make out his features, impressed by his composure and the strength she felt emanating from him. "I'm glad to meet you, too. I've wanted to for some time."

"My father and Aavik have been making things a little difficult."

Alanna saw him grin. "You're not frightened?"

"Of course I'm frightened. I'm not stupid." Aubrey sounded indignant. "Here's Minta. She can't climb as fast as I can."

As Aubrey completed his boast, Jerevan jumped down beside Alanna and pulled her to her feet. Thrym, helping Minta, followed and the mercenaries closed in around them.

"Let's go, then." Jerevan led Alanna through the rocks. Thrym, Minta and Aubrey followed with Ashe and the mercenaries guarding the rear.

Alanna clambered over the boulders at the foot of the cliffs back to where the boats had been left. The dazzle spots made it difficult to see where to put her feet. Her ears and mind were being bludgeoned by the screams of the dragons in the sky. The firedrakes flew higher now and well out over the bay, heading southwest, twin streaks of multi-colored flame, beautiful and terrible. The fiery form of the cock was gaining on the hen, but she was still higher in the air. As Alanna and the others approached the foot of the cliffs where the boats had landed, she heard musket fire. She broke into a run rounding the point. The open stretch of beach where the boats had been drawn up was full of soldiers. As Alanna watched, the patrol slew the last of the mercenaries who'd been guarding the boats and began to pull them farther up the beach. There appeared to be fourteen left.

"Who are they? Human or isklarin?" she asked.

"Isklarin!" Jerevan thought. "But they couldn't have been looking for us this soon. And there would've been more of them. They must be a routine patrol, but four of them are wizards and they've already killed Garth and Dinara. They must have known enough not to try looking at the firedrakes."

"What can we do?"

Jerevan smiled. "Fight them. We don't have any other way to escape."

Alanna swallowed but drew Vyrkarion from her bodice and reached out to Jerevan. He clasped her hand and their eyes met. "We should have practiced this more. I still don't know what to do," she whispered.

"Just look into Vyrkarion and let me draw from you, just as you did the last time."

She tore her eyes away from his and stared at the crystal. It glowed like a green sun and, as she looked into it, the jewel expanded until she found herself falling back down into the infinite green well. It wasn't what she had felt during her first combat, there was no raging funnel draining away her energy. Instead, the feeling was closer to what she felt when they first completed the linkage. Then she felt a drawing sensation, as though a part of her were being drawn off into the green swirl, or she herself had become a part of the whirlpool. When she thought she couldn't stand the spinning any longer, it ceased and she felt laved in warmth and light. She heard silence. The terrible shrieking that had surrounded her ever since the firedrakes rose had vanished. There in the green, warm limbo inside the crystal it was still, protected, safe. But she wasn't safe. She was on a beach. It was dark. They were in danger. She had to see.

With the thought came vision and she was back in her own body. She realized that what had seemed to be hours had, in fact, been seconds. Nothing had changed except that there was now a bridge of green force connecting her with Jerevan.

"I can draw on your energy now. It shouldn't hurt as much, with both of us linked through Vyrkarion." They started down the beach toward the boat.

Ashe, Thrym and the mercenaries crowded around and ahead of them. Minta and Aubrey hid in the rocks behind.

Alanna and the others charged onto the beach. Six soldiers turned to face them; the others formed a guard around the four isklarin wizards who also turned to face them. She stopped when Jerevan did, aware of Ashe coming up on her other side.

The link of green fire connecting her with Jerevan grew brighter. She felt Vyrkarion burn with the power being drawn from her. The jewel focused the energy in a bright emerald glow that flared higher and higher. Then the glow reached out and met three of the four fires arcing toward her. A white fire leapt out from Ashe to meet the fourth. Energies flared. Alanna felt fire in her brain, burning and burning. Time stopped. There was only flame.

Fire. She felt herself, her strength, her will, everything that was Alanna, melted down and drawn into that green flame. Then, when she was afraid that there was nothing left of her, that she was all fire, she felt a great wave of power come surging back at her, as if all her strength, which had taken ages to funnel out, was being forced back into her in one instant. The flash blinded her, leaving her stunned. She felt her body fall. The world around her was black, filled with enormous colored stars. The sand beneath her felt lumpy. Pain filled her. Then all feeling vanished.

XXVII

4731, 474TH CYCLE OF THE YEAR OF THE DRAGON
MONTH OF INGVASH

> So flaming dragons fought
> And fire rained from the sky;
> The Wanderer's doomed to exile
> And even the heavens cry.
> Cry, cry for the Wanderer
> Wherever he may be,
> For he is doomed to exile
> By the shore of Sorrow Sea.

— FROM *THE BALLAD OF AUBREY THE WANDERER* BY ANONYMOUS

E lath broke into a run. The last survivor of the mercenaries left to guard the boats fell just before she reached the beach. She drew her musket and charged, aware of Fianna, Thrym and the others behind her.

Missed, she thought, hearing the whine of a bullet going past her, and hoped it also missed Fianna at her back. She fired her musket into one of the six soldiers coming up the beach toward her. The isklar jerked but came on.

Elath threw the empty musket at his head and drew her sword, seeing Fianna coming up beside her out of the corner of her eye. It wasn't like having Fal at her back, but it would do. The Gandaharan, thin and dark, swung at her, his blade glinting in the faint moonlight. She dodged and swung. The isklar parried but he was slow; Elath's sword nicked his arm. He twisted away and she swung again. Her sword sank into his neck. Blood gushed and she pulled the blade free.

Varl, the white-haired giant off to her right, had killed, too, Elath noted as she swung to meet another Gandaharan and heard Fianna fighting at her back. The isklar facing her was bigger than the first, burly, with a long arm reach. Harder to kill quickly, Elath thought, and stepped aside as he swung at her. She returned the blow and he parried. She bent low and swung at his legs. He dodged, but stumbled. She ran him through the stomach and twisted the blade. He screamed and his hands went down to hold in the snaky mass of his intestines as they tried to fall out onto the sand. Elath finished him off. Looking around, she saw Thrym and Bruden, the fourth mercenary of their party, defending the wizards. She pulled her sword free and turned.

Too late. Fianna was falling with half her shoulder sheared off. Elath drove her sword through the isklar before he could free his blade from Fianna's body. Then, breathing hard, she glanced around again.

The wizards were all on the ground, human and isklarin, and the rest of the Gandaharan soldiers were coming up the beach. She heard shots and felt a sting on her arm. A bullet had grazed her. She flexed the arm. It still worked.

Varl had killed a second soldier and was fighting a third. Bruden was dead. Thrym had his hands full with two isklarin.

Another two soldiers came straight for her. Elath ran toward them. Taking a firm grip on her sword, she did a one-handed cartwheel between them toward Thrym. She came to her feet before they could turn to face her. Thrym ran his sword though one of the Gandaharans facing him and Elath struck down the other from the rear, her blade cutting halfway through his neck.

Then, pulling her sword free, she positioned herself at Thrym's back in time to parry the stroke of one of the two soldiers she'd dodged just moments before. Varl, coming from the isklar's rear, clove him nearly in two and Thrym took out the other.

Elath looked around. No living isklarin were left on the beach. She knelt and cleaned her sword on the sleeve of one of the dead soldiers.

"Are the wizards dead?" she asked.

"Only stunned, I think," Thrym said. "We'd better get them into the boat and get out of here."

"Boat's not going to help," Varl said. He was looking out to sea and Elath followed his eyes. The *Ilfargand* had come round the point and lay offshore, her railing lined with Gandaharan soldiers. A boat was being lowered over the side.

Thrym swore. Then he went over to the fallen wizards and swung Ashe over his shoulder. "Come on, Varl, Elath. We've got to get out of here."

Elath sheathed her sword. "Where can we go? We're cut off from *Morning Star*."

"Up the cliffs and through the Park." Thrym waved to Minta and Aubrey who had been hiding among the boulders at the foot of the cliff. They rose and started toward him, but he gestured them back. Then he set off at an angle toward the cliff, carrying Ashe. Varl picked up Leyburn and followed him. Elath swung the Tamrai over her shoulder and brought up the rear. Minta and Aubrey met them at the start of a faint trail that climbed up what had seemed a sheer cliff face.

The path was steep and treacherous. In the dark and unbalanced by the heavy weight of the woman she carried, Elath had to feel for each step. She was exhausted by the time they reached the top of the cliff and sank to her knees on the grass, lowering Alanna to the ground. Minta and Aubrey collapsed next to her.

"We can't stop here," Thrym gasped, breathing nearly as hard as Elath. "There are guards patrolling the Park. We have to get to shelter."

"How far?" Varl asked. The white-haired giant was the only one of them, Elath saw, who wasn't out of breath.

"There's a bank of bushes that way," Thrym panted, pointing southeast.

Varl nodded and, shifting Jerevan to one shoulder, picked up Alanna as well. "Can you make it now?" he asked Elath.

She nodded and climbed to her feet as Thrym hoisted Ashe up onto his shoulder and set out across the Park. The ground was gently rolling and the grass was well kept. Without the extra weight, Elath recovered quickly but she saw that both Minta and Aubrey were tiring.

Thrym made no allowance for weariness, setting a fast pace through the open area, seeking out cover wherever he could find it. He led them into a stand of rhododendrons near the southern edge of the Park, moments before a patrol of mounted guards rode past.

"How much farther and where are we going?" Elath asked when the soldiers had passed.

"I don't know but Ashe's coming round." Thrym propped Ashe up and examined him.

Ashe blinked and put his hands to his head. "What happened? Where are we?"

"Ssh! We're in the Royal Park," Thrym whispered.

"What happened to the *Morning Star*?"

"We couldn't reach her," Thrym said. "Do you know if Lord Leyburn made any plans for what we'd do if things went wrong?"

"Yes," Ashe said. "We have to reach my carnival in the Lamashrak."

"That's more than halfway across the city," Elath protested.

"We'll rest here for a few minutes." Thrym turned to Ashe, "Is there any chance of waking Leyburn and the Tamrai?"

Ashe examined the two bodies Varl had laid out on the ground near him. "No. I can't even examine them while the firedrakes are singing. They were both burned by the backlash when the isklarin wizards died. I think it will be some time before we can wake them."

"You don't know how long?"

"No. I've never seen a backlash like that before, three wizards taken out at once. I wasn't even linked to it and it knocked me out."

"They'll be all right though, won't they?" Aubrey asked.

"I don't know." Ashe shook his head. He was pale and his eyes looked bloodshot.

"The Gandaharans will be coming after us. How will we get away if Lord Leyburn can't help us?" Minta asked.

"The troops in the Tower don't even know we've gone yet; not with that wail blocking their senses." Aubrey gestured at the firedrakes, still brilliant against the stars in the distance.

"That may be true," Varl said, "but whoever's commanding the *Ilfargand* knows something's going on. He started putting men ashore while we climbed the cliff. They can't be far behind us."

Thrym looked up at the sky. "They won't be able to track us while the firedrakes are this near."

Ashe nodded. "We'll have to get as far as we can before the energies they broadcast get too weak to interfere with farseeing. Even then, if the isklarin try to see while the firedrakes are singing, they'll be burned out, unable to see anything for hours, maybe days."

"We'll do the best we can," Thrym said. "I know a place about half-way to the Lamashrak where we can rest safely. After that, we'll just have to see."

Thrym got them moving again after about ten minutes rest. Varl still carried both Alanna and Jerevan. It was soon obvious to Elath that Thrym knew the park very well indeed. Not once did they have to cross an open space of more than a fifty meters and they reached the wall at a point that was out of sight of the guard posts to either side.

They were hampered in the process of scaling the wall by the two unconscious wizards, but they made it without being detected. And they met no problems crossing the spacious gardens of the estates that surrounded the Park. Thrym always knew the route that offered the most cover and guided them unerringly.

For two hours they crossed streets, backyards and gardens, moving northeast, with the gradually diminishing song of the firedrakes constantly in their ears. When Aubrey grew too tired to continue, Thrym carried him. Ashe and Minta were also close to exhaustion, Elath noted. Only Varl, carrying both Jerevan and Alanna, was inexhaustible.

About an hour before dawn they reached a huge derelict mansion, and Minta exclaimed, "The Hetri of Caldor's house, where we came for our picnic!"

Thrym grinned. "We can rest here for what's left of the night." He picked the lock on a door leading into an enormous kitchen and ushered them in, pointing out the door to the stairs leading down. "The cellar's cut from solid rock. Down there, Aavik and his wizards won't be able to sense us, even after the firedrakes are gone. If you'll excuse me, I have to notify our host of our presence." He headed back across the yard.

Downstairs, Elath helped Varl make Jerevan and Alanna comfortable as possible on some of the pile of blankets they found folded in a corner. Obviously, others had used the cellar as a shelter or hideout before them. Minta and Aubrey curled up together in another blanket and fell asleep.

Elath's body was tired but her mind was restless. When Ashe went back upstairs she followed him. She had noticed him growing more and more disturbed during the last half hour and his expression worried her.

"What's bothering you?" Elath asked.

"The firedrakes," Ashe said. He climbed another flight of stairs to the top of the house and opened a window that faced to the southwest.

Elath looked out over his shoulder. The sky was just beginning to lighten. "What about the firedrakes?"

Thrym came up behind Elath. "So you heard it too. What does it mean?"

"I don't know. The noise was getting steadily fainter until about half an hour ago. Then it started growing louder again. I thought I was imagining the change at first but you heard it too."

Thrym opened the window wider and leaned out. "Jehan guide us, look at that!" He pointed at the southern sky.

Elath couldn't make out what disturbed him. All she could see was the black velvet of the night sky, paling slightly but still spangled with stars. "What's the matter?"

"Sweet Maera, mother of men, there are three of them," Ashe said.

"Three firedrakes?" Elath asked, disturbed by the stunned expressions on both their faces.

"What?" Ashe turned to Elath as though just realizing she was there. "Yes. Three firedrakes, the two we flew and another from Tarat knows where, and they're headed right for the city."

"Well," Thrym said, "at least we don't need to worry about Aavik's wizards tracking us for a while."

"I'll have to wake Jerevan," Ashe said, turning to go back downstairs.

"If you can, it's a good idea. But I doubt there's anything even he can do. From what I've heard, we're in for a firefight," Thrym said, following.

Elath watched them go and then turned back and studied the southern sky. Even knowing where to look, it was half an hour before she made out the three bright lights moving too rapidly to be stars, although she would have mistaken them for stars if she hadn't known better. She watched them for a time. They grew brighter as the stars dimmed and the sky to the east paled from black to gray: two brilliant, multi-colored forms close together and moving straight toward her and another larger, more splendid form just behind the first two and gaining on them.

Elath shivered. Firedrakes were creatures of the south, of desert regions where their aerial firefights affected little but rock or sand. Yet there were tales of cock firedrakes destroying cities.

"Help me, Ashe. I have to see them. Where in all of Agnith's fires could a third firedrake have come from?" Elath turned sharply at the sound of Jerevan's voice.

"I don't know, but he's bigger than the other two. They're both flee-ing him. The trouble is, it looks as though they're going to meet over the city." Ashe had an arm around Jerevan to support him.

"Who would have dreamed there'd be a wild firedrake north of Zamarga? Where could he have lived that no one's heard of him?" Jerevan reached the window and gripped the frame to support himself. He looked pale with dark hollows under his eyes.

It was still not quite dawn but the eastern horizon had gone from gray to pale rose. The flaming shapes of the firedrakes were now clearly visible against the brightening sky. The newcomer pursuing the others was much larger, much older than the original two. His fires burned in deeper colors: garnet and vermilion, cadmium yellow, viridian and indigo. Even as Elath watched, he overtook the smaller male and sent a gout of flame at him. The other cock twisted away, screaming, and the flame fell past him and out of sight. The firedrakes could only be a few kilometers away, certainly over some part of Ninkarrak.

"Can't Vitry and Basel turn them somehow?" Ashe asked.

"Nothing could distract them now, right in the middle of a mating battle. *Ilthev taela taelin nith*," Jerevan added in a murmur.

"What?"

"That was part of Inanda's prophecy, 'The sky will cry with tears of fire.'" Jerevan shook his head. "I thought it meant some sort of meteor shower, a sign sent by the gods. And then I helped set it up myself."

"You couldn't have known."

"Making excuses for me, Ashe. I should have foreseen this."

Thrym came up behind them. "What part of the city are they over, can you tell?"

"Somewhere back from the harbor," Jerevan said. The smaller cock sent a streamer of fire at the larger one. The newcomer was bigger but not as maneuverable; the flame caught the edge of his wing. He screamed and the sound was terrible.

"Jehan, if the city isn't wiped out by fires, the sonics will get whatever's left," Ashe said, holding his ears.

"Isn't there anything anyone can do?"

Elath turned at the question to see that Aubrey had also awakened and come to watch the firedrakes fly their fiery dance.

"Not now, your highness. It's too late. I'm sorry." Jerevan shook his head. "We should have found some other way to rescue you. I should have remembered the wording of the prophecy and been warned, but regrets are useless now." He leaned against the window sill, still needing its support to stay erect. His eyes were full of pain.

Elath thought of the area in from the harbor: Farinmalith, where Fal sat helpless in their small, cramped room. She had arranged for one of their neighbors to take care of him while she was gone, but she knew the woman wouldn't think of him at a time like this. "Couldn't you make it rain?" she asked. "Wouldn't rain put out the fires, drive them away?"

Jerevan looked surprised, then thoughtful. "I don't know. I don't think it's ever been tried. They're desert creatures. It would be too hard to make rain in a desert, but here it might work." He leaned out the window and looked up at the paling sky. The sun had not yet cleared the horizon, but its rays reflected off clouds, great fluffy clouds, piled up like pink and orange whipped cream to the north. He turned to Ashe, "Could you do it? Could you pull the clouds and make rain from them?"

Ashe shook his head. "Not with the firedrakes projecting like that. I could manage it without them, but there's no way I could gather in clouds in a period of time that would do any good, when most of my energy would have to be spent shielding myself."

Jerevan sighed. "If you can't do it, that leaves me and I don't know if I have enough energy left." He looked back at the firedrakes and their fiery duel. "Nevertheless, I'll have to try. I'll need Alanna's help; I have no chance without it. I'm not sure she'll be up to it either, but the interference won't be our main problem. Vyrkarion shields us from the most harmful levels. I noticed it earlier." He rubbed his hand across his eyes. "We'll need food and an hour's rest to restore some level of energy. Then we'll see."

"In the meantime," Ashe said, "shouldn't we be trying to get across the city while the isklarin are still blinded."

Jerevan sighed. "I'll leave that up to you and Thrym. Right now I need to try and heal Alanna and recoup some energy."

Alanna was in a place where there was no light, yet no darkness, a place where sounds and sensations echoed feebly through an enveloping mist. When she first arrived there she heard the sharp bark of gunfire and the clang of metal ringing on metal. She wasn't able to move or struggle and she wondered if she were dead.

After that, she heard voices call her and she tried to answer, but there in the mists she had no body with which to speak, no power to respond.

Alanna felt someone carry her, her body bent across someone's shoulder. That sensation lasted for a long time. At some point the shoulder grew broader and she was set down and lifted several times. The motion went on and on. Then, finally, she felt herself laid on a hard, flat surface.

She tried to call Jerevan, but there was no answer. She wasn't even sure she was sending. She might have just been thinking about it. Then he reached her.

"Alanna?"

"Jerevan! What's happened. Why can't I move?"

"You're suffering from backlash. We both are, but we'll recover. Look, you can speed the healing this way."

Alanna wasn't able to grasp the series of actions his mind demonstrated. She felt the thoughts in her head, but she didn't understand them.

"Never mind. I can do it for you."

How strange, she thought, to have one part of my mind communicate with the other part and not to understand. After that she lost consciousness altogether.

Alanna woke to pain. Her head throbbed and her limbs felt leaden, but she was no longer paralyzed or afloat in limbo. She opened her eyes and blinked at the light of a lantern and the sight of dusty wine racks above her. Where was she?

"We're in Ninkarrak. We didn't make it to the Morning Star," Jerevan thought.

The events of the past night came back to her. *"How long have I been unconscious?"*

"About three hours."

Alanna turned to see Jerevan sitting beside her on the floor. *"I need your help again."* The tone of his thought expressed concern and regret.

"Whatever I can do, I'll do, but I don't think I can even stand up," she said, her voice little more than a harsh whisper.

He grimaced but accepted her rejection of the mind link. "Ashe or Minta can hold you up. It's what's left of your mental reserves that worries me. I wouldn't ask if it weren't a real emergency. The whole city will go up in flames if we can't produce some rain. At least there won't be a backlash in this type of operation."

"You can make it rain?"

"Not without your help."

Alanna realized how weak he was when she saw he had to struggle to get to his feet and the effort left him shaking. It startled her when Ashe came to his assistance; until then she hadn't noticed that Ashe and the Nahar's nurse were both present.

"Help me up, too," Alanna said, trying to rise.

The nurse looked at Jerevan for confirmation. He nodded and went to the door, leaning heavily on Ashe. "I'll leave Minta to help you get ready," he said as he left.

Even with Minta's help it was hard for her to stand, but she felt a little better when she was on her feet. She was still fully dressed in the rough, dark clothes Jerevan had supplied to everyone to avoid being seen, but the shirt was torn and the pants stained with seaweed and salt water. Her underthings felt full of sand.

"Can you get me a basin of water so I can wash up a bit?"

"I'll have Thrym bring you one." Minta went to the door and called up the stairs for water to be brought.

Alanna steadied herself against a chest and wished that the shrill, keening noise that cut though her skull would go away.

"Alanna."

She shied away from Jerevan's contact. She felt filthy and uncomfortable. She didn't want to be exposed to intimacy now.

Thrym arrived with a pitcher of water and she was able to wash, after which she felt better and was able to climb the stairs leaning only slightly on Minta.

Upstairs, Alanna saw that they had taken shelter in an abandoned mansion. Jerevan, Ashe and the two surviving mercenaries were in the back courtyard inspecting a wagon hitched to four horses. Aubrey was helping Thrym rummage for food in the large kitchen.

The sun crested the horizon, shrugging itself up over the top of the hills to the southeast. The shriek of the firedrakes was worse now it was no longer muffled by the stone walls of the cellar and through the window she could see their fiery forms as they swooped and fought.

Alanna let Minta lead her outside and help her into an improvised bed in the back of the wagon. Aubrey, Ashe and Jerevan were already inside. Thrym and the female mercenary climbed up onto the driver's seat as soon as Alanna and Minta were seated. The huge white-haired man stood by the horses.

"Where did you get the wagon?" Minta asked.

Thrym grinned. "Our host lent it to us." He turned to Alanna. "Leyburn says you'll need an hour or so to gather energy before you can make it rain. We're going to try to make it as far across town as we can while the firedrakes are flying," he added, slapping the horses on their backs with the reins.

The horses lurched forward and the wagon jerked into motion down the rutted drive. Alanna grabbed the side and hung on. Once they reached the level surface of the paved road, however, the ride smoothed out and Alanna relaxed slightly. She took the fruit and cheese that Jerevan handed her and ate it. She still felt weak but minute by minute her strength was returning despite the terrifying din from the sky.

Even though it was still early, the road was full of traffic, all of it going in the opposite direction, away from the city. Alanna realized with shock that people were fleeing. If the roads were already this heavily trafficked here, in one of the richest of the residential districts, what would they be like in the densely populated areas they were trying to reach?

"We'll undoubtedly have to abandon the wagon soon," Jerevan answered her thought.

Again, Alanna shied away from the contact, disturbed that Jerevan was able to hear her thoughts, even when they weren't directed at him.

"You can pick up mine, too. Here, like this." He showed her how to open her mind to his awareness, a simple shifting of focus.

She still felt uncomfortable, but strangely she felt better when he moved over to her and put his arm around her.

Tired as she was, Alanna saw their progress through the rapidly filling streets in a chiaroscuro of images. Light from the rising sun glinted off the enamel paint of elaborate carriages as they vied for advantage with peddler's carts piled high with furniture and pots and pans. Men and women half-dressed, and others with weird combinations of clothing, pushed wheelbarrows and even baby carriages full of prized possessions.

Thrym threaded a way through the traffic for another half hour. After that, they unharnessed the horses and abandoned the wagon. Alanna, Jerevan and Ashe rode, while Thrym led the fourth horse carrying Minta and Aubrey. The mercenaries walked. A faint smell of smoke rode the air at times and a yellow-brown haze clouded the sky.

Soon after they abandoned the wagon, they came to a crossroads where Alanna smelled a stronger whiff of smoke and saw clouds of it rising from an area to the west.

"The market's on fire," Ashe said. "If you're going to do anything, you'll have to do it soon or the whole town will go up."

"Won't the firedrakes blind us?" Alanna asked.

"I can block out most of my vision. I'll only need to see the water vapor in the air. It will be painful, but Vyrkarion shields us from the worst of the interference," Jerevan reassured her. "The question is, are you strong enough?"

"I'll have to be, won't I."

Jerevan dismounted and helped her off her horse. Alanna drew out Vyrkarion and put her hand in Jerevan's. There was no swirling green well this time, only a sensation of merging. His mind intertwined with hers. Then they reached out, far out, their minds extending like a gossamer web to catch clouds. Again a sense of timelessness overcame her. She felt great swirls of energies, moving currents of air. She saw the sun reflect off drops of water making prisms. Elsewhere water vapor condensed to tiny droplets on the wing of a bird.

Yet, through all the separate moments of awareness, she felt pain. She was stretched thin across the sky and there was only a frail, precarious barrier between her and a terrible fire. At times the barrier thinned. Then the fire roar burned and deafened her, and always the wind tore at her, and spread her awareness farther and farther.

Jerevan's thought, directed at her rather than focused on the clouds, shocked Alanna back to awareness. "The storm's forming. We must guide it over the city and pull as much rain from it as we can. Are you all right?"

"I don't know," she thought. "I feel like I'm coming apart, unraveling in the wind."

Jerevan hesitated and Alanna sensed his unwillingness to put further strain on her. His strength was also dissipating as the shrieks of the firedrakes tore at their mental net despite their shield. Alanna tried to summon more energy, but she had no reserves left. Their thin web began to shred in the winds of the upper air. She cried out and felt Jerevan's mind as he strove to strengthen her and draw her back.

At the last possible moment, when Alanna knew they were defeated and would have to withdraw, she found herself drawing on one strand that didn't give way, a green thread leading to Vyrkarion.

Although she still tended to shy away from mind-speech, she had used it enough with Jerevan to recognize it, but it had never occurred to her to mind-speak Vyrkarion. Yet now, Vyrkarion mind-spoke her down that thin green thread. Somehow she saw through Vyrkarion that there was energy all around her; all she had to do was reach out and draw it to her, but she didn't know how to reach.

Then she felt Jerevan with her, joined in the web and somehow the method became clear. She reached. The energy came, fiery hot and burning. It licked at the fragile remaining threads of the web, but instead of charring them it reinforced them. The threads grew, and still the air was filled with energy. She drew more of it, a tremendous wave. It buoyed the threads up, filled them with new strength. Alanna watched in awe as Jerevan took this new energy and reached out to swirl the clouds over the city, mass the water in them and multiply it again and again, until she felt the rain start to fall. She let go of the green thread and the power that had flowed through her was gone.

Alanna opened her eyes. She was propped against the side of a building. She was weak and her brain felt as though it were on fire. "*What was it? Where did the energy come from?*" She turned to Jerevan whom she could feel sitting next to her.

His appearance shocked her. His eyes were deep sunk pits, his face pale and beaded with sweat. He smiled, however. "*From you. Vyrkarion showed you how to access the ambient energy all around us. I never dreamed it was so simple.*"

Their eyes went to the southern sky. The firedrakes flew southwest, fleeing a dangerous foe. One of the smaller dragons, presumably the female, soared beside the largest. The third one fled on a different heading, closer to due south, so that the gap between him and the others steadily increased.

"*It worked!*" she thought.

"*Yes.*" He turned to Ashe who was standing next to them. "We have to find a place to rest."

"We'll get you both to shelter," Ashe said, putting his arm down to help Jerevan to his feet. "I know just the place."

Thrym helped Alanna to her feet and onto the back of one of the horses.

XXVIII

4731, 474TH CYCLE OF THE YEAR OF THE DRAGON
MONTHS OF INGVASH AND CERDANA

Sen ua lordom ya, bal abwin larin e he lomcaul ean. Jao ac ean;
bajal ac ean. Va resrionwe quen tonod.
Sen ua ba nalor e lordom ya, ua puat mit nik itne he lomcaul. Bal
abwin mawhen e ean hedal, senit ilmekod boril uase va. Nalorin
bores papailin a lorin.

"If you worship me, go out among the people and give
them pleasure. Sing to them; dance for them. Life is meant
to be enjoyed.
"If you are a wizard and you worship me, you must stop
pain as well as bring pleasure. Go among the oppressed
and rescue them, even at the cost of your own life. Wizards
bear the responsibilities of the gods."

— FROM *LESSONS TAUGHT TO WIZARDS*
ATTRIBUTED TO JEHAN THE PLAYER

Elath watched as Thrym and Ashe helped the Tamrai and Leyburn
remount. The rain was cold and penetrating, saturating her clothes
and hair. All around her people milled in confusion. Until moments
before they had been in flight, desperate for their lives. Now, most of
them wanted to return to their homes but their attempts to turn around
in the already congested streets created a traffic jam of gargantuan
proportions.

Elath, clutching the reins of the Tamrai's horse, followed Thrym as he
wove through the crowds. He led the horse carrying Minta and Aubrey
while Varl led Leyburn's horse behind her and Ashe brought up the rear.
They ducked through alleys and around wagons and carriages amid
crowds gone surly with frustration and discomfort, everyone pushing
and pulling to make a path. Coaches and carts overladen with goods
were angled every which way across the streets while the owners yelled
at each other.

"Where are we going?" Elath shouted ahead to Thrym.

He turned to look back at her. "The Temple of Jehan on the edge of
the Lamashrak. We can rest there. All of Jehan's Temples are shielded;

even when Aavik's wizards recover from the firedrakes, they won't find us in a Temple sanctuary."

Elath nodded and pulled the horse through a gap Thrym found into a less crowded alley. The rain was beginning to taper off. Elath hoped it had done its job. Reaching the temple took some two hours and through the whole journey Elath's mind was on Fal. Had the fires reached their room in Farinmalith? That area had appeared to be the one the firedrakes flew over most often. Had the fires been put out in time?

The Temple of Jehan was a small, rectangular building of black marble devoid of ornamentation. They left the horses tied to a post before going inside. Varl carried Aubrey, who had fallen asleep. The main floor of the interior was one enormous, vaulted room filled with the rich, lilting sound of a skillfully played jalith, the twelve-stringed, pear-shaped instrument said to be the favorite of Jehan. A screen at the far end concealed the musician.

The room was crowded with people. Some sat on the chairs that filled about a third of the room, but most sat or lay down on the bare floor. A priest was distributing blankets. While most of the people were obviously refugees from the confusion outside, the Temple of Jehan turned no one away and the music soothed exacerbated tempers. Thrym found them a space near a back corner and Minta and Ashe spread out their driest blankets for Aubrey and the wizards, who still looked incredibly pale.

"You'll all be safe here," Thrym said, "while Ashe and I find his carnival."

"I have to check on Fal," Elath said. "I can't go anywhere until I know what's happened to him. I'll come back to complete my contract but I have to know. It won't take me more than a couple of hours and Varl should be a sufficient guard here in the temple."

Thrym looked at her and nodded. "All right. We won't be able to get away before then anyway. But we need you, Elath. We're shorthanded as it is. Be sure you do get back here." He hesitated and added, "If you find Fal and you can't find anyone to take care of him, bring him along. There'll be space in one of the caravans."

"Thanks, Thrym." Elath left the temple at a run. Outside, the streets were still clogged with traffic but it was easier for Elath to force a way through than it had been for Thrym to find a way for the horses. She kept to a fast pace. At first, she retraced part of the distance they'd covered earlier but Farinmalith was northwest of the Lamashrak and she was soon well to the west of their earlier path.

The closer Elath got to Farinmalith the more damage she saw. That morning they'd seen and smelled smoke in the distance but witnessed no actual fires. Now she passed burned out buildings every few blocks. In some places fire had destroyed whole blocks of houses and the sharp smell of wet ashes filled the air.

VYRKARION: THE TALISMAN OF ANOR

When Elath reached the street where she lived, she was relieved to see most of the buildings still intact. On coming closer, however, she saw that half of the building next door had burned. Miraculously, the fire had been put out before it crossed to the house containing the room she shared with Fal.

Elath yelled at Sanyi, the woman she'd trusted to take care of Fal. Sanyi's apartment had been in the building that burned and she was sifting through the rubble. "Have you seen Fal? Is he all right?"

Sanyi looked up and called back, "Haven't seen him. Fire didn't get to your place."

Elath ran up the stairs to her room.

"Fal," she called. She jerked the door open and ran inside.

He lay on the bed just as she'd left him. He sat up when she entered. "El, is that you?"

"Are you all right?"

"No worse than yesterday. What're you doing here? I thought you'd be gone for at least a week."

"I'm taking you with me. Plans got changed and we'll be going overland. It'll take longer before I can get back. Anyway, Sanyi's burnt out," Elath said, going to his things. She bundled them into a sack, except for the clothes he'd need to wear.

"I can't travel like this."

"You can ride in a wagon. That's all you'll need to do." She stripped him of the robe he was wearing and started to put his clothes on him.

"Why, El? Why drag me around with you? I'd have been better off if the fire had hit this building," Fal said, but he didn't resist.

When Elath had him dressed she threw the sack over her shoulder, grabbed his elbow and guided him out of the room.

Alanna fell asleep the moment she sat down after reaching the temple. She woke to find Magra shaking her. "I'm sorry. We let you sleep as long as possible but we have to leave now."

"How long have I been asleep?" Alanna asked, raising her hand to her head. It ached like three toothaches rolled into one. "And how did you get here?"

"I don't know when you fell asleep," Magra said. "I came with Thrym and Ashe after they found the carnival."

"You were with the carnival?" Alanna asked, suddenly taking in Magra's motley costume.

Magra laughed. "Jerevan's contingency plan. When you didn't make it to the *Morning Star*, Rainal, Tana and I landed with some of the mercenaries and headed for the carnival. Everyone's outside now with the caravans but we have to move."

Magra helped Alanna to rise and Alanna reflected that her first experiences as a wizard had included a great deal more pain and dependency than she'd have previously believed possible.

At least the music soothed her aching head and she was relieved to hear no trace of the firedrakes. "We put out all the fires?"

"Most of them," Magra said. "It rained pretty hard for a while. Even if a few are still smoldering, they won't spread, and the firedrakes lit out of here in a hurry so there won't be any new ones. The rain's stopped now. The streets will be clear soon."

Alanna went outside with Magra and watched while Jerevan supervised the loading of the last of the caravans. He looked better. He'd washed and changed his clothes and, except for the deep shadows under his eyes, he looked almost himself again. His clothes startled her, however: tight fitting black pants and a loose-sleeved, scarlet shirt. They'd obviously been supplied by someone with the carnival. Then she noticed that all their party now wore carnival costumes.

"You'll feel better when you've bathed and changed," Jerevan said. "I've ordered a tub of hot water brought to our caravan. You'll have to bathe while we travel, but you'll get used to that in the next few days."

"A hot bath does sound good," she agreed, staring at the closed wagons with their colorfully painted sides in amazement. "Is this Ashe's carnival? I suppose it's an excellent cover, but are you sure no one will betray us?"

Rainal, who was with them, gaped. "You haven't told her, Jere?"

"I suppose I forgot. There's been so little time," Jerevan said ruefully.

"Told me what?" Alanna asked.

"About carnivals and wizards," Rainal said, grinning.

"What about carnivals and wizards?" She frowned as the answer surfaced in her mind, Jerevan's memories coming to her as though they were her own. "The Varfarin uses the carnivals as a cover, a disguise. How marvelous!"

As though the word Varfarin were a key, another vast series of images emerged in her mind, years of journeying in caravans through hot deserts and humid jungles, years of danger and privation.

Jerevan frowned and she realized that her access to his memories bothered him as much as his access to her thoughts bothered her. "Most of the carnivals all over Tamar are worked by our people. All the employees of any of our carnivals are loyal, wizards or not. Unfortunately, because of the fighting in Cibata and because the carnivals generally go south for the winter, we're short of wizards in Ilwheirlane. We've never had to worry about a rescue here at home before and it's not on our routes except, of course, in the summer for recruiting."

Alanna caught another association from Jerevan's mind and looked back at the Temple they had just left. "Are all the members of the Varfarin worshipers of Jehan?"

"Yes. We've all taken oaths as priests of Jehan. That's part of the reason we use the carnivals. Jehan teaches that it's our duty to give pleasure as well as to keep others from harm. The carnivals entertain in addition to supplying camouflage for less overt activities."

She tucked her arm in Jerevan's and was about to climb into the caravan he'd indicated as theirs when she saw the female mercenary who had been with them earlier come running up pulling a blind man behind her. Elath and Fal, Jerevan's memory supplied the names. The man was tall, almost skeletal and looked exhausted but there was something about his face that seemed familiar. Then she noticed that Elath wasn't holding his hand, but a stump. This was the man from the Basilica. The man who'd been with the isklarin.

"I'm sorry I'm late getting back," Elath said, "but it was hard getting Fal across town."

"Just as long as you made it. Get in that caravan over there." Jerevan pointed to the one ahead of the one to which he'd been taking Alanna.

"He was one of the thieves who tried to steal Miune's staff," she said.

"Yes, I know," Jerevan said. "But he's not dealing with the isklarin now."

Alanna climbed into the caravan she would share with Jerevan. As soon as she got in, she felt it start to move. She bathed as quickly as she could and changed into the clothes Jerevan gave her. Her hair was a wild tangle and she wasn't used to dressing it herself but she did her best and then joined Jerevan and Rainal on the driver's seat in the front.

"Where are we going?"

"Northwest around the bay to Peverel, north to Harby and then back along the Great West Road to the Mallarnes. If Aavik doesn't catch us, we'll reach the mountains in time for the fruiting and then we'll take Aubrey on to Akyrion," Jerevan said.

"Why Akyrion?" Alanna asked.

"Aubrey is the legitimate heir to the throne of Ilwheirlane. In any of the human lands he'd be in danger of being used as a pawn in some political game. He'll be safer growing up in Akyrion with the baneslarin," Jerevan said.

"But what about his training? Are you planning on going to Akyrion too?"

"*No.*" He smiled at her, his eyes warm. "*We may visit the northlands, but the Varfarin must be run out of Ilwheirlane. As soon as we've delivered Aubrey to safety, I must return here and try to make my peace with Rhys.*"

This time the current of the mind link between them felt more natural, but Alanna still felt restless. She edged sideways on the hard wooden seat until her shoulder touched Jerevan's. The contact soothed her.

"Won't it seem unusual for the carnival to travel at night?" she asked.

"Carnivals always travel at night," Rainal said. "That way they don't miss a show. It's our traveling in the daytime that may draw attention."

Jerevan grinned. "We're being paid to do a big show in Ethdale, but we have to be there by the nineteenth of Cerdana."

"What's our cover after we reach Ethdale?" Rainal asked.

"Same story, only it will be Sallus of Lachan who offered us a bonus if we got there in time for the Spring Fair," Jerevan answered. "We'll probably have to do a performance in Ethdale and Barmur to avoid raising suspicion, but that shouldn't present a problem."

"No. It's a good plan, if Aavik doesn't trace us," Rainal said.

"I'm hoping he thinks we made it to the *Morning Star* and chases her. The landing you made to join us may help," Jerevan said.

"What good will it do him to chase us now? I thought the only person we had left to fear was Rhys?" Alanna asked.

"The last thing Aavik wants is to see Rhys take the throne. He knows that a strong leader in Ilwheirlane will put a major cramp in his plans to pick off the human nations one by one." Jerevan paused and Alanna could feel him gathering his thoughts, estimating the chances of his opponent doing this or that. She felt the echo of other such thoughts down the years. It was a game he'd played again and again, risking his life and the lives of the others who followed him, always believing that he'd outguess his enemies one more time.

Alanna was startled when Jerevan spoke again, she'd been absorbed in his memories. "Aavik will follow us if we haven't left the coastal area before he locates us. In any event, he's bound to set some of his wizards to tracing us. He has too much to lose if we get away, too much to gain if he catches us. We just have to hope that he's fooled by the *Morning Star* and that our disguise holds up."

The streets were clearing and the caravans had to make few detours on their route out of Ninkarrak. Jerevan chose to go by the coast road to Halse. Although not one of the flint toll roads, it was well maintained and there were frequent inns where the horses could be changed. The carnival personnel slept in their caravans and took turns driving through the night and all the following day. The caravans reached Halse late on the second morning of the journey, the first day of Cerdana.

Halse was a small town, really more a large fishing village than a port, but it was also the place where the coast road joined a spur of the Great Southwest Road, one of Ilwheirlane's three main highways. They could make better time on the smooth flint surface. But so could anyone pursuing them.

XXIX

4731, 474th Cycle of the Year of the Dragon
Month of Cerdana
The thief became the servant
Who'd serve him through the years,
Two hundred long and lonely years,
The sorrows and the tears.
Tears, tears for the Wanderer
Wherever he may be,
For he is doomed to exile
By the shore of Sorrow Sea.

— FROM *THE BALLAD OF AUBREY THE WANDERER* BY ANONYMOUS

The caravans reached Peverel in the middle of the third day after leaving Ninkarrak. There they turned north away from the well-kept toll road and their speed immediately suffered. The dirt track that connected Peverel with Harby on the Great West Road was rutted and often muddy. The horses pulling the heavy caravans strained to keep them from sinking into the mire and, as inns with fresh horses were rarer, the teams had to be rested frequently. The carnival took over two days to reach Seton.

On their eighth day of traveling, while still some hours from Mareswood, Thrym was taking his turn at driving one of the caravans with Minta beside him. Both of them wore the bright garments typical of the carnival people. Aubrey slept in the back. They passed an orchard with ordered rows of lomcan trees covered with blooms.

"I don't like it, Minta," Thrym complained. "I feel like a lame seral trying to outrun a malik."

"I know, but Aubrey says we're inconspicuous." Minta looked rather doubtfully at her brilliant yellow and green finery.

Thrym grinned, pointing to his own orange and tan motley. "Be thankful for yellow and green. I don't know about inconspicuous, but we're certainly slow. If it were me in charge, I'd take Aubrey and the tamrai with Vyrkarion and put them on fast horses and ride for Lachan. None of this sixty kilometers a day routine, and that's only if we're lucky."

"It'll be faster when we reach Harby and get back on a main road again."

"I hope so."

They lapsed into silence and Minta studied the green hills now clothed with copses of budding jula, elm and chestnut trees, their branches sporting the soft green of new leaves.

After a time the forested hills gave way to meadows gay with wild flowers, the brilliant red drops of love-lies-bleeding sprinkled through patches of white sylphin hair and golden buttercups.

"I'm a widow now," Minta said, her eyes fixed on the colored hills. She had taken her sweater off some time before. Her pale face was beginning to tan from the hours in the fresh air and sunlight.

Thrym turned to her. "You're sure?"

"I saw him die in the courtyard." She kept her eyes focused on the hills. Her voice was flat, emotionless. "He was disemboweled. He couldn't have survived."

"Then you're free," Thrym said tentatively, her expression confusing him. "You're not going to mourn for him, are you?"

"No. I am glad. That's the problem," Minta said, facing him at last. Her eyes were angry. "I can't mourn him. I can't even regret that he died so painfully. I wanted him to die like that. I wanted him to suffer, but it was all so ugly." She turned into his arms and buried her head in his shoulder.

Thrym shifted both sets of reins into his left hand and put his other arm around her. "Hey. It's all right. I understand. You're not to blame for what happened. He didn't die because you wished for it. He died in the line of duty, fighting to protect the Estahar."

She sniffed and wiped at her eyes. "It's just, I'd wanted it for so long."

"I know." He hugged her. "But he died well, and you mustn't feel guilty about that. Everything he put you through, it's over."

She rested her head on his shoulders and sighed. "I'm sorry. I didn't mean to cry all over you."

He grinned. "Just as long as you don't go crying on anyone else." He hesitated, then continued, "We can get married now, if you want. Maybe someday we'll even have children of our own." He turned her chin up and kissed the tears that still streaked her cheeks. "You do want to marry me, don't you?"

"Why do you think I told you I was a widow?" Minta's eyes were brilliant but no longer just with tears. "I wasn't sure you'd want to make it official."

Thrym looked startled, but he recovered and grinned. "I don't see that I have much choice if we're both going to be living in the same household. That is, unless you thought I was going to give up sleeping with you?"

She blushed "I didn't think…"

"No, you didn't. Minta, don't you know I'd have married you any time after our first evening together if I'd seen a way to make it possible.

I wanted to take you away with me, but I realized that, while you might hate your husband, you'd never leave Aubrey."

Minta sighed, snuggling her head against his shoulder. "You never said anything about marriage."

"How could I?" Thrym hugged her tight to his side. "But I'll see to it now."

"I'm glad you have that settled," Aubrey said, squeezing up from the back of the wagon to sit on the seat beside Minta.

Minta saw the heat rising in Thrym's face at the same time she felt it in her own. She was about to protest, but Aubrey added, "It'll be easier if we live together like a family when we get to Akyrion." Then his grin vanished and Minta saw a flash of pain in his bright blue eyes and knew he was remembering what had happened to his mother.

"Vanith was brave," she said.

Aubrey closed his eyes and nodded, but then he looked up and the mischief was back in his face. "I wouldn't ordinarily have interrupted you, but this caravan is rather small."

"I thought you were asleep," Minta said.

"I couldn't sleep. I'm sensitive to emotional levels, remember."

"So we're going to Akyrion?" Thrym asked.

"Jere says that Elune Minrai, the Ahar of Akyrion, has offered me sanctuary. He said I'd be safe there from Aavik, and from any human rulers who might want to use me. No one will invade the lands of the baneslarin, no matter what the prize."

"Will Lord Leyburn go with us to continue your training?" Minta asked.

Aubrey frowned and shook his head. "No. He's needed here in Ilwheirlane. But he says that Kaaremin, a wizard trained by Iskkaar and Minneth, has volunteered to take over my apprenticeship. Jere thought he'd died, but he spoke to Jere by mind touch about a month ago." Aubrey swallowed. "He may be a bit strange, but Jere says he could have qualified for the Council a thousand years ago, if he'd wanted to. And he must be a good teacher, because he trained the Wizard Ashe and Jere thinks Ashe is one of the best teachers he knows."

"You'll need friends by you," Thrym said.

"Yes."

"I always wished for a son like you," Minta said, hugging him with her free arm. They sat like that for some time, Minta with an arm around each of those she held dear. The sun smiled on them and the caravans wound through the flower covered hills.

In the late afternoon, with the sun sinking below the western hills and casting long shadows, the peace was disrupted. Aubrey, who had been napping with his head in Minta's lap, sat up. "No!"

"What is it?" Minta was alarmed by the boy's expression.

"Jerevan just called me. The isklarin are behind us, a troop of a hundred, thirty of them wizards led by Aavik himself. They're near Seton now. They'll catch us tomorrow before we reach Harby. And Rhys has disappeared. He's no longer with his army and no farseeing can find him."

XXX

4731, 474TH CYCLE OF THE YEAR OF THE DRAGON
MONTH OF CERDANA

> *Ilahar puat harwe a dao*
> *a rion e larin ea har.*

> "A ruler must be ruled by the good
> of the state and the people he rules."

> — FROM *THE ART OF GOVERNMENT*
> BY VYDARGA V OF ILWHEIRLANE

As camouflage had failed, Jerevan abandoned it for speed. They left the carnival and purchased horses at Mareswood. Valla, Jerevan's chestnut karioth, had kept away as long as they had any hope of secrecy but she joined them there. Jerevan put Aubrey up on the karioth in front of him and Alanna on the fastest of the horses at his side. Minta, who had never learned to ride, clung to Thrym. Elath rode with Fal up behind her and Varl, Magra, Ashe, Rainal, Tana and twenty-seven mercenaries, all they could find horses for, brought up the rear. The others remained with the carnival. By morning they were close to Harby and Alanna's thigh muscles ached. She wasn't accustomed to such long hours in the saddle.

"You're not afraid that we've left the others to their deaths?" Alanna asked Jerevan.

"Aavik won't bother with the carnival folk when he has us to pursue."

Alanna felt the weariness that weighted his thoughts and her mind filled with images of other close escapes.

"*So Morning Star didn't fool him?*" she asked.

"*He did think we were aboard to begin with,*" Jerevan thought, "*but he caught her too quickly and then had the ship he was on deliver him to Halse.*"

"*What about Rhys?*"

A sudden stillness descended over his mind. Alanna turned to look ahead. A karoth and rider came to meet them. The karoth was much larger than the kariothin Alanna had met previously and as black as night.

"*Tarat's fury!*" Jerevan swore.

"*Who is he?*"

"He whose whereabouts you just questioned. Our new monarch," Jerevan said. *"It seems you're going to have your audience with the Estahar after all."*

Valla stopped and Alanna reined in her mare beside the karioth, the horses drawing up behind them. They stood still as the karoth and his rider halted in front of them.

He's beautiful, Alanna thought. Rhys looked as she imagined a god might look, perfect of face and form, his features as immobile as if they'd been carved from stone. She realized with a start that he fit the image she'd held in her mind of what the Estahar should be.

"Good day," Jerevan thought.

"What do you want of us?" Alanna demanded when Rhys didn't immediately respond to the greeting.

Rhys had been eyeing them expressionlessly, but the spoken words seemed to surprise him. *"To meet you. As you wouldn't come to me, I came to you."* There was no trace of emotion revealed in his thoughts.

"Where is your army?" She didn't know where the courage to question him came from. Perhaps it was just that she was tired and had struggled too long for all her efforts to be wasted without her making even a protest.

"I left it behind." This time a trace of amusement colored the baneslar's response. *"I need no army's help to take the throne of Ilwheirlane. Idrim, Vanith and Arrel are dead; the boy is fleeing the country and my grandfather is senile, confined in a tower in the north. I am Estahar of Ilwheirlane."*

"And the isklarin, will they flee before you too?"

Rhys smiled and his smile was both charming and terrible. *"There are many of them, but I have Cyrkarion and the knowledge Cormor gave it. If they're wise, they'll flee."*

Jerevan thought, *"There are a number of them behind us now."*

"Yes. That is one of the reasons I'm here."

"You described the boy as fleeing the country; you don't intend to interfere?"

"I wish to meet him first. That's all."

"Why?" Jerevan demanded.

Rhys laughed. *"You are both members of my family. You both give promise of being my peers some day. Would it not truly be stranger if I didn't wish to meet you."*

"That's your only reason?" Alanna asked.

"There is no such thing as a straight line; no act with but one motive." The great black karoth that Rhys rode gave a sudden snort and half reared. *"Aubrey, stand before me!"* Rhys demanded and dismounted.

Aubrey looked up at Jerevan, but Jerevan made no comment. "What do you want of me?" the boy asked. Alanna was reminded of his calm when they escaped from the Tower. He sounded the same now, self-possessed, but she sensed he was afraid.

"Stand before me, cousin."

VYRKARION: THE TALISMAN OF ANOR

Aubrey glanced once more at Jerevan, who remained motionless. Then he slid down from Valla and limped forward to stand before Rhys. He looked even smaller than usual facing the perfectly proportioned height of his half-eslar cousin.

"You need not fear me, child. I want to talk with you for a time. I want to know you and I want you to remember me. In the years to come there'll be few opportunities for us to meet. It would be a pity to waste this one. Come." Rhys reached down a hand from his greater than two meter height and tousled the child's hair. Then he walked toward a stand of jula trees some distance from the road.

Aubrey followed. There was a cry from behind them as Minta slipped from her horse and ran toward the boy, but Thrym caught her before she could reach him.

"Easy, Minta," Thrym said, holding her back.

"You can't go out there with him, Aubrey. He'll kill you," Minta cried.

Aubrey hesitated, then said, "It's my decision, Minta. Don't be afraid." He turned and started after Rhys.

His cousin hadn't paused and had almost reached the trees. The morning air was chill; the grass damp with dew. Alanna shivered, comparing Aubrey's short, uneven steps and small tracks with the footprints left by Rhys.

"Why didn't you stop him?" she demanded of Jerevan.

"He did the right thing."

Minta sobbed in Thrym's arms and Magra and Rainal watched Jerevan as though waiting for a signal.

"You needn't worry, you know. He's unpredictable at times, but he won't hurt the boy."

Alanna turned as the clear thought images came from the black karoth who still blocked the road. She felt Jerevan relax in response. *"You sound certain of that."*

"I can't predict what he will do, but I've learned something of what he won't do," the karoth thought. *"The boy is quite safe."*

"You're Rakshe, aren't you?" Jerevan questioned. *"Why did you give up your herds to serve him?"*

"The others feared him. In the past, kariothin were called by youths just beginning their climb to knowledge. Never before has one called who was already at the peak of his power, and yet young, still sometimes childish, and unschooled in its use. Not to mention cursed by Tarat." Rakshe arched his neck and snorted. *"I do not fear him. His rage can truly shake the world, but his madness is never absolute. There are things he would not do even in one of his worst rages."*

Jerevan nodded. *"I thank you. You have eased my mind."*

Time passed and they waited. Alanna shifted uncomfortably in her saddle and wished she could get off, but she was still too uncertain of what was going to happen next. When she reached the point where she thought she would go after Rhys herself if he didn't return with the boy, the two figures emerged from the trees, Aubrey riding on his cousin's shoulder.

As Rhys crossed the grass to the road, Alanna heard the sound of horses galloping hard. She reined her mount around and saw a troop of Gandaharan soldiers draw up behind them. The thirty riders in front rode forward at a walk, Aavik at their head, until no more than eight meters separated them from the rear rank of mercenaries.

"Surrender the boy and the woman who bears Vyrkarion," Aavik demanded.

"And if they do not?"

Alanna turned to Rhys when that calm, musical voice rang out its question. He was drawing a sword from the sheath on his back, Aubrey still perched on his shoulder.

"Then we'll take them."

"That may not be easy," Rhys said.

"We outnumber you," Aavik said, drawing a crystal from a chain around his neck. The thirty other riders who had ridden forward with Aavik also drew crystals and Alanna realized with shock that they were all wizards.

"But the karionin make nonsense of your numbers," Rhys said. Then he turned to Alanna and Jerevan. *"Link with me."*

She looked at Jerevan. He reached out a hand to grasp hers and said, *"We have no choice."*

She gripped his hand and drew Vyrkarion, feeling the linkage and the way that Jerevan then reached out to Rhys.

Rhys stood still, holding the sword in front of him. A blue glow gathered around the hilt. Alanna felt the linkage form and felt the other wizards with them drawn in. Magra, Tana, Rainal and Ashe all felt like points of heat in a web. The glow around Rhys' sword shifted to aquamarine. It wasn't the flaming focus of energy that she'd seen used in the previous wizard battles she'd witnessed. It was more like a dense, glowing fog. It seemed to drift toward the isklarin.

Their energies took the same form she was used to, lancing out at the blue-green mist like spears of fire. She felt pain, as though the lances of force were thorns tearing at her flesh. Still, the lances couldn't stop the fog, which continued to advance. When that insubstantial haze reached the isklarin, she felt them as though a part of her own body reached out to engulf them. They felt hot, like hard knots of energy. The heat of them burned some of the fog away, but more billowed from Cyrkarion to replace what was lost. Alanna felt the drain, but it was steady and even. She had no trouble drawing energy enough to replace what was lost.

Then she heard a shout and realized that the isklarin soldiers were attacking, and the mercenaries had moved to defend them, despite the fact that the mercenaries were outnumbered nearly two to one.

"I can hold the wizards now," Rhys thought. *"Help your men."*

Alanna felt the link that connected Jerevan, herself and the other wizards to Rhys snap shut. She no longer felt a part of the fog, but she still sensed the linkage between Magra, Tana, Rainal and Ashe. She felt Jerevan's attention shift to the oncoming attack and forced her own awareness outward as Jerevan hurled a lance of power at one of the Gandaharan soldiers.

Seventy soldiers bore down on the mercenary troop of less than thirty, but the mercenaries positioned their horses to block the isklarin from reaching Aubrey or herself. Alanna concentrated on supplying Jerevan and the others still linked with them energy for their lances.

The fog thinned and turned blue again when the linkage to Rhys closed but it still surrounded Aavik and his associates. Light flared around the wizards as they fought the fog, but their lances did not seem able to do significant damage.

Further, the fog limited the area through which the Gandaharans could attack, as both they and the mercenaries avoided contact with it. That gave Jerevan and the other wizards time to bring down more than sixteen isklarin before the two forces joined in combat.

Both sides fired their muskets, but only one isklar fell. The other isklarin had enough wizard power to divert the balls and the mercenaries were protected by Ashe. Then the two sides merged into a mass of confused combat. It grew harder for the wizards to choose clear targets.

Alanna watched as Varl, the white-haired giant, pulled one isklar off his horse, disarmed him, broke his neck, and hurled him in the face of another, knocking him off his mount. A lance from Tana struck the fallen Gandaharan before he could rise and Varl, after leaning over to recover his sword from the ground, swung round just in time to decapitate another.

Even the blind cripple Alanna had thought totally helpless, turned on the back of the horse he shared and fought back to back with his black-haired companion, the hooks on his arm stumps making surprisingly effective weapons despite his lack of sight. She remembered then how he had fought in the Basilica.

She reached out for more power as the wizards began to make sense of the combat and find targets, but the air around them seemed drained of energy. She drew on Vyrkarion and her own reserves, which had not recovered from the strain of Aubrey's rescue from the Tower. Jerevan struck down two isklarin who had almost managed to penetrate the mass of mounted mercenaries, and Alanna flinched at the drain. Ashe struck another, then Magra, and Alanna felt the drain, with nothing left to draw upon, snap the linkage. "*Jerevan*," she thought.

"*It's all right*," he thought, "*Rhys has already drained all the available energy controlling Aavik and the other isklarin wizards. Ashe and the others will have to depend on their own reserves. I've enough left for a few more bolts, but hopefully we won't need them. I think the sides are almost equal now.*"

Alanna forced her attention outward once more to survey the battle. Jerevan was right. A large number of Gandaharans littered the ground in a semi-circle around them, a full circle being impossible with the line of fog that still projected from Rhys and enclosed the isklarin wizards.

While many mercenaries had also fallen, the Gandaharans no longer seemed to outnumber those that remained and the fighting was breaking up into individual combats. Even as she watched, Varl grabbed the body of an isklar he'd slain and swung it by its feet left-handed to knock another isklar off his horse. He then rode over the downed isklar and cut off his head with the sword in his right hand.

Some of the remaining isklarin began to withdraw. One of them yelled something in a harsh sounding language and the remaining nineteen retreated. She saw them hesitate as they passed the fog still encompassing their wizards, then another one shouted something and they turned and galloped back the way they had come.

Alanna dismounted and joined Jerevan and the other wizards in tending to the wounded. Sixteen mercenaries had been killed, but most of those who survived had only minor wounds quickly healed.

When they'd done all they could, Alanna turned and looked at Rhys, still standing as motionless as a statue, and at the wizards in the fog. The flashes of light around them were dimming. Their crystals dulled, became almost opaque. As she stared at him, Aavik struggled for a moment, then fell to the ground. The other wizards around him slumped in their saddles or fell. When the last one lost consciousness, the fog thinned, dissipated.

"Are they dead?" Alanna asked, turning from the isklarin wizards to look at Rhys.

He stretched, then laughed, the sound rich and musical yet full of mockery. "Aavik and three more of the strongest are dead. The rest are merely unconscious. They'll come round in a few hours, but they won't have enough energy to light a candle for weeks. They're no danger to you now."

Rhys shook his head as though clearing it. Then he walked up to Valla and swung Aubrey from his shoulder to Valla's back. "Cousin, if you wear a plain cape and go to the back door of Ninkarrak you'll be welcome. Tell my guard the name 'Rhyanna' and you'll be brought before me whatever the hour. But you must remember the password."

"You'd welcome me to your court?" Aubrey sounded curious.

VYRKARION: THE TALISMAN OF ANOR

"I'll welcome you, but not to my court. I told you, wear a plain cape and a false name. If I welcomed you officially, I'd have to give up my throne to you," Rhys thought wryly, "and that is not the destiny the gods have chosen for me."

Alanna blinked. As she felt Rhys' thought, she saw an image of Aubrey and the wizard king as pieces on a game board moved by immense, ghostly hands.

"Why?" Aubrey demanded.

"Perhaps because we both worship the Guide of the Crooked Path, perhaps for other reasons." Rhys turned from the boy and faced Jerevan. "I'll have need of you and of those who answer to you."

"I sent a message to you and you answered that you'd grant no favors," Jerevan's thought was wary. He walked up to where Rhys stood by Valla.

"To anyone who will not face me." Rhys smiled. "You've not only faced me now, you've linked with me. What favors would you ask?"

"The freedom to live and study here in Ilwheirlane as we've always done; the freedom to recruit the young as we have done."

"I will grant you more than that." Rhys walked to Rakshe and mounted, then turned back to them and said aloud, "From the day I take the throne of Ilwheirlane, it will be the law that all children be tested by the age of five. If a child has talent above a certain degree, then that child *shall* be trained. I need you both," and Alanna felt herself included in his gaze, "to teach at Onchan and to train other teachers. The College will be re-opened within the year. Take the boy to safety and then return."

"Why?" Jerevan asked. "You have no need of other wizards to serve you. There's no one on Tamar your equal."

"It is indeed fortunate for the human lands that Aavik and the other isklarin wizards share the same delusion. As he was not yet really master of the high sight, he thought me more powerful than I am. I'd have thought better of you but, as your linkage is new and you've had distractions, perhaps you haven't yet explored Vyrkarion's potential."

"What do you mean?"

"Every isklar in the army of Gandahar is a wizard to some extent and they number more than two hundred thousand. Granted, most of them can merely light a fire without a flint, simple things, but they all have some power. When Aavik's successor, or one of his kindred, links with one of the karionin — which will happen, don't doubt it — then he'll learn that more than two or three, or even half a dozen, can be linked as we linked in combat today. Not the same linkage as that you share with your lady; it isn't permanent or binding, but it is a linkage. Without the karionin such linkages are limited to a half dozen or a dozen at most. But with the one of the karionin, I don't know the limits myself. And then the isklarin will conquer the world. Unless there are enough human wizards to stop them."

"How do you know this?"

"How do you know that the sky is blue or that grass grows. Cyrkarion is now a part of me and with it came much of the knowledge of Cormor. I know the nature of the power I use."

"Can you create such multiple linkages?" Jerevan asked.

"Not until I've taken a mate and Cyrkarion is complete. In the linkage we just formed, I used your bond with Vyrkarion as the opposite pole, but that's an unstable configuration. Once I've taken a mate, Cyrkarion will be much more effective."

Jerevan looked at her and Alanna felt his question inside her. "We'll return and teach at Onchan," she said aloud as though taking an oath. Then she looked up at Rhys and asked, "Your majesty, may I make a request?"

"You have wizards enough, either with you now or on their way to meet you on your journey west, to service the sylvith trees this year. Next year there'll be teachers at Onchan to help, and, if necessary, I'll come myself."

"Is there no way you can make peace with the eslarin?"

Again Rhys smiled. "That's in the hands of the Lorincen. There may be a way, but it will be some years yet before I'm free to explore it. In the meantime we will make do."

"Why did you come south before the spring?" Jerevan asked.

Rakshe curvetted and Rhys' face froze as the karoth landed. *"You know how to hit close to the bone."*

"I don't understand," Jerevan said.

Rhys grimaced. *"An error of judgment. I lost my temper. Rakshe here,"* he patted the karoth on the neck, *"considers it a fault of my youth as much as Tarat's curse. But for whatever cause, my temper is uncertain at times."*

"Then you aren't omniscient?"

"I never said I was. Even the gods are not omniscient or what pleasure would they get from their contests?" He shook his head, and for a moment Alanna felt a sense of overwhelming sorrow. *"No! They are not omniscient, for the universe itself is random beyond any being's power to ultimately control it. All any of us can do is struggle, and sometimes weight the odds."*

"Perhaps you just implied your control over destiny?"

Rhys laughed his beautiful, musical laugh but this time the sound seemed more real to Alanna, as though he was actually pleased. *"We'll work together well, Jerevan."*

"I hope so, sire."

"And you, Aubrey," he looked down again at the boy, *"will you come to visit me?"*

"I'll try, cousin, but I can't see the future."

"Even Cormor didn't see the future, only possibilities. In fact, that's all the gods can see."

"Don't the sibyl witches see the future? Surely Inanda saw what was going to happen?" Alanna asked.

Rhys snorted. *"She saw nothing but what Maera sent her to see. The gods don't predict the future, they try and force it into the paths they wish it to take."*

"Then even you are a counter on their board?" Alanna questioned.

"One with less freedom than most. A common soldier may be overlooked, but the wizard-king is the most prominent of pieces," Rhys thought. He looked around at the bodies that littered the ground around them. *"I'll see that the dead are buried, and the isklarin sent on their way."* Then he commanded Rakshe back off the road.

Alanna noted that most of the surviving mercenaries had remounted. She allowed Jerevan to help her onto her horse and watched as he mounted Valla.

"Have a good journey. You'll not be followed," Rhys thought.

Elath watched the confrontation between Leyburn, the Tamrai and Rhys Cinnac, bemused by the long silences. By some miracle, neither she nor Fal had been wounded, although they'd done their share of wounding. In her euphoria after the battle, the sight of the baneslar reminded her of the advice Thrym had given her.

She waited until everyone else remounted and Rhys made way for them to pass. Then she ran to kneel in front of the black karoth.

"Lord," she cried, "I request mercy. They say you're to be the new Estahar of Ilwheirlane. My man was judged too harshly by the god your predecessor revered. If you have mercy, you'll undo the punishment of Miune and give my man back his sight and the use of his hands."

Rhys stared at Elath for a moment. Then his eyes went to Fal where Fal sat on the back of her horse. The action of the battle seemed to have restored something to Fal and he sat erect.

Rhys nodded. "The punishment was indeed harsh, but he did intend to steal from Miune. What makes you think that I can undo what the agent of a god has done?"

"They say your powers are like a god's," Elath said. "You could heal him, if you wished. Do you deny it?"

Rhys shook his head. "No. His maiming is within my power to heal, but every act has repercussions and this one would have more than most. What will you give me, if I give you another chance at justice?"

"Whatever you ask that's within my power," Elath said. "I saved the money we were paid for the job, hoping it would be enough for a wizard, but money would mean nothing to you."

"No. You can keep your money." Rhys turned to Fal and said, "Fallon Gavi, what would you give me in return for another chance at justice?"

Fal made a sound that was halfway between a laugh and a croak. "I have nothing and I don't believe in justice."

"You have nothing." Rhys nodded. "And you are nothing. Therefore, if I said my price was nothing, would you pay it?"

Fal jerked as though he were a puppet on strings someone had pulled. His face turned in Rhys' direction. Then he sat even straighter in the saddle and nodded. He was pale.

Rhys turned to Elath. "You are also nothing to me. Do you understand the price of my justice? And are you also willing to pay it?"

Fal said quickly, "It's for me to pay the price, not her."

Rhys ignored him, his eyes still on Elath. "Well?"

She looked at Fal and then back to the indifferent face of the wizard-king, the baneslar who would soon be the new Estahar of Ilwheirlane. She bit her lip and nodded as Fal had done.

Rhys looked at Fal. There was no gesture, only the momentary refocusing of his eyes, but Fal screamed and fell off the horse to the ground where he began to writhe, the stumps of his arms going up to cover his face.

"What have you done?" Elath cried. She ran to Fal and tried to hold him.

Rhys smiled. "I have granted your request."

Fal's thrashing grew less violent and Elath grabbed one of his arms, pulling it away from his face. One eye squinted up at her, his left eye. The right socket was still empty. "I can see," Fal said. "It hurts, but I can see. And my hands," he looked down at the ends of his arms.

Elath looked at the arm she held and where the stump had ended saw instead his hand, looking as it had looked before he lost it except much cleaner. Then she looked at Fal's left arm and saw the same. She looked back at his face but the right eye was still missing.

Rhys said, "He was punished by the High Priest of Miune, woman. And he was guilty of the crime. You asked for justice, not total forgiveness, which I couldn't have granted in any case. He can live and do his work with only one eye."

"How can we repay you," Elath asked, turning back to Rhys.

"I thought I made that clear," Rhys said. "You are bound to me now. That is the price you paid."

"You gave me back my life. I give it to you gladly," Fal said.

"And you, Elath Orm?"

"I, too, swear to serve you," she said.

Rhys nodded. "Then you, Fallon Gavi, will train my soldiers to fight in the ways you learned in Ravaar and both of you will serve me in whatever way I require for the rest of your lives. I cannot wait for you now, and Elath has a contract she must complete, but you'll come to me in Ninkarrak by the end of the month of Anor."

VYRKARION: THE TALISMAN OF ANOR

EPILOGUE

Be nalorin jast ameam ba acad tamar.
Mare rham ba put.

"Two wizards linked together are all the world.
Nothing else is needed."

— FROM THE WRITINGS OF
THE WIZARD ANOR

It was spring in the Mallarnes and a time of celebration. Aubrey, Thrym and Minta had left the week before. They were on their way to Akyrion with their escort of wizards, including Tana, Rainal, Magra and Ashe. Aubrey would be safe from the isklarin there, as well as from human rulers. The baneslarin were only slightly less powerful than the eslarin, their kin. No one would enter their territory for any but legitimate purposes.

The wizards had stayed until the fruiting was almost complete and what remained could be handled by Jerevan and herself with the aid of Vyrkarion. And now it was nearly done.

Alanna inhaled the faint sweet-dusty smell of the pollen laden air as it wafted through the sylvith trees lining the driveway of her home. She could feel Jerevan's concentration as he spread the last of the pollen, making sure no blossom was missed.

She sighed and looked around at the group gathered to celebrate the end of the fruiting. All the members of the Council of Idris were present and most of her neighbors. It was a warm day. Everyone had taken the opportunity to don new spring finery. They made a brilliant sight spread out amid the terraced gardens in front of Sylvithon.

"That's it, then," the Hetri of Carahel stated with satisfaction. The hawklike face with its hooked beak of a nose twisted into a smile.

If anything, Alanna thought, he's thinner than he was at the Council meeting last fall. But Carahel would radiate authority from his death bed.

"Yes. It's done, and we have Rhys' word that the sylvith will be seen to every year until he can make a new peace with the eslarin," Alanna said. There would be sylvith harvests in the Mallarnes, not just the next year but for all the years to come.

"Can we depend on this new estahar to keep his word, though? What makes you think he'll be any better than Idrim in the long run?" Councilman Selith demanded, his thick, black eyebrows beetled above his shrewd eyes.

"That's not a fear that need concern us," Jerevan said coming up behind Alanna and putting his arm around her lightly. She relaxed, his touch soothing her.

Milas Arrock, the Tamrai of Dworkin, snorted. "If he has eslarin blood, as they say, then you can count on his word being good. An eslar may slit your throat, but he'll never lie to you."

"We don't know whether that holds for a half-breed, though," Councilman Eggar said doubtfully, rubbing his stomach.

"It holds true for this one," Jerevan said with certainty.

"I'll grant he took care of the isklarin, all right," Councilman Selith said. "They say not a single soldier was killed and the Tower was cleared just as slick as you please."

"It was more than just the Tower he cleaned out," remarked Carahel. "No soldiers may have died, but I hear a few officers and officials weren't so lucky."

Alanna leaned back further against the comfort of Jerevan's arm and let the current that flowed between them drown out the flow of voices.

"*It's done. In a little while we'll be able to relax.*" She could feel his image of how they would relax.

Alanna laughed. "*It doesn't occur to you that I might be tired and want to sleep?*"

"*Of course not. I know you too well.*"

Jerevan was teasing, but Alanna knew that his comment was true. The linkage between them was none of the things she had feared and everything she might have hoped. The complete merging they had felt when they first completed the linkage did not occur now, unless they deliberately initiated it. The normal state of the link was more subtle and yet, over the weeks, they had come to depend on it so much that Alanna knew she could never again live without it. Jerevan was her life now, as she was his, and not just because of the pleasure they found in each others arms.

She had come to accept his access to her thoughts, and he had accepted her access to his memories, even the horrible ones of the years he had suffered under Derwen's curse. She understood him better now, with access to the past which had shaped him. Even his sensuality and his often fastidious tastes took on new meaning for her in the context of those memories.

She had been impatient with him when he pushed the camp food away one evening, not taking more than a taste. "We can't always eat at first class inns or have your personal chef in attendance," she said. "You have to eat something."

"No I don't," he said, curtly.

But the words triggered a flood of memories of when he had been forced to eat, and eat. She closed her eyes, overwhelmed by what he had lived through while afflicted with Derwen's curse. The massive quantities of food he had eaten, the way his flesh had ballooned around him, confining him in a soft, smothering prison he could not escape, she remembered it all.

"*Once I broke the curse,*" he thought, bringing her back from his memories, "*I swore I'd never again take a bite of food that didn't taste good to me. It took me as long to recover my palate as it took me to restore my body, but I've lived by that vow.*"

"*You told that you'd been cursed and Witha said you'd been a recluse. I wondered what kept you from society, but I never imagined…*"

"*No, I know you didn't,*" Jerevan thought ruefully. "*Imagination rarely reaches such depths. If I could have cut those memories out of my mind so you'd never see them, I'd have done so.*"

"*But they're part of what made you the man I love,*" she thought simply. "*Having painful memories isn't something shameful, to be concealed.*"

"*Degrading memories,*" he thought. "*My condition was degrading. It degraded me.*"

"*No. You may have thought it did at the time, but your pain was a fire that tempered you. Sometimes your sensuality has troubled me, but now I see it differently. Your body gave you pain. Now you appreciate that it can give you pleasure, too.*"

He had smiled his most sensual smile and thought, "*Then let's both appreciate that we can give each other pleasure now.*"

She shook her head, casting off her own memories, and looked around the garden to see if anyone had noticed her distraction.

Jerevan brought her hand up to his mouth and kissed it. "*Only me.*"

She turned her head to rest it against his chest, seduced as always by his touch. "*You feel so good.*"

"*So do you.*" He bent and kissed the top of her head but his mind pictured a much more suggestive act.

"*We've got to see everyone off,*" she protested.

"*You shouldn't be so tempting.*" He sighed. "*I don't know if I can wait until after they're gone.*"

She drew apart and took his hand, damping the level of linkage so that she could again concentrate on the voices around her. The afternoon was nearly over. Soon they would be able to be alone. At least for a time.

Magra and Ashe would return to Ilwheirlane later in the summer. Then they would all leave for Jerevan's estates at Leyburn, which fortunately were only a short journey from Onchan. The College of Wizards would reopen that summer for the first time in over a thousand years. She sighed, still intimidated by the thought of so great a responsibility.

"*We'll face it together.*" Jerevan's arm went back around her, deliberately increasing the current that ran between them. They rarely went anywhere alone in these days. If they did there was a faint discomfort, a feeling of incompleteness, though the mind link still joined them and would do so even over hundreds of kilometers.

It was somehow better to touch. So they moved around each other, adjusting their lives and activities so that they never had to be apart. A kiss, the brush of a fingertip, the amount of contact didn't matter as long as there was contact. This dependency developed so naturally they had hardly been aware of it until one of the other wizards brought it to their attention. Even then, it was not something they could worry about. It was too enjoyable.

"*It says in Anor's diary that most linked wizards hate to be apart, but she and Torin hated it most of all. I never realized the degree of togetherness that implied,*" Jerevan told her when she asked him if he might not find it irritating in the future. "*But how can I be annoyed when I'm as dependent on your presence as you are on mine.*"

She had been reassured and now rarely thought about it. It was natural for them to be together. Thus, when the last of their guests had gone, they strolled back to the house arm in arm.